I0562725

What Led To The Discovery of the Source Of The Nile

John Hanning Speke

Contents

WHAT LED TO THE DISCOVERY OF

THE SOURCE OF THE NILE

BY

John Hanning Speke

Journal of Adventures in Somali Land.
Chapter I. Introduction to the Journal.

Projects and Hobbies--life in India--lord Clyde and Sir James Outram--the Position and Physical Geography of the Somali Country--the Nogal Country, and Historical Sketches--Costume and Customs.

It was in the year 1849, at the expiration of the Punjaub campaign, under Lord Gough, where I had been actively engaged as a subaltern officer in the (so-called) fighting brigade of General Sir Colin Campbell's division of the army, adding my mite to the four successive victorious actions--Ramnugger, Sadoolapore, Chillianwallah, and Guzerat--that I first conceived the idea of exploring Central Equatorial Africa. My plan was made with a view to strike the Nile at its head, and then to sail down that river to Egypt. It was conceived, however, not for geographical interest, so much as for a view I had in my mind of collecting the fauna of those regions, to complete and fully develop a museum in my father's house, a nucleus of which I had already formed from the rich menageries of India, the Himalaya Mountains, and Tibet. My idea in selecting the new field for my future researches was, that I should find within it various orders and species of animals hitherto unknown. Although Major Cornwallis Harris, Ruppell, and others had by this time well-nigh exhausted, by their assiduous investigations, all discoveries in animal life, both in the northern and southern extremities of Africa, in the lowlands of Kaffraria in the south, and the highlands of Ethiopia in the north, no one as yet had penetrated to the centre in the low latitudes near the equator; and by latitudinal differences I thought I should obtain new descriptions and varieties of animals. Further, I imagined the Mountains of the Moon were a vast range, stretching across

Africa from east to west, which in all probability would harbour wild goats and sheep, as the Himalaya range does. There, too, I thought I should find the Nile rising in snow, as does the Ganges in the Himalayas.

The time I proposed to myself for carrying this scheme into operation was my furlough--a lease of three years' leave of absence, which I should become entitled to at the expiration of ten years' service in India; but I would not leave the reader to infer that I intended devoting the whole of my furlough to this one pursuit alone. Two of the three years were to be occupied in collecting animals, and descending by the valley of the Nile to Egypt and England, whilst the third year was to be spent in indulgent recreations at home after my labours should be over.

I had now served five years in the Indian army, and five years were left to serve ere I should become entitled to take my furlough. During this time I had to consider two important questions: How I should be able, out of my very limited pay as a sub-altern officer, to meet the heavy expenditure which such a vast undertaking would necessarily involve? and how, before leaving India, I might best employ any local leave I could obtain, in completing my already commenced collections of the fauna of that country and its adjacent hill-ranges?[1]

Previous experience had taught me that, in the prosecution of my chief hobby, I would also solve the problem of the most economical mode of living. In the back-woods and jungles no ceremony or etiquette provokes unnecessary expenditure; whilst the fewer men and material I took with me on my sporting excursions the better sport I always got, and the freer and more independent I was to carry on the chase. I need now only say I acted on this conviction, and I think, I may add, I managed it successfully; for there are now but few animals to be found in either India, Tibet, or the Himalaya Mountains, specimens of which have not fallen victims to my gun. Of this the paternal hall is an existing testimony. Every year after the war I obtained leave of absence, and every year I marched across the Himalayas, and penetrated into some unknown portions of Tibet, shooting, collecting, and mapping the country wherever I went. My mess-mates wondered how it was I succeeded in getting so much leave; but the reason was simply this, and I tell it that others may profit by it:--The Commander-in-Chief, Sir William Gomm, observing to what good account I always turned my leave, instead of idling my time away, or running into debt, took great pleasure in encouraging my hobby; and his Staff were even heard to say it would be a pity if I did not get leave, as so much good resulted from it.

The 3d September 1854 completed my tenth year's servitude in India, and on the succeeding day, the 4th, I embarked on board one of the P. and O. Company's steamers at Calcutta, and left the Indian shore for Aden; but previously to my departure I purchased various cheap articles of barter, all as tempting and seductive as I could find, for the simple-minded negroes of Africa. These consisted principally of cheap guns, revolving pistols, swords, cheap cutlery of all sorts, beads, cotton stuffs of a variety of kinds, and sewing material, &c. &c. &c., to the amount of L390 sterling. Arrived at Aden, my first step was to visit Colonel Outram, the political resident, to open my views to him with regard to penetrating Africa, and to solicit his assistance to my doing so, by granting introductory letters to the native chiefs on the coast, and in any other manner that he could. But to my utter astonishment and discomfiture, with the frank and characteristic ardour which has marked him through life, he at once said he would not only withhold his influence, but would prohibit my going there at all, as the countries opposite to Aden were so extremely dangerous for any foreigners to travel in, that he considered it his duty as a Christian to prevent, as far as he was able, anybody from hazarding his life there. This opposition, fortunately, only lasted for a time. After repeated supplications on my part, the generous kind nature of the Colonel overcame him, and he thought of a pretext by which, should anything serious happen to me, there would not remain any onus on his conscience.

The Bombay Government at that time had been induced to order an expedition to be organised for the purpose of investigating the Somali country--a large tract of land lying due south of Aden, and separated only from the Arabian coast by the Gulf of Aden--and had appointed three officers, Lieutenant Burton to command, and Lieutenants Stroyan and Herne to assist in its conduct. To this project Colonel Outram had ever been adverse, and he had remonstrated with the Government about it, declaring, as his opinion, the scheme to be quite unfeasible. The Somali, he said, were the most savage of all African savages, and were of such a wild and inhospitable nature that no stranger could possibly live amongst them. The Government, however, relying on the ability of one who made the pilgrimage of Mecca, were bent at least on giving the Lieutenant a chance of showing what he could do in this even darker land, and he was then occupied in Aden maturing his plans of procedure.[2]

This, then, was the opportunity the Colonel took advantage of, advising me to ask Lieutenant Burton to incorporate me in his expedition, at the same time saying that, if it was found to be agreeable to Lieutenant Burton, he would back my application to the Indian Government, obtain a cancel of my furlough, and get me put on service-duty as a member of the expedition.

Nothing could have suited me better, as it brought me on service again, and so saved my furlough leave for a future exploration. Lieutenant Burton consented, and I was at once installed in the expedition. My travelling, mapping,[3] and collecting propensities, it was thought would be of service to the ends of the expedition; and by my being incorporated in it, there would be no chance of my running counter to it, by travelling on its line of march, and possibly giving rise to disturbances with the natives.

Before proceeding further in the narrative of events as they occurred, it may be as well, perhaps, to anticipate a little, and give a general impression of the geography, ethnology, history, and other characteristics of the country under investigation--the Somali land--and the way in which it was intended that those investigations should be carried out. As will appear by the following pages, my experiences were mostly confined to the north central parts, in the highlands of the Warsingali and Dulbahanta tribes. The rest of my information is derived from conversations with the natives, or what I have read in some very interesting pages in vol. xix. of the 'Transactions of the Royal Geographical Society,' written by Lieutenant Cruttenden.

The Somali country is an elbow of land lying between the equator and the 11th degree of north latitude, which, from its peculiar form, might well be designated the Eastern Horn of Africa. The land is high in the north, and has a general declination, as may be seen by the river system, to the south and eastward, but with less easting as we come westward.

It is separated from the main body of Africa by the river Jub, a large and fertilising stream, which, rising in the mountains of southern Abyssinia, passes between the territories of the Gallas on the west and the Somali on the east, and debouches in the Indian Ocean at the northern extremity of the Zanzibar coast. According to Lieutenant Cruttenden's map, there are only two other rivers besides this of any consequence in the land,--the Webbe (river) Shebeli, or Haines river, which is of considerable importance, having a large flow of water, trending down a cultivable district of rich red soil, and another less important to the eastward of these two, called very unfortunately by him the Wadi[4] Nogal. The proper specific name for this river has never, to my knowledge, been given; but the Jid Ali Tug is one of its head branches. It rises in some small hills close overhanging the north coast, and runs south-easterly into the Indian Ocean, dividing two large territories, called Ugahden, or Haud, on the west, and Nogal on the east, mouthing at Ras Ul Khyle. Ugahden is said to be a flat grassy country, of red soil, almost stoneless, and having water everywhere near the surface. It is considered by the pastoral Somali a famous place for keeping cattle, of which by report they possess a great abundance, such as camels, ponies, cows, and Dumba sheep--a fat-tailed animal, like the Persian breed. Game also abounds in this country, of which the gazelles and antelopes, I was assured, roamed about in vast herds like sheep.

The Nogal country is the opposite of this, containing nothing of any material value in it. The rock-formation is all lime, very pure and white like marble, which consequently makes the soil white, and, being very stony, it is almost barren. The Somali keep cattle here, but with much apparent difficulty, being, from the scarcity of springs and want of water, obliged to march about, following the last falls of rain, to obtain fresh herbage for their cattle. My first and greater journey gave me an insight into this portion of the interior of the country south of Bunder Gori. It was very interesting, though not profitable, from its never having been visited by any Europeans before. I observed here two distinct leading features in its physical geography. The first is a narrow hill-range, about 180 miles long and 20 or more broad, which is occupied by two large tribes--the Warsingali on the east, and a branch of the Habr Gerhajis on the west. It is situated at an average distance of from 200 yards to three or four miles from the sea-shore, separated from it by a sandy flat or maritime plain, and, like the line of coast, extends from east to west. Immediately due south of Bunder Gori, the sea-face, or northern slopes of this range, are very steep and irregular, being trenched down by deep ravines, which, during the rainy season, shed their water across the maritime plain into the Gulf of Aden.

The lower folds on this side of the range are composed of brown rocks and earth, having little or no vegetation upon them, and are just as uninviting in appearance as the light-brown hills which fringe the coast of Arabia, as seen by voyagers on the Red Sea. Further up the hill, in the central folds of the range, this great sterility changes for a warm rich clothing of bush-jungle and a little grass. Gum-trees, myrrh, and some varieties of the frankincense are found in great profusion, as well as a variety of the aloe plant, from which the Somali manufacture good strong cordage. The upper part of the range is very steep and precipitous, and on this face is well clad with trees and bush-jungle. The southern side of the range is exactly the opposite, in all its characteristics, of the northern. Instead of having a steep drop of from 6000 to 7000 feet, it falls by gentle slopes to successive terraces, like a giant staircase, to scarcely half that depth, where it rests at the head of the high plateau land of Nogal, and is almost barren. Nogal, as I have said before, is also very barren, only producing trees, such as the hardy acacia and jujube, in sheltered places, in the valleys or watercourses which drain that land to the south-east. I had no means of determining it, but should judge this second great geographical feature, the plateau of Nogal, by the directions its streams lie in, to have a gradual decreasing declination, like all the rest of the interior, from the north, where it averages an altitude of from 3000 to 4000 feet, down to the level of the sea on south and by east.

According to traditional histories furnished me by the natives who accompanied me on the journeys I undertook, it appears that the present Somali are of rather recent origin, not more than four and a half centuries old. About the year 1413, an Arab chieftain, Darud-bin-Ismail, who had been disputing with an elder brother for certain territorial rights at Mecca, was overpowered and driven from the Mussulman Holy Land, and marched southwards, accompanied by a large number of faithful followers,--amongst whom was an Asyri damsel, of gentle blood and interesting beauty, whom he subsequently married,--to Makallah, on the southern shores of Arabia. Once arrived there, this band of vanquished fugitives hired vessels, and, crossing the Gulf of Aden, came to Bunder Gori. Here they were hospitably received by the then governing people, who, for the most part, were Christians--probably Gallas and Abyssinians--who, judging from the few archaeological remains they subsequently left behind them, must have lived in a far more advanced state of civilisation than the present Somali enjoy. Those Christian people were governed by one man, Sultan Kin, who had a deputy called Wurrah, renowned alike for his ferocity of character and his ability to govern.

For some years Darud and his Arab followers led a quiet, peaceable life, gaining the confidence of his host, and inspiring Kin's subjects with reverence for their superior talents. In process of time, by intermarriage and proselytising, these Mussulmans increased in number, and gained such strength, that they began to covet, and finally determined to take the country from the race that had preceded them. This project, by various intrigues and machinations, was easily effected; and Kin, with all his Christians, was driven back to his native highlands in Ethiopia.[5] Darud now was paramount in all this land, and reigned until he died, when an only son by his Asyri wife succeeded to him. This man's name was Kabl Ullah, who had a son called Harti. On succeeding his father, Harti had three sons, called respectively, in order of birth, Warsingali, Dulbahanta, and Mijjertaine. Amongst these three he divided his kingdom, which to this day retains the names. The Mijjertaine dispersed over the eastern portions of the land, the Warsingali held the central, and the Dulbahantas the western territories.[6]

Subsequently to this period, an Arab called Ishak came across from Southern Arabia and established himself forcibly at Meit, and founded the three different nations who now occupy all the coast-line from Ras Galweni on the eastward to Zeyleh on the extreme west of the Somali country. Ishak, it appears, had three wives, who gave in issue three sons, and among these three men was divided the whole country which he subdued.

Forming themselves into tribes, the senior or Habr Gerhajis, by constant feuds and other causes, are much distributed about the country, but mostly occupy the hilly grounds to the southward of the coast-line; whilst the Habr Owel, or second in order of birth, possess all the coast of Berbera between Zeyleh and Kurrum; and the third, or Habr Teljala, hold all the rest thence eastwards to Heis.

The Somali have been chiefly known to us since the time of our taking occupation of Aden, whither many of them resort with their wives and families to carry on trade, or do the more menial services of porterage and donkey-driving. They are at once easily recognised by the overland traveller by their singular appearance and boisterous manner, as well as by their cheating and lying propensities, for which they are peculiarly notorious; indeed, success in fraud is more agreeable to them than any other mode of gaining a livelihood, and the narration of such acts is their greatest delight in conversation. They excel as donkey-boys even the Egyptians. As may be concluded from their history, they are a mixed Ham-Shemitic race, but differing considerably from both in their general appearance, though retaining certain characteristics of both these breeds. They are a tall, slender people, light and agile as deer; slightly darker than, though much the colour of Arabs, with thin lip, and noses rather Grecian when compared with those of blacks, but with woolly heads like the true negroes. Their natures are so boisterous and warlike, that at Aden it has been found necessary to disarm them. When they first arrived there, it was not an unusual sight to see the men of different tribes, on the hillsides that form the face of the "crater," fighting battles-royal with their spears and shields; and even to this day, they, without their arms, sometimes have hot contests, by pelting one another with sticks and stones. There is scarcely a man of them who does not show some scars of wounds received in these turmoils, some apparently so deep that it is marvellous how they ever recovered from them.

Their costume is very simple. The men, who despise trousers, wear a single sheet of long-cloth, eight cubits long, thrown over the shoulder, much after the fashion of the Scotsman's plaid. Some shave their head, leaving it bare; others wear the mane of a lion as a wig, which is supposed by them to give the character of ferocity and courage to the wearer, while those who affect the dandy allow their hair to grow, and jauntily place some sticks in it resembling the Chinaman's joss-sticks, which, when arranging their toilette, they use as a comb, and all carry as weapons of defence a spear and shield, a shillelagh, and a long two-edged knife. The women clothe more extensively, though not much so. Fastening a cloth tightly round the body immediately under their arms, they allow it to fall evenly down to the ground, and effectually cover their legs. The married ones encase their hair in a piece of blue cloth, gathering it up at the back of the head in the fashion of English women of the present day; this is a sign of wedlock. The virgins wear theirs loose, plaited in small plaits of three, which, being parted in the centre, allows the hair to fall evenly down all round the head like a well-arranged mop. On approaching these fairs, they seductively give their heads a cant backwards, with a half side-jerk, which parts the locks in front, and discloses a pretty little smiling face, with teeth as white as pearls, and lips as red as rubies. Pretty as they are when young, this beauty fades at once after bearing children, and all their fair proportions go with it. After that marked peculiarity of female negroes, they swell about the waist, and have that large development behind, which, in polite language, is called steatopyga. Although they are Mussulmans, none wear the yashmac. Beads are not so much in request here as in other parts of Africa, though some do wear necklaces of them, with large rings of amber. This description, however, applies to the Somali in his own land. When he comes over to Aden he takes shame at his nakedness, dons the Arab's gown and trousers, and becomes the merchant complete.[7]

In consequence of the poorness of their land, almost all the Somali are wandering pastorals, which of itself is enough to account for their turbulent natures. The system of government they maintain is purely patriarchal, and is succeeded to by order of birth generally in a regular and orderly manner, attributable, it would appear, to the reverence they feel for preserving their purity of blood. The head of each clan is called Gerad or Sultan, who would be powerless in himself were he not supported by the united influence of all the royal family. When any disturbances or great disputes arise, the sultan is consulted, who collects his elders in parliament to debate the matter over, and, through them, ascertain the people's feelings. Petty disputes are settled by the elders without any further reference. In most cases war arises from blood-feuds, when a member of one clan kills the subject of another, and will not pay the recognised valuation of the party injured, or allow himself to be given up to the vengeance of the family who has sustained the loss. In such cases as these, whole tribes voluntarily march out to revenge the deed by forcibly taking as many cattle from the aggressor as the market valuation may amount to.

Thus a war, once contracted, does not subside for years, as by repeated deaths among the contending parties the balance of blood-money never can be settled. Moreover, the inflicted punishment seldom falls on the party immediately concerned; added to which, in wars of tribes, everybody helps himself to his enemy's cattle in the best way he can, and men formerly poor now suddenly become rich, which gives a zest to the extension of the contest nothing else could produce. Indeed, the poorer orders of Somali are only too glad to have a good pretext for a fight, as a means of bettering their condition, by adding a few more head of cattle to their stock. Were this not the case, there would be no fighting whatever, as the sultan would be powerless to raise an army against the inclination of the people. War only ceases when both sides become exhausted, and withdraw as by mutual consent. The great object in these encounters is to steal away as many cattle as possible without risk of person, and such feats are boasted of with rapture by those returning home with any prize. In the administration of justice they consult the Mosaic law, as given in the Koran, taking life for life, and kind for kind.

The northern Somali have no permanent villages in the interior of the country, as the ground is not cultivated; but they scatter about, constantly moving with their flocks and herds to any place within their limited districts where water is to be found, and erect temporary huts of sticks, covered with grass mats; or, when favourable, they throw up loose stone walls like the dykes in Scotland. But on the sea-coast, wherever there are harbours for shipping, they build permanent villages on a very primitive scale. These are composed of square mat walls, supported by sticks, and all huddled together, and partitioned off for the accommodation of the various families, near which there are usually one or more square box-shaped stone buildings, the property of the chief of the place, which are designated forts, though there is nothing in their artless construction to deserve this name. They are all composed of blocks of coralline, cemented together with mortar extracted from the same material.

Like nearly all places within the tropics, beyond the equatorial rainy zone, this country is visited by regular monsoons, or seasons in which the winds prevail constantly in one direction; consequently vessels can only come into the harbours of the northern coast when the sun is in the south, or during five months of the year, from the 15th November to the 15th April, to trade with the people; and then the Somali bring the products of their country, such as sheep, cows, ghee, mats made by the women from certain grasses and the Daum palm, ostrich feathers, and hides, and settle on the coast to exchange them in barter with the outer merchants, such as Arabs and men from Cutch, who bring thither cloths, dates, rice, beads, and iron for that purpose.

Of all the trading places on the coast, the most important is Berbera; it is, in fact, the great emporium of Somali land, and we must call the reader's particular attention to it, since it forms the chief point of interest in these pages. It is on the same meridian as Aden, and only divided from it by the gulf of that name. Although it is of such great importance, it is only inhabited during the five months of the favourable monsoon, when great caravans come up from the rich provinces which lie to its south and south-west, the principal ones being those from Ugahden and Harar.

Having now given a general sketch of the country, we shall enter upon the objects of the expedition. It was obvious, by the lay of the land, that the richest and most interesting part of the country must be that which lies between the Jub and Webbe Shebeli rivers, and it was the most accessible to inspection, as large and powerful caravans, travelling southwards through Ugahden, much frequent it. Seeing this, Lieutenant Burton conceived the idea of waiting until the breaking up of the Berbera fair, when the caravans disperse to their homes, to travel by the ordinary caravan route, through the Ugahden country to the Webbe Shebeli, and on to Gananah, and then to proceed further by any favourable opportunity to the Zanzibar coast.

It was now, however, early October, and fully five months must elapse ere we could finally enter on our march. In the mean time, Lieutenant Burton, desirous of becoming acquainted as far as possible with the habits of the people we were destined to travel amongst, as well as the nature of the country and the modes of travelling in this *terra incognita*, determined on making an experimental tour to Harar, a place which had never been entered by any European, and was said to be inaccessible to them. Harar, as I have said before, sends caravans annually to the Berbera fair, and therefore comes within the influence of British power. Taking advantage of this, Lieutenant Burton ordered Herne to go to Berbera whilst he was on this expedition, to keep up a diversion in his favour, arming him with instructions, that in case he was detained in Harar by the Amir of that place, Herne might detain their caravan as a ransom for the release of his party.

Further, to obtain more accurate knowledge concerning the march of the Ugahden caravans, to gain an insight into the market transactions of Berbera, and to collect cattle for our final march, it was deemed advisable he should go there. Stroyan, as soon as he could manage it, was also to go to Berbera to assist him. Thus everybody had a duty to perform during this interregnum but myself.

Dreading the monotony of a station life, I now volunteered to travel in any direction my commandant might think proper to direct, and to any length of time he might consider it advisable for me to be away. This proposition had its effect, as affording an extra opportunity of obtaining the knowledge desired, and instructions were drawn up for my guidance. I was to proceed to Bunder Gori, on the Warsingali frontier, to penetrate the country southwards as far as possible, passing over the maritime hill-range, and, turning thence westwards, was to inspect the Wadi Nogal, and march direct on Berbera, to meet Stroyan and Herne, at a date not later than the 15th January 1855. Whilst travelling I was to remark upon the watershed of the country, plot the route I travelled, keep *copious* notes on everything I saw, and collect specimens of natural history in all its branches, as well as observe and register all meteorological phenomena, and buy camels and ponies for the great future expedition.

Funds for the expenses of this undertaking were not available at that time from the public purse, as the Indian Government had stipulated that the whole sum they would advance for this great expedition should not exceed L1000, and, for security's sake, had decided on paying it by instalments of L250 at a time. I therefore, desirous to render as much assistance as lay within my power to further the cause I had embarked upon, volunteered to advance the necessary sum from my own private resources, trusting to Lieutenant Burton's promises in the future for being repaid.

This project settled, I at once set to work, and commenced laying in such stores as were necessary for an outfit, whilst Lieutenant Burton, who had been long resident in Aden, engaged two men to assist me on the journey. The first was a man named Sumunter, who ranked highly in his country, who was to be my *Abban* or protector. The duty of abbanship is of the greatest importance, for it rests entirely on the Abban's honesty whether his client can succeed in doing anything in the country he takes him through. Arabs, when travelling under their protection, have to ask his permission for anything they may wish to do, and cannot even make a march, or purchase anything, without his sanction being first obtained. The Abban introduces the person under his protection to the chief of his clan, is answerable for all outrages committed on the way, and is the recognised go-between in all questions of dispute or barter, and in every other fashion. The second man was also a Warsingali,[8] by name Ahmed, who knew a slight smattering of Hindustani, and acted as interpreter between us. I then engaged two other men, a Hindustani butler named Imam, and a Seedi called Farhan. This latter man was a perfect Hercules in stature, with huge arms and limbs, knit together with largely developed ropy-looking muscles. He had a large head, with small eyes, flabby squat nose, and prominent muzzle filled with sharp-pointed teeth, as if in imitation of a crocodile. Farhan told me that when very young he was kidnapped on the Zanzibar coast by the captain of a small Arab vessel. This captain one day seeing him engaged with many other little children playing on the sandy seashore, offered him a handful of fine fruity-looking dates, which proved so tempting to his juvenile taste that he could not resist the proffered bait, and he made a grab at them. The captain's powerful fingers then fell like a mighty trap on his little closed hand, and he was hurried off to the vessel, where he was employed in the capacity of "powder-monkey." In this position he remained serving until full grown, when, finding an opportunity, he ran away from his master, and has ever since lived the life of a "free-man."

As a soldier, he had been tried in warfare, and was proved valorous and cunning in the art, and promised to be a very efficient guard for me. The next thing of most importance to be considered was the dress I should wear. I first consulted the Colonel (Outram), who said he was averse to our going in disguise, thinking that lowering ourselves in this manner would operate against me in the estimation of the natives. But this did not suit Lieutenant Burton's plans, who, not wishing to be conspicuous whilst travelling to Harar, determined on going there disguised as an Arab merchant, and thought it better we should appear as his disciples, in accordance with which Herne had already purchased his dress, and now I bought mine. It was anything but pleasant to the feel. I had a huge hot turban, a long close-fitting gown, baggy loose drawers, drawn in at the ankles, sandals on my naked feet, and a silk girdle decorated with pistol and dirk. As an outfit for this especial journey, I bought at Aden L120 worth of miscellaneous articles, consisting chiefly of English and American sheeting, some coarse fabrics of indigo-dyed Indian manufacture, several sacks of dates and rice, and a large quantity of salt, with a few coloured stuffs of greater value than the other cloths, to give away as presents to the native chiefs. As defensible and other useful implements for the scientific portion of the expedition, I took rifles, guns, muskets, pistols, sabres, ammunition in great quantity, large commodious camel-boxes for carrying specimens of natural history, one sextant and artificial horizon, three boiling-point and common atmospheric thermometers, and one primitive kind of camera obscure, which I had made at Aden under the ingenious supervision of Herne.

Chapter II.

The Voyage--An Akil--The Somali Shore--Sultan (Gerad) Mahamed Ali--
Hidden Treasure--The Warsingali--A Royal Reception--Somali Appetites-
-Difficulties and Impediments--Sultan Tries My Abban or Protector.

On the 18th October 1854, having got all my preparations completed, I embarked in an Arab vessel, attired in my Oriental costume, with my retinue and kit complete, and set sail that same evening at 6 P.M. The voyage, owing to light and varying breezes, was very slow and tedious. Instead of performing the whole voyage in three days, the ordinary time, it took us nine. According to the method of Arab navigation, instead of going from port to port direct, we first tracked eastward along the Arabian shore three successive days, setting sail at sunrise, and anchoring regularly at sundown. By this time we were supposed to be opposite Bunder Heis, on the Somali coast, and the Nahkoda (captain) thought it time for crossing over the Gulf. We therefore put out to sea at sunrise on the morning of the 21st, and arrived the same evening, by mistake, assisted with a stiffish easterly breeze, at a small place called Rakodah, which, by report, contained a small fort, three mat huts, and many burnt ones, a little to the westward of Bunder Heis. My Abban accounted for the destruction of this place by saying it had been occupied surreptitiously for a long period by a people called Rheer Dud, who sprang from a man called Sambur-bin-Ishak; but about four years ago, the Musa Abokr--a sub-tribe of the Habr Teljala, who were the former and rightful owners of the place--suddenly returned, took the usurpers by surprise, and drove them off by setting fire to the village. The next day, by hard work, tacking up the wind, which still continued easterly, we succeeded in reaching Bunder Heis, which, like the last place, was occupied by the Musa Abokr. There were four small craft lying here, waiting for cargoes, under lee of a spur of low hills which constituted the harbour; in which, fortunately, there was very good fishing to be obtained. We were detained here by adverse and light winds two days, during which time I went on shore and paid my respects to the Akil (chief) of the place, who lived in a small box-shaped stone fort, on the west flank of the village of Heis, which was very small, composed, as usual, of square mat huts, all built together, and occupied only by a few women, who made mats, collected gums, and stored the produce of the interior, as sheep, cows, and ghee, which their men constantly brought down to them, for shipping off to Arabia.[9] The Akil's reception was very warm and polite. He offered me everything at his disposal, and gave as an honorary present a Dumba sheep and a bowl of sour camel's milk, which I thought at the time the most delicious thing I ever drank. It is sharp and rough, like labourers' cider, and, drunk in the heat of the day, is most refreshing. When first taken, and until the stomach becomes accustomed to it, it operates like medicine, and I on this occasion was fairly taken in. The fish we caught were not very good, but comical in appearance, and of a great variety of the most beautiful prismatic colours, changing in tint as different lights and shades struck upon them.

We left Heis on the 25th, with very light and unfavourable winds, and tracked along shore to the eastward, making very little way. The weather continuing the same, on the 26th I forced the Nahkoda, much against his will, on at night, as during the darker hours the winds were much stronger, and by this means we arrived at our destination, Bunder Gori on the Warsingali frontier, at sundown on the 27th of October. I had now seen the Somali shore, and must confess I was much disappointed. All that was visible, besides the village mentioned, was a sandy tract of ground, the maritime plain, which extended in breadth from the sea-shore to some brown-looking hills in the background, from a few hundred yards to one or two miles distant; and hills and plains--for I could, by my close approximation to them, only see the brown folds of the hills near the base--were alike almost destitute of any vegetation; whilst not one animal or any other living creature could be seen.

28th October.--The Abban would not allow anybody to go on shore until certain parties came off to welcome us and invite us to land, such being the etiquette of the country when any big-wigs arrive. After the sun rose we were duly honoured by the arrival of many half-naked dignitaries, who tenderly inquired after the state of our health, the prosperity or otherwise of our voyage, the purpose of our coming there, and a variety of other such interesting matters. Then again they were questioned by our people as to the state of the country, whether in peace or war; how and where the Sultan Gerad Mahamed Ali was residing; if rain had lately fallen, and where; if the cattle were well in milk;--to which it was responded that everything was in the most promising order; the cattle were flourishing in the hills, where rain had lately fallen, about twenty miles distant from that place; and the sultan, with all the royal family,[10] were there, revelling on milk, under the shade of favouring trees, or reposedly basking in the warm morning sun--the height of Somali bliss. The order was now given to go ashore, and we all moved off to a fort which the Abban said was his own property, in Goriat (little Bunder Gori), three miles to the westward of Bunder Gori. There were two of these little forts near, and a small collection of mat huts, like those already described, and of the same material as all Somali forts and huts. The kit was now brought across and placed within the fort I occupied, all except the salt, which afterwards proved a bone of contention between me and the Abban, and the sultan was at once sent for. No one could move a yard inland, or purchase anything, without his sanction being first obtained.

Although Gerad Mahamed Ali was living only twenty miles distant from Gori-at, it was not until repeated messages had been sent to him, and eleven days had elapsed, that he answered the summons by his presence. In the meanwhile, having nothing better to do during this tedious interval, as no people would bring cattle or anything for sale, I took walks about the plain, shooting, and killed a new variety of gazelle, called Dera[11] by the Somali, and Salt's antelopes, here called Sagaro, which fortunately were very abundant, though rather wild; catching fish, drawing with the camera, bathing in the sea, luxuriating on milk, dates, and rice, or talking and gossiping with the natives.

On one occasion my interpreter came to me with a mysterious air, and whispered in my ear that he knew of some hidden treasures of vast amount, which had been buried not far off, under rocky ground, in such a way that nobody had been able to dig them up, and he wished that I, being an Englishman, and consequently knowing secret arts, as well as *hikmat* (scientific dodges), would direct how to search for these treasures. By inquiring farther into the matter, it appeared that an old man, a miser, who had been hoarding all his life, was suddenly taken ill about forty years ago, and feared he would die. Seeing this, his relatives assembled round him to ask his blessing; and the old man, then fearing all his worldly exertions would end to no good purpose, asked them to draw near that he might tell them where his riches were hidden; but even then he would not disclose the secret, until he was in the last dying gasp, when he said, "Go to a pathway lying between two trees, and stretch out a walking-stick to the full length of your arm, and the place where the end of your wand touches is that in which my treasures are hidden." The wretched man then gave up the ghost, and his family commenced the search; but though they toiled hard for many days and weeks, turning up the stones in every direction, they never succeeded in finding the treasure, and had now given up the search in despair. The fact was, they omitted to ask their parent on which side of the path it was concealed, and hence their discomfiture. At my request the said family came to me, corroborated the statements of the interpreter, and begged imploringly I would direct them how to search for the money; saying at the same time they would work again, if I thought it of any use; and, moreover, they would give me half if the search proved successful. I lent them some English pick-axes, and went to see the place, which certainly showed traces of very severe exertions; but the strong nature of the soil was too much for them, even when armed with tools, unless they were fortunate enough to hit upon the exact spot, which they did not, and therefore toiled in vain again.

The Warsingali complained to me sadly of their decline in power since the English had interfered in their fights with the Habr Teljala, which took place near Aden about seven years ago, and had deprived them of their vessels for creating a disturbance, which interfered with the ordinary routine of traffic. They said that on that occasion they had not only beaten the Habr Teljala, but had seized one of their vessels; and that prior to this rupture they had enjoyed paramount superiority over all the tribes of the Somali; but now that they were forbidden to transport soldiers or make reprisals on the sea, every tribe was on an equality with them.

They further spoke of the decline of their tribe's morals since the time when the English took possession of Aden and brought in civilisation with them. This they in most part attributed to our weak manner in prosecuting crime, by requiring too accurate evidence before inflicting punishment; saying that many a dishonest person escaped the vengeance of law from the simple fact of there being no eye-witnesses to his crime, although there existed such strong presumptive evidence as to render the accusation proved. When speaking against our laws, and about their insufficiency to carry out all governmental points with a strong and spirited hand, they never forget to laud their own sultan's despotic powers and equity in justice.

Of course no mortal man was like their Gerad Mahamed Ali. In leading them to war he was like the English French,[12] and in settling disputes he required no writing office, but, sitting on the woolsack, he listened to the narration of prosecution and defence with his head buried in his hands, and never uttering a word until the trial was over, when he gave his final decision in one word only, ay or nay, without comment of any sort. In confirmation of their statements, they gave the description of a recent trial, when a boy was accused of having attempted to steal some rice from a granary; the lad had put his hand through a chink in the door of it, and had succeeded in getting one finger, up to the second joint, in the grain; this, during the trial, he frankly acknowledged having done, and the sultan appointed that much of his finger exactly to be cut off, and no more--punishing the deed exactly according to its deserts. This, to Somali notions, seemed a punctiliousness in strict equity of judicial administration which nothing could excel, and they bragged of it accordingly.

Becoming dreadfully impatient at so much loss of precious time whilst waiting here, unable to prepare in any way for the journey, I sent repeated messages to the sultan, demanding his immediate attendance; but it was not until the 6th of November that I heard definitely of his approach, and then it was that he was coming down the hill.

On the 7th he came with a host of Akils to Bunder Gori, and put up in a Nahkoda's hut. This indignity he was obliged to submit to, as he had not cautioned the merchants who occupied his forts of his intended approach, and now no one would turn out for him. Finding him so near me, I longed to walk over to him and settle matters personally at once; but dignity forbade it; and as he had come with such cautious trepidation, I feared any over-hastiness might frighten him away again. He seemed to observe the same punctiliousness towards me, so I split the difference by sending an embassy by my Abban, assisted by other powerful Akils, early the following morning, when they held durbar, and my intentions of travelling were fully discussed in open court. For a long time the elders on the sultan's side were highly adverse to my seeing their country, considering no good could possibly arise from it, and much harm might follow; I might covet their country, and eventually take it from them, whereas they could gain nothing. Hearing this, the Abban waxed very wroth, and indignantly retorted he would never allow such a slur to be cast upon **his honour**, or the office which he held. He argued he had come there as my adviser and Abban; his parentage was of such high order, his patriotism could not be doubted. Had he not fought battles by their side, of which his scars bore living testimony? and now they wished to stigmatise him as a traitor to his country! The sultan must decide it. How could jungle-folk like them know anything of the English and their intentions?

The sultan listened silently during this discourse, which, though written in a few lines, took many hours of hot debating, by their turning and turning every little particular over and over again; and finally decided it in his usual curt and conclusive manner, by saying, "The Warsingali were on the most friendly and amicable relations with the English; and as he was desirous of maintaining it, he would give me leave to travel anywhere I liked within his dominions, and to see and examine anything I chose. But out of fear for the consequences, as the English would hold him answerable should any disasters befall me, he could not sanction my crossing over his frontier in any direction, and more especially into the Dulbahanta country, where wars were raging, and the country so unsafe that even Warsingali dare not venture there." This announcement was brought back in high exultation by Sumunter, who thought his success complete, and at the same time announced to me the sultan's intention of honouring me with a visit in the evening, which was duly done.

He came a little before sunset, with his bare head shaven, a dirty coloured tobe thrown over his shoulders, and hanging loosely down to his sandaled feet.[13] He looked for all the world like a patriarch of the olden times, and passed me, marching in martial order in the centre of a double line of men sloping their spears in bristling array over their shoulders, all keeping step in slow marching order, a scene evidently got up in imitation of our soldiers. Not a word was spoken, and the deepest solemnity prevailed. On his arrival in front of the fort, I drew up my men, and fired a salute to give him welcome. This was done in right good earnest, by every man cramming his gun with powder, to excel his neighbour in a loud report, to show the superiority of his weapon; for such is the black man's notions of excellence in a fowling-piece. The march concluded, the sultan with his followers all huddled together and squatted on the ground outside the second fort, deeply agitated, and not knowing what to do, as they evidently dreaded what might follow. To dissipate their fears, I approached his royalty, salaamed, and tried to beguile the time by engaging them in conversation.

Finding that this had rather the opposite effect, I then retired, and soon found them all intently wrapped up in prayer, prostrating and rising by turns, with uplifted hands, and muttering for hours together without cessation. I then ordered a regal repast to be served them of rice swimming in ghee, and dates *ad libitum*. This, notwithstanding their alarm, was despatched with the most marvellous rapacity, to such an alarming extent, that I required to know how many men were engaged in eating it. The Abban replied that there were only a few: he would not allow many to come over here out of a spirit of economy, knowing I had not much property to spare, though all the rest had wished to come, and were greatly disappointed. But these men, as is usual amongst Somali, had prepared themselves for a feast by several days' previous fasting, and each man would, if I allowed it, swallow at one meal as much as a sheep's skin could contain. As a gun is known by the loudness of its report, and ability to stand a large discharge of powder, to be of good quality, so is a man's power gauged by his capacity of devouring food; it is considered a feat of superiority to surpass another in eating.

I have seen a Somali myself, when half-starved by long fasting, and his stomach drawn in, sit down to a large skinful of milk, and drink away without drawing breath until it was quite empty, and it was easy to observe his stomach swelling out in exact proportion as the skin of liquor decreased. They are perfect dogs in this fashion. I may here add, that although the Abban in this speech seemed to show so much consideration for my property, by several recent tricks of his I entertained much suspicion of his honesty; and this little address, though uttered plausibly, was too common and transparent a trick in the East to beguile me. All Orientals have a proverbial habit of saving their master's property to leave greater pickings for themselves, and such I considered was Sumunter's dodge now.

8th November.--This morning the sultan, having now recovered, came to return my salaam of the previous evening, when I opened to him the purport of my expedition in minute detail: how I wished to visit the Southern Dulbahantas, cross and inspect the Wadi Nogal, and thence proceed west to meet my friends, Stroyan and Herne, at Berbera. He listened very attentively and politely, but at the conclusion repeated the words I had already heard; adding that the Dulbahantas had intestine wars; they had been fighting many years, and were now in hot strife, dividing the government of their country. Not many days since a report had arrived that the southern portion of them, who occupied the countries about one hundred miles due south of Bunder Heis, had had a fight with the northern ones, who were living on the same meridian, immediately to their northward, and had succeeded in capturing 2000 horses, 400 camels, a great number of sheep and goats, and had wounded one man severely: it was therefore impossible I could go from the northern division to the southern, for I should be treated as an enemy; and that was the only line on which water could be found during this, the dry season. Had I come here during the monsoon, I might have travelled directly in a diagonal line, from the south of the mountain-range to the rear of this place, into their, the southerners', country, who were the older branch, and were now governed by the hereditary and rightful chief, Gerad Mahamed Ali, who was on the most friendly terms with the Warsingali, and who, being an old chief, and well respected by his adherent subjects, might have granted me a hospitable reception.

On the other hand, the northern Dulbahantas, who were also friendly with the Warsingali, were under no control: the Gerad, by name Mahamed Ali also, was recently installed in government, and was consequently very little respected. He (the Warsingali chief) could not, therefore, give his sanction to my going amongst them, by which my life would be endangered, and he, for permitting it, would be held responsible by the English. No arguments of mine would alter the decision of the inflexible chief; I therefore changed the subject by asking him to assist me in procuring camels, by which I might go into the interior, and feel my way thereafter. This he readily agreed to, and begged permission to return to Bunder Gori to give the necessary orders to his subjects. His escort then demanded a cloth apiece from me, to be given them for their trouble in coming over here; arguing that, had I not required the sultan's attendance, they would not have had to come;--a plausible, but truly Somali notion of justice; they knew their proper master would give them nothing for coming to support his dignity, but thought I might be softer.

10th.--The sultan, not able to do business hurriedly with his rabble subjects, did not appear again until this morning, and then, instead of proceeding at once to work, hinted he should like to have the presents I had brought from Aden for him, as the best method of showing our feelings to one another. This was not so easily concluded. I portioned out the things that were intended for him, and wished he would take them at once away and clear the room, thinking, in my inexperience of savages, I had only to give, and it would be received with a hearty Bism-illah; but I was soon undeceived: the things were taken with a grunt of discontentment; all looked over one by one. If a cloth was soiled, it must be changed; and then the measurements began by cubits = 18 inches, or from the point of the elbow to the tip of the middle finger, just as Noah must have done when he built the ark. But as all forearms are not of equal length, much delay was occasioned by the sultan trying the length of his forearm against everybody's in the room, and then by measuring every cloth by turn, and remeasuring them again for fear of mistake; then they were divided into lots, to be disposed of to his wives, and children and Akils and servants, and, of course, found insufficient to meet everybody's expectations, and I must give more.

Tedious hours passed in this way; as a final petition, the sultan said I must give him for himself a gun and my silk turban, as I had given up wearing anything on my head, and did not require it: these were, after a certain amount of haggling, surrendered, on condition that the sultan would exert himself a little more energetically on my account. The way he handled the musket was very amusing: he had never had one in his hands before, and could not get it to sit against his shoulder; and when his people placed it for him, he persisted in always cocking the wrong eye, which tickled Farhan's fancy so much, that he burst into loud roars of laughter. Nevertheless, the sultan took things quietly, and would not allow himself to be discomposed, but coolly said the gun would be of no use unless I gave him some powder to feed it with. This last straw broke the camel's back; all things must have an end, and I promised I would give him some after he procured enough camels for my wants, but not before. This settled the matter, and he walked off, with all the things I had given him, as sulkily as if he had been injured.

Camels were then brought for sale, and purchasing commenced. When the sultan was present, he had to determine if the prices asked by the sellers were reasonable or not, and took for his office as mediator a tithe on all purchases; but in his absence, Akils were appointed to officiate on the same conditions. This system of robbing, I was assured, was the custom of the country, and if I wanted to buy at all I must abide by it. Cloth was at a great discount on the coast, for the men there had, by their dealings with Aden, become accustomed to handle dollars, and were in consequence inspired with that superior innate love for the precious metal over all other materials, with which all men, and especially those newly acquainted with it, become unaccountably possessed. No one would believe that my boxes could be made for any other purpose than for locking up money; and I was obliged to leave them open to inspection before they would sell anything for cloth.[14]

The sultan now lived at Bunder Gori, and seldom showed himself, promising to come to me every day, without the least intention of doing so; and only at last, after three days' absence, when I threatened to invade his dwelling, did he appear, bringing several camels with him: of these I purchased some good ones, and sent the rest away: this was the 15th November. He then returned home again, and promised faithfully he would bring on the morrow a sufficient number of camels to carry all my kit.

16th.--For the first time the sultan kept his promise by returning, but the animals he brought were weak and useless, and I could plainly see I was being trifled with, and detained here for the mere purpose of being robbed in an indirect manner, so that no accusation could be laid against any one. Nothing, I may say, in all my experiences, vexes the mind so much as feeling one's self injured in a way that cannot be prevented or avenged. Some might take such matters quietly, but I confess I could not. Indeed, I stormed and expostulated with the sultan until he agreed to assist me in a move. I had now eleven camels, and wanted some five more, but thought it better not to wait; for as long as I remained in a comfortable dwelling, I knew my men would not exert themselves. That day, then, packing up what I most required, I started for Bunder Gori, and unloaded, after a three miles' march, at an old well in rear of the village, selecting as a camping-ground the least comfortable place I could find, and not allowing the tent to be pitched, though the sun-heat was 112 degrees, and the sand was blowing in perfect clouds. Some days previous to my leaving Goriat, Sumunter induced me to give him twenty rupees to hire donkeys for conveying the heavier things over the hills, and repeatedly assured me he had got them, but they never came; and now I asked him to return the money, as I had brought it with me as a reserve fund, to provide against any possible difficulty, and not to be parted with for any ordinary purpose. This commenced a series of rows between Sumunter and myself: he had made away with the money, and could not produce it. The salt also was never forthcoming.

17th.--I could not succeed in making up my complement of camels. The sultan said he and his men must be fed before they could do work, and sat upon the date-bags so resolutely I was fain to open them that some business might be done. After feasting they all dispersed, under pretence of bringing other camels, and I went into the town to inspect the place. There were five small forts, occupied by merchants, of whom one was a Hindi from Cutch, and a large collection of mat huts, mostly oc-cupied by women. Instead of finding a harbour (Bunder), as the name of the village implied, the shore was a gradual shelving open roadstead, in which two buggaloes were lying at anchor, waiting for cargoes, and four small sailing-boats were prepar-ing, with harpoon and tackle, to go porpoise-hunting for oil.

18th.--Having made everybody as uncomfortable as I could wish, sitting in the sandy open plain, all the men were equally desirous with myself for a move on the journey; but still I was five camels short, and saw no hopes of getting them. The plan then settled was to move southwards half-way up the hill, leaving the few things still in the fort as they were, until I arrived at the camping-place, and could send the animals I was taking with me back to fetch them. Having now desired the sultan, Sumunter, and Farhan to return to Goriat, and leave the rear property in safe cus-tody with the fort-keeper, I commenced the march across the maritime plain with Ahmed, Imam, a number of Somali camel-tenders armed with spear and bow, and the sultan's youngest son, Abdullah, to direct the way until his father and the other two should arrive, which they promised they would do by the evening. The track first led us across the maritime plain, here about two miles broad, and composed of sand overlying limestone, with boulders in the dry shallow watercourses, and with no vegetable life save a few scrub acacias and certain salsola. This traversed, we next wound along a deep ravine called Tug (river) Tura,[15] lying between the lower spurs of the mountain-range, and commenced a slight ascent up its cracked, uneven passage, until we reached a halting-place called Iskodubuk. The distance we had made was only about five miles from Bunder Gori, but the camels were so fatigued by travelling over boulders, that we were obliged to unload and stop there for the day. The sultan and Abban now overtook us to say that the rear things were in safe custody in the fort; and, leaving instructions with the young Prince Abdullah about the road we should follow on the morrow, returned ***nolens volens*** back to Bunder Gori, saying, as they went away, we might expect them at the next camping-ground as soon even as we could get there with the camels. A little after sunset, some interesting rock-pigeons--very similar to the Indian painted bird, which I found there frequenting ground much of the same nature--lit at some pools in the bed of the ravine, and enabled me to shoot and stuff several of them.

19th.--We got under way in the early morning, and commenced ascending the same ravine, when a messenger from the sultan arrived, and desired we would stop until he came. We had scarcely accomplished two miles, and the morning was yet young and cool, and I strove with every effort in my power to induce the men to go a little further forward, but without the slightest effect; they were as obstinate as mules, and just as unruly. This was a fair specimen of Somali travelling; any pretext to save the trouble of moving is accounted too precious to be lost. The ground here was a little more wooded; tall slender trees, with thick green foliage, grew in the bed of the ravine, in which there were some occasional pools of stagnant rain-water, and the brown rocky hill-sides were decorated with budding bush acacias, which afforded a good repast for the weary camels, whose journey over the boulders must have been very fatiguing to them.

20th.--As the sultan did not arrive, and the young prince would not allow my men to load, I ordered the interpreter and Imam to remain where they were, whilst I returned to Bunder Gori to see what was the matter, and on no account were they to issue any food until I came back again. As soon as I had gone two or three miles, I found the young prince and all the camel-men hastening after me, and entreating me to return; they said the sultan was on his way, and would arrive in camp in the evening. I complied, conditionally that they bound themselves to march in the morning whether he came or not. Once again in camp, I had my food prepared, and sat savagely watching the effect its odour had upon my starving men, who, fearing they would get none, formed in a body, and came petitioning me to forgive them, as they consented to do my bidding for ever after. They were then fed.

21st.--After loading in the morning, with a great deal of beating and thumping, all the camels, save two or three weakly ones, were whipped up a winding steep ridge, one of the buttresses of the mountain, to a camping-ground, six miles farther on, called Adhai. Here we were at the station originally assigned for the first day's march, and, for the first and last time during the whole journey, I pitched the tent. The higher we ascended the hill the more abundant became the wooding, and green grass for the first time was visible amongst the stones. This freshness was attributed to a recent fall of rain. Altitude, by boiling thermometer, 4577 feet.

22d.--I sent all the freshest camels off to Goriat for the remaining property, with orders that everybody should return on the following day. At this height the temperature of the air was very delightful, the range at noon being only 79o. I spent the whole day specimen-hunting, and found the rocks were full of fossil shells. I killed a new snake or variety of **Psammophis sibilans**, and shot an interesting little antelope, **Oreotragus saltatrix**, the "klip-springer" of the Cape Colonist, as well as hyraxes and various small birds, which we duly preserved. My collections in this country were sent by Lieutenant Burton to the Asiatic Society's Museum, Calcutta, and have been described in their journals by Mr E. Blyth, the Curator.

23d and 24th.--Passed without anybody appearing, and I was becoming much alarmed at repeated stories I heard of the Abban's dishonesty. It then transpired that Sumunter was heavily in debt, and one of his principal creditors was at Bunder Gori detaining him there. A pony had been hired for my riding, and on this animal I wished to send Imam back, to find out the truth of everything, and to return to me the following day; but the wicked young prince, Abdullah, got wind of my intention, and had the pony driven away, so that the unfortunate Imam had to walk.

25th.--Still nobody came. I now despatched the interpreter on the same mission, and was left alone with the young prince and two or three camel-drivers. After a little while had elapsed, a number of savage hungry-looking men came up the hill and settled themselves in my encampment, squatting on the date-bags and clamouring for food. The prince and camel-drivers joined them, and became so importunate, I was obliged to rebuke them with angry demonstration. No sooner did they see me vexed than they began hovering tauntingly around me, jeering and vociferating in savage delight at the impunity they enjoyed in irritating me when all alone and helpless. However, I stood by the date and rice bags with my gun, and prevented anybody coming near me. The prince and camel-men now seeing me determined, and no farther discomposed by their manoeuvres, came supplicating for their daily rations. I gave it them at once, but could not satisfy them; they must have some more for all their brothers (meaning the ***blackguards*** who had just arrived), or they would strike work. This stirred my blood; I took back what I had given, and resolutely declined to be passively cajoled out of anything, let happen what may. They saw I was determined not to submit to them; and suddenly, as if the same thought struck every one of them at the same instant, they dashed down the hill, flying over the bushes and stones in their way, with yells and shouts, and, seizing a goat from a neighbouring flock, killed and quartered it without a moment's hesitation. At this juncture, just as the robbed shepherd came crying to me for the price of his goat, Imam arrived from Goriat, and tried to reason with him that it was no business of mine, and I could not be expected to pay it. The injured man then swore he would have justice done him at the sultan's hands, and all yelled again for dates and rice. As they could not get it, the young prince, ever full of boyish tricks, now seized up a mussack (water-skin), and said I should have no more water until I complied with their demands. The others, following his example, picked up as many more as they could find, and left but one mussack remaining. This one I immediately captured, and requested Imam to fill from a spring farther down the hill; but the men, thus far outdone, rather than allow it, said they would kill him if he dared attempt to go now. As Imam showed alarm at their wild threats, I took the water-skin myself and walked off to fill it, upon which the savages threw themselves out in line, flourishing their spears and bows, and declared they would kill me if I persisted in going. On I went, however, and had just passed through their line, when the sultan's eldest son, Mohamed Aul, fortunately arrived, and rebuked them, together with his brother, for allowing me to be ill-treated. Finding Mohamed Aul very reasonable and obliging, I begged him to send Abdullah away as a nuisance, for I could never permit him to eat any more salt of mine.

Imam now disclosed to me the results of his investigations at Goriat and Bunder Gori. The Abban, as I had heard before, was detained there by a creditor to whom he had contracted debts in Aden, and now, in part liquidation of them, he had given away all my salt, the twenty rupees he took for hiring donkeys, several pieces of cloth, and he had changed my good rice for bad; and, knowing Farhan to be cognisant of all his villanies, had tried by bribes to induce him to desert. The sultan now arrived, and excused his long absence, saying that he had lost the time in fruitless endeavours to induce Sumunter to come with him. He said he had been remonstrating with Sumunter, and thought him very culpable in not obeying me. Hoping the sultan was in earnest in what he said, I now told him of all I had seen and heard about Sumunter, and begged he would assist me in sending him back to Aden, for no reliance could possibly be placed on a man who had proved himself so dishonest and unprincipled as he was. The interpreter also thought this would be a good plan, and advised my employing the sultan's brother Hasan as abban or protector in his stead. However, the sultan said he could not undo what the English had done in Aden, but said if I wished he would send for Sumunter and rebuke him in my presence. I replied that I thought he could not get Sumunter to leave Bunder Gori, or he should have done so ere this. This touched his pride, and he raised his body indignantly, and said, "If I command, he must obey." "Then, for goodness' sake," said I, "order him with all--all my things at once, and lose no more time."

The following day they all arrived, and Sumunter with them, riding on a pony. I felt much incensed as the Abban came cringing up to me, and proclaimed him in presence of the sultan and all my men a traitor and robber, mentioning all his villanies in detail, and begging he would leave my camp at once, for I could not travel with him. He appeared very humble, and denied flatly all the accusations I brought against him. Upon this I begged the sultan, flattering him with his great renown for administering justice, that he would do me justice as his guest. He said he was willing to do anything for me if I would direct the way in which I wished him to proceed; he did not understand the English law, and I must submit to Somali methods. This was agreed to, and we all assembled in my tent, and arranged the court as follows:--I sat at the gable end of the tent with Imam, Ahmed, and Farhan, with Sumunter facing us. The sultan mounted on the bales of cloth, and all his retainers and princes, and my camel-drivers, sat in a group on the ground at his feet.

In opening the proceedings of the prosecution, I first said to Sumunter--

P. Speke.--"Where is the salt which you confess came with us to Goriat, and which you have told me daily you would give; but as yet, though everything, you say, is in the camp, it has not arrived?"

D. Sumunter.--"I did not bring it because it was so heavy, and thought you would not want it."

P.--"Then why did you not land it at Goriat, and give it me there, or why did you even buy it at all at Aden if it was of no use?"

D.--"Because the Nahkoda took it to Bunder Gori."

After a few more questions and answers, and the subject was exhausted, the sultan (judge), who had been sitting in silence with his head buried in his hands, now gave a grunt and motioned us to continue.

P.--"Where are the bales of cloth which by my account and Imam's are missing?"

D.--"I did not take them; somebody else must have."

P.--" They were in your charge, and you are answerable for them; besides which, Farhan here knows you gave them away."

Judge.--"Ahem!" and the prosecution continued.

P.--"Where are the twenty rupees I gave you for hiring donkeys, and which I particularly ordered should not be expended for any other purpose?"

Sumunter, putting his hand fixedly in his breast, said, "I've got them; they are all right. I will give them to you presently."

Speke.--"No! give them to me now; I want them this instant."

Sumunter, confused, and fumbling at his pocket, much to the delight of all the court, who burst with laughter, said, "No! I've left them at home in Bunder Gori, and will give them by-and-by."

Judge.--"Ahem!" and the prosecution continued.

P.--"Why did you change my good rice for bad?" (opening and showing the contents of the nearest sack).

D.--"I thought it would not signify: bad rice is good enough for the camel-drivers, and I have left enough good for your consumption. An old friend asked me for it, and I did it to oblige him."

Judge.--"Ahem!" and the prosecution continued.

P.--"Why did you attempt to bribe Farhan to leave my service, and say nothing to me about it?"

D.--"Farhan is a bad man; and I was afraid he would steal your things."

Judge.--"Ahem!"

Thus ended the prosecution and defence. The sultan raised his head, and in answer to my appeal as to what judgment he would give, calmly said, he could see no harm in what had been done--Sumunter was my Abban, and, in virtue of the ship he commanded, was at liberty to do whatever he pleased either with or to my property. Words, in fact, equivalent to saying I had come into a land of robbers, and therefore must submit to being robbed; and this I plainly told him. Further, I even threatened the sultan with a pretended determination to return to Aden, where I said the matter would be settled at our police court without bias or favour. I then desired the interpreter to look out for any vessel that would give me a passage to Aden, as it was obvious to me Sumunter had more power in the land than the sultan. This took them all by surprise, abashed the old sultan and his family--for they were proud of their strength--and induced them to say I need not fear anything on that score;--was the sultan of the Warsingali, indeed, not the greatest chief in the land, and, moreover, a great ally of the English? This, of course, was only a feint on my part to bring them to a proper sense of their duty towards me; for I had brought letters of recommendation from the Government at Aden to their chief, and knew they would rather do anything than let me go back in a huff.

29th.--I had been now nine days waiting here, and had taken many walks about the hill-sides, investigating the place, and making sundry collections. The most interesting amongst these was a small lizard, a new species, afterwards named by Mr E. Blyth, the Curator of the Asiatic Society, *Tiloqua Burtoni*, after my commandant. The Somali brought a leopard into camp, which they said they had destroyed in a cave by beating it to death with sticks and stones. They have a mortal antipathy to these animals, as they sometimes kill defenceless men, and are very destructive to their flocks. Besides the little antelope described, I only saw the Saltiana antelope, and the tracks of two other species which were said to be very scarce. Rhinoceroses were formerly very abundant here, but have been nearly all killed down with spear and bow (they do not use firearms) by the Somali hunters, in consequence of the great demand for their skins for making shields. Amongst the bush and trees there were several gum-producing ones, of which the frankincense, I think, ranked first. These gums are usually plucked by the women and transported to Aden. The barks of various other trees are also very useful; for instance, they strip down the bark of the acacia in long slips, and chew it until only fibres remain, which, when twisted in the hand, make strong cordage. The acacia bark also makes a good tan for preserving leather; but of far greater account than this is the bark of a squat stunted tree, like the "elephant's foot," called by the Somali mohur, which has a smooth skin, with knotty-looking warts upon it like a huge turnip, reddish inside, with a yellowish-green exterior. It has a highly aromatic flavour, and is a powerful astringent. When making mussacks, the Somali pull a sheep or goat out of his skin; tie its legs and tail, where incisions had been made, to make it a waterproof bag, and then fill it with bits of this bark, chopped up and mixed with water. They then suspend it in a tree to dry, and afterwards render it soft and pliable by a severe course of manipulation. The taste of the bark is considered very wholesome, and a corrective to bad and fetid water. Besides possessing this quality, the mohur is useful as a poultice-when mashed and mixed with water; and the Somali always have recourse to it when badly wounded.

During my peregrinations at this place, I often dropped bits of paper about the jungle, little suspecting what would become of them; and, to my surprise, one day the interpreter came to me in some alarm, to say that several Dulbahantas had arrived at Bunder Gori, and were sharply canvassing amongst themselves the probable objects of my visit. I could not be travelling without a purpose, at so much expense; and they thought these bits of paper, which they had carefully picked up, conclusive evidence I was marking out some spots for future purposes. They abused the Warsingali for being such fools as to let me travel in their country, and said I should never cross over to them. This little incident of dropping paper, though fully explained to them, was ever afterwards brought up in accusation against me, and proved very perplexing.

30th.--Camp Habal Ishawale. Altitude 5052 feet.--We were now all together, and I thought ready to march; but the men had first to be paid their hire in advance--a monthly stipend of five tobes each. When that was settled, many other men, and amongst them the sultan's second brother Hassan, coveting my clothes, wished to be engaged. Some tedious hours were wasted on this subject. The sultan, at the instigation of these advocates for service, would have it, if I wished to travel according to the custom of the country, I must take more men with me as a guard. I, on the other hand, neither wanted them nor could afford to pay them, as I had been so extensively plundered--but wished to exchange Sumunter for his brother, and promised high rewards if he would take me through the journey. To put an end to the discussion, I struck my tent, never to be pitched again, and waited patiently until the camels came. It was not until near sundown that the camels were ready and the march commenced. The sultan then ordered Hassan and the naughty boy Abdullah, against my wish, to accompany me on the journey; and we set off, leaving two or three loads behind to be brought up on the morrow. The march was a short one, made to relieve the one beyond; for the spring of water we were now drinking from was the last on this side the range. It led us up a gradual but tortuous ascent, very thickly clad with strong bushes, to a kraal or ring-fence of prickly acacias, which was evidently made to protect the Somali's sheep from lions, leopards, hyenas, and freebooters suddenly pouncing on them.

We remained here three days, sending the things I had brought in relays across the mountain, and fetching up the rear ones. The sultan could not lose the opportunity afforded by my detention to come again and beg for presents, and I gave him a razor to shave his head with and make a clean Mussulman of him. On finding he could get nothing further from me gratis, he demanded that a cloth should be paid to the man whom my camel-drivers had robbed of the goat at Adhai, and, before retiring, wished me urgently to take a letter for him to Aden, petitioning the English to allow him to form an expedition by sea, and take retribution on the Musa Abokr at Heis, who had recently killed one of his subjects.

Chapter III.

Yafir Pass--Rhut Tug--The Ruins at Kin's City--Abban Apprehends Future Consequences--Hyenas--The Dulbahantas--Camel Drivers' Tricks--Briny Water--Antelope-shooting--Elephant-hunting--Ostrich-hunting--Gazelles--Jealousy and Suspicions of the People--Troubles from Forty Thieves--Rapid Decline of Property.

4th December 1854.--At dawn of day the last of the camels was loaded, and we set out to clamber up to the top of the mountain-range and descend on the other side to the first watering-place in the interior of the country. It was a double march, and a very stiff one for the camels. Directly in our front lay an easy, flattish ground, with moderate undulations, densely wooded with such trees as I had already seen; but beyond it, about three miles from camp, the face of the mountain-top, towering to a great height, stood frowning over us like a huge bluff wall, which at first sight it appeared quite impossible any camel could surmount. At 9 A.M. we reached this steep, and commenced the stiffest and last ascent up a winding, narrow goat-path, having sharp turns at the extremity of every zigzag, and with huge projecting stones, which seemed to bid defiance to the passage of the camels' bodies. Indeed, it was very marvellous, with their long spindle-shanks and great splay feet, and the awkward boxes on their backs striking constantly against every little projection in the hill, that they did not tumble headlong over the pathway; for many times, at the corners, they fell upon their chests, with their hind-legs dangling over the side, and were only pulled into the path again by the combined exertions of all the men. Like Tibet ponies, when they felt their bodies slipping helplessly over the precipices--down which, had they fallen, they would have met instantaneous and certain death--they invariably seized hold of anything and everything with their teeth to save their equilibrium. The ascent was at length completed after an infinity of trouble, and our view from the top of the mountain repaid me fully for everything of the past. It was a glorious place! In one glance round I had a complete survey of all the country I was now destined to travel over, and what I had already gone over.

The pass was called Yafir, and, by the boiling thermometer, showed an altitude of 6704 feet. It was almost the highest point on this range. From a cedar tree I cooked my breakfast under, on facing to the north I saw at once the vast waters of the Gulf, all smooth and glassy as a mill-pond, the village of Bunder Gori, and the two buggaloes lying in its anchorage-ground, like little dots of nut-shells, immediately below the steep face of the mountain. So deep and perpendicular was it, that it had almost the effect of looking down a vast precipice. But how different was the view on turning to the south! Instead of this enormous grandeur--a deep rugged hill, green and fresh in verdure, with the sea like a large lake below--it was tame in the extreme; the land dropped gently to scarcely more than half its depth, with barely a tree visible on its surface; and at the foot of the hill, stretched out as far as the eye could reach, was a howling, blank-looking desert, all hot and arid, and very wretched to look upon. It was the more disappointing, as the Somali had pictured this to me as a land of promise, literally flowing with milk and honey, where, they said, I should see boundless prairies of grass, large roomy trees, beautiful valleys with deep brooks running down them, and cattle, wild animals, and bees in abundance. Perhaps this was true to them, who had seen nothing finer in creation; who thought ponies fine horses, a few weeds grass, and a puny little brook a fine large stream. At noon we reloaded, and proceeded to join the camels and men sent forward on the previous day. The track first led us a mile or two across the hill-top, where I remarked several heaps of stones piled up, much after the fashion of those monuments the Tibet Tartars erect in commemoration of their Lahma saints. These, the Somali said, were left here by their predecessors, and, they thought, were Christian tombs. Once over the brow of the hill, we descended the slopes on the south, which fell gently in terraces, and travelled until dark, when we reached a deep nullah, here called Mukur, in which we found our vanguard safely encamped in a strong ring-fence of thorn bushes.

The distance accomplished was seventeen miles; the altitude 3660 feet. The two following days (5th and 6th) we halted to rest the cattle, whilst I went shooting and collecting. There were a great number of gazelles and antelopes, some bustard, many florikan and partridges, as well as other very interesting birds and reptiles. These were mostly found in ravines at the foot of the hills, or amongst acacia and jujube trees, with patches of heather in places. We now held ***durbar***,[16] to consult on the plan of proceeding. It was obviously impossible to march across the plateau directly upon the southern Dulbahantas, as there was not a blade of grass to be seen nor any water on the way beyond the first ten miles from the foot of the hills. To go to Berbera, then, I must perforce pass through the territories of the northern Dulbahantas; and this was fixed upon. But hearing of some "ancient Christian ruins" (left by Sultan Kin) only a day's march to the south-eastward, I resolved to see them first, and on the 7th made a move five miles in that direction to a kraal, called Karrah, where we found a deep pool of stagnant water.

8th.--My kit was now so much diminished that we all marched together down a broad shallow valley south-eastward, in which meandered a nullah, called Rhut Tug, the first wadi I came upon in Nogal. The distance accomplished was eight miles when we put up in the Kraal of Rhut; for, as I have said before, there were no villages or permanent habitations in the interior of the Nogal country. All the little wooding there is, is found in depressions like this, near the base of hill-ranges, where water is moderately near the surface, and the trees are sheltered from the winds that blow over the higher grounds of the general plateau. Rhut is the most favoured spot in the Warsingali dominions, and had been loudly lauded by my followers; but all I could find were a few trees larger than the ordinary acacias, a symptom of grass having grown there in more favoured times when rain had fallen, a few puddles of water in the bed of the nullah, and one flock of sheep to keep the place alive. Gazelles were numerous, and many small birds in gaudy plumage flitted about the trees, amongst which the most beautiful was the ***Lamprotornis superba***, a kind of Maina, called by the Somali Lhimber-load (the cowbird), because it follows after cows to feed.

9th.--Halt. Kin's City, or rather the ruins of it, I was told, lay to the northward of my camp, in the direction of the hills, at a distance of about two miles; so I proceeded at once to see it, hoping by this means I should be able to advance westward on the following day. After an hour's walk I came upon those remains of which I had heard so much at first on landing in the country, as indicative of the great advancement in architectural art of Kin's Christian legion over the present Somali inhabitants; but I was as much disappointed in this matter as in all others of Somali fabrication. There were five objects of attraction here:--1. The ruins of a (said to be) Christian church; 2. The site and remains of a village; 3. A hole in the ground, denoting a lime-kiln; 4. A cemetery; and, 5. The ground-lines of a fort. This certainly showed a degree of advancement beyond what the Somali now enjoy, inasmuch as they have no buildings in the interior, though that does not say much for the ancients. The plan of the church is an oblong square, 48 by 27 feet, its length lying N.E. and S.W., whilst its breadth was directed N.W. and S.E., which latter may be considered its front and rear. In the centre of the N.W. wall there was a niche, which evidently, if built by Christians, was intended to point to Jerusalem; and this might have been conclusive evidence of its having been a Christian house of worship, and consequently of great antiquity, did it not unfortunately point likewise in the direction of Mecca, to which place all Mohammedans turn when saying their prayers. Again, I entertained some suspicion that the walls, which were in some parts ten feet high, had not sufficient decay to warrant their being four and a half or more centuries old. But one thing was remarkable at this present time--there were no springs or any water nearer than my camping place, which could not have been the case when this place was occupied; but it denoted a certain amount of antiquity, without any doubt. The walls of the church were composed of limestone rocks, cemented together with a very pure white lime.

The entrance fronted the niche, and was led up to by a street of round pebbles, protected on each side by semicircular loosely-thrown-up stone walls. There was nothing left of the village but its foundation outlines, which at once showed simplicity of construction, as well as economy of labour in building. It lay about 50 yards to the east of the church. One straight wall ran down the centre, from which, as supports, ran out a number of lateral chambers lying at right angles to it.

To the northward of the church was the cemetery, in which, strange to say, if the Somali believe their own story, they even at the present time bury their dead, and erect crosses at the head of the tombs, in the same manner as we Christians do. The kiln was an artless hole in the ground, in which there was a large collection of cinders, and other debris not worth mentioning. Lastly, the fort, or rather remains of what the Somali said had been one, was situated on an eminence overlooking the village, and about 70 yards to the S.W. of the church. Now, having completed my investigations of the ruins, I returned to camp, where I was met by the Abban, looking as sulky as a bear with a sore head, and frowning diabolically. He had been brooding over my late censures, and reflecting on the consequences his bad conduct would finally have upon him, if he could not obtain a pardon from me. And should he not be able to elicit it by fair means, he thought at any rate he would extract it by foul, then and there, without condition or any clause whatever. This was preposterous. I frankly told him exactly what I thought of him, saying I could not forget what had happened; that he had abused the trust reposed in him by the English, and I was bound in duty to report the whole matter in every detail to the Government; but should he discontinue his evil ways, and take me safely to my journey's end, I would promise him a full pardon as soon as I arrived at Berbera. This would not an-swer his purpose--bygones must be bygones without any condition whatever, and he went to his bed as wrathful as he rose.

10th.--I rose early and ordered the men to load, but not a soul would stir. The Abban had ordered otherwise, and they all preferred to stick, like brother villains, to him. And then began a battle-royal; as obstinately as I insisted, so obstinately did he persist; then, to show his superior authority, and thinking to touch me on a tender point, forbade my shooting any more. This was too much for my now heated blood to stand, so I immediately killed a partridge running on the ground before his face. Seeing this, he wheeled about, prepared his pony, and, mounting it, with his arms agitated and ready for action, said to the people standing by that he would kill me if I dared shoot again. I was all this while standing prepared to shoot, without understanding a word of what was said, when the interpreter rushed towards me pale and trembling, and implored me not to shoot, but to arrange matters quietly. He would not tell me, however, what had occasioned the great anxiety his excited manner showed. I of course was ready at any time to do anything I could to help me on the journey, and again stated the terms on which I would grant the man a pardon. At this juncture, Hassan, the sultan's brother, who had been absent a few days, came and interceded between us. I told him everything that had happened, how the Abban had even superseded the sultan's order, by forbidding me to do what I wished in his country, and again begged him to be my Abban in Sumunter's stead. This he said he could not do, but gave Sumunter a wigging, and desired me to go and shoot anywhere I liked. Thus ended this valuable day.

11th.--Last night I shot a female spotted crocuta hyena (here called Durwa) in the act of robbing. These tiresome brutes prowl about at night, and pick up anything they can find. Their approach is always indicated by a whining sound, which had prepared me on this occasion. She was caught in the act of stealing away some leather thongs. The specimen was a fine one, but until dissected I could not, from the hermaphrodital form of these animals, determine which sex it was that I had killed. We now prepared for the march westward, when Hassan said he would go back to near the Mijjertaine frontier, where rain had lately fallen, and all the Warsingalis had migrated with their cattle, to fetch some ponies, which he would bring to me in a few days, even before I could arrive at the Dulbahanta frontier, and begged a gun at parting as Judge's fee for his settlement of the Abban question, and as an earnest that he would bring the five ponies which I wanted. We then got under way, and travelled westward, bidding Rhut Tug adieu, but every one was stiff and formal. Sumunter had not confessed contrition, and I had not committed myself to saying that I would hush the matter up, assuring him that in duty as a public officer I could not, that I was bound to report every circumstance, though privately I promised a pardon as before. After travelling a little way, we emerged from the low land of the valley, and ascended a higher track to the normal level of the plateau, which, as I have said before, was all bleak and barren, with scarcely a tree growing on it, and very stony. Here I saw a large troop of ostriches and numberless gazelles stalking away out of the line of the caravan's march. My men were all highly anxious I should shoot them, but I would not, to try what effect it would have on the Abban, saying, sport was of secondary importance to me, and I now only wished to finish the journey quickly.

By his detentions I had lost so much time, I despaired of reaching Berbera agreeably with my instructions, and, moreover, he had not begged my pardon, from which I doubted his intention to serve me faithfully. This caused a halt. Sumunter and all the men alike said, "Of what good is your coming here, if you do not enjoy yourself? We all came on this journey to reap advantages from serving you, and now if you don't shoot, what may we expect?" I said, Prove to me that I shall not be thwarted again, and I will shoot or do anything to create good-will. Then appointing three men as Sumunter's advisers to hold him in restraint in case any wrongheadedness on his part should get the mastery of him, I begged they would proceed. This proved successful for the time. Sumunter wrote me a letter, stating his intention of abject servitude, and ratified it by presenting his spear and shield, through the hands of the interpreter, for me to return to him as an acknowledgment that I would henceforth forgive him; and we again proceeded on the journey.

After travelling ten miles without seeing a single habitation or human being of any sort, we arrived at a nullah, in which there were several pools of bitter spring-water, and some Egyptian geese swimming on them. This place was called Barham. On the right or northern side of the line of our march was the hill-range, about ten miles distant, at the foot of which, in the beds of small ravines, grew some belts of the jujube-tree and hardy acacias; but to the south the land was all sterile, and stretched away in a succession of little flat plains, circumscribed by bosses or hillocks of pure white limestone rock, which appeared standing unaffected by the weathering which had worn down the plains that were lying between them. Again these little enclosed plains sank in gentle gradation to their centres, where nullahs, like the one I was encamped upon, drained the land and refuse debris to the south and eastward, possibly to join eventually the Rhut Tug.

12th.--At 9 A.M. we were again in motion on our westward course, rising by a gentle incline to about half-way between Rhut Tug and a second Wadi Nogal farther on, called Yubbe Tug. Here, at the water-parting between these two large watercourses, was the tomb of the great founder of these mighty nations, Darud bin Ismail, and an excavated tumulus. There were also several bitter springs in the neighbourhood, with stone enclosures and numerous flocks of sheep tended by Somali. On passing the tomb I scarcely remarked it, so insignificant did it appear, whilst the Somali paid no homage to it whatever. But the tumulus excited more attention, and I was requested to examine it. Six years ago, the interpreter said, a Somali who wished to bury his wife in it, broke through its exterior, and found a hollow compartment propped up by beams of timber, at the bottom of which, buried in the ground, were several earthenware pots, some leaden coins, a ring of gold such as the Indian Mussulman women wear in their noses, and various other miscellaneous property.

I was very much struck with the sleekness of the sheep, considering there appeared nothing for them to live upon; but I was shown amongst the stony ground here and there a little green pulpy-looking weed, an ice plant called Buskale, succulent, and by repute highly nutritious. It was on this they fed and throve. These Dumba sheep--the fat-tailed breed--appear to thrive on much less food, and can abstain longer from eating, than any others. This is probably occasioned by the nourishment they derive from the fat of their tails, which acts as a reservoir, regularly supplying, as it necessarily would do, any sudden or excessive drainage from any other part of their systems.

After crossing over this high land we began descending to the westward, and at the completion of the twelfth mile dropped into a nullah tributary to the Yubbe Tug, made a kraal for protection against hyenas close to a pool of water, and spent the night. This plain was called Libbahdile (the haunt of lions).[17]

13th.--The air was so cold, the men could not bestir themselves until after sunrise, when, to my great surprise and delight, without one angry word or attempted impediment from the Abban, we were on the move at 8 A.M. I now fondly hoped the Abban had really turned over a new leaf, but was soon undeceived, and also disappointed. He was married to a Dulbahanta woman, and this wife, for he had two others, with her family, was residing in that country. I was therefore, unawares to myself, travelling directly on his home. Hence these three consecutive marches. Gradually we descended into a broad valley, down the centre of which meandered the Yubbe Tug, or the second Wadi Nogal of my acquaintance. This formed a natural boundary-line, separating the Warsingali from the northern Dulbahanta frontiers. Where we first came upon the nullah it was deep and broad, with such steep perpendicular sides that camels could not cross it. We therefore turned suddenly northward, and followed up its left bank till we turned its head, which begins abruptly, and marched five miles to the Yubbe Kraals. Had this valley been blessed with a moderate quantity of rain, there is no doubt it would have been available for agricultural purposes; and as it was, there were more trees growing in the hollow here than in any other place I had seen, and several flocks and herds were congregated in it. Whilst travelling to-day the interpreter narrated the circumstances of a fight which the Warsingali had with the Dulbahantas about ten years ago in this valley, in which it appeared the Dulbahantas were the aggressing party, having sent a foraging-party over their frontier to lift some cattle. The Warsingali, seeing this, mustered their forces and repelled the enemy; but would not follow them up, preferring rather to tease them into submission than to engender a bloody contest. This they effected by exposing all their flocks and herds to the view of the Dulbahantas on the bank of the impassable nullah, whilst they guarded its head and protected their flank by stationing a strong party of warriors there. The Dulbahantas, tantalised at this tempting yet aggravating sight, for they had not strength enough to cope with the Warsingali in full force, waited covetously gazing across the nullah for some time, and then retired in such great disgust, they have never attempted to steal again.

When once ensconced in the new camp, the Abban came to me with an air of high importance, to announce that we were now on the Dulbahanta frontier, and that, if I wished to see their land, I must allow him to precede me, and pave the way, taking the young prince Abdullah with him to magnify the purport of his mission, as the Dulbahantas were a terrible and savage nation, governed, not like the Warsingalis, by an old and revered chief, but by a young sultan whom nobody listened to. Moreover, the Dulbahantas had sent word to say they had heard of my marking the Warsingali country out with paper, and would not admit me on any consideration. Besides which, it was a custom in the country that strangers should ask permission to enter through the medium of an abban, and as I had acted on that custom in the Warsingali country, so also must I do it here.

I was kept at this station eight days, sometimes hearing ominous announcements of the terrible Dulbahantas, sent to frighten me by the Abban, and sometimes amusing myself in other and various ways. The Dulbahantas could not conceive my motive for wishing to travel in their land; no peddling Arab, even, had ever ventured there, so why should I desire to go? Fortunately I had a good deal of employment with my gun; for, besides gazelles, antelopes, a lynx, florikans, and partridges, I shot many very beautiful little honey-birds, as well as other small birds. Of these former the most beautiful was the ***Nectarinia Habessinica***. It has an exceedingly gaudy plumage, that glistens in metallic lustre as the rays of light strike upon its various-coloured feathers. This is the more remarkable on a warm sunshiny day, when the tiny bird, like a busy humble-bee, bowing the slender plant with its weight, inserts his sharp curved bill into the flower-bells to drink their honey-dew, keeping its wings the whole time in such rapid motion as to be scarcely distinguishable.

Without animal flesh I do not know what I should have done here. The water was so nitrous I could not drink it. To quench my thirst, I threw it in gulps down my throat; and rice, when boiled in it, resembled salts and senna. After returning from sport one day, the interpreter brought up one of the camel-drivers, to be punished for having stolen some deer flesh when sent to clean it. He was a Midgar, or low-caste fellow, who does not object to indulge in cannibalism when hard pressed by hunger. I would not decide the case myself, but handed him over, much against his wish, to the *tender* mercies of the interpreter and two other men whom the sultan, at parting, appointed judges on any sudden occasion. It was everybody's interest to make him guilty, and therefore he was condemned to find two sheep, to be killed and eaten in the camp. Another case of theft, much more vexatious than this, occurred when I first arrived here, and turned off some spare camel-drivers, who took away all the packing-ropes with them, and I have been obliged to employ the remaining men ever since in chewing acacia bark into fibres to make new ones.

I was now becoming so much alarmed at the Abban's delay and tricks, that I wrote a letter to Lieutenant Playfair, Assistant Political Resident at Aden, complaining of what he had done, saying I felt very uncertain of being able to reach Berbera by the time appointed, and requesting him to send a letter of remonstrance to the sultan. This I forwarded by a man called Abdie, *via* Bunder Gori. Prudence would have suggested my returning with the letter, for I had now received intelligence that the Abban was in his home, and after experience gained by the tragedies on the coast, I could have expected no good from him. But as long as life and time lasted, I was resolved to go ahead.

It was very remarkable to see the great length of time animals in this country can exist, even under hard work, without drinking water. In an ordinary way, the Somali water camels only twice a-month, donkeys four times, sheep every fourth day, and ponies only once in two days, and even object to doing it oftener, when the water is plentiful, lest the animals should lose their hardihood. I do not think antelopes could possibly get at water for several months together, as every drop of water in the country is guarded by the Somali. We were now in "the land of honey," and the Somali nomads constantly came to me to borrow my English pickaxe for digging it out of the ground; for the bees of this country, instead of settling in the boughs of trees, as they do in England, work holes in the ground like wasps, or take advantage more generally of chinks or fissures in the rocks to build their combs and deposit their wax. It was a great treat to get a little of this sweet nutriment, to counteract the salts which prevail in all the spring waters of the interior. When out shooting specimens, I often saw the Somali chasing down the Salt's antelopes on foot.

I killed many of them myself right and left, when running like hares, with common shot, much to the astonishment of the Somali, for they are too small a mark for their bow-and-arrow shooting. The little creatures cannot stand travelling in the mid-day sun, and usually lie about under favouring trees which line the watercourses. Knowing this weakness, the cunning Somali hunter watches him down from feeding to his favourite haunts, and, after the sun shines strong enough, quietly disturbs him; then, as he trots away to search for another shady bush, they follow gently after to prevent his resting. In the course of an hour or so, the terrified animal, utterly exhausted, rushes from bush to bush, throwing itself down under each in succession, until at length it gets captured.

Somali, from their roving habits of life, are as keen and cunning sportsmen as any in the world. They told me of many dodges they adopted for killing elephants, ostriches, and gazelles, which they do as follows:--If an elephant is ever seen upon the plains, a large body of men assemble on foot, armed with spears, bows, and sharp double-edged knives, with one man mounted on a white horse, to act as teaser. This man commences by riding in front of the animal, to irritate and absorb his entire attention by riding in repeated circles just in front of him. When the huge beast shows signs of distress by fruitlessly charging on his nimble adversary, the footmen rush in upon him from behind, and hamstring him with their knives, and then with great facility soon despatch him with their arrows and spears.

Ostriches, again, are killed in two ways; the more simple one is by finding out what places they usually resort to in search of food, and then throwing down some tempting herb of strong poisonous properties, which they eagerly eat and die from. The other method adopted in catching them is not so easy, but is managed with great effect. The ostrich is, as is generally known, a remarkably shy bird, and is so blind at night it cannot feed. Again, the Somali pony, though wonderfully hardy and enduring, is not swift; therefore, to accommodate existing power to knowledge of these various weaknesses, the Somali provides himself with a pony, and provisions for two or three days, and begins his hunt by showing himself at such a considerable distance from the birds he has formed his design upon, that they quietly stalk off, and he, at the same rate, follows after, but never draws near enough to scare them out of sight of him. At night, the birds stop in consequence of the darkness, but cannot feed. He, on the other hand, dismounts to rest and feed with his pony, and resumes the chase the following day. After the second or third day, when he and the pony are as fresh as ever, the ostriches, from constant fasting, become so weak, he is able to ride in amongst them, and knock down one by one as many as may be in the flock. The flesh is eaten, and the feathers are taken to the sea-coast for transportation to the Aden market. I once saw a donkey-load of feathers carried to market that had been taken in this way.

There are two methods, also, of killing gazelles; the more usual one is effected by two men walking into a bushy ground to search for them, and when discovered, walking in such large circles around them as will not scare them; gradually they draw their circles in, until a favoured bush, down wind, is found, which the herd is most likely, when once moved, to pass by, and behind this one of the men stops, with his bow and arrows, whilst the second one, without ever stopping to create alarm, continues drawing in the circles of circumvention until he induces the gazelles to walk up to the bush his friend is concealed in, when one or more may be easily shot. The other plan for killing them is extremely artful, and is done on horseback, and therefore on the open plain. Fleet animals, like antelopes and gazelles, always endeavour to head across their pursuers, no matter in which direction they go. The Somali, therefore, taking advantage of this habit, when they wish to catch them on ponies, which are not half so swift as the gazelles in fair open chase, economise their strength by directing their animals' heads towards the leading gazelle, and thus inducing the herd, as they continue heading on, to describe double the circumference of ground their ponies have to traverse. In process of time, the gazelles, by their extra exertions, begin to flag and drop, and the hunters rush in upon them, and cut them up in detail.

20th.--To-day the young prince, Abdullah, returned to say the Dulbahantas had been conferred with, and had shown the strongest objections to my seeing their country, enumerating at the same time all their reasonings, such as I had already heard; but added, as a great concession on their part, as a particular favour they wished to show to my Abban, that I might be permitted to advance a little way to the next valley; but then only on condition that I would surrender to them the whole of my remaining property.

I now heard more particulars of the Dulbahantas' fights, and the manner in which they first originated. For full thirteen years they had been disputing amongst themselves, and many cabals had sprung out of it. Whilst these intrigues were gaining ground, a minor chief, named Ali Haram, with a powerful support in connections, about five years ago determined on alienating himself from the yoke of the government, which was headed by an old Gerad, called Mahamed Ali, the rightful and hereditary chief. Since then the original kingdom has been divided into two portions, called the Northern and Southern Dulbahantas; but although the northerners declare themselves independent, the chief of the south still fights for his lawful rights, and at this present time had driven the northerners, with all their cattle and stock, to Jid Ali Tug, the next valley beyond this, which I was now desirous of visiting. Ali Haram was an old man, and consequently incapacitated from taking an active part in these tumultuous filibusterings; he had therefore, since his first accession to power, deputed a son called Mahamed Ali Gerad to act as Regent in his stead, and this was the man of whom the Warsingali spoke to me at Bunder Gori so disparagingly.

21st.--I was now preparing to start again westward, when an order came from the Abban to my men, that no property should accompany me, excepting what little I felt disposed to part with in presents to the Dulbahantas; as an Akil, by name Husayn Hadji, the senior man present at Jid Ali, had decided, as a final measure, on seizing everything I brought with me immediately I set foot in Jid Ali. Though I had had experience enough of the Abban's tricks to see that this was merely a farce, though a very useless and inconvenient one, I permitted the arrangement rather than make a row and retard my progress, and set out with the young prince, Hamed, Farhan, and two camels and drivers, leaving Imam and the other nine camels, with their drivers, behind, to follow as soon as I should send back.

At the western extremity of the valley we came upon a small mound of earth, all white and glistening, covered with nitre in an efflorescent form, which shone so conspicuously in the sun, it could be seen at many miles' distance; from the base of it a clear spring of water trickled, so disagreeable in taste that no one, save Somali, could possibly drink it. Now, emerging from the low land, we again left the trees behind us, and rose by a well-beaten foot-track to the primary level of the country, where stone and bare ground prevailed. Each of these elevations and depressions was a mere reflection of the other, only varying more or less according to their size; and as my line was directed due west, I always had the mountain-range at even distance on the north, whilst every feature on the south remained the same. It was monotonous in the extreme. At the fifth mile we came upon some springs of bitter water, sunk in deep cavities in the earth, from which we filled our water-skins, and travelled on till night; when, dark overtaking us, we slipped into a hollow in the ground, called Ali, cooked a little rice with the water we had brought, and slept it out till morning. Distance, thirteen miles.

22d.--As soon as the morning was well aired with the sun, and the black men had recovered from the torpor which the cold seemed to produce on them as it does on lizards and snakes, I struck out for Jid Ali, hoping to surprise the Abban, and thereby counteract, if possible, his various machinations. But this was not to be done. At the thirteenth mile, as we were descending in full view of Jid Ali, at a place called Birhamir, I was met by the Akil Husayn Hadji himself, who, instead of show-ing any disposition to hinder my approach, was very affable and kind in manner. He politely begged me to remain where I was and rest the day, and on the morrow he would take me to the Tug (river) below. He had never felt indisposed towards me; but one Galed Ali, an Akil superior to himself, was averse to my proceeding further. Unfortunately for the Somali, their lies are very transparent, and they were too fond of uttering falsehoods ever to be trusted. I neither believed in the existence of Galed Ali, nor in his own kind intentions towards me, and therefore begged him to prove it by allowing me to pass. This began a long discussion. The wars were raging. The Dulbahantas would not let me see their country, as they could not see why an Englishman should wish to travel where even beggars were afraid to go; and then followed a hundred other excuses, all of which I rejected as freely as he advanced them.

Then at length, Somali fashion, the true meaning of his unwelcome visit trans-pired. He then said--"Well, if you have no fear of anything, and will join us in our fight, to represent your nation's disposition in our favour, I will give you as many horses as you may wish to have, and a free passage to Berbera, as soon as it is con-cluded." This was certainly a tempting offer, as I told him; but I said, Although, as far as I was individually concerned, there was nothing which would please me better, still, being a servant of the Government, I could not represent anything they had not sanctioned; and, moreover, I was bound to be at Berbera by a certain date, which I could not if I went southwards with them. They argued, There would be no delay in finishing the battles, if I merely showed myself as a representative of the English, for the enemy would retire before a shot was fired, concluding that the opinion of the world was against them. They all declared the war had lasted so long, and had been so harassing, they wished ardently to put an end to it. I told them, in my opinion, it was all their own fault; that they ought never to have commenced the war, for the chief they now recognised was a mere usurper--a traitor, in fact, who ought to be punished.

The Abban's mother, Mrs Awado, of whom I knew nothing until now, and who was living at Birhamir, in a hut close by, then hastened towards us, joined our party, and interrupted the conversation by clapping her hands and beating her knees, exclaiming, in wild dismay and terrifying words, "Oh! why have you come to this land, where there are no laws, or any respect for life? You don't know what these people are you've come amongst! Come with me now to my place; rest the night, and refresh yourself: tomorrow morning your Abban will come and conduct you safely on your way." This was a climax to the day's journey; the men smelt grub in an instant, and hurried off with the old lady to some empty stone enclosures (sheepfolds), and at once unburdened and "lay-to" for the night. As before, I had many conferences about the THE WADI NOGAL, which Lieutenant Burton had desired me to investigate, but could obtain no satisfactory information. They said there were many wadis in Nogal, but the largest one was in the Mijjertaine country, where its waters were deep and large, with extensive forest around it, frequented by numerous herds of elephants. Those in advance of my line of march, on the road to Berbera, were all mere nullahs, like Yubbe Tug, or Jid Ali Tug, and were not used for agricultural purposes. However, in the southern Dulbahanta country, south by west of this, at a distance of five or six marches, there was a nullah, with many springs in it, which united in certain places, and became a running stream. This I now, from subsequent inquiries and inspection of Lieut. Cruttenden's map,[18] suspect is the watercourse set down in my instructions as the Wadi Nogal. This watercourse, I was assured, bounded the Nogal or white stony country on the west, and divided it from the Haud or red stoneless country, which is occupied in most part by the southern Dulbahantas, who have "the finest grazing-grounds in the world, and possess incalculable numbers of camels and horses (meaning ponies), and cows, sheep, and goats; whilst the game which roamed about there covered the ground like flocks of sheep." Of these the largest were giraffes, rhinoceroses, and lions, elephants being confined to the Mijjertaine country, the Koolies hills to the south of Berbera, and the Webbe Shebeli, or Haines River.[19]

23d.--Early in the morning, accompanied by Husayn Ali, who opposed me no longer, we commenced our descent to the valley of Jid Ali, an expansive flat several miles in breadth, fuller and better wooded in the north than any place I had yet seen, but tapering away to the south and eastwards, until it became lost to sight in the barren plateau. After marching a mile or so, we found the Abban hastening to meet us, in high dudgeon with my men for having advanced contrary to his mandates, before he had time to arrive and smooth the way; for now the great impressive spell, his influence, which I was to understand could alone save me from the terrors of the unruly Dulbahantas, was proved to me of secondary importance, and he, consequently, insignificant. This occasioned a little delay; but at last, the Abban becoming reconciled to this defeat of his projected plans, we were permitted to resume the march, and, soon arriving in the bed of the valley, encamped near the watercourse of Jid Ali Tug, on the meridian of Mai. The water in the nullah extended upwards of half a mile, when it became absorbed in the thirsty soil. It consisted of a chain of pools, connected by little runners, the produce of some bitter springs, and made the country green in consequence. Attracted by my dates and rice--for I had brought no other property save my specimen-boxes and ammunition--many of the Dulbahantas forgot their occupations in war, and flocked around my camp all day and night, bothering my servants incessantly whilst cooking, and begging presents from me every moment. I remained here three days, trying to negotiate with the head men for permission to advance, but obtained no practical result. They insisted, for even coming thus far, that I should give them as many cloths and material as I had given to the Warsingali, for they would take no less. When told all my worldly goods did not admit of such a payment, they quietly said, I had come there against their will; they did not believe me; and if I did not open my boxes to their inspection, they would smash them up and help themselves. This was an everyday occurrence, which became only insignificant, as it was repeated without being carried into execution. Most of the time the Abban was away, stopping at his home, and no business could be done. I therefore took short excursions about the valley shooting, and inspecting the various habitations.

Animals were more abundant, in consequence of the greater extent of water; and I shot gazelles, little saltiana antelopes, hares, Egyptian geese, rock-pigeons, ducks and teal, and snipe and partridge, besides a choice collection of small birds. In one place I found a small stone hut, occupied by an old man who had once been on a pilgrimage to Mecca, and had seen the art of cultivating ground. He was now turning his experience to account by growing jowari (a species of millet), and effected it with some success; for he had two small enclosures, which he irrigated by cuts from the nullah, that produced grain, which grew from eight to nine feet high. He was loud in praise of the advantages which he derived from his farm, saying it saved his flocks, and assisted him in the means of food when his ewes were pregnant, or giving lamb. I patronised this farmer, and offered to lend him some tools for digging with, when he said he did not want that so much as some hints about sowing, and wished I would send a man to instruct him. Farhan, who was with me, delighted at the prospect of showing his skill in any manner--for he styled himself professor of all things--at once took the hint, and bargained to do a day's work, and furnish him with some wrinkles for his future guidance, for the payment of a goat, which was readily agreed to.

The people here were highly superstitious, and, like all ignorant races, very punctilious in their ceremonies of worship. As *true* Mussulmans, they were constant in their time of prayer, and abused my interpreter for never saying his. When I made him cut the deer's throats a little lower down the throat than their canons permit, to save the specimen, they spat on the ground to show their contempt, and abused him heartily. If I threw date-stones in the fire (the seed of paradisiacal food), they looked upon it as a sacrilege. They were also very suspicious. If I walked up and down the same place to stretch my legs, they formed councils of war on my motives, considering I must have some secret designs upon their country, or I would not do it, as no man in his senses could be guilty of working his legs unnecessarily.

Considering all the northerners were said to have been driven up here by the war, I was much surprised to see so few habitations or flocks in the valley; all there were consisted in a few kraals scattered over the plain, which were constantly moved as soon as each plot of ground in turn was eaten up by the cattle. In chang-ing ground, these nomads pack up everything on their camels, mat and stick, hut and all, and placing the wife, with perhaps a baby also, on a donkey, march to any unoccupied watering-place they can find. Their food is very limited, except in the rainy season, when milk prevails: in consequence of this, it being now the dry sea-son, my servants accounted for their increasing appetite for my dates. Some of the poorer men are said to pass their whole lives without tasting any flesh or grain, but to live entirely on sour milk, wild honey, or gums, as they may chance to come across them, and they are almost naked; but notwithstanding this, disease is scarce-ly known, and excepting in a few cases of endemic ophthalmia, which appears to attack the country periodically, at intervals of two or three years, I never heard of any. The climate was very delightful at this season, and the nights so cold I had to wrap myself well up in flannels. But perhaps that which best illustrates the healthi-ness of the country and pleasantness of its atmosphere, is the fact that I, although I had no bedstead, but always slept on the ground, never pitched my tent a single day in the interior, and neither wore a hat or shoe throughout the journey, save on one or two occasions, when, severely stabbed with thorns, I put on a sandal. I never knew a moment's illness.

25th.--This evening, Husayn Hadji, who I now found out was brother-in-law to Sumunter, approached me as I came in from shooting, and said, "We are sur-prised to see you return alive; did you not meet some armed men when you were shooting?" I replied, "No, not one." "Then," said he, "there are many men come here, who from the first have forbid your coming into this country; they are under no control, but, in open defiance of the Gerad, do and act just as they like: indeed, every head man is a Gerad here, and those who are strongest carry the day." This was the prelude to another farce; presently the men came of whom Husayn Hadji spoke, and, surrounding my camp, boisterously demanded to know what I was do-ing in their country against their orders. A violent altercation then ensued. They must have all my property given up at once, or they would take it by force; and re-mained trying to bully me into compliance, until I said I would sooner die than give them anything. Seeing me determined, they then walked off, saying I had not one night left to live, for they would return and kill me after dark. The place was now getting too hot to be pleasant, for the fact was, we were so near the watering-place, that my camp offered a convenient and tempting lounge for all the idle blackguards of the country to assemble at.

26th.--I sent orders back for the rear traps to come on as quick as possible, and at the suggestion of my servants, who were just as tired as myself of these incessant provocations, changed camp to a place three miles farther up the valley, much more remote from water, but nearer to the Abban's home, by which I hoped I should be able to get at him easier; for the aggravating wretch, whenever I sent messages to recall him, invariably returned plausible excuses, showing the necessity of his having stopped away, and as repeatedly said he would not fail in coming immediately; but at the same time, as the sequence showed, never intending to do so.

It would be useless, as well as painful, to narrate in detail all the daily and hourly incidents which occurred in the next few days whilst I was detained here by the artful and dishonest machinations of this vile-conditioned man, from whom I could never get one true word, and whose absence, although I was striving to induce his coming to me, really seemed a relief. A wicked feeling was almost coming over me, which made me shudder again when I reflected more calmly on what my mind was now dilating. He seemed to me only as an animal in satanical disguise; to have shot him would have given me great relief, for I fairly despaired of ever producing any good effect upon his mind. Again I tried the old scheme of forcing him to leave me, and even begged an Akil of the Dulbahantas, offering him large rewards, to be my guide to Berbera. This, as might be imagined, provoked a severe row. The man I was endeavouring to seduce to favour me was one of the gang of forty thieves, and as birds of a feather all Dulbahantas flocked together to assist the victim of my displeasure; for Sumunter was, by his intermarriage with these northerners, naturalised amongst them. However, I had my wicked will, by relating, in presence of all his now rapidly congregating friends (a row always brings a crowd), the whole of his misdemeanours since he first came with me to this country, and threatened him with the lasting displeasure of our Government, and ruin to his trade at Aden, if he still persisted in his tricks. This brought matters home much closer than anybody liked to hear, and set all parties cogitating on what course had best be followed. I now retired to cool myself by shooting, and on returning again was met by the Abban, interpreter, and many Dulbahanta Akils, who, now trying the conciliating dodge, came to report the good news that a victory had been gained by the northerners, and the southerners were in full retreat to their provinces, by which the road to Berbera would be open to my proceeding onwards. Moreover, the rear traps had arrived at Abi, by which accident everything seemed to harmonise. This sounded very cheering for the moment, but I soon was damped again.

I wanted to move at once, and lose no time in taking full benefit of the opportunity thus offered; but this, like every other proposal that I made, was immediately checked by a cruel device, as unforeseen as it was objectionable. Hassan had not come with the ponies he went after from Rhut Tug; I must therefore, before advancing, send back to the farther frontier of the Warsingali to purchase, by bills on Aden, five ponies at thirty dollars a-head, to be afterwards given away in presents to chiefs on the road for allowing me to pass through their territories, and this, at a minimum calculation, would occupy a fortnight's time, and even then I should have to go single-handed, without a servant, instrument, or article of any bulk with me. Of course this, as the Abban knew, I never would consent to. On no account would I suffer my being separated from my men and property when the time for my return to Berbera was so close at hand; and, moreover, without the instruments the journey would be of no avail. Row succeeded row when I pushed matters closely; the Abban sometimes affected repentance, but more often became defiant, and forbade anybody's assisting me without his entire consent. Such, in fact, were the effects of these angry ebullitions of temper on the minds of my people, that the young Prince Abdullah, fearing to be witness to them any more, took his leave and departed home.

31st.--At length the rear traps arrived, but one camel, having been taken ill on the march this morning whilst coming from Abi, was slaughtered to "*save*" his flesh, and devoured by my hungry men. As soon as everything had arrived, and the men were made aware of my intention to push forward, they requested their discharge, affecting fear to enter on a strange land, but in reality seeing I had no cloths left to pay them, as afterwards transpired. This deficiency I visited on the Abban, who, in trying to excuse himself for inefficiency in his protectorship, meekly said he had been grieved to see the very rapid decline of my property, but he could not help it, as I had so many thieves in my employment!!! Mrs Awado now came over from Birhamir, bringing a sheep and some ghee as a present for me; but I refused taking anything from the relative of the Abban, and this appeared to grieve her much. She said she had heard of all my disputes with Sumunter, her son, and had remonstrated with him about them; he was a proud man, and easily led away by vanity. She could see his being at variance with me would not end to his advantage on his return to Aden, and tried coaxing him to journey with me; but at the same time told me he would have to be well upon his guard, as in former years he had married clandestinely with a damsel of the Rheer Hamaturwa, a sub-tribe of the Habr Gerhajis, who occupy the hill-range overlooking Bunder Heis; and her loss to those people would be avenged at once, if he ever came within their power. The Rheer Hamaturwa had heard of my intention to journey westwards, and would be in readiness to descend upon and intercept our march, kill Sumunter, and destroy the whole of us; indeed, they had sent messages to that effect.

Chapter IV.

Meditations among the Tombs--A Fracas--The Return March--The Northeast Monsoon--Relief from Persecution--Interesting Animals--Gori Again--Shooting a Woman--Arrival at Aden--Fresh Projects--Arrangements.

3d January 1855.--During these three days I visited a ruined musjid and a cemetery, which, though much resembling the one at Rhut in every respect, was said to be of more recent origin, and built by Mohammedans. On my walking amongst the tombs, and inspecting the crosses[20] at their heads, the interpreter rebuked me for sacrilegious motives, and desired me to come away, lest the Dulbahantas should find it out, and be angry with me. Besides this, I daily tried to draw Sumunter, like a badger, from his hut, which was four miles distant from my tent, but without effect. He and his wife, two dwarf sisters (little bits of things, who, the interpreter said, were too small to be of any use), and some children, all lived together in a small beehive hut, so low that they had to crawl in on all-fours, and so small that it was marvellous how they could turn round in it. At length to-day he arrived in a sullen angry mood, and said, haughtily, he was displeased at my trying to force him into compliance, as if I had the power to make him move unless he chose. It was impossible to keep one's temper under such constant provocation; so I abused him vehemently, and warned him off the camp, again repeating he had abused his commission, as well as the Government authorities who engaged him,--and entreated he would "get away," and let me take my chance of proceeding how I could, for his presence simply made my position one of purgatory. He laughed in scorn, wishing to know if I thought I could do anything without him,--and said he had only to turn his back an instant, and the Dulbahantas were ready to devour me. I still persisted; and then he said, "If you say go once more, I take you at your word; and see you to the consequences."

My resolution was fixed; for I plainly saw I could not by any possibility be worse off. He now tried frightening me by assembling the Dulbahantas to confirm his words, making them say they only permitted my residence there out of the love they bore to their brother Sumunter, and that they certainly would kill me if he once left the place. They did not fear guns. The English could not reach them; besides, their fathers had driven Christians from these lands; and if an army was to attack them, they would assemble so many cavalry, and ride in such rapidity around them, that their gunners could not take aim in consequence of the clouds of dust which this feat would occasion. In addition to this, they thought the English only efficacious behind walls; else, why did they not take revenge upon the Arabs at Lahej, two years ago, for the murder of an officer? They had often heard of the English threatening and preparing to do it, but somehow they never carried their intention into execution. I treated these vain bombastic words with the contempt which they deserved,--but said, I only wanted Sumunter to take me on, or otherwise to leave me to my fate. They then tried weakening my party by bribing Farhan to side with them and leave; but the noble-hearted Seedi disclosed their treachery, and gallantly said he would share misfortunes with me, and fight, if necessary, to the last extremity.

Imam, tame-hearted Indian, got in a dreadful fright, and implored I would compromise the matter; for by this time all the camels had been driven away; and the Warsingali moved off with Sumunter, saying I brought the rupture by my obstinacy on my own head, and that as soon as they were out of sight, the Dulbahantas would walk in and kill us all in a heap. I then loaded all the guns, and, giving one to each of the servants, sat on the boxes waiting to see the up-shot. I was clearly outmanoeuvred--unable to move or get anything--but still was, to use their own expression, "obstinate." After proceeding a certain distance, the retiring band, with Sumunter at their head, sitting fully equipped with spear and shield on his war-steed, came to a halt, and invited the interpreter to meet them, presuming, they said, there might be some mistake, and therefore they wished to open negotiations afresh. Sumunter then gave me back my own words, saying, "If the Sahib would only say he wished me to take him to Berbera, I will give some small presents to the Akils of the Dulbahantas as a passport for him, and proceed at once;" for they were only endeavouring to feel my disposition towards them, and did not intend desertion, if I was not irredeemably incensed against them. They then came back, and work began afresh, by the distribution of presents, which, as is usual when no man can bear to see the smallest trifle slip from his grasp to be given to another, was a matter of no small difficulty in adjusting. If the Dulbahantas did not succeed in skinning me of all my effects, they naturally thought the next tribe would; and a whole day was consumed in wrangling and disputing how much they should get. This ended by my giving one musket, thirteen tobes, and my reserve silk turban; and now I was at liberty to quit Jid Ali.

11th.--At 10 A.M. we were loaded, and commenced the journey westward; whilst the Abban said he would bid his friends adieu at home, and bring five horses with him to Biyn Hable, where he would meet us on the following day. The track led us across a flat alluvial plain, still in the valley, which was well covered with a thick growth of acacias, and dry short grass, nipped short by cattle. After walking five miles, we arrived at our destination, not far from a well, and made a ring-fence of prickly boughs.

Here for the last time I boiled the thermometer, to ascertain the altitude of the plateau along my line of march, and found its average height was 3913 feet: the minimum, at Rhut Tug, being 3077 feet--and the maximum, at Yubbe Tug, 4498 feet.

The following day two Dulbahantas paid us a visit, and demanded to know by whose authority we had come upon their grounds; we were trespassers, and must pay our footing. The ground was theirs, and they recognised no authority over them. What I had given at the last place was no concern of theirs, but I must give them also a quantity of cloth equivalent to it. This being refused as a preposterous imposition, they turned hastily away, and, tossing their heads, said, I might soon expect to see them again in larger numbers, when they would help themselves. Moreover, for my satisfaction, they could assure me that a number of men, who had learned which road I was bent on travelling, were fast gathering on ahead, to oppose my advance. In the evening the Abban arrived, bringing only two ponies with him.

17th.--It would be needless to recount all the varied incidents of the next five days which were wasted here, by the thousand and one stories which the Abban produced to fritter away my time near his home, and swindle me out of my property. The time had now arrived when by appointment I should have been at Berbera; and as I was not then aware at what time the fair usually broke up, I felt much afraid of being too late to join my companions. Sometimes Sumunter raised my hopes by saying he would certainly proceed on a certain date; and when that day arrived, the journey was deferred again, but not without severe rows, so exactly like the past ones as to be unworthy of description. One day we were ready, and I was to pass through any people that might fall in the way by giving large credits on Aden under his security, when the tide was turned again in another moment by the arrival of some accomplices, who dropped in like unexpected evils, to say the southern Dul-bahantas had gained a great victory, slaughtering men and cattle, and the road to Berbera would be thronged with people, so that advance would be impossible for the present. This was a settler to my westward march; and now I thought of escaping from this land of robbers by turning northwards, and marching over the hills to Bunder Heis, where I could either ship off, or march along the coast to Berbera.

Negotiations were then set on foot with the Rheer Hamaturwa, and several of their Akils came at my bidding, but were as implacable about obliging a stranger as any of their neighbours. The whole distance was not three days' travel; still they said I should not see their country, and acknowledged themselves a lawless band, who would take everything from me if I ventured there: adding, if the Warsingali and Dulbahantas, who were stronger than themselves, would only withdraw from me one day, they would come down at once, and demolish my whole camp. They then demanded cloths for the trouble I had given them, but, not receiving any, re-tired in huge disgust.

18th.--In final despair I faced about, and marched north-easterly, by a new route, to reach Bunder Gori again, to ship for Aden, as there only could I be certain of finding a vessel to convey me over the Gulf. After six miles' march across the head of the valley, we arrived at Mirhiddo Kraal, on elevated ground, and found a large party assembled there. Some of them were the Rheer Hamaturwa, with whom I tried again for permission to cross their hills, but this time by the gap at the head of the valley in front of Bunder Jedid. This they were ready to permit, and give security of passage to my people, if I gave them all my remaining cloths; but they thought I should not find a vessel there, which settled the question. I had no time to lose, and, moreover, should save my cloths by continuing on the line I was travelling. For though I should have to cross the hills where they were occupied by the Habr Gerhajis, in the new way my track would pass so near to the Warsingali frontier, that that tribe would not have strength enough to demand anything from me, and passport fees are only given in such places to the extent to which they can be enforced.

The other people I met here were some Dulbahantas arming for the fight. They said they were 4000 strong in cavalry, and were slaughtering sheep wholesale for provision on the road. Each man carried a junk of flesh, a skin of water, and a little hay, and was then ready for a long campaign, for they were not soft like the English (their general boast), who must have their daily food; they were hardy enough to work without eating ten days in succession, if the emergency required it. Here a second camel was on the point of dying, when his flesh was saved from becoming carrion by a knife being passed across his throat.

21st.--The Abban slipped away on the 19th, when I was out specimen-hunting, and would not come again till to-day, and then even returned to give his wife a last salute, permitting me to advance to a watercourse called Hanfallal, whilst he would join me on the following day. This day we accomplished ten miles, and made a kraal about four miles north of our old line of march.

22d.--As the Abban did not keep his promise, and none of us knew the road, I now tried to prevail on his mother Awado, who was tending her flocks close by, to be my guide, which she readily consented to do, as she was anxious herself to go to Bunder Gori. The water found here was in a circular cleft of limestone, sixty feet below the surface, which was so small, only one person at a time could descend to it; and the supply was so limited, I was obliged to keep my men down there all night, to be the first for drawing in the morning. Gazelles were very abundant, and in the evening we were visited by a very singular-looking canine animal, which unfortunately I could not get a shot at. It was a little less in size than the Crocuta hyena, but inclined rather more, in its general shape, to a wolf than a hyena. The body was a pure black, like the black Tibet wolf, but the tail was tipped with white. I am not aware that this animal has ever been described.

23d.--At the usual starting-hour the Abban arrived, with two ponies belonging to his brother-in-law, Husayn Ali, but which he tried to pass off as his own, being ever very anxious to make me believe he was a large stock proprietor, to magnify his importance. But, unfortunately for him, the interpreter, who was as treacherous a man as any of the breed, although he often confounded me by his innate deceit, also peached at times upon his brother Sumunter. The Abban, on seeing his mother equipped and ready on her donkey to go with me, scolded her heartily for presuming to undertake the journey without his leave, and sent her home faster than she came. We now commenced the march, and travelled five miles diagonally across some low spurs of hills, and encamped in the evening in a broad, deep, dry nullah, at a place called Dalmalle. We brought water with us, and fortunate it was so, for none could be found anywhere near the camp.

24th.--We started early in the morning, ascending the hill-range by a steep winding footpath up one of its ridges, which, in respect to its barrenness and soil, resembled the descent I had from Yafir. After completing eleven miles' march, the caravan crested the hill opposite Ras[21] Galweni, travelled a short way on the flat of the summit, and encamped in the evening amongst some thick jungle on its north or seaward side, at a kraal called Gobamire.

Immediately on arriving, as we commenced to unload the camels, a number of men who were occupying that district--the Urus Sage section of the Habr Gerhajis tribe--seized the camels by their heads, and demanded their customary fees, at the same time boisterously gesticulating that they would help themselves if their request was not complied with. Farhan enjoyed the row in the boisterous characteristic manner of a Seedi--began dancing frantically the negro war-dance, cocking his gun, and pointing it at everybody by turns; whilst Sumunter and the other Warsingali began thumping them with their clubs, and swearing a fearful vengeance would be wrought upon them by their tribe, who were living within an hour or two's call, should they not desist. The fact was, my men knew their power here, and, guided only by animal passions, enjoyed showing it. The poor discomfited Urus Sage now slunk off like defeated dogs, or schoolboys returning from a fight, just wishing to know if they were only to be considered in the light of women, who could not maintain their own right, and, snarling and snapping, threatened they would return again in stronger force before the morning.

We then unloaded, and lay-to for the night. Immediately on reaching the top of this range, a most interesting and novel sight was presented to our view. We stepped in one instant from constant sunshine into constant clouds, and saw what accounted for the dense verdure of the north, as well as the extreme barrenness of the south side of the hills. For two months we had not seen the vestige of a cloud, or felt a drop of rain, and now we were at once launched into the middle of the "Dairti" or north-east monsoon, which had been pouring for some time previously against the north face of the mountain, and was arrested there by it. It reminded me at once of that marked phenomenon with which all travellers in the Himalaya Mountains, who spend their "hot-weather" season at Chini, on the banks of the Sutlege river, to escape rain, must be acquainted, when the clouds of the great Indian monsoon envelop all the mountain-range for months together on the weather or south-west side, and hang suspended on the top of a high hill in sight of that place, but never pass over, looking as if the mountain was too high to be surmounted by them, when trying to reach the dry plateaux of Tibet. The clouds were rolling in thick successive volumes at our feet, and obscured the view below us.

25th.--We were detained until noon in consequence of the Abban's ponies, which had gone astray, and until then could not be found. In the meanwhile the Urus Sage came again, and tried to prevent us loading, on the same plea as yesterday, but without effect; but when we were starting, a compromise was effected on condition they would escort us down the hill and guide the way. The road was steep and very slippery, so that the camels could hardly get along, and this was further increased by the thick strong green jungle-bushes, as well as rocks and other difficulties incidental to mountain travelling with such large and ungainly animals as laden camels. At the fourth mile we found a large roomy cave under a rock, and put up for the night. Sheep had been kept here, and the place was so full of fleas that the ground was literally browned with them. I never saw such an astonishing quantity congregated in one place; but we soon disposed of them by burning certain boughs, which the Somali justly said was a specific remedy against them.

26th and 27th.--During these two days we descended by a tortuous winding footpath under no mean difficulties, and finally arrived, after twelve miles' marching, at a place called Hundurgal, situated in the hollow of a watercourse which divides the Warsingali from the Habr Gerhajis frontiers, and transmits its waters to the Gulf at Ras Galweni. During the journey the Somali pointed out some of their richest gum-trees, of which the finest in order is a species of frankincense, called by them Falafala, or Luban Maiti. The gum of this tree is especially valued by the

Somali women for fumigating purposes, which they apply to their bodies by sitting over it, when ignited, in the same manner as Cashmeres sit over their little charcoal-pots to keep themselves warm when resting on their travels. They enshroud themselves in a large wrapper, place a pot with the burning gum between their legs, and allow the perfume to rise to every portion of their body simultaneously. We gave our guides five cloths for escort, and sent them away.

I was informed by my men that under lee of Ras Galweni there is a better harbour than any on the whole coast-line, having deep water close in to the shore, but, being neutral ground, the Warsingali will not allow anybody to occupy it. They do not allow the Habr Gerhajis to do so, as they would monopolise the trade; and they will not take it themselves, as their sultan sagely remarks it would draw all their force to one side of their possessions, and thus leave the other exposed to attack from the Mijjertaines. Now the Dulbahantas are obliged to come to Bunder Gori if they want to traffic with outer nations, but were the Habr Gerhajis at Galweni, this custom would be drawn from them.

28th.--The inexpressible delight I felt at snuffing the fresh sea-air, and being comparatively free from the tyranny of my persecutor Sumunter, was truly indescribable; and I felt so impatient to end this useless journey, and join my friends for the larger and more promising one, I could hardly restrain my spirits. I stepped out before the caravan was ready, and began the journey alone, when presently a rapid fire, the discharge of a six-barrel revolver, attracted my attention. This was done by the Abban, who said that whilst travelling there his life was in jeopardy from the Habr Gerhajis, in consequence of an old feud he had contracted with them, on account of which they had forbidden this road to him. He thought to frighten them by the report of firearms, but it seemed to have the opposite effect, for many men at once gathered around the caravan, and for the time prevented its onward course. As usual, they wanted me not only to pay for travelling in their country, but to liquidate their claim on the Abban, as I had brought him there, and only out of consideration for the respect they felt towards me, they permitted his passage in safety.

They might as well have tried to skin a flint as obtain anything from me, and I told them so, for Sumunter had fleeced me of all my effects. This parley concluded, we travelled on without any further molestation, and, crossing over the foot of some low spurs, arrived at noon in a broad watercourse on the maritime plain to eat some breakfast.

Here I shot and stuffed a very interesting rat, with a bushy tail, very much resembling the little gilleri squirrel of the Indian plains, but plumper in face and body, like a recently born rabbit. I had seen many of them in rocks about the hill's side, but until now had not secured a good specimen.[22] Again at this place I saw those large black canine animals with white-tipped tail, but could not get a shot: there were three hunting together, like jungle dogs in India. After refreshing ourselves we resumed the march, and travelled along the sandy shore eastward to a halting-place called Farjeh, completing a march of twelve miles.

29th.--This day we completed our journey by marching into Gori, when I again took occupation of the old fort. An answer from the Government at Aden to my appeal against the sultan and Abban had now arrived, and affected Sumunter severely. He was ready to sink into the earth, and said to me, "Oh, why did you not whip me when I was in fault? I could have borne that well, but writing to the English at Aden is more than I can bear. What will be the consequences now if I return to Aden?" I said I could not answer for it, as it was now beyond my control, and if he went over there he must take his chance; but I strongly advised his not going at all. "Indeed," I said, "I wish you would depart from me at once. From the first, I told you I was obliged, by order, to write accurate accounts of everything as it happened, and the English, as you have often said yourself, are remarkable for not telling lies." The sultan, into whose hands the letter first went, would not show himself, but remained in the distant jungles, although I sent repeatedly for him to converse concerning Sumunter.

The buggalow in which I came from Aden was now anchored in Bunder Gori. It had made a voyage somewhere in the meanwhile, but the captain had been afraid to go to Aden in consequence of the salt question, in which Sumunter had made him confederate, fearing lest I might have since written to the authorities there about it. However, I now wanted to hire it again, and made sundry overtures to the captain, who at first showed a disposition to treat, hoping thereby I should forgive him; but he was finally hindered from doing so by the insidious machinations of Sumunter, who doubtless was afraid by this means of collecting at Aden more witnesses against himself. Sumunter now saw his position clearly, and must have felt equally with myself it was a great pity the letter of reproof from the Brigadier of

Aden[23] did not arrive sooner, and keep him on a course of rectitude, for he was obliged to return to Aden and take his chance, as there he had not only a wife and family, but it was the headquarters of all his mercantile transactions. During this time, whilst I was in the old fort, an odd accident occurred to an Akil's wife. She was playing with my interpreter, who, for a frolic, snatched up one of my six-barrelled revolver pistols and gave her chase. Suddenly she darted into the room I was sitting in, bounced on a bench and poked her tail in my man's face. He, not knowing the pistol was loaded, pulled at the trigger, and discharged the contents of two barrels at once into her fleshy projection. In an instant their fun came to an end, and great consternation ensued. She thought she must die from it, and bolted off home to give up the ghost. Her husband now came and clamoured for revenge--her value was so-and-so, and my man must pay it. The interpreter, hearing this, came crying to me, and wished to know if I thought she would die; for should she do so, he, by the laws of the land, would have to pay her price. I said I could not tell without seeing her wounds, but, under any circumstances, the bullets ought to be extracted. This appeared to them still more alarming than ever. They did not wish me to inspect the wounds, and the woman herself was very bashful. However, the Sahib was the only surgeon present, and votes gave me the practice. It was certainly very amusing to witness the struggle between virtue and necessity, and the operation was so far satisfactory that I succeeded in extracting one of the balls. The other ball, however, was so deeply imbedded I could not find a probe that would reach it. Fortunately it was not fired in a dangerous direction, and the ball being small, I thought it would not occasion her any serious inconvenience. In short, I set their minds easy on that score, though it did not keep their tongues quiet from importunate begging. I was now dreadfully impatient to get away, but day by day I had to suffer disappointment. I was assured by Sumunter he was doing everything in his power to facilitate it, and as often told by the interpreter, when he had gone away, that he was doing nothing of the sort, but, on the contrary, had sent to the interior to get three ponies, which would make five with what he had, the complement required by Lieutenant Burton, to make a present to him on arrival, as a bribe to overlook his faults. I besought he would desist from this hopeless speculation, as time was now more precious than any other matter. Still he persisted, and in a fortnight's time the animals arrived, and then, without further trouble, we chartered a vessel for thirty-five dollars, twelve times the fare I paid for coming over, with the whole vessel to myself; and embarked with eight camels and five ponies on the 15th February 1855. After five days' sailing we anchored in Aden harbour, and no sooner did the "let go the anchor" sound, than, Somali fashion, overjoyed at my release from three and a half months' persecution, I took a header into the sea, and hastily swam ashore to hurry off and meet old friends.

After the first greetings were over, and I had delivered for report all my sketch-notes[24] of the journey, as well as maps and collections, which latter were sent to the public museum in Calcutta, a discussion took place as to the disposal of the Ab-ban, who, I now found out, was not singular in the way of treating his clients, for Herne had been writing over complaints constantly about his man. I was averse to punishing him, from the simple fact of having brought him over; but my comman-dant thought otherwise, and that he had better be punished, if for no other reason than to set a good moral example to the others.[25]

Against my inclination I was appointed to be Sumunter's prosecutor, and with my servants as witnesses, a verdict of guilty was speedily effected against him in the Aden Police Court. He was then sentenced to two months' imprisonment, and to pay the sum of 200 rupees, or, failing to do that within the given time, he would be further subjected to imprisonment, with hard labour, for six months more, and was to be banished with his family for ever after the present punishment should cease.

I now advised Lieutenant Burton, after my late defeat in travelling, that it would be highly essential to the success of the great expedition that we should be escorted by some Somali picked from the Aden police force, as by this means alone should we have men on whom we could depend. He also was aware of this fact, from having been successfully taken himself into Harar by one of that corps; but, unfortunately for us, there were none to spare.

Though the Somali are rare blackguards in most respects, there are some traits in their character which have always won me to them. They love freedom and liberty, and enjoy a jolly row, added to which they are always in good spirits. In my humble opinion, they would make first-rate guerilla soldiers for Aden, if armed and trained to shoot with good rifles, and not restrained to wearing any particular clothes, or confined to steady-marching drills. They have a national antipathy to the Arabs, their elder brothers, and would glory in having scrimmages with them.

This was the climax of my first proceedings with Africa.

Stroyan and Herne were now both employed at Berbera or in its vicinity. The former had been making slight excursions inland, shooting, and had killed three elephants; whilst the latter was purchasing baggage-cattle for the expedition transport. After enjoying a short repose in civilised life, I again felt restless, and proposed a move to proceed thither in order to assist Herne in completing the desired complement of animals. This at once met the views of our commandant, who, doubting whether Berbera could supply a sufficient number of beasts of burden of itself, asked me to cross over the Gulf and see what I could do at Kurrum, to keep in communication with Herne, and as soon as I had got enough, to march with them along the sea-shore to Berbera.

Nothing could have suited me better. I saw before me, by this measure, active employment until the breaking-up of the Berbera fair.

A kind friend (Lieutenant Dansey of the Bombay army, late Assistant Political Agent of Aden, who knew the characters of all the Somali well) offered to procure me a man as guide and interpreter who had formerly performed, during the time of his appointment, some political service in the Somali country, with great credit both to his mission and himself. In consequence of this he was nicknamed El Balyuz, or the Ambassador.

Balyuz was a clever Hindostani scholar, and, as I ultimately found, possessed such honesty of purpose and straightforwardness of character, as rendered him a perfect *rara avis* amongst all Somali. He was of the Mijjertaine tribe. Travelling in his company, after my experiences with Sumunter and Ahmed, was verily a luxury. I parted with him at the termination of the expedition with pure feelings of affection.

Lieutenant Burton now conceived the idea of suppressing the system of Abbanship, thinking that, as the Somali had access to Aden without any impost, Englishmen ought to enjoy a corresponding freedom to travel in Somali Land. This perhaps was scarcely the right time to dictate a policy which would be distasteful as well as injurious (in a monetary sense) to the people among whom we were about to travel, and with whom it was highly essential to our interest to be on the most friendly terms.[26]

I now applied to the Government for some Somali policemen, but unfortunately there were then too few hands present to carry on the duties of the office, and I could not have them. I therefore engaged, by the orders of Lieutenant Burton, a dozen men of various races (Egyptians, Nubians, Arabs, and Seedis), to form an escort, and armed them with my sabres and muskets. They were all raw recruits, and unaccustomed to warfare. Still we could get no others. With a little practice they learned to shoot at a mark with tolerable accuracy.

Seven of these men, together with the eight camels I brought across from Bunder Gori, were despatched direct to Berbera, whilst the remaining five, and some ponies I purchased in Aden, remained with me. I then took a bag of dollars for purchasing camels; some dates and rice for the consumption of the party; and with the Balyuz and the old servants, Imam the butler and Farhan the gamekeeper, all was ready for my second adventure on the 20th March 1855.

Chapter V.

21st March 1855.--Having engaged a buggalow and stowed away all the traps, I embarked in the evening, weighed anchor, and set sail. Even before we could sail out of the harbour, the first row commenced. The Nakhoda (captain), as is often the case in these primitive countries, kept no regular sailors, but trusted to finding men desirous of going to their country, who would work his vessel for him--all Somali being by nature sailors.

The men he had now on board were of the Habr Gerhajis and Habr Teljala tribes, who occupy the coast-line near Kurrum, and had waited the opportunity of obtaining a passage over there in company with me. They were all dreadfully uproarious, and would not by any persuasion on my part keep quiet. On inquiring from the Balyuz the cause of their violent discussions, he informed me they were drawing lots to see who should be my Abban, and those of the seven foreign servants I had with me. The bare idea of eight Abbans was too ridiculous, and their persistency made it beyond a joke. I instantly ordered the sails to be hauled down, and had my instructions from Lieutenant Burton about Abbans proclaimed to the whole crew: that the Balyuz was my Ras Cafila, and the other foreigners my protectors. The Somali were evidently determined not to be done. If I had been allowed to have but one Abban with me, this could not have occurred. As it was, I said if they determined on wrangling any more, I should 'bout ship and settle the difference with them in a less ceremonious manner in the harbour. This effectually stopped their tongues, and we again proceeded on the journey. After two entire days' sailing across the

Gulf with variable and gentle breezes, we arrived at our destination, Kurrum, in safety, on the third evening, the 24th March, and at once sent some Government letters to the Akils, ordering their attendance, and to proclaim publicly the nature of my business, in order that camels might be brought for sale. I found all the people extremely obliging; they tried to make my residence as comfortable as they could; showed me great deference because I was an Englishman, and brought their camels readily, though, of course, as might be expected, they were canny in their mode of dealing, trying to dispose of their worst animals first, and asking prices much above the market tariff. For poor animals they asked from four to five and a half dollars, which, though not a third of the price I paid in the Warsingali country, was full price for the finest animals at Berbera. Berbera during the fair time is undoubtedly the cheapest place to purchase camels in of all the coast-line, and the farther you leave it the more expensive animals become, increasing in price at the same ratio as the extent of distance. Whilst halting here I heard of the existence of the Victoria N'yanza. The Somali described its dimensions as equal in extent to the Gulf of Aden, and further alluded to its being navigated by white men. None of the men present had been there to see it, though it was currently known as a positive fact amongst them. I did not believe the story in the light they expressed it, supposing they confounded an inland sea with the Western or Atlantic Ocean. Colonel Rigby, H.B.M. Consul at Zanzibar, tells me he also heard of this lake when he was travelling in this country some years previously. It is strange this story was never published earlier. The white navigators alluded to are evidently the expeditionists who were sent by Mehemet Ali, Viceroy of Egypt, up the White Nile as far as Gondokoro, about twelve or fourteen years ago, and the Nile and lake have been confounded as one water in the transmission of the intelligence, though both were seen.

The minds of the Kurrum people seemed greatly discomposed about various rumours which they heard. One was that the English intended to suppress the slave-trade, and they wished me to tell them if such was not a fact--saying it would be unjust for us to do so, as slaving was an acknowledged right given them in the Koran, and handed down by their Russool Mahamed.

The other bugbear which alarmed them was a report that the English intended either to take possession of Berbera, or that they would give it to Shermarky--a native chief and ally of ours who lives at Zeylah. In short, these numerous fears arose from Herne's long residence at Berbera. It looked suspicious seeing him take notes there of everything, and they naturally put the worst interpretation on all his actions. What could be the use of his watching the trade, if our Government did not want to take the country?--of watching the slave-trade, if it did not mean stopping it? And then the suppression of Abbanships was the crowning of all.

The village of Kurrum consisted of a single fort and a large collection of mat huts, all grouped together, situated close to the shore. The maritime plain consisted of sandy-brown soil, very uninteresting, with scarcely any vegetation growing on it, and was here only about half a mile broad. The hills in the background were very insignificant, not half so high as any I had seen, and were dull and brown, like those one sees when travelling down the Red Sea. The people say that in their recesses and ravines acacias and other gum-trees grow as they do elsewhere. Gum only exudes in the dry hot season; and the confined air in the ravines is described as being so hot that people can hardly stay there, and many of the gum-pickers who do, become deaf in consequence of it.

The water which the villagers used was so brackish as to be hardly drinkable. I lived here five days, enjoying sour camel's milk, gossiping with the natives, and roaming about the place. The difference between the life I was now living, attributable principally to the sagacity and good-heartedness of the Balyuz, was a charming contrast to my wretched existence when with the Warsingali. I bought twenty-five camels, at an average rate of five and a half dollars a-head, and then stopped purchasing, as I heard by letter from Herne he had then got nearly sufficient for our requirements--that camels were very plentiful at Berbera, and he was buying them at a cheaper rate than I could.

On the 29th March, at 4 P.M., I broke ground with all my camels and ponies, and commenced the march on Berbera. At sundown, after travelling three miles along the sea-shore, we encamped in a water-course called Goldera. The water we found here, in a little well in its bed, was deliciously sweet--so pleasant after the brackish Kurrum wells. No one who had not been deprived for a long time of the pure element, can conceive the greed with which a man first plunges his head into clear sweet water. It is the natural fluid for man, and for no other beverage does abstinence produce so keen an appetite.

The following morning, a little after daybreak, the caravan was ready, and we soon got under way. Travelling with tedious slowness, aggravated by the dreary monotony of the road and the sandy plain, constantly crossing dry, shallow water-courses, lined on both sides by fringes of stunted acacias or other salsolacious plants, we at last arrived at a hot spring of sweet water, called Golamiro, and rested here for several hours during the great heat of the mid-day sun. When the day became cooler we resumed the march, and travelled until after dark to a grazing-ground one mile short of Ain Tarad, and there spent the night. The farther we travelled westwards, the broader became the maritime plain, and the richer its clothing of shrubs and grass. Besides the ordinary acacias, which were finer and more numerous, there were many patches of the bastard cypress and tall rank grasses growing on sandy hillocks, in the same way as they do in India. The Somali exultingly pointed this out as a paradise, replete with every necessary for life's enjoyment, and begged to know if the English had any country pastures like it, where camels and sheep can roam about the whole year round without exhausting it.

31st.--To-day we made a short march, passing through Ain Tarad, and encamping on a grazing-ground one mile to its westward. The village, as usual, was close to the shore, for the convenience of shipping. It is not half the size of Kurrum, but boasts of a fort of recent construction, with six rusty pieces of cannon lying on the sand in front of it. An Akil, named Abdie, being chief of the place, is the lordly proprietor of these instruments of defence.

On first entering the place he advanced to receive me, and politely said, "Had you not dropped so suddenly in upon me this morning, it was my intention to have welcomed you with a royal salute, for the honour you have done, as the representative of the English, in paying me this visit." This speech, though showing what his feelings were towards me, was obviously a matter of simple palaver; for, in the first place, the guns could not have possibly been fired without occasioning their total destruction; and it was doubtful if he possessed any powder. Whilst sitting in his village, and drinking a bowl of sour curd--the first thing always offered to a visitor--I observed a group of old men sitting, in hot discussion on some knotty point, under the lee of the fort, and desired the Balyuz to ascertain the purport of the arguments under debate, as by their gesticulations I could plainly see it had some connection with my coming here.

After joining them and listening some time, he returned to say they were discussing the possibility of our expedition ever reaching the Webbe (River) Shebeli; to go as far as Ugahden, they thought, was out of the question. Hearing this, I went up to them, and asked what reasons they had for thinking so. They replied openly that the Somali would stop us before we got half-way. The Balyuz then interposed, saying, "But the British are strong, and can do anything, they like." Hearing this, they laughingly replied, "If the Somali came down to fight, and then ran away back into the fastnesses of their hills, what would the English do then, who cannot live a day without drinking beer and eating meat? whereas the Somali can do very well without anything, seldom requiring even water, and not more than one morsel of meat, for a whole week together." I concluded the argument by saying, "Without any exertion on our parts, we could cripple you at once; we have the seaboard in our hands, and at any moment could stop your trade, so that neither grain nor clothing would ever be supplied you; besides, if we wished, we could take quiet occupation of your hills and watering-places, and then what would become of you?" The sages mildly shook their heads, and said the English were indeed Shaitans (devils), and that they had never looked at their position in that light before. I then repaired to the camp, and found the cattle, as usual, gone out to graze, under charge of their drivers and two soldiers. In the evening, when the animals were brought home to be picketed, one pony and one camel were found wanting.

I sent men immediately to track the missing ones down, when it was discovered by footprints that some savages had singled them out from the herd, had driven them gently into a deep ravine, and when there out of sight had hurried them off to the hills lying beyond the plain. This open plunder on the coast, where British authority seemed to prevail, was monstrous. I summoned Abdie, as chief of the place, told him the whole story, and demanded that he should produce the missing animals immediately, as it was impossible for him not to be cognisant of the transaction. He said he did not then know who had stolen them, but I might rest satisfied he would find out by the morning, and they should be returned intact. He assured me he was lord of all he surveyed, and his power was infinite within the limits of his clan. The same night he brought back the pony, and said he would produce the camel in the morning. I believed he had played this trick himself to show the effect of his power, and so did the Balyuz; but he said he had been obliged to pay ten dollars to the thief before he would give it up. I now demanded he would produce the thief for trial, suspecting that thief to be himself, but he said he could not. This reply made the Balyuz knowingly cock his eye. The next day, as the camel did not come by noon, I wrote a letter to Aden reporting the circumstance, and begging some retribution would be taken from the Akil, as it was obvious to any man who knows these savages, that Abdie could not have been ignorant of one single feature in the whole of these transactions. Though the loss was small, I did not think it of little importance, as it remained a precedent, if overlooked, for the committal of greater deeds; and the place, being a port, was open to the exaction by blockade of any fines--which, without doubt, is the true way to make Somali feel.

During that day and the succeeding one we travelled along the coast to Siyareh, a small dilapidated fort,[27] standing alone without any other habitation, as if only intended for a traveller's lodge. Near it was an old well, said to be of antique construction, sunk by the former occupants of the land. As we increased our distance westwards, the maritime plain also enlarged, and was bounded to the southwards by small irregularly-disposed hills, all brown and dreary-looking as before. To judge from the quantity of vegetation, it would appear that water is nearer the surface here than elsewhere, though there was none of any importance to be seen. These few marches, slight as they were, served to prove the stamina of the soldiers, and showed the Seedis to have twice the heart and bottom of the Egyptians, who succumbed at once to the influences of the sun and fatigue of marching.

3d April.--The caravan broke ground at 2 A.M., and, after travelling over much the same ground as yesterday, nearly the whole day long without passing a single habitation, arrived in the evening at Berbera. Here I was warmly met by my companions, Herne and Stroyan, and began again a social life of great enjoyment. Berbera was in the plenitude of its prosperity. Its market was full of life and bustle, and the harbour was full of native Oriental craft. Our camp was pitched on a little rise in the land, facing the east and overlooking the fair. Our tents, three in number, were formed in line--Stroyan's on the right, Herne's in the centre, and mine on the left flank nearest the sea, and each about a dozen yards apart. Herne had procured his fair share of animals, and we mustered from forty to fifty camels and six or seven ponies and mules, including those I brought. These at night-time were all tethered in front of our tents, and guarded by a sentry. During the day they were always sent out to graze under an escort of soldiers, with Somali archers to look after them.

The boxes, pack-saddles, and grain were placed between the central tent and mine, whilst the dates and more precious cloths I kept underneath my tent. Including ourselves, servants, guards, and camel-tenders, we mustered in all about forty souls; amongst these were the two Abbans of Herne and Stroyan, who, now matters had gone so far, could not prudently be dispensed with; but my man, the Balyuz, was considered chief, or Ras Cafila.

During the four days succeeding my arrival I inspected the fair and shipping. The marketplace was supposed to contain upwards of 60,000 people,[28] Banyans from Cutch and Aden, Arab merchants and Somali, who had been gradually flocking in from about the 15th November; and as they arrived they erected mat huts as booths for carrying on their bartering trade. According to Herne's investigations, the Somali took coarse cloths, such as American and English sheeting, black and indigo-dyed stuffs, and cotton nets (worn by married women generally to encase their hair), small bars of iron and steel, as well as zinc and lead, beads of various sorts, and dates and rice. In exchange for these, they exported slaves, cattle, gums of all sorts, ghee, ivory, ostrich-feathers, and rhinoceros-horns.

7th.--At sunrise this morning a very interesting scene took place in the arrival of the great annual Harar caravan,--a large body, composed of an aggregate of numerous small caravans, which all march together that their combined strength may give mutual support. Down the whole breadth of the plain, like a busy stream of ants, they came in single file, one camel's nose tied to his leader's tail. Immediately on their flanks were Somali, armed with spear and bow, the men who tended them and looked after the loading. Outside them again were occasional detachments of men riding ponies, all armed, and guarding the caravan from sudden surprise or attack. In this caravan alone there were about three thousand people, as many head of cattle, and 500 or more slaves, all driven chained together for sale in the market. A little later the same morning a second excitement enlivened our little camp in the approach of a man-of-war, which came sailing up the coast in full sail, looking like a giant swan in contrast to the little ducks of native shipping. It was the Hon. East India Company's schooner Mahi, commanded by Lieutenant King, conveying our Captain, Lieutenant Burton, and the complement of the expedition. Arrived in the harbour, we saluted them with our small-arms, and went on board to pay respects and exchange congratulations. King then gave us a hospitable entertainment, and we all repaired on shore.

The same evening a thundering salute from the Mahi was fired, to assure the Somali we were travelling under the auspices of the British Government, and King departed with his vessel.

Lieutenant Burton now took occupation of the centre tent with Herne, and the party was complete.

We were then severally appointed to our respective duties, Lieutenant Burton commanding; Stroyan chief surveyor; Herne, photographer, geologist, and assistant-surveyor; whilst I was to be a Jack-of-all-trades, assisting everybody, looking after the interests of the men, portioning out their rations, setting the guards, and collecting specimens of natural history in all its branches. The central tent was fixed as a place of rendezvous for all to flock to in case of any sudden alarm. Here I appended my guns and sword, whilst my revolver-pistol and dirk were placed within my belt by day, or under my pillow by night. I made the whole guard sleep with their arms in rear of the camp, where it was most likely any attack might be expected. As so many men were necessarily brought on duty by watching the cattle grazing in the day-time, I only posted two sentries by night to watch the camp--one with the guard in the rear, the other over the cattle in front; whilst we Englishmen and the Balyuz occasionally patrolled the camp to see that the sentries were on the alert.

9th.--On this day the Gugi, or south-west Somali monsoon, in opposition to the Dairti, or north-east monsoon, commenced in the hills behind our camp, and warned us that we should soon have to start southwards. The fair had already begun to break. Caravan after caravan streamed out of the town, wending their way across the plain like strings of ants emerging from a hole, and, like the busy habits of those little insects, kept the whole maritime plain alive in motion. At this time we were daily expecting a vessel from Aden, which would bring us some letters and instruments that were on their way out from England, and saw the great Ugahden caravan preparing to leave, but were undecided what to do--whether to go with them without our things from England, or wait and rely upon our strength in travelling alone. The latter alternative was unfortunately decided upon, and we saw our wonted protector depart upon its journey.

15th.--Saw the shore and harbour, alike both destitute of any living thing, save a few diseased and dying cattle, and one poor forlorn girl, in whom the smallpox had begun to show its symptoms, and who was now mercilessly left by her parents, with only two or three days' provisions, to die like a dog on the inhospitable plain. Having suffered from that disease myself, and not fearing contagion, I went to her and administered some medicine, which she took without any hesitation; and I hoped to cure her, for she was really, barring the blackness, a very pretty creature, but the disease was beyond my skill to relieve. I then took her to a room in the tomb of an Arab sheikh, gave her some rice-water, and bade her keep out of the sun, but it was no use. She took fright at the idea of living with the dead, and wandered into the desert no one knows whither, and was seen no more. So completely was Berbera cleared out now, that even the matting and sticks which formed the booths, with two or three exceptions, were packed on the camels and carried away. We were now alone, and nobody came near us; our two Abbans had begged and obtained permission to go with their families to their homes in the hills close by, in company with the retiring caravans, leaving their sons for the time being, as substitutes, until we marched past their abodes.

In this isolated position we felt no alarm for our safety, as long at least as we remained upon the sea-shore, deeming the Somali would never be so imprudent as to attack us in such a vital place to them as Berbera, where their whole interests of life were centred, and where, by the simple process of blockading, we could so easily take retribution in any way we liked.

So confident were we in this assumption, that we did not take the precaution of standing sentry ourselves at night, thinking it more prudent to nurse our strength whilst here, to be better able to hold out when it would become necessary after our leaving the sea-shore.

Though Somali are cunning as foxes, they are not wise.

On the 18th April, by a providential coincidence, a small Arab vessel came into the deserted harbour to see if anything still remained of the fair. In her there were several men and four women, Somali, desirous of going to their homes. Finding we were the only people left, and not daring to travel in that country alone, they petitioned us to take them with us. It was hard to refuse these poor creatures; but fearing our supply of dates and rice would not hold out with so many additional mouths to eat it, we reluctantly refused the men. The four women, however, on their engaging to do the minor offices of the camp, to bring water, and lead the camels, were permitted to remain with us. That evening we invited the captain and his crew to dine in the camp; and it was fortunate that we did so, as the sequel will show. Shortly after sundown, as we were all sitting in our usual way, on an extempore divan in front of the tents, drinking coffee, telling stories, and enjoying the cool sea evening breezes, a challenge was heard by the sentinel placed on the rear right of the camp, followed by a sudden and rapid discharge of musketry, which took us by surprise. I had previously given strict orders that no ammunition was to be wasted in firing to frighten, or giving false alarms; therefore, hearing this, I instantly ran to the spot to see what was the matter, and found three men walking quietly into camp, leading ponies by their reins, whilst the guard, to intimidate them, were firing bullets in the air immediately over their heads. My anger knew no bounds. All hopes of security seemed annihilated by such direct disobedience to all order, and persistence in such a false principle as trying to frighten, which all black men, by a sort of natural instinct, invariably endeavour to do. I then assembled the men, and in presence of the intruders again proclaimed through the Balyuz my intention to punish with severity any person who might create a false alarm or fire a bullet vacantly in the air; directing that, in case of any opposition to a challenge, they should fire into, and not over, their object.

I then sent the Balyuz and the three newly-arrived men round to the front of the camp, where Lieutenant Burton and the other two officers were sitting, to be interrogated as to the purpose of their visit. We all at first naturally suspected them of being spies sent to inspect our dispositions and resources; but after a long palaver with Lieutenant Burton, he concluded that their coming there was accidental, and not designed. True to their nature as Easterns, who from constant practice can forge lies with far greater facility to themselves than they can speak simple truths, bringing in with the readiest aptitude the application of immediate circumstances to harmonise appropriately in the development of their tale, these men at once made use of the circumstance of the arrival of the vessel that evening, saying they merely came down to ascertain if the ship was not full of building material, as it was currently reported amongst their clan, the Habr Owel, that their old enemy, Shermarkey, the chief of Zeylah, was lying with other vessels in the port of Siyareh, waiting an opportunity to land at Berbera and take occupation of the place by building forts, as he had done on previous occasions. This story seemed the more probable from the fact that everybody knew Shermarkey wished to have the place, and that he would at any time have taken it, had it lain within his power to do so.

The more to impose on our credulity, they further asked, with an air of indignation, "How could you suspect us of any treacherous intentions towards you, when you know us to be men of the same tribe as your Abbans?" The palaver over, these wolves in sheep's clothing were allowed to sup on dates with our men, and depart at their pleasure.

At the usual hour we all turned in to sleep, and silence reigned throughout the camp. A little after midnight, probably at one or two A.M., there suddenly arose a furious noise, as though the world were coming to end: there was a terrible rush and hurry, then came sticks and stones, flying as thick as hail, followed by a rapid discharge of firearms, and my tent shook as if it would come down. I bounced out of bed, with pistol and dirk in hand, and ran across to the central tent to know what was the matter, and if we were to have any shooting. Lieutenant Burton, who was occupied in trying to load his revolver, replied there was:[29] "Be sharp, and arm to defend the camp." This I immediately did, stepping out in front of his tent; but though I saw many dusky forms before me, it was too dark to discern whether they were friend or foe.

Whilst standing, in hesitation how to act, stones kept whizzing over and around me, and I received a blow with one in the inside of my knee, which nearly knocked my leg from under me; it came from the left, where I had not been looking. I then ran under lee of the fly of the tent to take a better survey, and, by stooping low, could perceive the heads of some men peeping like monkeys over the boxes. Lieutenant Burton now said, "Don't step back, or they will think we are retiring." Chagrined by this rebuke at my management in fighting, and imagining by the remark I was expected to defend the camp, I stepped boldly to the front, and fired at close quarters into the first man before me. He was stooping to get a sight of my figure in relief against the sky; he fell back at the discharge, and I saw no more of him. Proceeding on, I saw some more men also stooping; I fired into the foremost, and he likewise fell back, but I do not know that I hit him. I then fired into a third man at close quarters, who also receded, possibly uninjured, though I cannot say. I was now close to the brink of the rising-ground, entirely surrounded by men, when I placed the muzzle of the Dean & Adams against the breast of the largest man before me, and pulled the trigger, but pulled in vain; the cylinder would not rotate; I imagine a cap had got jammed by the trigger-guard. In a fit of desperation, I was raising the revolver to hit the man in the face with it, when I suddenly found my legs powerless to support me, and I was falling, grasping for support, and gasping for breath, I did not then know why, though afterwards I discovered it was caused by the shock of a heavy blow on the lungs.

In another instant I was on the ground with a dozen Somali on the top of me. The man I had endeavoured to shoot wrenched the pistol out of my hand, and the way the scoundrel handled me sent a creeping shudder all over me. I felt as if my hair stood on end; and, not knowing who my opponents were, I feared that they belonged to a tribe called Eesa, who are notorious, not only for their ferocity in fighting, but for the unmanly mutilations they delight in. Indescribable was my relief when I found that my most dreadful fears were without foundation. The men were in reality feeling whether, after an Arab fashion, I was carrying a dagger between my legs, to rip up a foe after his victim was supposed to be powerless. Finding me naked, all but a few rags, they tied my hands behind my back, and began speaking to me in Arabic. Not knowing a word of that language, I spoke in broken Somali, and heard them say they had not killed any of the English, and would not kill me.

The man I had last endeavoured to kill was evidently the captain of the gang; he now made me rise, and, holding the other end of the rope to which my hands were attached, led me round to the rear of the camp, taking great precaution not to bring me in contact with many men at once, fearing lest they might take the law into their own hands, and despatch me against his will and authority. Arrived on the interior or rear side of the camp, men kept flocking round me, and showed a hasty anxiety to stab their spears into me; all, doubtless, were anxious for the honour of drawing the white man's blood, but none, in my captor's presence, dared do it.

I was now becoming very weak and faint, and almost unable to breathe; for the fact was, when I was knocked down, it was done with such violence by a shillelah on the lung breast, my whole frame was stunned by it, so that I could not feel; but now a swelling had set in, which, with the tightness of the skin drawn over the chest, by my hands being tied behind, nearly prevented respiration. I begged my captor to untie my hands and fasten them in front. He obligingly did so. I then asked for a little water and something to lie down upon; they were both supplied. Feeling myself somewhat revived, I began a rambling conversation with my captor, who sat by my side still holding the string, when several other men came and joined in the talk. They began a mocking tirade in their own language, of which I understood but little and could answer less; when an Aden donkey-boy (judging from his appearance) came with a jeering, sarcastic sneer, and asked me, in Hindustani, what business I had in their country, and where I had intended going, adding, were I a good Mohammedan like themselves, they would not touch me, but being a Christian I should be killed. This ridiculous farce excited my risible faculties, and provoked a laugh, when I replied, Our intentions were simply travelling; we wished to see the country of Ugahden, and pass on to Zanzibar. I was a Christian, and invited them, if it must be so, to despatch their work at once. On the donkey-boy's communicating this to the bystanders, they all broke into a rude boisterous laugh, spun upon their heels, and went off to open out the property. Nothing as yet had been taken away. Several wounded men were now brought and placed in a line before me; they groaned, and rolled, and stretched their limbs, as though they were in agonies of pain, and incessantly called for water, which was readily supplied them. In the rear I heard the sound of murmuring voices, the breaking of boxes, and ripping of bales of cloth, as though a band of robbers were stealthily dividing their unlawfully-gotten spoils in silence and fear of detection.

Just then the day began to dawn, and the light increased sufficiently to disclose what had been done. The tents were down, the property was lying in order on the ground, the camels and ponies were still picketed in their places, and all the robbers were standing looking on. At this juncture my captor and protector gave his end of my string over to the care of another man of very mean aspect, ordering him to look after me, and see that nobody came to injure me, whilst he retired in the direction of the property, and, selecting two fine stalwart men of equal proportions with himself, came again in front of me; then linking arms, and sloping spears over their shoulders, they commenced a slow martial march, keeping time by singing a solemn well-regulated tune, in deep, full, stentorian voices, until they completed the full circuit of the camp, and arrived again in front of me. This, I imagine, was their "Conquering hero comes," the song of victory. It was well sung, and had a very imposing effect, greatly increased by the dead silence which reigned in every other quarter. I felt quite sorry when this act was over, and would willingly have had it encored. From the orderly manner and regularity with which everything was done, I judge this to be a fair sample of the manner in which all plundering parties are conducted. The song and march were no sooner at an end than the whole ground became a scene of busy, active life. Every man, save the one who was holding my string, rushed in a regular scramble upon the property, and, like a legion of devils, began tearing and pulling at everything in promiscuous confusion, to see who could carry most away. Some darted at the camels and began pulling them along, others seized the ponies and began decamping; others, again, caught up the cloths, or dates, or rice, or anything they could lay hands on, and endeavoured to carry them off. But this was not so easy; there were too many men to be all satisfied, and those who had least began wrangling with their more fortunate competitors, who, on their part, not wishing to relinquish anything they had obtained, forcibly contested for their rights.

A more complete and ferocious **melee** I never witnessed. The whole ground was a scene of pull devil, pull baker, and victory to the stronger. As one man, hurrying along, was trailing his cloth behind, another rushed at it and pulled him back; clubs were unsparingly used, and destruction threatened with spears; what would not easily succumb to pulling, was separated with stabs of the spears or cuts of their knives. The camels and ponies were not more easily disposed of; by snatching from one hand and snatching from another, they were constantly in different people's hands. It was a scene very like that of an Indian poultry-yard, when some entrails are thrown amongst the chickens, and every fowl tries to rob the other.

Whilst all were intent with deep earnestness in this scramble, an alarm was suddenly given that another party were coming down the hills to fight and rob them of their spoils. The disordered band were instantly panic-stricken; for a moment or two there was the deadest silence; and then everybody, save some forty or fifty men who were probably more experienced hands, burst across the plain, flying in long jumps, and hurrying with all their might towards the hills. I heard afterwards it was not an unusual practice in this land of robbers for one party to get up an attack upon a caravan, and then another one, getting wind of their design, to project a plan of despoiling them as soon as they shall be in such a disconcerted **melee** that they would not be able to act in concert to support one another.

Whilst they were away, three fine-looking men came, with some of our soldiers' sabres; and one, standing over me, threatened, with ferocious determination in his countenance, to cut me in two. Twice he lifted his sword above his head, and brought it down with violence to within an inch or two of my side, and each time withdrew it, as if suddenly repenting of his purpose. I stared him earnestly in the face, but neither flinched nor uttered any noise. They then left me, and went to join the other forty thieves. I conceive this demonstration was made with a view of testing my pluck, and had I cried or implored for mercy, I should inevitably have been killed upon the spot. The last and worst scene in this tragedy was now to be performed.

My jailer, who was still holding the string, stepped up close to me, and coolly stabbed me with his spear. I then raised my body a little in defence, when he knocked me down by jobbing his spear violently on my shoulder, almost cutting the jugular arteries. I rose again as he poised his spear, and caught the next prod, which was intended for my heart, on the back of one of my shackled hands; this gouged the flesh up to the bone. The cruel villain now stepped back a pace or two, to get me off my guard, and dashed his spear down to the bone of my left thigh. I seized it violently with both my hands, and would not relinquish the gripe until he drew a shillelah from his girdle, and gave me such a violent blow on my left arm, I thought the bone was broken, and the spear fell helplessly from my hands. Finding his spear too blunt for running me through by a simple job when standing still, he now dropped the rope-end, walked back a dozen paces, and, rushing on me with savage fury, plunged his spear through the thick part of my right thigh into the ground, passing it between the thigh-bone and large sinew below.

With the action of lightning, seeing that death was inevitable if I remained lying there a moment longer, I sprang upon my legs, and gave the miscreant such a sharp back-hander in the face with my double-bound fists that he lost his presence of mind, and gave me a moment's opportunity to run away; which, by the Lord, I lost no time in doing, taking very good care, by holding my hands on one side, not to allow the dangling rope to trip me up. I was almost naked, and quite bare upon the feet, but I ran over the shingly beach towards the sea like wildfire. The man followed me a little way, but, finding I had the foot of him, threw his spear like a javelin, but did not strike me, for I bobbed, and allowed it to pass safely over my head; he then gave up the chase. Still I had at least forty more men to pass through, who were scattered all about the place, looking for what property they could pick up, before I could get safe away. These men, seeing the chase, all tried to cut off my retreat.

However, I dodged them all by turns, running fast across them, and bobbing as they threw their spears after me, until I reached the shore, when I had the satisfaction of seeing the last man give up the pursuit and leave me to myself. I was now fast fainting from loss of blood, and sat gently on a mound of sand, picked the knots which bound my hands open with my teeth, and exposed my breast to the genial influences of the refreshing sea-breeze, which at sunrise, as this was, is indescribably pleasant. But what a gloomy prospect was now before me!! I was growing weaker every minute; my limbs were beginning to stiffen and the muscles to contract, and I thought there was no help probably nearer than Ain Tarad; what was to be done? I could not travel the distance, and I must perish miserably by slow degrees, from starvation and exhaustion, in the dreary desert; far better, thought I, had the spear done its worst, and no lingering would have followed. Whilst reflecting in this strain, my eyes, wistfully gazing on the few remaining huts of Berbera, lit upon some female figures beckoning to me, but I could not divine who they were, or what was their meaning.

I rose as a last hope, and hobbled towards them, for my right leg was nearly crooked up double, and was so weak it could not support the weight of my body but for an instant at a time. Drawing nearer, I discovered them to be the four women whom we the evening before permitted to join our camp. Just then I saw some men hurrying from the eastward along the shore, endeavouring to meet me.

These, I soon perceived, were the old Balyuz and several of our servants. As soon as they arrived, they told me all that had happened. Immediately on the outbreak, the soldiers fired their guns, and all but one or two at once departed. Stroyan, he supposed, was killed at the outset; Lieutenants Burton and Herne had run away with him immediately after I left the central tent to fight. The former had been speared in the face, the latter had been much bruised with war-clubs, and some of our men had received severe sword-cuts. After escaping from the fight, Herne took refuge in the empty huts of Berbera, and at daybreak sent a servant to detain the Ain Tarad vessel, which had so providentially come in the previous evening. My companions were then on board of her, and had sent the Balyuz with the men to search for me, and pick up anything they could find.

I was now carried to the vessel, and stretched upon the poop in safety, and felt more truly thankful for this miraculous escape than words can tell. It is only after a deliverance of this kind one fully values or can properly appreciate the gift of life. My companions seemed downcast and full of sorrow for the sad misfortune which had so disastrously terminated our long-cherished hopes, and had deprived us so prematurely of an old and valued friend, especially dear to me, as he was a thorough sportsman. For courage, daring, and enterprise, as well as good-fellowship, there never lived a man more worthy of esteem than poor Stroyan.

Lieutenant Burton had sent a boat's crew off to near the site of our camp, a distance of three miles, to fetch away anything that might remain there, and bring it to us. They found the place deserted, with only such things left as the Somali could make no use of, and were too cumbersome to carry away; such, for instance, as grain, boxes, books, and various scientific instruments, which, after being wantonly injured, were left scattered on the ground. It appeared, by accounts brought back, that many of the men who ran off at the first false alarm never ventured back again to help themselves from the spoils. They had now destroyed about L1500 worth of property, but had enriched themselves but very little, for, whilst fighting, they had destroyed in the scramble nearly everything of any worth to themselves. When the boat's crew returned with Stroyan's body, it was found to be too late to sail that evening.

During the time of waiting, a poor man, with no covering on his body, crawled up to the vessel, and implored the captain, in the name of Allah--the fakir's mode of begging--to give him a passage to Aden. His prayer was answered, and he came on board. He was a Mussulman, born in Cashmere, and had been wandering about the world in the capacity of a fakir; but was now, through hunger and starvation, reduced to a mere skeleton of skin and bones. His stomach was so completely doubled inwards, it was surprising the vital spark remained within him. On being asked to recite his history, he said, "I was born in the 'happy valley' of Cashmere; but reduced circumstances led me to leave my native land. When wandering alone in some woods one day, I had a visitation, which induced me to turn devotee, and wander about the world to visit all places of pilgrimage, carrying only a bottle and a bag, and ask charity in the name of God, who supplies the world with every-thing, and takes compassion on the destitute. At first I travelled in India, visiting its shrines and temples, and then determined on crossing the sea to see what other countries were like. Taking passage at Bombay, I first went to Muskat in Southern Arabia, and thence travelled overland to Aden, begging all the way, and receiving kind hospitality wherever I spent the night. In Aden I remained a while, and by constant begging accumulated sufficient property to purchase food for a consider-able time, when I again set out, in the name of Allah, to see what the Somali Land was like. At first I went across to Kurrum, and lived there as long as my little stock held out, but I could get no assistance from the people of the place. The stock ex-hausted, I was spurned from every door. At last, despairing of obtaining anything on the coast, I ventured to see what the interior would produce, but I found the Somali everywhere the same; they were mere hywans (animals), with whom no human beings could live. A man might travel in Arabia or any other place in the world, but in the Somali Land no one could exist. Finding myself reduced to the last stages of life, for no one would give me food, I went to a pool of water in a ravine amongst the hills, and for the last fortnight have been living there on water and the gums of trees. Seeing I was about to die, as a forlorn hope I ventured in this direc-tion, without knowing whither I was going, or where I should come to; but God, you see, has brought me safely out."

20th.--This morning we weighed anchor, and in two days more arrived in Aden.

Thus then ended my first expedition,--a signal failure from inexperience, and with a loss of L510 worth of my own private property, which I never recovered. I had nothing to show but eleven artificial holes in my body. Had we gone straight from Aden, without any nervous preliminary fuss, and joined the Ugahden caravan at Berbera just as it was starting, I feel convinced we should have succeeded; for that is the only way, without great force, or giving yourself up to the protection of a powerful chief, that any one could travel in Somali Land. Firearms are useful in the day, but the Somali despise them at night, and consequently always take advantage of darkness to attack. Small-shot and smooth-bore guns, on this account, would be of far greater advantage as a means of defence than rifles with balls; and nothing but shot well poured in would have saved us from this last attack. We have been often condemned for not putting on more sentries to watch; but had the whole camp been in a state of ordinary preparation for war, with such cowardly hearts as our men all had, we should have been as signally defeated. We now set sail from Berbera, all highly disgusted with our defeat; and at Lieutenant Burton's request, we said we would go with him again if the Government would allow it.

On arriving in Aden, I was a miserable-looking cripple, dreadfully emaciated from loss of blood, and with my arms and legs contracted into indescribable positions, to say nothing of various angry-looking wounds all over my body. Dansey now gave me a room in his house, and bestowed such tender care on me as I shall never forget. Colonel Coghlan also, full of feeling and sympathy for my misfortune, came over and sat at the feet of my bed, with tears in his eyes, and tried to condole with me. Fever, however, had excited my brain, so I laughed it all off as a joke, and succeeded in making him laugh too. The doctors next took compassion on me, formed into committee, and prescribed, as the only remedy likely to set me right again, a three years' leave to England, where, with the congenial effects of my native home, they hoped I should recover. Lieutenant Burton now sent in an estimate of all loss to the Government, and advised, as the best plan of taking an effectual revenge upon the Somali, in whose territories we were attacked (the Habr Owel), that a ship should be sent to blockade their coast, with a demand that they should produce for trial in Aden the living bodies of the two men who so cruelly killed our lamented friend, and so wantonly endeavoured to despatch me. Further, that a sum of money equivalent to all our aggregate losses should be paid in full ere the blockade would be raised. This was considered the wisest method by which, in future times, any recurrence of such disasters might probably be avoided. It is needless to observe, considering the importance of Berbera to the welfare of the Habr Owel, their subsistence and their existence as a nation depending on it, that anything might have been exacted from them that we wished to extort, or they could afford to give. The Government, unfortunately for our pockets, were of a different opinion; they would have nothing to do with money exactions when human blood had to be avenged. Moreover, they had been wishing to suppress the slave-trade, and found in this occurrence a favourable opportunity to indulge their hobby. They therefore established a blockade of all the coast-line between Siyareh and Jibal El-mas, demanding, as the only alternative by which it would be raised, the surrender of the principal instigators of the outrage on us for trial in Aden, of whom the first in consequence was Ou Ali, the murderer of Stroyan. When the season for the fair arrived, the only vessel present in the Berbera harbour was a British man-of-war, and the Habr Owel then believed we were in earnest. Until then, it appeared, they would not believe it, thinking our trade in Aden would suffer by this proceeding as much as their own. They were, however, mistaken; trade found an outlet at other places; and they, by its suppression on their grounds, were fast sinking into insignificance. Seeing this, they showed by urgent prayers a disposition to treat on any conditions we might like to impose on them, and even sent in for trial to Aden a man who showed the scar of a gun-shot wound on his back, and at the same time declared their intention of forwarding all others to us as soon as they could catch them.

To make the matter short, I shall give intact the articles of a treaty which was signed at Berbera on the 7th November 1856, between the Honourable East India Company on the one hand, and the Habr Owel tribe of Somali on the other, as it appears in an appendix (D), in a 'History of Arabia Felix or Yemen,' by Captain R. L. Playfair, Assistant Political Resident, Aden.[30]

During my residence in Aden, which lasted three weeks, or until the second mail after my arrival took its departure for Suez, my wounds healed up in such a marvellously rapid manner, I was able to walk at large before I left there. They literally closed as wounds do in an India-rubber ball after prickings with a penknife. It would be difficult to account for the rapidity with which my wounds closed, knowing, as everybody who has lived in Aden must do, that that is the worst place in the world for effecting cures, had I not, in addition to a strong constitution which I fortunately possess, been living for many months previously in a very abstemious manner, principally, as appears in the body of the journal, on dates, rice, and sour curds.

I now left Aden on "sick certificate," and arrived in England in the early part of June 1855. The Crimean war was then at its height, and the military authorities were beating up for recruits in every corner of the land. This summons for war was irresistible. I was suffering a little from blindness, brought on probably by my late losses and impoverishment of blood.[31] Still I lost no time in volunteering my services to take part in this great national object, thinking it was a duty, as a soldier, I owed my country, and delighting in the prospect of immediate and active employment, where, at any rate, I should be in Europe and enjoying the temperature I had come home to seek. The Turkish Contingent was then being incorporated, and I was, being an Indian officer, competent to serve in it. With an introduction from friends, I wrote a letter to Major Graham, an officer appointed by the Horse Guards to engage officers for General Vivian's contingent, giving him an account of my past services, and asking for an appointment with the army. He at once closed with me, declaring "I was just the sort of man he wanted," and, granting two weeks' leave to prepare an outfit, told me to be off. In a fortnight more I arrived in Constantinople, and was posted to a regiment of Turks, with the commission of Captain. The Turkish Contingent was now at Buyukdere, but was soon ordered to embark in vessels and proceed to Kertch in the Crimea. I went with them, and remained serving until the close of the Crimean war. My commandant, Major Greene, being otherwise employed, I, as second in command and Kaimakan of the 16th regiment of infantry, took its headquarters back, and disbanded them at Constantinople.

Whilst I was engaged in these parts, and thinking there would be no further chance of my being able to return to Africa, I had made up my mind, at the expiration of the war, to try my hand in collecting the fauna of the very interesting regions of the Caucasian Mountains, and had even gone so far as to purchase guns and equip myself for it. Captain Smyth, of the Bengal Army, an old and notorious Himalayan sportsman, had agreed to accompany me, and we wrote home to the Royal Geographical Society to exert their influence in obtaining passports, by which we could cross over the range into the Russian frontier; but this scheme was put a stop to by Dr Shaw, the Secretary of that Society, writing out to say there would be very little hope of our being able to obtain the passports we required, and that he thought the time ill-advised for working in those regions, adding, at the same time, that an expedition to explore Africa was again being organised under the command of Captain Burton, and advising me to join it. By the same mail I received a communication from Captain Burton himself, inviting me to join him once more in exploring Africa, saying there would be no expense attached to it, as the Home and Indian Governments had each promised to contribute L1000. This settled the matter. Without a second thought I disposed of my Caucasian equipments, and, taking a passage to England by the first mail, travelled night and day until I again reached home, deeming, as I did on the first expedition, that I might just as well nurse my furlough for a future occasion,--the fact being that I was more of a sportsman and traveller than a soldier, and I only liked my profession when I had the sport of fighting.

JOURNAL OF A CRUISE ON
THE TANGANYIKA LAKE.
Chapter I.

The Royal Geographical Society--The Strange Lake on the Map--Set Off--
Arrive at Zanzibar--A Preliminary Excursion--A Sail along the Coast--The
Pangani River--A Jemadar's Trick--Journey up Country--Adventures--
Return to Zanzibar--Scenes there--Objects of the Expedition--Recruiting
for Followers--The Cafila Bashi--The Start--Fevers--Discussions about the
Mountains of the Moon and the Victoria N'yanza--The Tanganyika.

On my arrival in England, the first thing I did was to visit Captain Burton,
and obtain an introduction to the Royal Geographical Society, under
whose auspices I was about to travel. I next visited the Society, and
here was revealed to me, for the first time, the great objects designed
for the expedition in question. On the walls of the Society's rooms there hung a
large diagram, comprising a section of Eastern Africa, extending from the equator to the fourteenth degree of south latitude, and from Zanzibar sixteen degrees
inland, which had been constructed by two reverend gentlemen, Messrs Erhardt
and Rebmann, missionaries of the Church Mission Society of London, a short time
previously, when carrying on their duties at Zanzibar. In this section-map, swal-
lowing up about half of the whole area of the ground included in it, there figured a
lake of such portentous size and such unseemly shape, representing a gigantic slug,
or, perhaps, even closer still, the ugly salamander, that everybody who looked at
it incredulously laughed and shook his head. It was, indeed, phenomenon enough
in these days to excite anybody's curiosity! A single sheet of sweet water, upwards
of eight hundred miles long by three hundred broad, quite equal in size to, if not

larger than, the great salt Caspian.

Now, to the honour of Admiral Sir George Back be it said, a Fellow of the Royal Geographical Society, and an old explorer himself in the Arctic regions, that he had determined in his mind that this great mystery should be solved, and that an insight should be gained into those interesting regions, concerning which conjectures and speculations had been rife, and which had caused so many hot debates for so many ages past amongst all the first geographers of the day; debates which, hitherto, nobody had been found energetic enough to set at rest by actual inspection of the country.

Casting about for a man fitted to carry out his plans, the Admiral hit upon Captain Burton, who had recently returned from Constantinople, where he had been engaged with the Bashi-Bazuks; and it was thus, through Sir George's influence in the Royal Geographical Society, that Captain Burton had now been appointed to the command of this expedition.

A difference now arose about the Government L2000 in aid of the expedition. The Foreign Office had paid their L1000, but the India House thought Captain Burton's pay ought to be considered their share. Finding this was the case I objected to go, as I did not wish, for one reason, to put myself under any money obligations to Captain Burton; and, for another reason, I thought I had paid enough for a public cause in the Somali country, without having gained any advantage to myself. Captain Burton, however, knew nothing of astronomical surveying, of physical geography, or of collecting specimens of natural history, so he pressed me again to go with him, and even induced the President of the Royal Geographical Society to say there need be no fear of money if we only succeeded. I then consented to go, determining in my own mind, somehow or other, to have my old plans, formed in India, of completing my museum, carried into effect, even if, after all, the funds of the expedition did not suffice. Captain Burton now gave me a cheque for my passage out of the public funds;[32] but my incorporation with the expedition was not quite so easy as had been expected; for the Government in India at this time were using every endeavour in their power to increase their Indo-European forces, and had written home to Leadenhall Street an urgent desire that no officers should have their leave extended, or be placed on duty out of India; and for this reason, the India House authorities, although privately evincing a strong disposition to permit my going, felt it necessary to withhold their sanction to it. I was now between two fires. I had sacrificed my Caucasian expedition, and could not speak with the authorities in India. So, to cut the matter short, with a kind hint from my friend Sir Henry Rawlinson, as I had still nearly three years' furlough at my disposal, I ventured over with Captain Burton by the overland route to Bombay, and tried my luck again.

This time, fortunately, it turned up trumps; for I need only say that the Governor of Bombay at this time was Lord Elphinstone, a man whose large and comprehensive mind was not only able to discern the frown of a pending mutiny looming in the distance, but whose quick foresight, backed by a great and natural unremitting energy of body, was subsequently able to forestall and provide, as far as human powers extend, against its thundering outburst. He saw at a glance of how much importance to the improvement of the commercial objects of his presidency this exploring expedition was likely to be. The Secretary to Government, Mr Anderson, who was equally of this view, treated the matter as a great national object, and, at the request of Captain Burton, drew up an official application to incorporate me in the expedition, and sent it to the Government at Calcutta, with the recommendation of his lordship; whilst I, in anticipation of the sanction of the Governor-General, Lord Canning, was permitted to accompany Captain Burton to Zanzibar in the Hon. East India Company's sloop-of-war Elphinstone, commanded by Captain Frushard, I.N., and commence operations at once.

This vessel had been detached especially on this duty to meet Captain Burton's views, that a political importance should be given to the mission by our arriving in Government official state at the starting-point, in order to secure the influence and respect of the sultan reigning there.

After a residence of one week at Bombay, during which time I completed our outfit in scientific instruments and other minor points--for this charge was reposed in me, owing to my previous experience in those matters--we set sail on the 3d December 1856, taking two Goanese cook "boys," by name Valantine and Gaetano, with us as servants, and in eighteen days landed at our destination, Zanzibar. The kindness of Captain Frushard, who shared his cabin with us, as well as the constant attentions of his officers, combined with pleasant weather and a liberal fare, provided for us by the Bombay Government in the capacity of political envoys, made the time occupied on the voyage fly quickly and very agreeably.[33]

Immediately on arrival at the island of Zanzibar, we were warmly received and welcomed by our consul, Colonel Hamerton, an Irish gentleman, and one characterised by the true merry hospitality of his race. He had been a great sufferer, by the effects of the climate operating on him from too long a residence in these enervating regions; but he was, nevertheless, vivacious in temperament and full of amusing anecdotes, which kept the whole town alive. He gave us a share of his house, and what was more, made that house our homes. His generosity was boundless, and his influence so great, that he virtually commanded all societies here. Our old and faithful ally, the Imaum of Muscat, who, unfortunately for us, had but recently died, was so completely ruled by him, that he listened to and obeyed him as a child would his father.

The present ruler of Zanzibar--that is, of the coastline, with all the islands which lie between the equator on the southern confines of the Somali country and the Portuguese possessions in Mozambique--is Sultan Majid, the second son of the old Imaum; for it must be remembered that the Imaum, at his death, divided his territories, then comprising Muscat in Arabia, and Zanzibar in Africa, into two separate states, giving the former, or Muscat, to his eldest son, Sayyid (Prince) Suweni, whilst the latter was bequeathed to his favourite, the second son, Sayyid Majid, now styled Sultan. Sultan Majid was born of a Circassian woman, and in consequence is very light in complexion; and, taking much after the inclinations of his father, is likely to become as great a favourite as was the old Imaum. Zanzibar island is the seat of government, and consequently the metropolis. The town contains about sixty thousand inhabitants of all nations, but principally coloured people, of which the Suahili, or coast people, living on the opposite main, predominate in number, though they are the least important. Of the merchants, there are several European houses, comprising French, Germans, and Americans; and numerous Asiatics, mostly from Arabia and Hindostan,--the Suahili ranking lowest of the whole. There are also three consuls, an English, French, and American, who look after the interests of the subjects of their respective governments.

We found, considering it would take more than a month to organise an expedition, that we had arrived here at the very worst season of the year for commencing a long inland journey--the height of the dry season in these regions, when water is so very scarce in the more desert tracts of the interior of the continent, that travelling, from want of that material element, is precarious; and it was just before the commencement of the vernal monsoon, or greater rainy season, when everything would be deluged.

Considering this, and giving due deference to the opinions of the travelling merchants of this place against our organising at once for the interior journey to the great lake, Captain Burton bethought himself of gaining a little elementary training in East African travelling, by spending the remainder of the dry season in inspecting various places on the coast; and, if a favourable opportunity presented itself, he felt desirous of having a peep at the snowy Kilimandjaro Mountain, of which the Rev. Mr Rebmann, who first discovered it, had sent home reports, and which had excited such angry and unseemly contests amongst our usually sedate though speculative carpet-geographers in England as rendered a further inspection highly necessary.

Now, as the Royal Geographical Society had desired us to place ourselves in communication with Mr Rebmann, who was then at his mission-station, Kisulu-dini, at Rabbai, on a high hill at the back of Mombas, and to try and solicit him to go with us into the interior, where it was thought his experience in the native languages would be useful to the expedition,--my companion hired a small beden, or half-decked Arab vessel, by the month, to take us about wherever we pleased; and on the 5th January 1857, having engaged a respectable half-caste Arab Sheikh, named Said, to be our guide and interpreter, we took leave of our host, set sail, and steered northwards, coasting along the shores of this beautiful clove island, until we left it, and shortly afterwards sighted the still more lovely island of Pemba, or "The Emerald Isle" of the Arabs--named, doubtless, from the surprising verdure of its trees and plants. Here we called in at Chak-chak, the principal place, where there is a rude little fort and small garrison of Beluch soldiers, and a Wali, or governor. Starting the following morning, we put to sea again, and in three days--sailing against a strong southerly current, aggravated by a stiff north-easterly breeze, almost too much for our cranky little vessel, and which frightened the crew and our little timid Sheikh so much that they all lost presence of mind, and with the greatest difficulty were repressed from "'bouting ship," and wrecking themselves, together with us, on the shores of the coast--we harboured in the Mombas creek.

Mombas on the north, like Kilua on the south, are the two largest garrison

towns belonging to the Sultan on the main shores. They each have a Wali or governor, custom officers, and a Beluch guard; and have certain attractions to the an-
tiquarian in the shape of Portuguese ruins. We left our traps here to be housed by
a Banyan called Lakshmidos, the collector of customs,[34] and started on the 17th
January to visit Mr Rebmann, beyond the hills overlooking this place. It was a good
day's work, and was commenced by rowing about ten miles up the Rabbai branch of
the creek we were in, until we arrived at the foot of the hills bearing the same name,
beyond which his house stands. This inlet was fringed with such dense masses of
the mangrove shrub, on which clung countless numbers of small tree-oysters,--
adhering to their branches in clusters, and looking as though they subsisted thereon
after the manner of orchidaceous plants,--that we could obtain no view whatever,
save of the hills towering to the height of some ten hundred or twelve hundred
feet above us. The water-journey over, we commenced the ascent of Rabbai, and,
soon crowning it by a steep slope, passed into the country of the Wanyika, the first
true negro tribe of my acquaintance, and by a gentle decline passing through quiet
little villages, we entered, after a walk of five miles, the Kisuludini mission-house,
and there found Mr Rebmann, with his amiable English wife, living in their peaceful retreat. They gave us a free and cordial welcome and comfortable lodging, and
supplied us with all the delicacies of a dry Wanyika season, for there was now a
drought in the land, and consequently a famine. So hard were the times for the
unfortunate negroes, that they were forced against their wills to support the bulk of
their families by the sale of some of its junior members to keep themselves alive.

And now, according to Mr Rebmann, to aggravate their predicament, they
were on the eve of a more dreadful enemy still than famine,--that of the attacks of
a marauding party of the barbarous pastoral Masai, a neighbouring tribe, who were
now out engaged in pillaging some of the Wanyika villages, not far from this, of
the few heads of cattle which they keep as a "safety-valve" against the scourge of
droughts. The oddest thing to me was to see the placid equanimity with which Mr
Rebmann and his wife coolly delayed a day or two, notwithstanding the near proximity of this savage band of thieves, to pack up their kit comfortably before leaving
the place; but we were assured by the reverend gentleman that the Masai cared but
little for anything save beef, and they therefore did not apprehend rough usage at
their hands. The air of this high land is cool and pleasant, and the scenery from the

station overlooking the sea was very picturesque and serenely beautiful. The Rabbai hills are an outlying range running parallel to the coast, or more properly, I should say, an abattis, which supports a high but slightly depressed flattish interior, gently declining westwards.

After a good night's rest we returned to Mombas, housed ourselves in the dwelling appointed for our use by Lakshmidos, and had many civilities paid us by the Wali (governor) and coloured merchants of the place, who brought us fruits and paid us other delicate little attentions by way of showing their regard. The Wanyika having by this time sent to the Mombas fort for aid to support them against the attacks of their enemies, we felt some alarm at the position of Mr and Mrs Rebmann, and again returned to Kisuludini, to see if we could be of any use to them: but not so; they were as fearless as before, and would not leave their house until everything had been well packed up and sent away.[35] We now bade them adieu a second time, and returned to our house at Mombas. Here we heard that several of the Beluch troops had been despatched against the Masai, and that some skirmishes had taken place, but they were nothing of any material consequence.

Seeing that there was this little excitement on the direct road to Kadiaro and the Kilimandjaro, Captain Burton thought it unadvisable to venture on that line, the more especially so as he judged the Mombas people were not over-well disposed to our travelling into the interior. Further, he had heard of fresh attractions on the coast, in the shape of ruins, both Portuguese and Persian;--those places from which, in former ages, the Portuguese--who had been led there by the adventurous Vasco de Gama, and were the first European occupants of these dark lands--were driven southwards by the Arabs. Moreover, he heard that the mountain of Kilimandjaro was just as accessible to us from Tanga or Pangani, a little farther down the coast, where there would probably be no war-parties standing in our way, as the case was here.

I, on the other hand, did not see any cause of alarm, for I thought we could easily have walked round the Masai party; but I saw various reasons for abandoning the projected plan of looking at the Kilimandjaro. In the first place, it had been already discovered by Mr Rebmann; it was, moreover, rather distant for our limited time; it would require more money than our limited funds could admit of; and last, though not least, as we had some time to spare, I thought it would be much more agreeable to spend it in hippopotamus-shooting on the coast, and on what game we might find on the hills of Usumbara, if we perforce were to go through that kingdom on our way towards the Kilimandjaro, an idea that had struck us; for though Usumbara had been traversed formerly by the Church missionaries, it was still a maiden country for the sportsman. Considering Mombas as a starting-point for an excursion into the interior, I can conceive no direction more interesting or advantageous for any one to embark upon. Dr Krapf has already been as far as Kitui, in the country of Ukambani, fourteen marches distant only from Mombas, and there he heard of a snowy mountain called Kenia, lying probably to the northward of and on the same hill-range as Mount Kilimandjaro, which most likely separates the river-systems of the east from those which flow to the westward into the Nile. In confirmation of this impression, I would mention the fact that a merchant caravan of about two hundred men, whilst we were stopping here, arrived from Kitui laden with elephant ivories, which they had bartered for American sheeting, Venetian beads, and brass wire, &c. &c., in the district of Ukambani; and they described the country in the most glowing terms, as possessing a healthy climate, pleasant temperature, wholesome water, and an abundance of provisions, both flesh and grain: they had, moreover, camels and donkeys as beasts of burden, which alone denotes a great facility for travelling in Eastern Africa, where usually men take the place of beasts. The Wakambani porters belonging to this caravan, as many as there were, were boisterous, humorous savages, who, as they danced and paraded about the town, all armed in savage fashion with bows and spears and sharp knives, in fact anything but clothes, looked as wild as animals just driven from a jungle. Noise and dancing seemed their principal delight, and they indulged in it, blowing horns and firing muskets with a boisterous glee, which showed the strangest contrast to the tame Hindus and other merchant residents of the place.

Captain Burton now decided on quitting Mombas; and on the 24th January, after embarking in our little beden, we set sail southwards. Following the coastline, we touched at the villages of Gasi, Wasin, Tanga--where I had my first flirtations with the hippopotami, of which more hereafter--and Tangata, to inspect ruins and make inquiries about the interior condition of the country.

The coast-line was one continuous undeviating scene of tropical beauty, with green aquatic mangroves growing everywhere out into the tidal waves, with the beetal, palmyra, and other palms overtopping this fringe; and in the background a heterogeneous admixture, an impervious jungle, of every tree, shrub, and grass, that characterise the richest grounds on the central shores of this peculiar continent. The little islands we passed amongst, and all the reefs that make these shores so dangerous to the navigator, whether large or small, were the produce of the industrious little coral insect. The lime with which their cellular beds are composed being favourable to vegetable growth, leaves it no wonder that the higher grounds and dryer lands are thus so densely clothed. The few villages there are, bordering on the coast, are poor and meagre-looking, but their inhabitants were very hospitable, especially where there were any Banyans. Nothing could exceed the mingled pride and yearning pleasure these exotic Indians seemed to derive from having us as their guests. Being Indian officers, they looked upon us as their guardians, and did everything they could to show they felt it so. Our conversing in their own language, and talking freely of their native land, must, as indeed they said it did, have felt to them as if after a long banishment they were suddenly thrown amongst their old and long-lost friends. To us how strange did these things appear! that men so full of life, good-breeding, intelligence, and affections--so meaning and calculating in their conversation, so gentlemanly in their behaviour--should live this life of utter banishment, amidst these savages, devoid of all sympathetic affections, and knowing not even what things constitute the commonest business of life. And why? To make a little money for their latter days, when life's enjoyment has passed away. Their wretched case would not be so bad, only that, from being Hindus, they cannot marry or even bring their wives from India with them. It is a position even worse than that of hermits. Tanga was the most considerable of all the places we visited, being the grand terminus of those caravans, which, passing immediately to the south of the Kilimandjaro, traverse the Masai country to Burgenei, near the south-east corner of the Victoria N'yanza (Lake).[36] Here Captain Burton again commenced making inquiries about the route to Kilimandjaro, and how, if that could not be managed, considering the means at our disposal, we could march into Usumbara, see the capital Fuga, and pay the king, Kimueri, a cursory visit; but being more or less dissuaded from this, evidently, as it afterwards appeared, by the timorous inclinations rather than from any real difficulties which presented themselves to the mind of our Sheikh, Captain Burton thought it better to see first what could be done at Pangani.

We arrived in the mouth of the Pangani river on the 3d February; and, immediately on landing, were met by all the grandees of the place, who welcomed us as big men, and escorted us to a large stone house in the town overlooking the river. On the way to this domicile, a number of black singers were formed in line to serenade us, and they danced and sang in real negro peculiarity, with such earnest constancy that, although a novel sight, we were glad to be rid of them long before they were tired of performing. All inquisitive about other people's concerns, the Panganyites at once eagerly busied themselves to find out what our intentions were in coming there, and accordingly began to speculate on what they could make out of us. First the Diwans (head-men) wanted us to pay our footing in the town; but that only provoking a sharp rebuff, they began a system of "making difficulties." To go to the Kilimandjaro we must have a large and expensive escort, or nobody would go with us. But this we were not persistent in, for two reasons: in the first place, having frittered away so much time at Mombas, and in inspecting ruins on the way from it, we had no time left ere the kuzi, or little rains precursory to the great monsoon, which would shortly set in on the high lands near the Great Mountain, would fall and impede our progress; and, in the second, we were short of cash. Next we contemplated a flying trip to Fuga, for which alternative Sultan Majid had provided us with introductions to the king, Kimueri, living there; and this, of course, being known to the people through the medium of Sheikh Said, they at once beset our doors to meet our proposals and make fresh difficulties.

King Kimueri's son, who happened to be here on his way to Zanzibar, presuming we had presents for the king, mildly begged us to give them up to him at once, he securing us a passage to his father,--a cool request, which, of course, was just as coolly rejected. And now everybody, evidently actuated by him, stood in our way at every turn. We must not go the straight road, as the Wazegura living on the right bank of the Pangani river were "out," and in open hostilities with the Wasumbara, and would intercept our passage; and, instead, they proposed our going *via* Tangata, a much longer route, but open to us if we only took a sufficient number of men, and paid handsomely for the convenience. Considering that the value attachable to the undertaking would be magnified in our minds in proportion to the amount of obstacles which had to be surmounted, difficulty upon difficulty was now conjured up and produced as fast as they thought they were working upon our inclinations. Sometimes our advisers would go, and then the opposite. They were verily as coy in their advancements and retractions as a woman who, in love, gives and takes with a wavering man on whom she has set her heart at a time when he is fearful of giving way to her little seductive artifices.

At this perplexing juncture, quite unforeseen by us, the jemadar of a small Beluch garrison (Chogue), about seven miles up the river, came to pay his respects, and by a clever artifice--purely an Oriental dodge, as anybody who has lived in India will readily admit--at once perceiving an advantage to be gained by which he might profitably fill his own pocket at the same time that he would save ours, and give a job to his own Beluches to the prejudice of those avaricious Panganyites, offered us an inducement which was too good not to be at once accepted. The plan was simply this: He was to leave at once and return to Chogue, and make arrangements with his guard for our reception there, whilst we, feigning abandonment of all our plans, were to prepare for a shooting excursion up the river, with only one servant and our sporting gear with us. This trick succeeded admirably, without provoking the slightest suspicion on anybody's part. Leaving our Sheikh and one "boy" behind to take care of our property, we now set sail in a small canoe, on the 6th February, and made for Chogue. The river was extremely tortuous and filled with hippopotami, who, as the vessel advanced up the tidal stream, snorted and grunted as if they felt disposed to dispute our passage; but this never happened. Inquisitive in the extreme about the foreign intruders, they could not resist continually popping up their heads and apparently inviting us to take a shot, which, as may readily be imagined, I lost no opportunity in complying with. Whether I killed any or not is difficult to say, for as the guns were fired their heads immediately disappeared, to rise no more, or, if not struck, to peep above again some way distant at our stern. To shoot hippopotami properly, one must have time to wait for the receding of the tide, when, if killed, their bodies would be left exposed on the sandy bottom; or, if in deep water, to wait until, being filled with gases, they would float by the buoyancy of their bodies.

There was little to be seen in this voyage of any interest, for the curtains of mangroves, with palms and other trees growing in almost impenetrable denseness, veiled in our view to the limits of the stream's breadth. As the tide was running out at sunset, we halted for its return at Pombui, a small village on the left bank, and resumed the journey after midnight. In two hours we reached the mooring-place opposite the station, Chogue, fastened the canoe, and lay down to sleep. Early after dawn, the jemadar, with his guard, advanced to meet us, welcomed us with sundry complimentary discharges of their matchlocks, and escorted us to their post. The jemadar's guard was composed of twenty-five men, most of whom were here, whilst the other few held another fort on the top of a hill called Tongue. Volunteers were now called for to accompany us, who would carry each his arms, a little food, and such baggage as might be necessary--just enough to march up rapidly to Fuga, to have a little shooting in some favourable jungles near there, and return again as soon as possible. There was no difficulty, as the jemadar foresaw. The Beluches receive so little pay from their sultan that any windfall like this was naturally welcome; and out of the little garrison five men were readily enlisted; besides these, they supplied four slave-servants, and two men as guides.

With one day's delay in preparing, we left Chogue in the evening, and commenced a scrambling journey; all the men fully loaded, and ourselves much the same.

On the morning of the following day, after travelling by a footpath over undulating country, we mounted the hill of Tongue, and put up in the fort.

Mount Tongue is itself an outlying hill, detached from the massive clusters of Usumbara by a deep rolling valley of broken ground of desert forest, which as we afterwards saw by their numerous tracks, must contain, during the rainy season, vast herds of the elephant and buffalo, as well as antelopes and lions, though but few animals of any kind appeared to be here now. Looking south by west from this height over the broad valley of the Pangani, I was able to take compass bearings on some cones in the Uzegura country, belonging to the Nguru hills. The whole country below appeared to be covered with the richest vegetation, and in the river we could hear the murmuring sound of a waterfall, said by the Beluches to be a barrier to the navigation of the river any farther inland.[37]

10th February.--Early in the morning we bid Tongue Fort adieu, and, descending by its northern slopes, threaded our way, arching round by north to westward, through the forests below, until late in the evening we arrived within a short distance of a hill called Khombora; and here, as the darkness of night was closing in, the party by accident divided: some, taking a more northerly track--the proper one---soon came across a nullah containing water,--the thing we were then in search of; whilst we, following on the heels of the guide, lost the way, and, coming upon the same watercourse lower down the stream, bivouacked for the night alongside some green, fetid, stagnant pools, in which a host of young frogs were keeping up a merry concert. We fired guns, but without avail, the distance we were separated by being too great for the reports to be heard.

Next morning, after following up the nullah for some considerable distance, we lit upon the rest of the party, sitting by a chain of pools, where they had bivouacked like ourselves; and, mingling together, commenced the march. At this time it was discovered that the surveying compass had been left behind, and I wished to return at once; but as Captain Burton was knocked up, and would not wait for me, the instrument was abandoned. Then, with the party complete, we passed to the northward of Khombora, by an indenture of the ground lying between it and a much larger hill, called Sagama, which hill forms the south-eastern buttress of the Usumbara masses; and opening into the valley of Pangani again, we put up at a Wazegura village on its right bank, called Kohode, crossing the river by a ferry. Here my companion, with all the party--save one exceptional Seedi soldier, Mabarak Bombay[38] who knew a little Hindustani, and acted as my interpreter--stopped a day, to recover from the fatigues of the late harassing march, for they appeared thoroughly knocked up, and to revel on a feast of milk and flesh which, with great cordiality, was supplied them by Sultan Momba, a Wazegura chief. We were now fifteen miles distant from the compass, and I called on volunteers to forsake these festivities and follow me back to get it. It was a great trial, and Bombay of all the party was the only man who could be induced to go; but he, as will be seen in many subsequent parts of this book, was ever ready to do anything for anybody, and cheerfully started off with me. The first thing which we saw after crossing by the ferry was a dead hippopotamus, lying on the greensward of the alluvial plain, encircled by a number of savages (Washenzi), all armed with bow and arrows, looking wistfully at their prostrate game. The animal was scarcely cold, and lay on the ground like a large shapeless hog bristling with arrows. It appeared from their statements that these savage hunters had been waiting on the plain for several hours before daybreak, expecting the animal on his retreat from his nocturnal excursions under the lee of the Sagama hill, in quest of rank grasses and forest-trees growing there, which compose his ordinary food, to make for a certain deep place in the river, by which means he would have to cross the plain exactly where they posted themselves: they were not mistaken. The beast advanced at the usual time for going to his watery abode, and the savages at once surrounded him on the plain; by firing arrows from all sides at once in rapid succession, the huge awkward beast knew not which man to set on first, and in its constant, fruitless, angry endeavours to reach the last assailant, he soon became exhausted, and was eventually overpowered.

We now passed on to the nullah, followed it down to the place of bivouac, found the compass, and returned. In the bed of the nullah there were numerous pools, both large and small, but all were rapidly drying up, and destroying the numerous fish they contained; for as this desiccation increased, and the pools became smaller, the fervid sun heated the little remaining water to such an overpowering extent, that the fish, half suffocated, turned on their backs and became an easy prey to the numerous green-and-brown-striped iguanas that eagerly thronged their brinks for food. As we approached, these horrid-looking reptiles hurried off like frightened cats to their hiding-places, some bearing fish away in their mouths, whilst others, less composed, dropped what they had half devoured, to evade us all the more readily. This intense fear of man is caused by their being the negro's game, who eat them with the same kind of pleasure and relish which a Frenchman has for frogs. Cheerily did we trip along, for Bombay--astonished at my oddities or peculiarities, as he thought them, when I picked up a river shell, or dilated much on the antelopes and birds we sometimes saw--broke into a series of yarns about his former life, and of the wild animals with which he was familiar in his fatherland. He seemed to me a surprisingly indefatigable walker, for he joked and talked and walked as briskly at the end of thirty miles as he did at starting. As the sun was setting we repassed the place where the hippopotamus had been slain, but not a vestige of his flesh or a bone remained to mark the place--every morsel had been carried off for food. Ferrying across the river, we were heartily met by the boisterous, mirthful Sultan Momba, who instantly on our landing shook us heartily by the hand, commented on our walking powers with enthusiastic pride, invited us to his palace (grass hut), and gave us a royal repast.

13th February.--We started early in the morning, and after crossing the Pangani, took to the beaten track and followed up the valley. Nearly at the outset we passed over the Luangera river, close to its junction with the Pangani, by a tree thrown across it. The stream, though not broad, is deep and sullen, and, by native report, is infested with crocodiles. This may easily be imagined, for the Pangani, a much rougher, and therefore a less favourable river for them, undoubtedly is so. Here, near the junction of these two rivers, their united valleys cause a much greater expanse of alluvial ground; and had we turned northwards, we might have reached Fuga in two short marches, by crossing over a mountain spur called Vugiri; but in consideration of our men, who had to carry unusually heavy burdens, we determined to follow on our course up the valley by a lower and more easy road, passing round instead of over this spur. With the Vugiri hills overhanging us on the right, like a bluff high wall, prettily decked with bush and tree, and the boisterous Pangani murmuring on the left hand, which now in many places was divided by little inhabited islands, we tracked along the valley until we reached Pasunga, when we left the river still coming from the north-west, and then, turning sharply round the extreme western point of the Vugiri spur, we entered on a cultivated plain in a direct line facing Fuga. Here, on the second day, being overtaken by a fierce storm, we put up in some sheds outside a village. There were three small cones, called Mbara, close to us west by north; but besides these, to the northward, there was nothing save an uninterrupted plain of the densest jungle leading up to the Makumbara mountains, about ten miles distant. The village itself was enshrouded in a dense thicket, which was entered by the narrowest of passages, cut through branches for security's sake, and was further protected by piles and stakes against the attacks of enemies. Everybody here feels an insecurity to life and property, which makes people wonder how they ever can be happy. Prosperous they are not, and never will be, until such time as enlightened men may happen to come amongst them to teach their chiefs the art of governing. Of all villages the most secure from attack seem those that are situated on the river islands, where the division of the stream affords a natural moat, which no African art can overcome.

15th February.--After waiting for a few hours this morning for the rain to subside, we got under way and made straight for Fuga. The first half of the journey led us by well-beaten footpaths through flat cultivated fields of sugar-cane and bananas, tamarind-trees, papaws, and various jungle shrubs, filling up the non-arable surface; and then began a steep ascent by rudely-beaten zigzags, to ease the abrupt-ness of the hill, on which the capital is situated. The whole face of this hill was clothed with large timber trees, around which, here and there, entwining their trunks, clung the delicate sarsaparilla vine; and beneath them flourished, as by spontaneous growth, the universal plantain, a vegetable grown in this country as we do corn, and, like it also, regarded as the staff of life. At length, after a little hard toiling, we emerged from this prodigious wooding, and found ourselves on a naked, bold, prominent point overlooking the whole plain we had left behind, and from which we could clearly see its entire dimensions. To the northward, as already said, was the Makumbara range, a dense compact mass of solid-looking hills, much higher than the spur we stood upon, but joining it to the north-eastward; whilst its other extremity shot out to the north-westward, until it seemed as though it were suddenly cut off by the Pangani river.

Beyond the river, again, looking across the western extremity, but farther back than it, other large hills, bedimmed by distance, could be seen tending in a south-westerly direction, which in all probability are a link of the longitudinal chain, which, as our maps will show, fringe the whole of the southern continent of Africa. [39] The country directly beyond the river valley rose into gentle undulations, but on this side all was flat and densely wooded, save in one little spot to the north-west of the Mbara cones, where a sheet of water or small lake made a bald conspicu-ous place--and here it was, by native report, that elephants and other large game abounded.

Having now completed the survey, we proceeded along the shoulder of the hill just ascended, and passing by a ferruginous spring, soon arrived unexpectedly to its inhabitants at Fuga, the capital of Usumbara, and presented ourselves to the aston-ished Fugaites, who naturally began to question what could possibly be the meaning of this stolen march on them; for, contrary to the laws of the land, no permission to enter their *citadel* had been asked, and consequently no one was prepared to see or receive us. Access to the village was strictly forbidden to us strangers, until at least the king, whose palace is situated some distance from it, had been consulted with in a certain form of ridiculous ceremony, which, for politeness' sake, we felt ourselves bound to assent to, but in the meanwhile we took possession of some huts close to it, where Mr Krapf, our Church missionary, had some years previously, when visiting this place, taken up his abode.

A deputation was now sent with our compliments to the king, Kimueri, soliciting an audience; and just before sunset they returned to say we must remain where we were for the present, as the king was in doubt about our intentions, regarding us with suspicion, as we had come through the territories of his enemies, the Wa-zegura, which was tantamount to a hostile declaration; and, moreover, he required leisure for his mganga or magic-man to divine what time would be propitious for an interview. The old man was in the wane of life, being upwards, it was said, of one hundred years of age, and his people thought he must die. Hearing this, Captain Burton, playing with his superstitious credulity, devised a plan by which he at once gained access to him. The king was lying on a cartel in a small round hut, encompassed on his near side by swarthy-looking counsellors, who smoked small pipes and sat on low three-legged stools. Sultan Majid's introductory letter was now read, and all seemed satisfied as to who we were. We then returned to our lodgings, and found a bullock and some meal of Indian corn and plantains sent as a honorarium after us. Next morning, agreeably to promise, at the king's direction, a guide came to show us about the place, in order that Captain Burton might be able to pick some leaves or herbs to make a certain decoction which would insure longevity; but as none such could be found, and the old king had seen through the trick, entrance to the "town" was still forbidden.

Whilst wandering about, however, we chanced to see a number of negroes turn out and chase down an antelope. It was a very small rufous-brown animal, much about the size and shape of the Kakur deer of the Himalayas; but what struck me most was, the peculiarity of its having, unlike all hitherto known African species, four points of horns. In consequence of this great novelty, I tried to purchase its head, but the greedy savages who caught it, coveting the flesh, would not, for any consideration, let me have it, and I never saw another killed. Rain poured down in torrents at night, and the days remained so cloudy, that we felt the kuzi or little monsoon had now fairly set in, and the sooner we could get away from the high lands so much the better for us. In the evening (15th February), therefore, we sent our return presents to the king, and asked permission to be allowed to go. A very civil reply was given, with certain additions, for which I could not help admiring him; but he would not accept the present, and we might go whenever we pleased.

Thinking to obviate to the best of my ability any differences with these be-nighted but cunning people, and to leave as favourable an impression of our visit as I could, I advised Captain Burton to distribute amongst the ministers those things which had been brought for the king, and this accordingly was done, but not without considerable debate, and the finally reluctant sanction of the king.[40] The next morning (16th February) saw us descending the heights of Fuga, and in a few hours' walk we left the cool congenial air incidental to 4000 or 5000 feet, for the hot, damp, morbid, close atmosphere of the jungle plains below, in which, as Miss Nightingale would say, you could palpably smell a fever. Then following the old route, we came down to the Pangani; and in three days' travelling along it, as Captain Burton, being no sportsman, would not stop for shooting, we put up once more at Kohode, with Sultan Momba.

19th February.--To vary the way and gain a better knowledge of the river, we now determined to follow it all the way down to Chogue, which we made on the third day, spending the two intervening nights at the Wazegura villages of Kiranga and Kizungu. The valley, though much varied, was generally contracted by the closing in of the rolling terminal abutments of the Tongue hill, on the one side--with rising land, and little conical hills almost joining, which overhung the river on the right bank in Uzegura, on the other side. We seldom met any people on the line of march; and the land being totally uncultivated, excepting in the immediate vicinity of these villages, we felt as though we were travelling through a desert wild of dreary jungle--which, indeed, it was. No animals, and scarcely any birds, moved about to cheer and keep the road alive; and all was silent, save the constant gurgling, rumbling sound of the river's waters as they rushed rapidly over boulders and often plunged down many little falls in the bed of the stream. On passing the point opposite to Tongue Fort, we saw the cause which produced the sound like a cata-ract, which formerly we had heard when standing on its summit. It was, indeed, a cascade of considerable dimensions, and would, doubtless, be a sight of pleasing grandeur when the river is full.

In the afternoon of the 22d, as we approached Chogue, the little Beluch je-madar, with the rest of the guard, turned out to welcome us, and gloat over the successful termination of an artful trick he felt himself the father of. He spread mats for us to sit upon, and brought the universal coffee-pot and some sweetmeats as a relish to refresh us and increase the triumph; for the little man, no doubt, thought he had gained his prize.

The next three days were spent in making different excursions, shooting hippopotami in the vicinity of the outpost; and on the 26th February we returned to Pangani, Captain Burton dropping down the river in a canoe, whilst I, to complete the survey of the country and to check my former work on the river, walked with Bombay to Pombui, ferried across the stream there, and came by the right bank down to Bueni, on the shore of the Pangani Bay. Here I recrossed the river again, and found Sheikh Said and my "boy" Gaetano, with all the traps arranged, ready at the old house for our reception. Our vessel had been discharged at the expiration of the first month's engagement, and we were now expecting a second one from Zanzibar, to continue the cruise southward along the shore, and gain a fuller knowledge of the various entrepots of caravans. I had by this time become much attached to Bombay, for I must say I never saw any black man so thoroughly honest and conscientious as he was, added to which, his generosity was unbounded; and I thought (as we shall see afterwards proved to be the case) he would turn out a most valuable servant for the future journey--a regular "Friday." The only difficulty now was how to obtain his discharge from the service he was in; but this the jemadar, who followed us down to Pangani to receive the wages for the men who accompanied us to Fuga, said he would arrange, if Bombay felt willing, and would leave a substitute to act for him whilst he was away. A compact was accordingly concluded, by which Bombay became my servant for the time being, at five dollars per mensem, with board and lodging on the journey found him. The jemadar now left us, with a present for himself and the hire of his men, and we were all alone.

On the 1st March a violent bilious fever attacked me, and also floored Captain Burton and Valantine. It appeared in the form of the yellow jack of Jamaica, and made us all as yellow as guineas; and had we been able to perspire, I have no doubt we should have sweated out a sort of yellow ochre which a painter might have coveted. In this state we lay physicking ourselves until the 5th, when a vessel chartered by the Consul, and stored with delicacies of all kinds by our generous, thoughtful old host for the journey southwards, arrived, and took us off. Captain Burton being still under the influences of this terrible scourge, and very ill, even to absolute prostration, and occasionally wandering in his mind, he gave up his projected plans, and we returned at once to Zanzibar, reaching it on the 6th March.

The Masika, or great vernal rainy season which follows up the sun as it passes to the north, broke over the island of Zanzibar this year early in April, and was expected to last for its normal period of forty days. For this to subside we had now to wait here as patiently as we could, occupying the spare time so forced on us in purchasing an outfit and in preparing for the journey. It was highly interesting to see here at this season of the year, as we well could do, so near the equator, the regular systematic procession of the wind and rain following up the sun in its northward passage. The atmosphere, at this time and place, was heated and rarefied by the vertical rays of the sun; that produced a vacuum, which the cold airs of the south taking advantage of, rush up to fill, and with their coldness condense the heated vapours drawn up daily from the ocean and precipitate them back again on the earth below. This occurring and continually repeating day by day, for a certain time, nearly in the same place, fills the air with electric excitement, which causes thunder and lightning to accompany nearly every storm. The atmospheric air's being so surcharged with electricity was palpably felt by the nervous system; at any rate, judging from myself, I can only say I experienced a nervous sensibility I never knew before, of being startled at any sudden accident. A pen dropping from the table even would make me jump. Whilst stopping here, the Colonel's house was one continuous scene of pleasure and festivities. The British Consulate was the common rendezvous of all men: Arab, Hindi, German, French, or American, were all alike received without distinction or any forced restraint. Indeed, the old Consul literally studied the mode of making people happy; and Zanzibar, instead of being an outlandish place, such as to make one wonder how men could exile themselves by coming here, was really a place of great enjoyment. The merchants, on the other hand, were not less hospitably inclined, and constantly entertained and gave very handsome dinners.

Besides our Consulate, there is a French and an American one, and the European merchants were composed of French, Germans, and Americans,--the dark-coloured ones being principally confined to Arabs, Hindis, and the Wasuahili, or coast people. Taking advantage of the time, especially the evenings, I spent most of them in rating the chronometers and getting all the surveying instruments into working order; whilst Captain Burton, besides book-making, busied himself in making all the other arrangements for the journey, such as purchasing Venetian beads, brass wire, and American sheetings, &c., which come here in shiploads round the Cape of Good Hope, or in buying donkeys for our riding and their transport. Then in the cool of the mornings we took social walks or rides through the clove plantations, or amongst the palms, mango-trees, and orange gardens, treating pine-apples, which grew like common weeds on the roadsides, as if they were nothing better than ordinary turnips, though when placed upon the table they are certainly as delicious as any living fruit. The only fine houses are those occupied by the Europeans and the Sultan, and they front the harbour, which is considered a very good one, and is very constantly filled with shipping, the Sultan's men-of-war, foreign square-rigged vessels, and a host of buggaloes from Aden, Muscat, Catch, and Bombay. The back of the town is very much like a common Indian bazaar, but there is a hollow square in its centre, which nowadays is peculiar to this place--it is the slave-market. Immediately after every fresh importation, you can see in the early morning unhappy-looking men and women, all hideously black and ugly, tethered to one another like horses in a fair, and calculating men, knowing judges of flesh and limb, walking up and down, feeling their joints and looking out to make a bargain. Women, of course, sell better than the men, being fitted to more general purposes. For a good wife any sum might be given. But the saddest sight which came under my observation was the way in which some licentious-looking men began a cool, deliberate inspection of a certain divorced culprit who had been sent back to the market for inconstancy to her husband. She had learnt a sense of decency during her conjugal life, and the blushes on her face now clearly showed how her heart was mortified at this unseemly exposure, made worse because she could not help it.

The amount of information gathered by the expedition concerning the interior of Africa at Zanzibar, I may say was *nil*, to use Captain Burton's own words, in a letter written at the British Consulate, 22d April 1857, and published in the Proceedings of the Royal Geographical Society, page 52 of No. 1, vol. ii., where these remarkable words may be found:--"We could obtain no useful information from the European merchants of Zanzibar, who are mostly ignorant of everything beyond the island. The Arabs and Sawahilis, who were averse to, and fearful of, white travellers, *did* give us information, but it was worse than none."

The orders of the Royal Geographical Society to Captain Burton were these, in short:--"The great object of the expedition is to penetrate inland from Kilwa, or some other place on the east coast of Africa, and make the best of your way to the reputed Lake of Nyassa; to determine the position and limits of that lake; to ascertain the depth and nature of its waters and tributaries; to explore the country around it, &c. Having obtained all the information you require in that quarter, you are to proceed northwards towards the range of mountains marked upon our maps as containing the probable sources of the Bahr el Abiad, which it will be your next great object to discover."

Bearing these instructions in mind, Captain Burton naturally felt desirous of penetrating from Kilwa to attack the missionaries' great slug-shaped lake in the tail. The reason why Captain Burton was prevented from doing so, I shall show again by a reference to the same letter. He writes thus:--"The accounts formerly made in Europe about the facility of penetrating inland from Kilwa (Quiloa), and the economy of travel in that region, are fabulous. The southern Sawahili are more hostile to explorers than the inhabitants of the northern maritime towns, and their distance from the seat of government renders them daring by impunity. But last year they persuaded the Waginda tribe of the interior to murder a peaceful Arab merchant, in order that strangers might be deterred from interfering with their commerce. Messrs Krapf and Erhardt, of the Mombas mission, spent a few hours at Kilwa, where they were civilly received by the governor and citizens, but they were sadly deceived in being led to imagine that they could make that port their starting-point." "We shall probably land at Bagamoyo."

Now we did land at Kaole, close to Bagamoyo, but the route from Kilwa to Nyassa was afterwards safely traversed by Dr Boscher, though, after that, Boscher was murdered by some thieves in Whiyow.[41] Having said this much, which shows that Captain Burton was bent on going by the great caravan road to Ujiji, I shall first of all dwell on the nature of the men we took with us, what agreements they made, and what pays they received. I feel bound to state this, as I was called on by the Consul to witness the agreements, and much of the journey was performed by myself alone; added to which, the funds of the expedition fell short, and as soon as it did so, I made a compact with Captain Burton that, in the event of the Government not paying our excess of expenditure, I would pay him the half of all those expenses; and I did so to the extent of L600 after the journey was over.

Our cafila bashi (head of caravan) was Sheikh Said, who went with us to Mombas. He said he would go with us if we only went to Ujiji on the Tanganyika Lake, but he would not go on any other line, as his relatives feared some accident might befall him. For this he received from Colonel Hamerton 500 dollars; and he was promised, if he succeeded in pleasing us, 1000 dollars more, and a gold watch, on his return. There was a little more difficulty in getting a Beluch escort, for the Consul cautioned us that we could not expect the Sultan to give one gratis. He asked the Sultan, however, for men, and we were told we might have them out of his army if they would volunteer. The head jemadar then came to make a bargain, and we said we would give to each man five dollars a-month, besides rations and clothing the same as Bombay got. This bait would not take, and we could not get one man until the Consul again spoke to the Sultan about it. A party then were marched up to the Consulate, when, in addition to the pay already offered, they demanded flesh as often as we killed a goat, bullock, or sheep, but they would not serve more than six months. To this last stipulation, arguing on my Somali experiences, I stoutly objected, but was overruled both by Colonel Hamerton and Captain Burton. The Colonel then gave the jemadar of our party a present of 25 dollars, and to each of the privates 20 dollars, to set themselves up for the journey. Further, he promised them a handsome reward on their return if they served us well, to be paid out of some public fund in the same way as he paid Sheikh Said.

The rest of our escort consisted of some slaves, who were furnished us by a Banyan named Ramji. They were armed with muskets, and enlisted not to carry loads, but to guard us and treat with the native chiefs on the line of march, as they were familiar with the road to Ujiji, and were friends with the chiefs we should find there. Their pay was fixed at 5 dollars a-month, half of which they were to keep themselves, and the other half to be given to their master in compensation for the loss of their services. Further, six months' wages at this rate was to be paid in advance, and the remainder when the journey was over; but leaving a clause to the effect that they might be discharged at any time, supposing we did not require their services further.

Everybody at Zanzibar did his best to assist us, from the Sultan downwards. The European merchants gave us most hospitable entertainments on a very grand scale, and Mr Oswald, in particular, transported our spare boxes to England. Ladha, the customs master, was our banker, and found our outfit of beads, brass wire, and cloths, which is the circulating medium in inner Africa instead of money. Colonel Hamerton was so anxious for the success of the expedition, that he obtained a man-of-war--the corvette Artemise--from the Sultan on the 16th June 1857, and accompanied us over to Kaole on the mainland, notwithstanding at the time he was dangerously ill. For some time we were detained here collecting baggage animals to carry our property. All we wanted could not be procured, as the bulk of the pagazis (porters) had been previously hired by the ivory merchant traders. However, thirty-six men were sent forward to Zungomero by Ladha, and we bought thirty donkeys. When all was done that could be done in a hurry, we bade the generous old Colonel adieu, as well as his medical attendant, Mr Frost, and commenced the journey inland on the 27th June--Ladha promising to send the rest of our property after us as soon as he could find carriage for it.

I have already published, in my 'Journal of the Discovery of the Source of the Nile,' a description of the countries we had to pass through to reach Kaze, so I shall not trouble the reader with the details on that point, contained in my previous publication. Suffice it to say that Kaze is a place in the centre of Unyamuezi, the Land of the Moon, situated in S. lat. 5o, and E. long. 33o. It is occupied by Arab merchants as a central trading depot, and is fast expanding into a colony. At the time of our starting we did not know that, but imagined we should find a depot of that sort at Ujiji. Travelling through the country of Uzaramo, both Captain Burton and I contracted fevers. Mine occasionally recurred at various intervals, but his stuck to him throughout the journey, and even lasted till some time after he came home.

At Zungomero we overtook the porters that Ladha had sent forward. I calculated our rate of expenditure, found we had not enough for the necessities of the journey, and prevailed on Captain Burton to write back for more, notwithstanding our Government subsidy was out; for I could not brook the idea of failure, even though we might have to pay our future travelling expenses out of our own pockets.

I was also shocked here to hear that our good stanch friend, Colonel Hamerton, had died shortly after we left him. It struck a blow also on the minds of Sheikh Said and the Beluches, for they naturally thought their security was gone. Sheikh Said, however, I must say, very much to his credit, soon shook off his fears, and even told the Beluches to do the same, for another consul would come who would see justice done to them.

We then left Zungomero and crossed the East Coast Range. During this stage the Beluches one day struck for food, as they were disappointed at our not killing goats, the fact being that I had supplied our table with guinea-fowls. An altercation took place which I had to settle, as was invariably the case when any difficulties arose in the camp. I managed the matter by ordering a march. This brought them to reason, for hitherto they thought we should be afraid to go without them. The consequence was that, finding themselves left behind, they forgot their wrath and followed us. On the way they found Captain Burton lying by the roadside prostrate with fever, and, taking compassion on him, brought him into camp. They were forgiven; but another difficulty arose in consequence of our donkeys dying faster than their loads were consumed, so that we could not have proceeded had not some of Ramji's slaves carried some loads for us. Our supplies were already too short for our journey; nevertheless, Captain Burton said he would pay them if they carried our loads.

They did so; but Captain Burton, on my saying we should find it difficult to keep faith with them, mildly replied, "Arabs made promises in that way, but never kept them; and, moreover, slaves of this sort never expected to be paid." I grew angry at this declaration--for I had seen Tibet ruined by officers not keeping faith with their porters--and argued the matter, but without effect. On arrival at Ugogi, on the west flank of the East Coast Range, our cattle were so completely done up that we could not have proceeded, had it not happened, by the greatest luck in the world, we found some pagazis here desirous of going to their homes in Unyamuezi. They had been left there by a caravan in consequence of a quarrel which originated in seduction. This lift took us over the interior plateau across Ugogo and Mgunda Mkhali to Kaze, where we arrived on the 7th November 1857. The Arabs we found collected here were extremely obliging, especially one Sheikh Snay, who furnished us with a house, looked after our wants, and supplied us with much useful information.

On my opening Messrs Rebmann and Erhardt's map, and asking him where Nyassa was, he said it was a distinct lake from Ujiji, lying to the southward. This opened our eyes to a most interesting fact, for the first time discovered. I then asked what the word Ukerewe meant, and was answered in the same way, that it was a lake to the northward, much larger than Ujiji, and this solved the mystery. The missionaries had run three lakes into one. In great glee at this I asked Snay, through Captain Burton, whether or not a river ran out of that lake? to which he replied, he thought the lake was the source of the Jub river; and he strongly advised us, if our only motive in coming here was to look at a large piece of water, to go to it instead of on to Ujiji. Captain Burton and I argued that we thought the lake in question, which was the Victoria N'yanza, would more likely prove to be the source of the Nile, from the simple fact of our knowing the Jub to be separated from the interior plateau by the East Coast Range. Time wore on. Our pagazis all left us, as is usual, on their arriving at their homes, and we had to procure more to carry our traps on to Ujiji.

Captain Burton attempted to get porters by giving presents to the best two men we had for that purpose, but without the least effect. They promised and kept us waiting, but never performed. In the mean time Captain Burton got desperately ill, whilst I picked up all the information I could gather from the Arabs, with Bombay as an interpreter.[42] I heard that the Babisa, who live on the west of Nyassa, came to the southeast corner of Tanganyika in quest of ivory for the Kilua merchants. That caravans sometimes reached the Cazembe country by land, crossing the Manungu river, and also went to Katata for copper, which is of a dark rich red colour, and more prized than the imported copper. Some Arabs also went down the Tanganyika, disembarked at Manungu, and reached Cazembe. Further, I heard from Snay and his associates that the Kitangule and Katonga rivers ran out of the Ukerewe Lake (Victoria N'yanza), and that another river, which is the Nile, but supposed by them to be the upper portions of the Jub river, ran into the N'yanza. Further conversation explained this away, and I made them confess that all these rivers ran exactly contrary to the way they first stated; as it was obvious, if the N'yanza was the source of the Jub, the last river alluded to must flow out of the lake instead of into it, as they had said. Still more extraordinary than this, I heard from Snay that vessels frequented some waters to the northward of the equator, which confirmed some statement I had heard of the same nature in 1855 when travelling in the Somali country. I could not fix in my own mind exactly what this alluded to; but I felt so curious to find out, and so sure in my own mind that the Victoria N'yanza would prove to be the source of the Nile, I proposed going to see it at once, instead of going on to Ujiji. The route, however, to the northward was said to be dangerous--Usui alone would seize all our property--and Captain Burton preferred going west. How this even was to be managed then seemed very dubious, for not one of Ramji's slaves would come near us, and the Beluches were so tired of the journey they begged for their discharge, crying it was their due, as they had served their turn of service. They wanted no pay if we would only give them certificates of satisfaction. We would not do this; and then they said, as they saw we wanted them, they would not desert us.

We had now been at Kaze rather more than a month, and I thought Captain Burton would die if we did not make a move, so I begged him to allow me to assume the command *pro tem.*, and I would see what I could do to effect a move. Accordingly, as he agreed, I made arrangements with Snay, and transported half our property to Zimbili, where I prepared a house for Captain Burton's reception on the 5th December. Three days after he was carried over, and he begged me to take account of his effects, as he thought he would die. I cheered him up, and found the change of air had the effect I desired. Still Ramji's men would not come out to camp, so I tried with Bombay to see what they had at heart, and then it transpired they had not been paid for carrying loads on from the East Coast Range to Kaze. In a minute I recollected Captain Burton's promise to them, brought them into the camp, and paid them their dues.

Bit by bit we pushed on to Msene, another small colony occupied chiefly by Wasuahili, and here we ate our Christmas dinner. The country was rich in the extreme, and well under rice cultivation. Ramji's men were quite in their element here, and even Bombay became so *love-sick* we could hardly tear him away. We broke ground on the 10th January 1858, but not until three days after did the whole of our men join us. I saw now we had too many mouths to feed; and as Ramji's men had been hired more for show than work, their term of service had just expired, and I did not think we should require their guns any more, I begged Captain Burton to give them a present each, with leave to go to their homes--for it must be remembered they possess homes in Unyamuezi as well as at Zanzibar. The men craved to be allowed to go on with us, but I, more than any one else, insisted we ought to get rid of them, for the reasons stated above; and so they were discharged. I found we were on a great decline of the country draining to the westward; the soil was deeper and richer, and the vegetation proportionately richer as we went on with the journey. Shortly we crossed the Malagarazi river in a bark canoe at the Mpete ferry, and found that, after having travelled along this decline from Kaze about one hundred and fifty miles, we began to ascend at the eastern horn of a large crescent-shaped mass of mountains overhanging the northern half of the Tanganyika Lake, which I am now about to describe.

This mountain mass I consider to be THE TRUE MOUNTAINS OF THE MOON, regarding which so many erroneous speculations have been ventured. I infer this because they lie beyond Unyamuezi (country of the Moon), and must have been first mentioned to geographical inquirers by the Wanyamuezi (people of the Moon), who have from time out of mind visited the coast, and must have been the first who gave information of them. I am the more satisfied of the correctness of this view from observing the missionaries' map; for what could have induced them to call their great lake, in general terms, the Sea of the Moon, except that it lay beyond the country of the Moon?[43] The mountains form a crescent overhanging the north end of the lake, large and deep in the body to the north, and tapering to horns as they stretch southwards down the east and west sides of the lake. Our line of march, about six hundred rectilinear geographical miles, had been nearly due west from Zanzibar. Here you may picture to yourself my bitter disappointment when, after toiling through so many miles of savage life, all the time emaciated by divers sicknesses and weakened by great privations of food and rest, I found, on approaching the zenith of my ambition, the Great Lake in question nothing but mist and glare before my eyes. From the summit of the eastern horn the lovely Tanganyika Lake could be seen in all its glory by everybody but myself. The fact was, that fevers and the influence of a vertical sun had reduced my system so, that inflammation, caught by sleeping on the ground during this rainy season, attacked my eyes, brought on an almost total blindness, and rendered every object before me enclouded as by a misty veil. Proceeding onwards down the western slopes of the hill, we soon arrived at the margin of the lake, and hired a canoe at Ukaranga to take us to Ujiji, the chief place on the lake which Arabs frequent. This is a name we had long been familiar with, and is the term by which the Arabs in general call this lake. This mode of nomenclature is quite in accordance with the usual custom of semi-civilised people, as we see in Arabia, where the Arabs call the Red Sea by the names of the different ports which they frequent. Thus, for instance, at Jeddah, it is called by them the Sea of Jeddah, whilst at Suez it is the Sea of Suez, &c. &c. The Tanganyika Lake, lying between 3o and 8o south latitude, and in 29o east longitude, has a length of three hundred miles, and is from thirty to forty broad in its centre. The surface-level, as I ascertained by the temperature of boiling water, is only eighteen hundred feet, and it appears quite sunk into the lap of these mountains. Its waters are very sweet, and abound with delicious fish in great variety. The fertility of the northern end of the lake surpassed anything we had hitherto seen; but this was not surprising when duly considered. The hills, instead of being, as on the great plateau we had recently left, outcrops of granite, were composed of argillaceous sandstone. Rains there lasted all the year round, and the temperature was very considerable. In consequence of this the sides of the lake are thickly inhabited by numerous tribes of the true negro breed, amongst which the most conspicuous are the Wabembe cannibals, into whose territory no Arabs durst ever venture. Bombay, my interpreter, describes them as being very dreadful creatures, who are "always looking out for some of our sort." The port we finally arrived at is called Kawele, a small village in the Ujiji district. Here we landed all our property, and took up our abode in a deserted house, which had been left to decay by some Arab merchants. The Beluch guard received a present of cloth; they seemed very glad the land march was at an end. In that respect we felt the same as our men; but we found ourselves in the hands of a very ill-disposed chief, called Kannina--tyrannical, and, as such savages invariably are, utterly unreasonable. A heavy tribute was paid for the advantages of this savage monster's ***protection***, and we were too short of beads and cloth to search out for and pay another chief of more moderate inclinations. This was a serious misfortune; for, having once entered his dominions and established our headquarters there, we could not very well leave them. This was the more distressing, as comfort, pleasure, and everything is at the mercy of these headsmen's wills, and we were destined for a long sojourn here. To war with these chiefs is like "cutting off the nose to spite the face." Nobody, let his desire be what it may, dares assist you without the chief's full approbation; and Kannina's austere government we had occasion to feel from first to last. Our first object on arrival was to get boats for the survey of the lake; but here arose a difficulty. Hostilities were rife with nearly all the border tribes; and the little cockle-shell canoes, made from the hollowed trunks of trees, are not only liable to be driven ashore by the slightest storm, but are so small that there is but little stowage-room in them for carrying supplies. The sailors, aware of this defect, fear to venture anywhere except on certain friendly beats, and therefore their boats were quite unfitted for our work.

This dilemma made us try to hire a dhow or sailing-vessel, belonging to Sheikh Hamed bin Suleyim, living at Kasenge Island, on the opposite or western shore, as it was the only boat afloat on these waters fitted for carrying provisions and moving about independent of the border clans. On arriving here, we were so disabled by sickness--Captain Burton utterly, and I suffering from ophthalmia, and a weakness in the lower extremities resembling paralysis--that my companion proposed sending our Ras-cafila, Sheikh Said, across the lake to bargain for the dhow, and applied to Kannina for the means of transport. At first he seemed inclined to treat, though at an exorbitant rate; but when we came direct to terms, he backed entirely out. Fortunately we obtained a boat and crew from another chief, at the extortionate charge of four kitindis and four dhotis merikani, besides the usual sailors' fee. The dhoti is a piece of American sheeting measuring eight cubits. The cubit is still the negro's yard, the same as was adopted at the time of the Flood; they have no other measure than that with which nature has provided them--viz., the first joint of the arm, or from the elbow to the top of the middle finger. These kitindis are a sort of brass-wire bracelet worn on the lower arm by the negro females, coiled up from the wrist to the elbow, like a wax taper circling up a stick or stem. Sometimes this wire is reformed and coiled flat out round the neck to a breadth of about eight inches, and gives the wearer's head much the appearance of John the Baptist's standing in the middle of a charger. These necklaces are never taken off, so at night, or resting-time, the wearer on lying down places a block of wood or stone beneath his head, to prevent the wire from galling. This concession of the chief was given under the proviso that Kannina would not object, which, strange to say, he promised not to do; and hopes were entertained of an early departure. However, this, like every other earthly expectation in these black regions, was destined to be disappointed. In the first place, an African must do everything by easy stages, nor can he entertain two ideas in his head at the same moment. First a crew had to be collected, and when collected to be paid, and when paid the boat was found to be unseaworthy, and must be plugged; and so much time elapsed, and plans were changed. But after all, things, it happened, were wisely ordained; for the time thus wasted served to recruit my health, as I employed it in bathing and strolling gently about during the cool of the mornings and evenings, and so gained considerable benefit. There is a curious idea here with regard to the bathing-place, in fancying the dreaded crocodile will obey the mandates of a charm. They plant the bough of a particular tree in the water about fifty yards from the shore, which marks the line of safe bathing, for within it they say the animal dares not venture. At noon, protected by an umbrella, and fortified with stained-glass spectacles, I usually visited the market-place, with beads in hand, to purchase daily supplies. The market is held between the hours of 10 A.M. and 4 P.M., near the port, and consists of a few temporary huts, composed of grass and branches hastily tied together. Most of these are thrown up day by day. The commodities brought for sale are fish, flesh, tobacco, palm oil, and spirits, different kinds of potatoes, artichokes, several sorts of beans, plantains, melons, cotton, sugar-cane, a variety of pulse and vegetables, ivories, and sometimes slaves. Between these perambulations, I spent the day reclining with my eyes shut. At length, after eighteen days' negotiations, improved by these constitutional diversions and rest, and longing for a change, especially one that led across the sea, and afforded the means of surveying it, I proposed to go myself, and treat directly with Sheikh Hamed. Captain Burton threw obstacles in my way at first, saying canoes were not safe on such a large lake, but he finally gave in when I pressed the advisability of my doing so. This intention soon reached the ears of Kannina, who, fearing that he might thus lose much cloth, threw obstacles in the way, and most unjustly demanded as large a passport-fee for my crossing as had been given to the other chief; which demand we were obliged to comply with, or the men would not take up an oar.

Chapter II.

Canoes--The Crews--The Biography of Bombay--The Voyage--Crocodiles-
-The Lake Scenery--Kivira Island--Black Beetles--An Adventure with One
of Them--Kasenge Island--African Slavery.

3d March 1858.--ALL being settled, I set out in a long narrow canoe, hollowed out of the trunk of a single tree. These vessels are mostly built from large timbers, growing in the district of Uguhha, on the western side of the lake. The seats of these canoes are bars of wood tied transversely to the length. The kit taken consists of one load (60 lb.) of cloth (American sheeting), another of large blue beads, a magazine of powder, and seven kitindis. The party is composed of Bombay, my interpreter; Gaetano, the Goanese cook-boy; two Beluch soldiers; one Nakhuda or sea-captain, who sometimes wore a goat-skin; and twenty stark-naked savage sailors: twenty-six in all. Of these only ten started, the remainder leaving word that they would follow down the coast, and meet us at a *khambi* (encampment), three miles distant, by 12 o'clock. The ten, however, sufficient for the occasion, move merrily off at 9 A.M., and in an hour we reached the rendezvous, under a large spreading tree on the right bank of the mouth of the river Ruche.

The party is decidedly motley. The man of quaintest aspect in it is Sidi Mabarak Bombay. He is of the Wahiyow tribe, who make the best slaves in Eastern Africa. His breed is that of the true woolly-headed negro, though he does not represent a good specimen of them physically, being somewhat smaller in his general proportions than those one generally sees as stokers in our steamers that traverse the Indian Ocean. His head, though woodeny, like a barber's block, is lit up by a humorous little pair of pig-like eyes, set in a generous benign-looking countenance, which, strange to say, does not belie him, for his good conduct and honesty of purpose are without parallel. His muzzle projects dog-monkey fashion, and is adorned with a regular set of sharp-pointed alligator teeth, which he presents to full view as constantly as his very ticklish risible faculties become excited. The tobacconist's "jolly nigger," stuck in the corner house of ---- street, as it stands in mute but full grin, tempting the patronage of accidental passengers, is his perfect counterpart. This wonderful man says he knows nothing of his genealogy, nor any of the dates of the leading epochs of his adventurous life,--not even his birth, time of captivity, or restoration.

But his general history he narrated to me as follows, which I give as he told it me, for this sketch may be of interest, presenting, as it does, a good characteristic account of the manner in which slave-hunts are planned and carried into execution. It must be truthful, for I have witnessed tragedies of a similar nature. The great slave-hunters of Eastern Africa are the Wasuahili or coast people; formerly slaves themselves, they are more enlightened, and fuller of tricks than the interior people, whom they now in their turn catch. Having been once caught themselves, they know how to proceed, and are consequently very cautious in their movements, taking sometimes years before they finally try to accomplish their object. They first ensnare the ignorant unsuspicious inlanders by alluring and entangling them in the treacherous meshes of debt, and then, by capturing and mercilessly selling their human game, liquidate the debt, insinuatingly advanced as an irresistible decoy to allure their confiding victims.

Bombay says: "I am a Mhiyow; my father lived in a village in the country of Uhiyow (a large district situated between the east coast and the Nyassa (Lake) in latitude 11o S.) Of my mother I have but the faintest recollection; she died whilst I was in my infancy. Our village was living in happy contentment, until the fated year when I was about the age of twelve. At that period a large body of Wasuahili merchants and their slaves, all equipped with sword and gun, came suddenly, and, surrounding our village, demanded of the inhabitants instant liquidation of their debts (cloths and beads), advanced in former times of pinching dearth, or else to stand the consequences of refusal.

"As all the residents had at different times contracted debts to different members of the body present, there was no appeal against the equity of this sudden demand, but no one had the means of payment. They knew fighting against firearms would be hopeless; so after a few stratagems, looking for a good opportunity to bolt, the whole village took to precipitate flight. Most of the villagers were captured like myself; but of my father, or any other relatives, I never more gained any intelligence. He was either shot in endeavouring to defend himself, or still more probably gave leg-bail, and so escaped. As soon as this foray was over, all the captives were grouped together, and tethered with chains or ropes, and marched off to Kilua, on the east coast (in latitude 9o S.) Arrived there, the whole party embarked in dhows, which, setting sail, soon arrived at Zanzibar. We were then driven to the slave-market, where I was bought by an Arab merchant, and taken off to India. I served with this master for several years, till by his death I obtained my liberation. My next destination was Zanzibar, where I took service in the late Imaum's army, and passed my days in half-starved inactivity, until the lucky day when, at Chongue, you saw and gave me service."

Shortly after we had encamped under the rendezvous tree, and begun our cooking, some villagers brought ivories of the elephant and hippopotamus for sale, but had to suffer the disappointment of meeting a stranger to merchandise, and straightway departed, fully convinced that all Wazungu (or wise, or white men) were mere fools for not making money, when they had so good an opportunity. Noon and evening passed without a sign of the black captain or the remaining men. We were in a wretched place for a halt, a sloping ploughed field; and, deceived by the captain's not keeping his promise, were unprepared for spending the night there. I pitched my tent, but the poor men had nothing to protect them. With the darkness a deluge of rain descended; and, owing to the awkwardness of our position, the surcharged earth poured off a regular stream of water over our beds, baggage, and everything alike. To keep the tent erect--a small gable-shaped affair, six feet high, and seven by six square, made of American sheeting, and so light that with poles and everything complete it barely weighs one man's load--I called up the men, and for hours held it so by strength of arm. Even the hippopotami, to judge by the frequency of their snorts and grunts, as they indulged in their devastating excursions amongst the crops, seemed angry at this unusual severity of the weather. Never from the 15th of November, when the rainy season commenced, had we experienced such a violent and heavy downpour.

4th.--Halt. The morning is no improvement on the night. The captain now arrives with most of the remaining crew, fears the troubled waters, and will not put out to sea. In consequence of this disappointment, a messenger is sent back to Kawele, to fetch some fresh provisions and firewood, as what little of this latter article can be gathered in its saturated state is useless, for it will not burn. During the afternoon the remainder of the crew keep dropping in, and at nightfall seventeen hands are mustered.

5th.--At 3 A.M. the sea subsides, and the boat is loaded.--To pack so many men together, with material, in so small a space as the canoe affords, seems a difficulty almost insurmountable. Still it is effected. I litter down amidships, with my bedding spread on reeds, in so short a compass that my legs keep slipping off and dangling in the bilge-water. The cook and bailsman sit on the first bar, facing me; and behind them, to the stern, one-half the sailors sit in couples; whilst on the first bar behind me are Bombay and one Beluch, and beyond them to the bow, also in couples, the remaining crew. The captain takes post in the bows, and all hands on both sides paddle in stroke together.

Fuel, cooking-apparatus, food, bag and baggage, are thrown promiscuously under the seats. But the sailors' blankets, in the shape of grass matting, are placed on the bars to render the sitting soft. Once all properly arranged, the seventeen paddles dash off with vigour, and, steering southwards, we soon cross the mouth of the Ruche. Next Ukaranga, the last village on this line down the eastern shore, lying snugly in a bay, with a low range of densely-wooded hills about three miles in its rear, is passed by dawn of day, and about sunrise the bay itself is lost to sight.

The tired crew now hug a bluff shore, crowned with dense jungle, until a nook familiar to the men is entered under plea of breakfasting. Here all hands land, fires are kindled, and the cooking-pots arranged. Some prepare their rods and nets for fishing, some go in search of fungi (a favourite food), and others collect fuel. Gaetano, ever doing wrong, dips his cooking-pot in the sea for water--a dangerous experiment, if the traditions of Tanganyika hold good, that the ravenous hosts of crocodiles seldom spare any one bold enough to excite their appetites with such dregs as usually drop from those utensils; moreover, they will follow and even board the boats, after a single taste.

The sailors here have as great an aversion to being followed by the crocodile as our seamen by a shark, and they now display their feelings by looks and mutterings, and strictly prohibiting the use of the cooking-pot on that service again. Breakfast ready, all hands eagerly fall to, and feast away in happy ignorance of any danger, when suddenly confusion enters the camp, and, with the alarming cry that foes are coming, all hurry-skurry for the boat, some with one thing, some with another. The greater part of the kit is left upon the ground. A breathless silence reigns for several minutes. Then one jumps off and secures his pot; another succeeds him, and then more, till courage is gained to make a search, and ascertain the cause of the alarm. Sneaking, crawling in the bush, some peering this way, others listening that, they stealthily move along, until at length a single man, with arrow poised, in self-defence I suppose, is pounced upon.

His story of why he came there, who and how many are his comrades, what he wants in such a desert place, and why he carries arms, though spoken with a cunning plausibility, has no effect upon the knowing sailors. They proclaim him and his party, some eight or ten men, who are clamorously squabbling in the jungle at no great distance, to be a rough and lawless set of marauders, fearing to come out and show themselves on being challenged, and further insist that none ever ventured in such wilds who had not got in view some desperate enterprise. In short, it was proverbially men of their sort who were the general plunderers of honest navigators. They therefore seize his weapons, cut and break his bow and arrows, and let him go; though some of the crew advocate his life being taken, and others, that the whole party should be chased down and slaughtered. The sailors then return to the canoe, each vaunting his part in this adventurous exploit, and bandying congratulations in the highest spirits. They are one and all as proud of this success, and each as boastful of his prowess, as though a mighty battle had been fought and won.

On starting again we pass alongside another bluff, backed by small well-wooded hills, an extension of the aforesaid east horn of the Moon, and cross a little bay, when the lazy crew, tired by two hours' work, bear in with the land, and disembark, as they say, to make some ropes, or find some creepers long and strong enough for mooring this *mighty* canoe. It is now eleven o'clock; there is more rest than work, a purely negro way of getting through the day; three hours went in idleness before, and now five more are wasted. Again we start, and after crossing a similar small bay, continue along a low shelving shore, densely wooded to the water's edge, until the Malagarazi river's mouth is gained. This river is the largest on the eastern shore of the lake, and was previously crossed by the caravan on its way from Kaze, in small bark canoes, much rougher, but constructed something similarly to those of the Americans. Each of these canoes contains one man and his load, besides the owner, who lives near the ferry, and poles the vessel across. Still to the eastward we have the same tree-clad hilly view, beautiful in itself, but tiresome in its constant sameness. After a stretch, and half an hour's pipes and breathing, we start afresh, and cross the bay into which the river debouches.

Here tall aquatic reeds diversify the surface, and are well tenanted by the crocodile and hippopotami, the latter of which keep staring, grunting, and snorting as though much vexed at our intrusion on their former peace and privacy. We now hug the shore, and continue on in the dark of night till Mgiti Khambi,[44] a beautiful little harbour bending back away amongst the hills, and out of sight of the lake, is reached at 11 P.M. Could but a little civilised art, as whitewashed houses, well-trained gardens, and the like, vary these evergreen hills and trees, and diversify the unceasing monotony of hill and dale, and dale and hill--of green trees, green grass--green grass, green trees, so wearisome in their luxuriance,--what a paradise of beauty would this place present! The deep blue waters of the lake, in contrast with the vegetation and large brown rocks, form everywhere an object of intense attraction; but the appetite soon wearies of such profusion, without the contrast of more sober tints, or the variety incidental to a populous and inhabited country. There are said to be some few scattered villages concealed in these dense jungles extending away in the background, but how the shores should be so desolate strikes one with much surprise. The naturally excessive growth of all vegetable life is sufficient proof of the soil's capabilities. Unless in former times this beautiful country has been harassed by neighbouring tribes, and despoiled of its men and cattle to satisfy the spoilers and be sold to distant markets, its present state appears quite incomprehensible. In hazarding this conjecture, it might be thought that I am taking an extreme view of the case; but when we see everywhere in Africa what one slave-hunt or cattle-lifting party can effect, it is not unreasonable to imagine that this was most probably the cause of such utter desolation here. These war-parties lay waste the tracks they visit for endless time. Indeed, until slavery is suppressed in Africa, we may expect to find such places in a similarly melancholy state.

Immediately on arriving here I pitch my tent, and cook a meal; whilst the sailors, as is usual on arrival at their camping-grounds, divide into parties,--some to catch fish, others to look for fungi, whilst many cook the food, and the rest construct little huts by planting boughs in a circle in the ground and fastening the tops together, leaving the hut in the shape of a haycock, to which they further assimilate it by throwing grass above; and in rainy weather it is further covered by their mats, to secure them against getting wet. As only one or two men occupy a hut, to accommodate so large a party many of them have to be constructed. It is amusing to see how some men, proud of their superior powers of inventiveness, and possessing the knack of making pleasant what would otherwise be uncomfortable, plume themselves before their brethren, and turn them to derision: and it appears the more ridiculous, as they all are as stark naked as an unclothed animal, and have really nothing to boast of after all.

6th.--The following morning sees us under way, and clear of the harbour by sunrise; but the gathering of clouds in the south soon cautions the weather-wise sailors to desist from their advance. Timely is the warning; for, as we rest on our oars, the glimmer of lightning illuminates the distant hills; whilst low heavy rolling clouds of pitchy darkness, preceded by a heavy gale and a foaming sea, outspread over the whole southern waters, rapidly advance. It is an ocean-tempest in miniature, which sends us right about to our former berth. Some of our men now employ themselves in fishing for small fry with a slender rod, a piece of string, and an iron hook, with a bait of meat or fish attached; whilst others use small handnets, which they place behind some reeds or other cover, to secure the retreating fish as he makes off on being poked out of his refuge on the opposite side by a wand held for that purpose in the sportsman's other hand. But the majority are occupied in gathering sticks and cooking breakfast till 1 P.M., when the sea abates, and the journey is resumed. During this portion of the journey, a slight change of scenery takes place. The chain of hills running parallel with the shore of the lake is broken, and in its stead we see small detached and short irregular lines of hills, separated by extended plains of forest, thickly clad in verdure, like all the rest of the country. After two hours' paddling, we stand opposite the Luguvu river, and rest awhile to smoke; then start again, and in an hour cross the mouth of the little river Hebue. Unfortunately these streams add nothing to the beauty of the scenery; and were it not for the gaps in the hills suggesting the probable course of rivers, they might be passed without notice, for the mouths are always concealed by bulrushes, or other tall aquatic reeds; and inland they are just as closely hidden by forest vegetation. In half an hour more we enter a small nook called Luguvu Khambi, very deep, and full of crocodiles and hippopotami. On landing, we fire the usual alarm-guns--a point to which our captain is ever strictly attentive--cook our dinners, and turn in for the night. Here I picked up four varieties of shells--two univalves and two bivalves--all very interesting from being quite unknown in the conchological world. There were numbers of them lying on the pebbly beach.

7th.--We started at dawn as usual; but again at sunrise, the wind increasing, we put in for the shore, for these little cranky boats can stand no sea whatever. Here a herd of wild buffaloes, horned like the Cape ones, were seen by the men, and caused some diversion: for, though too blind myself to see the brutes at the distance that the others did, I loaded and gave them chase. Whilst tracking along, I saw fresh prints of elephants, which, judging from their trail, had evidently just been down to drink at the lake; and sprang some antelopes, but could not get a shot. The sea going down by noon, we proceeded, and hugged a bluff shore, till we arrived at Insigazi, a desert place, a little short of Kabogo, the usual crossing-point. Although the day was now far advanced, the weather was so promising, whilst our stores were running short, that impatience suggested a venture for the opposite shore to Kivira, an island near it, and which, with the Uguhha heights in the background, is from this distinctly visible. This line is selected for canoes to cross at, from containing the least expanse of water between the two shores, between Ujiji and the south end. The Kabogo Island, which stands so conspicuously in the missionaries' map that hung on the Royal Geographical Society's walls in 1856, is evidently intended for this Kabogo or starting-point, near which we now are, and is so far rightly placed upon their map as representing the half-way station from Ujiji to Kasenge, two places on opposite sides of the lake, whither the Arab merchants go in search of ivory. For Kabogo, as will be seen by my map, lies just midway on the line always taken by boats travelling between those two ports--the rest of the lake being too broad for these adventurous spirits. In short, they coast south from Ujiji to Kabogo, which constitutes the first half of the journey, and then cross over.

On the passage I carefully inquired the names of several points and places, to take their bearings, and to learn the geography of the lake, but all to no purpose.

The superstitious captain, and even more superstitious crew, refused to answer any questions, and earnestly forbade my talking. The idea was founded upon the fear of vitiating their *uganga* or "church," by answering a stranger any questions whilst at sea; but they dread more especially to talk about the places of departure or arrival, lest ill luck should overtake them, and deprive them of the chance of ever reaching shore. They blamed me for throwing the remnants of my cold dinner overboard, and pointed to the bottom of the boat as the proper receptacle for refuse. Night set in with great serenity, and at 2 A.M. the following morning (8th March) when arriving amongst some islands, close on the western shore of the lake--the principal of which are Kivira, Kabizia, and Kasenge, the only ones inhabited--a watch-boat belonging to Sultan Kasanga, the reigning chief of this group, challenged us, and asked our mission. Great fraternising, story-telling, and a little pipe ensued, for every one loves tobacco; then both departed in peace and friendship: they to their former abode, a cove in a small uninhabited island which lies due south of Kivira; whilst we proceeded to a long narrow harbour in Kivira itself, the largest of all these islands. Fourteen hours were occupied in crossing the lake, of which two were spent in brawling and smoking. At 9 A.M. the islanders, receiving intelligence of our arrival, came down the hill of which this island is formed, in great numbers, and held a market; but as we were unprovided with what they wanted, little business could be done. The chief desideratum was flesh of fish or beast, next salt, then tobacco--in fact, anything but what I had brought as market money, cloth and glass beads. This day passed in rest and idleness, recruiting from our late exertions.

At night a violent storm of rain and wind beat on my tent with such fury that its nether parts were torn away from the pegs, and the tent itself was only kept upright by sheer force. On the wind's abating, a candle was lighted to rearrange the kit, and in a moment, as though by magic, the whole interior became covered with a host of small black beetles, evidently attracted by the glimmer of the candle. They were so annoyingly determined in their choice of place for peregrinating, that it seemed hopeless my trying to brush them off the clothes or bedding, for as one was knocked aside another came on, and then another; till at last, worn out, I extinguished the candle, and with difficulty--trying to overcome the tickling annoyance occasioned by these intruders crawling up my sleeves and into my hair, or down my back and legs--fell off to sleep. Repose that night was not destined to be my lot. One of these horrid little insects awoke me in his struggles to penetrate my ear, but just too late: for in my endeavour to extract him, I aided his immersion. He went his course, struggling up the narrow channel, until he got arrested by want of passage-room. This impediment evidently enraged him, for he began with exceeding vigour, like a rabbit at a hole, to dig violently away at my tympanum. The queer sensation this amusing *measure* excited in me is past description. I felt inclined to act as our donkeys once did, when beset by a swarm of bees, who buzzed about their ears and stung their heads and eyes until they were so irritated and confused that they galloped about in the most distracted order, trying to knock them off by treading on their heads, or by rushing under bushes, into houses, or through any jungle they could find. Indeed, I do not know which was worst off. The bees killed some of them, and this beetle nearly did for me. What to do I knew not. Neither tobacco, oil, nor salt could be found: I therefore tried melted butter; that failing, I applied the point of a penknife to his back, which did more harm than good; for though a few thrusts quieted him, the point also wounded my ear so badly, that inflammation set in, severe suppuration took place, and all the facial glands extending from that point down to the point of the shoulder became contorted and drawn aside, and a string of boils decorated the whole length of that region. It was the most painful thing I ever remember to have endured; but, more annoying still, I could not masticate for several days, and had to feed on broth alone. For many months the tumour made me almost deaf, and ate a hole between the ear and the nose, so that when I blew it, my ear whistled so audibly that those who heard it laughed. Six or seven months after this accident happened, bits of the beetle--a leg, a wing, or parts of its body--came away in the wax.

It was not altogether an unmixed evil, for the excitement occasioned by the beetle's operations acted towards my blindness as a counter-irritant, by drawing the inflammation away from my eyes. Indeed, it operated far better than any other artificial appliance. To cure the blindness I once tried rubbing in some blistering liquor behind my ear, but this unfortunately had been injured by the journey, and had lost its stimulating properties. Finding it of no avail, I then caused my servant to rub the part with his finger until it was excoriated, which, though it proved insufficiently strong to cure me, was, according to Dr Bowman, whom I have since consulted, as good a substitute for a blister as could have been applied.

9th.--The weather still remaining too rough for sailing, I strolled over the island, and from its summit on the eastern side I found a good view of the lake, and took bearings of Ujiji, Insigazi, and a distant point southwards on the eastern shore of the lake, called Ukungue. Kivira Island is a massive hill, about five miles long by two or three broad, and is irregularly shaped. In places there are high flats, formed in terraces, but generally the steeps are abrupt and thickly wooded. The mainland immediately west is a promontory, at the southern extremity of the Uguhha Mountains, on the western coast of the Tanganyika; and the island is detached from it by so narrow a strip of water that, unless you obtained a profile view, it might easily be mistaken for a headland. The population is considerable, and they live in mushroom huts, situated on the high flats and easier slopes, where they cultivate the manioc, sweet potato, maize, millet, various kinds of pulse, and all the common vegetables in general use about the country. Poultry abounds in the villages.

The dress of the people is simple, consisting of small black monkey skins, cat-skins, and the furs of any vermin they can get. These are tucked under a waist-strap, and, according to the number they possess, go completely or only half-way round the body, the animals' heads hanging in front, and the tails always depending gracefully below. These monkeys are easily captured when the maize is ripe, by a number of people stealthily staking small square nets in contiguous line all round the fields which these animals may be occupied in robbing, and then with screams and yells, flinging sticks and stones, the hunters rush upon the affrighted thieves, till, in their hurry and confusion to escape, they become irretrievably entangled in the meshes. But few of these islanders carry spear or bow, though I imagine all possess them. They were most unpleasantly inquisitive, and by their stares, jabber, and pointings, incessantly wanting me to show them everything that I possessed, with explanations about their various uses, quite tired out my patience. If I tried to get away, they plaguingly followed after, so at last I dodged them by getting into the boat. To sit in the tent was the worst place of all; they would pull up the sides, and peer under like so many monkeys; and if I turned my head aside to avoid their gaze, they would jabber in the most noisy and disagreeable manner in order to arouse me.

10th.--We quit Kivira early, and paddling S. 25o W., make the famous fish-market in the little island Kabizia, just in time to breakfast on a freshly-caught fish, the celebrated *Singa*,--a large, ugly, black-backed monster, with white belly, small fins, and long barbs, but no scales. In appearance a sluggish ground-fish, it is always immoderately and grossly fat, and at this season is full of roe; its flesh is highly esteemed by the natives. This island is very small, with a gradual rising slope from the N.W. extremity; and at the S.E. end assumes the form of a bull's hump. There is but one village of twenty odd mushroom-shaped huts, chiefly occupied by fishermen, who live on their spoils, and by selling all that they cannot consume to the neighbouring islanders and the villagers on the mainland. Added to this, they grow maize and other vegetables, and keep a good stock of fowls. I tried every mode of inducement to entice the crew away to complete the journey, for the place of my destination, Kasenge, was in sight; but in vain. They had tasted this to them delicious fish, and were determined to dress and lay by a good store of it to carry with them. About noon Khamis, a merchant from Kasenge, bound for Ujiji, arrived, and kindly gave me a long needle to stir up the beetle in my ear; but the insect had gone in so far, and the swelling and suppuration of the wounds had so imbedded him, that no instrument could have done any good. Khamis, like myself, was very anxious to complete his journey, and tried every conceivable means to entice his crew away, but he failed as signally as I did. On the mainland opposite to this, we see the western horn of these concavely-disposed mountains, which encircle the north of the lake, and from hence the horn stretches away in increasing height as it extends northwards. Its sea-ward slopes are well wooded from near the summit down to the water's edge; but on the top, as though strong currents of air prevailed, and prevented vegetation from attaining any height, grass only is visible. Westward, behind the island of Kasenge, and away to the southward, the country is of a rolling formation, and devoid of any objects of interest.

11th.--The morning wind was too high for crossing from Kabizia to Kasenge, but at noon we embarked, and after paddling for ninety minutes S. 80o W., we arrived at the latter island, my destination. Sheikh Hamed bin Sulayyim, with many attendants and a host of natives, was standing ready to receive me. He gave us a hearty welcome, took my hand, and led me to his abode, placing everything at my disposal, and arranging a second house for my future residence. These Arab merchants are everywhere the same. Their warm and generous hospitality to a stranger equals anything I have ever seen elsewhere, not forgetting India, where a cordial welcome greets any incidental traveller. Hamed's abode, like all the semi-civilised ones found in this country, and constructed by the Wasuahili (or coast people), is made with good substantial walls of mud, and roofed with rafters and brushwood, cemented together with a compound of common earth, straw, and water. The rooms are conveniently partitioned off for domestic convenience, with an ante-room for general business, and sundry other enclosures for separating his wives and other belongings. On the exterior of the house is a *palaver* platform, covered with an ample verandah, under which he sits, surrounded by a group of swarthy blacks, gossiping for hours together, or transacting his worldly business, in purchasing ivory, slaves, or any commodities worthy of his notice. The dhow I had come for, he said, was lying at Ukaranga, on the eastern shore, but was expected in a day or two, and would then be at my service. Indeed he had sent a letter by Khamis, whom I met at Kabizia, offering it to Captain Burton, as soon as he had been made acquainted (by native report, I imagine) with our desire of obtaining her. He thought, however, that there might be some difficulty in forming a crew capable of managing her, as this craft was too large for paddles, and no natives understood the art of rowing, and, moreover, like all Easterns, they are not disposed to learn anything that their fathers did not know before them. His own men were necessary to him, for in a few days he intended marching to Uruwa, a territory belonging to Sultan Kiyombo, about a hundred miles south-west of this island. During that trip, every one of the dhow sailors (who are slaves, and the Arabs' gun-bearers) would be in requisition. But he thought, if I had patience to wait, he might be able to prevail on a few of the dhow's present crew, men in his temporary employ, to take service with me. My host gave me a full description of the lake. He said he had visited both ends of it, and found the southern portion both longer and broader than the northern. "There are no islands in the middle of the sea, but near the shores there are several in various places, situated much in the same way as those we are amongst; they are mere projections, divided from the mainland by shoals or narrow channels. A large river, called Marungu, supplies the lake at its southern extremity; and on a visit to the northern end, I saw one which was very much larger than either of these, and which I am certain flowed out of the lake; for although I did not venture on it, in consequence of its banks being occupied by desperately savage negroes, inimical to all strangers, I went so near its outlet that I could see and feel the outward drift of the water." He then described an adventure he once had when going to the north, with a boisterous barbarous tribe called Warundi. On approaching their hostile shore, he noticed, as he thought, a great commotion amongst the fishing-boats, and soon perceived that the men were concocting a plan of attack upon himself, for they concentrated forces, and came at his dhow in a body of about thirty canoes. Conceiving that their intentions were hostile, he avoided any conflict by putting out to sea, fearing lest an affray would be prejudicial to future mercantile transactions, as stains of blood are not soon effaced from their black memories. He further said he felt no alarm for his safety, as he had thirty slaves with guns on board. My retrospective opinion of this story--for everybody tells stories in this country--is, that Hamed's Marungu river more likely runs out of the Tanganyika and into the Nyassa, forming a chain of lakes, drained by the Shire river into the Zambeze; but I did not, unfortunately, argue it out with him. I feel convinced also that he was romancing when talking of the northern river's flow, not only because the northern end of the lake is encircled by high hills--the concave of the Mountains of the Moon--but because the lake's altitude is so much less than that of the adjacent plateau. Indeed, the waters of the lake are so low they would convey the impression that the trough they lie in has been formed by volcanic agency, were it not that Dr Livingstone has determined the level of the Nyassa to be very nearly the same as this lake; and the Babisa, who live on the west of the Nyassa, in crossing the country between the two lakes to Luwemba,[45] cross the Marungu river, and yet cross no mountain-range there. With reference to the time which it would take us to traverse the entire lake, he said he thought we should take forty-six days in going up and down the lake, starting from Ujiji. Going to the north would take eight days, and going to the south fifteen. As Hamed had said nothing about the hire of the dhow, though he had offered it so willingly, I thought it probable that shame of mentioning it in public had deterred him from alluding to the subject--so begged a private conference. He then came to my house with Bombay and a slave, a confidant of his own, who could also speak Hindustani, and was told, through my medium Bombay, exactly what things I had brought with me, and requested to speak his mind freely, as I had called him especially for business, and we were now alone. He still remained mute about the price; but again saying I could have his dhow whenever I chose, he asked permission to retire, and departed. Puzzled at this procedure, I sent Bombay to observe him, and find out if he had any secret motives for shirking so direct an appeal, and empowered him to offer money in case my cloth and powder did not afford sufficient inducement. Bombay soon returned as much puzzled as myself, unable to extract any but the old answer--that I was welcome to the dhow, and that he would try and procure men for me. As a hint had reached me that Hamed cast covetous eyes on my powder-magazine, I tried enticing him to take some in part payment for her; but he replied that he did not require anything in payment, but would gladly accept a little powder if I had any to spare. To this I readily assented, as he had been so constant and liberal in his attentions to me ever since I landed on the island and became his guest, that I felt it was the least I could do in return for his generosity. Indeed, he was constantly observing and inquiring what I wanted, and supplied everything in his power that I found difficult to obtain. Every day he brought presents of flesh, fowl, ducks (the Muscovite, brought from the coast), eggs, plantains, and ghee (clarified butter).

The island of Kasenge is about one mile long, a narrow high ridge of land lying nearly due north and south, and is devoid of trees, and only a small portion of it is under cultivation. The lake washes its northwestern end; the remainder is encircled by a girdle of water about eighty yards broad. It appears, from being so imbedded in the land, to be a part of the coast, to anybody approaching it from the open lake. The population is very considerable, more so than that of the other ports. They are extremely filthy in their habits, and are excessively inquisitive, as far at least as gratifying their idle curiosity is concerned. From having no industrial occupations, they will stand for hours and hours together, watching any strange object, and are, in consequence, an infinite pest to any stranger coming near them. In appearance they are not much unlike the Kaffir, resembling that tribe both in size, height, and general bearing, having enlarged lips, flattish noses, and frizzly woolly hair. They are very easily amused, and generally wear smiling faces. The women are better dressed than the men, having a cloth round the body, fastened under the arms, and reaching below the knees, and generally beads, brass necklaces, or other ornaments; while the latter only wear a single goat-skin slung game-bag fashion over the shoulder, or, when they possess it, a short cloth tied, kilt fashion, round the waist. They lie about their huts like swine, with little more animation on a warm day than the pig has when basking in a summer's sun. The mothers of these savage people have infinitely less affection than many savage beasts of my acquaintance. I have seen a mother bear, galled by frequent shots, obstinately meet her death, by repeatedly returning under fire whilst endeavouring to rescue her young from the grasp of intruding men. But here, for a simple loin-cloth or two, human mothers eagerly exchanged their little offspring, delivering them into perpetual bondage to my Beluch soldiers.

Talking about slaves makes me always feel for this unfortunate land, and reflect how foolish are all those outer nations who allow the slave trade to go on. One quarter of the globe--and that, too, one which might, if relieved of this scourge, be of the greatest commercial advantage to us, both as a consuming and exporting country--is entirely ruined. The horrors of the "middle passage" are familiar to us by report, but they are nothing as compared with what happens in the interior of the country when the capturing goes on. There whole villages are destroyed in the most remorseless manner by the slave-hunters to obtain their victims, for no one will yield so long as he can fight for his freedom. The slave-hunters are not merely confined to the coast men, for the interior chiefs are as fond of gain as they are, and this sets one against the other until the whole country is in a flame. It is true that the slaves whom the Arab merchants, or other men, have in their possession, never forsake their master, as if they disliked their state in bondage; but then, when we consider their position, what pleasure or advantage would they derive by doing so? During the slave-hunts, when they are caught, their country is devastated, their friends and relatives are either killed or are scattered to the winds, and nothing but a wreck is left behind them. Again, they enter upon a life which is new to them, and is very fascinating to their tastes; and as long as they do remain with such kind masters as the Arabs are, there is no necessity for our commiserating them. They become elevated in their new state of existence, and are better off than in their precarious homes, ever in terror of being attacked. On the other hand, foreign slavery is a different thing altogether. Instead of living, as they in most part do, willingly with the families of the Arabs, men of a superior order, and doing mild and congenial services, they get transported against their will and inclinations to a foreign land, where, to live at all, they must labour like beasts; and yet this is only half the mischief. When a market for slavery is opened, when the draining poultice is applied to Africa's exterior, then the interior is drained of all its working men. To supply the markets with those slaves becomes so lucrative a means of gain that merchants would stick at no expedient in endeavouring to secure them. The country, so full as we have seen it of all the useful necessaries of life, able to supply our markets and relieve our people by cheapening all commodities, is sacrificed for the very minor consideration of improving Cuba, Arabia, Persia, and a few small islands in the Indian Ocean. On the contrary, slavery has only to be suppressed entirely, and the country would soon yield one hundredfold more than it ever has done before. The merchants themselves at Zanzibar are aware of this, for every Hindi on the coast with whom I ever spoke on the subject of slavery, seemed confident that the true prosperity of Africa would only commence with the cessation of slavery. And they all say it would be far better for them if slavery were put down altogether than allowed to remain as it is, subject to limited restriction; for by this limitation many inconveniences arise. Those who were permitted to retain slaves, have a great and distressing advantage over those who have not. The restriction alluded to by our Indian subjects at Zanzibar is the result of a most unfortunate treaty our Government made with the Sultan of that country, wherein slavery was permitted to be carried on within certain limits of latitude and longitude. The subjects of the Sultan by this means trade at a considerable pecuniary advantage over our subjects, who, were they English instead of being Indians, would never rest satisfied until they were placed on an equal footing with the Arabs and Wasuahili. They argue amongst themselves, and very properly, that in consequence of these slave-hunts the country is kept in such a state of commotion that no one thinks it worth his while to make accumulations of property, and, consequently, the negroes now only live for the day, and keep no granaries, never thinking of exerting themselves to better their condition. Without doubt it is mainly owing to this unfortunate influence of slavery on African society that we have been kept so long ignorant of the resources of Equatorial Africa--a vast field of surprising fertility, which would be of so much value to Zanzibar and neighbouring India, were it only properly developed. But I have been digressing, and must again return to Kasenge.

The village is very large and straggling, and consists of a collection of haycock-looking huts, framed with wood or boughs, and covered over with grass. Kasanga's palace is the grandest one amongst them. This monarch is a very amiable despot, and is liked in consequence. He presented me with a goat and some grain, in return for which I gave a **hongo** (or tribute-fee) of three dhotis, two kitindis, and two fundas, equal to twenty necklaces of large blue beads. The food of these people consists chiefly of fish and fowls, both of which are very abundant. All other articles of consumption, except a very little grown on the spot, are imported from the mainland, and are, in consequence, dear. The surrounding country, however, is very highly cultivated--so much so, that it exports for the Ujiji and other distant markets. The Africans have no religion, unless Fetishism may be considered such. They use charms to keep off the evil eye, and believe in fortune-tellers. Their church is called Uganga, and the parson Mganga, the plural of which, priests, changes to Waganga. The prefixes, *U*, *M*, and *Wa*, are used uniformly throughout this land from Zanzibar, to denote respectively, U, country or place, M, an individual, and Wa for plurality, as in tribe or people: thus, Uganga, Mganga, Waganga; or, Unyamuezi, Myamuezi, Wanyamuezi. The composition of this latter name is worthy of remark, as it differs from the former, and therefore must tend to perplex. For instance, Uganga is composed of *U*, place, house, church, or country, and **ganga**, magic; whilst Unyamuezi is a triple word, divided into *U* country--**ya**, of--and **muezi**, moon. Then, the language being euphonious, an accidental n is thrown in between the *u* and *y* to tone down the pronunciation.

13th.--The dhow came in this evening, bringing cows and goats, oil, ghee, and other articles of consumption not found immediately in this neighbourhood. She looked very graceful in contrast to the wretched little canoes, and came moving slowly up the smooth waters of the channel decked in her white sails, like a swan upon "a garden reach." The next day Hamed declared himself endeavouring to secure some men, but none appeared. The day following he told me that the dhow was out of repair, and must be mended. And the succeeding day he coupled shifts and excuses with promises and hopes, so likely to be further deferred, that my patience was fairly upset; and on the 17th, as nothing was settled, we had a little tiff. I accused him of detaining me in the hopes of getting powder, for as yet his armourer had not succeeded in opening my chest, from which I knew he wanted some; at any rate, I could see no other cause for his desiring my further stay there, when even Bombay had notified his displeasure at these long-continued procrastinations. Hamed, however, very quietly denied the imputation, declaring that he desired nothing but what I might frankly give, and continued his former kindnesses as though nothing had happened. I then begged his counsel as to the best mode of proceeding, upon which he advised my returning to Ujiji, where an Arab merchant called Said bin Majid, with many men of the sort I required, was reported to be arriving. In the meanwhile, during his absence at Uruwa, he would authorise his agent to make the dhow over to me whenever I should come or send for it. It is needless to say how easily, had my hands now been free to act, I might have availed myself of this tempting opportunity of accompanying Hamed on his journey to Uruwa, and have thus nearly connected this line from Zanzibar with the Portuguese and Dr Livingstone's routes to Loando on the western coast. It would also have afforded a more perfect knowledge of the copper mines at Katata, a quantity of which comes to Uruwa. Hamed describes the roads as easy to travel over, for the track lay across an undulating country, intersected by many small insignificant streams, running from north to south, which only contribute to fertilise the land, and present no obstacles whatever. The line is cheap, and affords provisions in abundance. It may appear odd that men should go so far into the interior of Africa to procure ivory, when undoubtedly much is to be found at places not half so distant from Zanzibar; but the reason of it is simple. The nearer countries have become so overstocked with beads and cloth, that ivory there has risen to so great a price, it does not pay its transport. Hence every succeeding year finds the Arabs penetrating farther inland. Now, it will be seen that the Zanzibar Arabs have reached the uttermost limits of their tether; for Uruwa is half-way across the continent, and in a few years they must unite their labours with the people who come from Loando on the opposite coast.

As to obtain the dhow would, in our hampered state, have been of much importance--for our cloth and supplies were all fast ebbing away--I did not yet give in applying for it, and next day tried another device to tempt this wily Arab, by offering 500 dollars, or L100, if he would defer his journey for a short time, and accompany us round the lake. This was a large, and evidently an unexpected offer, and tried his cupidity sorely; it produced a nervous fidgetiness, and he begged leave to retire and con the matter over. Next day, however, to my great distress, he said he was sorry that he must decline, for his business would not stand deferment, but declared himself willing to sail with us on his return from Uruwa, three months hence, if we could only stay till then.[46]

Feeling now satisfied that nothing would prevail upon Hamed to let us have the dhow, I wished to quit the island and return to Ujiji, but found my crew had taken French leave, and gone foraging on the mainland, where, all grain being so much cheaper than at Ujiji, they wanted to procure a supply. I therefore employed the day in strolling all over the island, and took bearings of some of the principal features of the lake: of Thembue, a distant promontory on the western shore, south of this, which is occupied by a powerful sultan, and contains a large population of very boisterous savages; of Ukungue, on the east shore; and of the islands of Kivira and Kabizia. I could also see two other small islands lying amidst these larger ones, too small for habitation. Though my canoe arrived on the 20th, bad weather prevented our leaving till the 22d, morning, completing twelve days at Kasenge. I now took leave of my generous host; and, bidding adieu to Kasenge, soon arrived and spent the day at Kabizia, mourning in my mind that I had induced Captain Burton to discharge Ramji's slaves, for Bombay said they were all sailors, and would have handled the dhow in first-rate style.

23d.--We crossed over to Kivira, and pitched the tent in our former harbour. Next day we halted from stress of weather; and the following day also remaining boisterous, we could not put to sea; but, to obtain a better view of the lake, and watch the weather for choosing a favourable time to cross, we changed Khambi for a place farther up the island.

24th.--We moved out two miles in the morning, but returned again from fear of the weather, as the sailors could discern a small but very alarming-looking cloud many miles distant, hanging on the top of one of the hills, and there was a gentle breeze. In the evening, as the portentous elements still frowned upon us, the wise crew surmised that the *uganga* (church) was angry at my endeavouring to carry across the waters the goat which the sultan had given me, and which, they said, ought never to have left the spot it was presented in alive; and declared their intention of applying to the *mganga* (priest) to ascertain his opinion before venturing out again. As the goat had just given a kid, and produced a good supply of milk, I was anxious to bring her to Ujiji for my sick companion, and told the sailors so; yet still they persisted, and said they would run away rather than venture on the water with the goat again. Fearing detention, and guessing their motive was only to obtain a share in the eating her, I killed both kid and mother at once, and divided them amongst my party, taking care that none of the crew received any of the flesh. At night we sallied forth again, but soon returned from the same cause that hindered us in the morning. And I did not spare the men's feelings who had caused the death of my goat in the morning, now that their superstitious fears concerning it, if they ever possessed any, were proven to be without foundation.

27th.--We took our final departure from Kivira in the morning, and crossed the broad lake again in fourteen hours, two of them, as before, being spent in pipes and rest. I have now measured the lake's centre pretty satisfactorily by triangulation, by compass in connection with astronomical observation, and twice by dead reckoning. It is twenty-six miles broad at the place of crossing, which is its narrowest central part. But, alas! that I should have omitted to bring a sounding-line with me, and not have ascertained that highly interesting feature--its depth. There is very little doubt in my mind that its bed is very deep, owing to the trough-like formation of it, and also because I have seen my crew haul up fishing-baskets, sunk in the sea near to the shore, from very considerable depths, by long ropes with trimmers attached. For the benefit of science, and as a hint to future travellers, I may mention that, had I brought a lead, I might, as if by accident, have dropped it in the sea when they were resting--have tapped the bottom, and ascertained its depth--whilst the superstitious crew would have only wondered in vain as to what I was about.

28th.--We started up coast early, and at 10 A.M. put in amongst some reeds opposite the Luguvu river, as the wind, rain, and waves had very nearly swamped the boat, and drenched us all from head to foot. I pitched the tent in the canoe, to protect me from the storm, but it only served to keep the wind from blowing on my wet clothes and chilling me, for wave after wave washed over the gunwale, and kept me and all my kit constantly drenched through. Three lingering miserable hours were passed in this fashion; for there was no place to land in, and we could not venture forward. The sea abated in the afternoon, and we gained Mgiti Khambi. After a day's halt, the weather being stormy, and everything being wet and comfortless, we hailed with delight the succeeding sunny day, and, making good our time, reached the old tree on the right bank of the mouth of the Ruche by 9 P.M.

31st.--We arrived at Ujiji by breakfast-time, when I disclosed to Captain Burton, then happily a little restored, the mortifying intelligence of my failing to procure the dhow. This appeared doubly distressing to him, for he had been led to expect it by Khamis, whom I passed at Kabizia, and who had delivered Hamed's letter, stating that the dhow was at his service. Hamed's manoeuvring with the dhow bears much the appearance of one anxious to obtain the credit of generosity without incurring the attendant inconvenience of its reality. Otherwise I cannot divine what good his procrastinations and the means he took for keeping me near him so long could have been to him; for he made no overtures to me whatever. Bombay now thought, when it was too late, that if I had offered to give him 500 dollars' worth of cloth, landed at his house, he could not have resisted the offer. I give this notice for the advantage of any future explorers on the lake. I could not form a true estimate of the lake's average breadth, in consequence of the numberless bays and promontories that diversify the regularity of its coast-line; but I should say that from thirty to forty miles is probably near the truth.

We had now no other resource left us but to proceed with the investigation of the lake in common canoes; for we could not wait any longer, as our supplies were fast on the wane. I was sorry for it, as my companion was still suffering so severely, that anybody seeing him attempt to go would have despaired of his ever returning. Yet he could not endure being left behind. Travelling in canoes, as I could now testify from my late experiences, is, without joke, a very trying business to a sick man, even in the best weather; and here we were still in the height of the monsoon. Negotiations for the means of carrying out our object (of proceeding to the north of the lake, surveying it, and ascertaining whether Hamed's story about a large river running out of it was based upon a true foundation) were then commenced, and Kannina was applied to. He likewise, it appeared, had a plan in view of carrying on some ivory transactions with the Sultan of Uvira, governing a district at the northern end and western shore of the lake, and agreed to take us there, and also show us the river in question. It was settled that we should go in two canoes; Captain Burton, with Kannina, in a very large one, paddled by forty men at once, and I in another considerably smaller--our party to pay all expenses; and, in fact, to do Kannina's business in consideration of his protection. This we did do, and no more; for, after arriving at Uvira, nothing could induce him to take us to the river at the end of the lake, although the remaining distance could have been accomplished in about six hours' paddling. His reason, which he must have known before, was, that the savages resident there, the Warundi tribe, were inimical to his people, the

Wajiji. This was a sore disappointment, though not so great as it would have been had we not ascertained that Hamed's story was a mere fabrication. He had never been to the north end of the lake, nor had he had the fight he described with the natives; and, moreover, Bombay assured both Captain Burton and myself that Hamed really meant that the river ran into the lake. Had I thought of it, I should then have changed the course of the Marungu river on my map, and made it run out of the lake, but I did not. Next the sultan's son, who visited us immediately on our arrival at Uvira, told us that the river, which is named Rusizi, drained the high mountains encircling our immediate north, and discharged its waters into the lake. I should not have been satisfied with this counter-statement alone, had I not ascended some neighbouring heights, and observed the mountains increasing in size as they extended away to the northward, and effectually closing in this *low* lake, which is not quite half the altitude of the surface-level of the general interior plateau. Although wrong in most respects, Hamed was right about the distance the lake's northern end lay from Ujiji; for, properly divided, it takes eight days, the time he specified, exactly. On coming up the lake, we travelled the first half up the east coast, then crossed over to the end of a long island called Ubuari, made for the western shore, and coasted up it to Uvira. It would have amused any one very much to have seen our two canoes racing together up the lake. The naked savages were never tired of testing their respective strengths. They would paddle away like so many black devils--dashing up the water whenever they succeeded in coming near each other, and delighting in drenching us with the spray. The greatest pleasure to them, it appeared, was torturing others with impunity to themselves. Because the Wazungu had clothes, and they had none, they cared not how the water flew about; and the more they were asked to desist, the more obstinately they persevered. For fear of misapprehension, I must state that though these negroes go stark naked when cruising or working during a shower of rain, they all possess a mantle or goat-skin, which they sling over their shoulders, and strut about in when on shore and the weather is fine.

It is a curious sight, when encamped on a showery day, to see every man take off his skin, wrap it carefully up, and place it in his mzigo or load, and stand, whilst his garment is thus comfortably disposed of, cowering and trembling like a dog which has just emerged from a cold pond.

Now we have done with the Tanganyika Lake, I must say for it, that in no part of Africa hitherto visited by us had we seen such splendid vegetation as covers its basin, from the mountain-tops to its shores. To the northward, rain falls all the year round in frequent showers, but on the southern half rain only falls during those six months when the sun is in its southern declination. Hence the northern half must be richer than the southern; and the lake must owe its existence to the constant inflows from the north.

Chapter III.

Leave Tanganyika--Determine to Visit the Ukerewe Lake, **_alias_** Victoria N'yanza--Confusion about Rivers Running in and out--Idea that it is the Source of the Nile--Arrangements for the Journey--Difficulties--The March--Nature of the Country--Formalities at the Meeting of Caravans--A Pagazi Strike--A Sultana--Incidents--Pillars of Granite.

On returning to Ujiji after a rather protracted sojourn at Uvira, occasioned by Kannina's not completing his work so quickly as had been anticipated, we found our stock of beads and cloth, which had been left in charge of the Ras-cafila, Sheikh Said, and under the protection of the Beluches and our Wanyamuezi porters, reduced to so low an ebb that everybody felt anxious about our future movements. The Sheikh, however, I must add, on a prior occasion, very generously proposed, in case we felt disposed to carry on the survey of the lake, to return to the Arab depot at Kaze, and fetch some more **_African money_**, to meet the necessary expenses. I wished to finish off the navigation of the lake; but Captain Burton declared he would not, as he had had enough of canoe-travelling, and thought our being short of cloth, and out of leave, would be sufficient excuse for him. Though admiring so magnanimous a sacrifice on the part of this energetic Sheikh, it was voted, in consequence of my companion's failing health, as well as from the delay it would occasion, that we should all return at once to Kaze, where we expected to meet our reserve supplies. This once agreed upon, I then proposed that, after reaching Kaze, we should travel northwards to the lake described by the Arabs to be both broader and longer than the Tanganyika, and which they call Ukerewe, after the island where their caravans go for ivory--in short, the Victoria N'yanza--for I was all the while burning to see it. To this Captain Burton at first demurred. He said we had done enough, and he would do no more; but finally gave way when I said, If you are not well enough when we reach Kaze I will go by myself, and you can employ the time in taking notes from the travelled Arabs of all the countries round. This was agreed to at last by Captain Burton, as he said the journey hitherto had been so uninteresting, a month with Sheikh Snay would be very necessary to completing his book. Delighted at this announcement, I begged for leave to take Sheikh Said with me. Captain Burton, however, wanted to keep him, as he was a great friend of all the Arabs, and could procure him news better than any one else. I argued that the road was dangerous, and without him I thought I could not succeed, as there was no one else to argue with the native chiefs, and bring them to terms if they were headstrong. Captain Burton to this appeal finally gave way, but said I must ask the Sheikh myself, as he was not bound to go on any other line than the one we were now on. I did ask the Sheikh, some time after, at Usenye, and he said he would see about it when we reached Kaze. Just as we were preparing to leave Ujiji, by great good fortune some supplies were brought to us by an Arab called Mohinna, an old friend whom we formerly left at Kaze, and who had now followed us here to trade in ivory. Had this timely supply not reached us, it is difficult to conceive what would have been our fate, left as we should have been with a large amount of non-marketable property, and having numbers of people to feed, whilst my companion was unable to move without the assistance of eight men to carry him in a hammock, we being totally without the means of purchase in the territory of one of the most inhospitable of all the tribes with whom we have had connection.

This timely supply was one of the many strokes of good fortune which befell us upon this journey, and for which we have so much reason to be grateful. Help had always reached us at the time when least we expected it, but when we most required it. My health had been improving ever since I first reached the lake, and enjoyed those invigorating swims upon its surface, and revelled in the good living afforded by the market at Ujiji. The facilities of the place giving us such a choice of food, our powers in the culinary art were tried to their fullest extent. It would be difficult to tell what dishes we did not make there. Fish of many sorts done up in all the fashions of the day--meat and fowl in every form--vegetable soups, and dishes of numberless varieties--fruit-preserves, custards, custard-puddings, and jellies--

and last, but not least, buttered crumpets and cheese,--formed as fine a spread as was ever set before a king.

But sometimes we came to grief when our supply of milk was, on the most foolish pretexts, stopped by Kannina, who was the only cow-proprietor in the neighbourhood. At one time he took offence because we turned his importunate wives out of the house, in mistake for common beggars. On another occasion, when I showed him a cheese of our manufacture, and begged he would allow me to instruct his people in the art of making them, he took fright, declared that the cheese was something supernatural, and that it could never have been made by any ordinary artifice. Moreover, if his people were shown the way to do it one hundred times, they would never be able to comprehend it. He further showed his alarm by forbidding us any more milk, lest, by our tampering with it, we should bewitch his cows and make them all run dry. The cattle this milk was taken from are of a uniform red colour, like our Devonshire breed; but they attain a very great height and size, and have horns of the most stupendous dimensions.

A year's acclimatisation had by this time produced a wonderful effect on all the party; so that now, with our fresh supplies, most of us marched away from Ujiji in better condition than we had enjoyed since leaving the coast. The weather was very fine, the rainy season having ceased on the 15th May; we marched rapidly across the eastern horn of the mountains back to the ferry on the Malagarazi, but by a more northernly route than the one by which we came.

We reached this river in early June, and found its appearance very different from what it was on our former visit, at the beginning of the monsoon. Then its waters were contained within its banks, of no considerable width; but now, although the rains had ceased here long ago, the river had not only overflowed its banks, but had submerged nearly all the valley in which it lies to the extent at least of a mile or more. The rains about 5o south latitude had just lasted out the six months during which the sun was in the south; and now, as the sun had gone north, the rains had gone there also. This was a very important fact, by which the rise of the Nile on the other side of the axis of this mountain-group might be determined, proving, as it does, that whilst rain falls most wherever the sun is vertical, it is greatly augmented on the equatorial regions by these mountains, where also, as our maps show, is the rainy zone of the world.

After crossing the river, we hurried along by a more southernly and straighter road than we formerly came by, and reached Kaze towards the latter end of June. Here Sheikh Snay received us with his usual genuine hospitality, arranged a house especially for our use, and with him we again established our headquarters. This man, when we were formerly detained here to form our second caravan on our journey westwards, housed us, and carefully attended to our wants. He took charge of our kit, provided us with porters, and finally became our agent. Living with him, surrounded by an Arab community, felt like living in a civilised land; for the Arab's manners and society are as pleasant and respectable as can be found in any Oriental family. Snay had travelled as much as, or more than, any person in this land; and from being a shrewd and intelligent inquirer, knew everybody and everything. It was from his mouth, on our former visit to Kaze, that I first heard of the N'yanza, or, as he called it, the Ukerewe Sea; and then, too, I first proposed that we should go to it instead of journeying westward to the smaller waters of Ujiji. He had travelled up its western flank to Kibuga, the capital of the kingdom of Uganda, and had in his employ men who had lived and traded in Usoga. Snay, narrating his own experiences, said to me, "I was once three years absent on a visit to King Sunna, at his capital (Kibuga) in the Uganda kingdom, occupied by a tribe called Waganda. Starting from Kaze, it took me thirty-five marches to reach Kitangule (bearing N.N.W.), and twenty more marches going northwards, with the morning sun a little on my right face (probably north by east), to arrive at Kibuga. The only people that gave me any trouble on the way are the Wasui, situate at the beginning of the Karague kingdom; but that was only trifling, as they did not fight, and lasted but three or four marches. The Karague kingdom (a mountainous tract of land, containing several high spurs of hill, the eastern buttresses of these Lunae Montes, and washed on the flanks by the Ukerewe Sea) is bounded on the north by the Kitangule river, beyond which the Wanyoro territory (crescent shape) lies, with the horns directed eastwards. Amidst them, situate in the concave or lake side, are the Waganda, to whose capital I went. Anybody wishing to see the northern boundary of the lake should go to Kibuga, take good presents, and make friends with the reigning monarch; and, with his assistance, buy or construct boats on the shore of the lake, which is about five marches east of his capital.[47] North, beyond the Waganda, the Wanyoro are again met with; and there quarrels and wars were so rife, from a jealousy existing among them and the Waganda, that had these people known of a northern boundary, I still might not have heard of it. On crossing the Kitangule river, I found it emanating from Urundi (a district in the Mountains of the Moon), and flowing north-easterly. The breadth of the river is very great--I should imagine, some five to six hundred yards--and it contains much water, overflowing as the Malagarazi does after rains. There are also numerous other little streams on the way to Kibuga, but none so great as the Katonga river. This, like the rest, comes from the west, and flows towards the lake. It has a breadth of two thousand yards, is very deep when full, but sinks and is very sluggish in the dry season, when water-lilies and rushes overspread its surface, and the musquitoes are very annoying. The cowrie-shell, brought from the Zanzibar coast, is the common currency amongst the more northern tribes; but they are not worth the merchant's while to carry, as beads and brass (not cloth, for they are essentially a bead-wearing and naked people) are eagerly sought for and taken in exchange. Large sailing-craft, capable of containing forty or fifty men, and manned and navigated after the fashion of ocean mariners, are reported by the natives to frequent the lake (meaning the Nile at Gondokoro). We Arabs believe in this report, as everybody tells the same story; but don't know how it happens to be so, unless it is open to the sea. The Kitangule river is crossed in good-sized wooden canoes; but the Katonga river can only be passed in the dry season, when men walk over it on the lily leaves: cattle, too, are then passed across in certain open spaces, guided by a long string, which is attached to the animals' heads."

Other Arab and Wasuahili merchants have corroborated Snay's statement, as also a Hindi merchant, called Musa, whom I especially mention, as I consider him a very valuable informant--not only from the straightforward way he had of telling his story, but also because we could converse with one another direct, and so obviate any chance of errors. After describing his route to the north in minute detail, stage by stage, with great precision, which was to the same effect as all the other accounts, he told me of a third large river to the northward of the Line, beyond Uganda; this he spoke of as much larger than the Katonga, and generally called the Usoga River, because it waters that district. Although he had recently visited Kibuga, and had lived with Sultan Mtesa, the present reigning monarch in place of Sunna, who died since Snay was there, he had no positive or definite idea of the physical features of any of the country beyond the point which he had reached;

but he produced a negro slave who had been to Usoga, and had seen the river in question. This man called the river Kivira, and described it as being much broader, deeper, and stronger in its current than either the Katonga or Kitangule river; that it came from the lake, and that it intersected stony hilly ground on its passage to the north-west.

This river Kivira, I now believe (although I must confess I did not until I made Snay alter his original statement about the direction of its flow, and so proved he meant this for his Jub), is the Nile itself. On a subsequent occasion, when talking to a very respectable Suahili merchant, by name Sheikh Abdullah bin Nasib, about the N'yanza, he corroborated the story about the mariners, who are said to keep logs and use sextants, and mentioned that he had heard of the Kidi and Bari people living on the Kivira river. Now, the Bari people mentioned by him are evidently those who have long since been known to us as a tribe living on the Nile in latitude 5o north and longitude 32o east, and described by the different Egyptian expeditions sent up the Nile to discover its source. M. Ferdinand Werne (says Dr Beke) has published an account of the second expedition's proceedings, in which he took part; and which, it appears, succeeded in getting farther up the river than either of the others. "The author states that, according to Lacono, King of Bari, the course of the river continues thence southwards a distance of thirty days' journey." This, by Dr Beke's computation, places the source of the Nile just where I have since discovered the N'yanza's southern extremity to be--in the second degree south latitude, lying in the Unyamuezi country.[48]

Here we see how singularly all the different informers' statements blend together in substantiating my opinion that the N'yanza is the great reservoir or fountainhead of that mighty stream that floated Father Moses on his first adventurous sail--the Nile. It must appear marvellous to the English reader how it happened that these traders obtained so much and such good information to the northward of the equator, and especially of the White Nile traders. The reasons are these:--For several years these Arabs have not only traded with Karague, Uganda, and Usoga, but they have had trading-stations in Uddu-Uganda and in Karague. The Uganda station has since been broken up by order of the king, as the Arabs were interfering too much with his subjects. In Karague, on the contrary, they still have establishments; and as they cannot go into Unyoro themselves, they have induced the Wahaiya and Waziwa to bring them ivory from that country and from Kidi, in exchange for which they give beads. These Zanzibar merchants are very inquiring men, and have learnt a great deal from this source. Far more, however, they have learned from the King of Karague, who is much respected by all the surrounding kings, and is continually exchanging presents and news with them. The King of Unyoro, for instance, whose territory extends to Madi, once sent him a present of beads and coral ornaments which must have come up the Nile, for at the same time the sailing-vessels on the Nile were heard of, and ornaments of that nature were never brought into the country from the Zanzibar side. Omitted in these accounts was a statement of Musa's I did not believe at first concerning the rise of the Nile, which was this: The natives had told him when the N'yanza (Nile) rose, it tore up and floated away islands. Further, Abdullah told me of a wonderfully high and steep mountain beyond Karague--doubtless the Mfumbiro--being constantly covered with clouds; and I heard from him of a salt lake--doubtless the Little Luta Nzige--which had some connection with the N'yanza. These details were, however, so obscurely given, I feared to place them on my map at that time.

I began the formation of the new caravan for exploring Northern Unyamuezi immediately after our arrival, but found it difficult to do things hurriedly. There was only one man then at Unyanyembe who knew the coast language, and would consent to act as my Kirangozi;[49] and as he had come all the way from Ujiji with us, he required a few days to arrange things at his home, in a village some distance off. Whilst he was absent the Arabs paid us daily visits, and gave many useful hints about the journey in prospect. One hint must especially be regarded, which was, to take care, on arrival at the lake, that I did not enter the village of a certain sultan called Mahaya, to whose district, Muanza, at the southern extremity of the lake, they directed me to go. This precautionary warning was advanced in consequence of a trick the sultan had played an Arab, who, after visiting him in a friendly way, was forcibly detained until he paid a ransom; an unjust measure, which the Arabs pointedly advert to as destructive to commercial interests. Further, the Arabs had learnt from travellers just arrived from Usukuma that the whole route leading to the N'yanza was in a state of commotion, caused by civil wars, and therefore advised me to go as strongly armed as possible.

To lose no time whilst the Kirangozi was away--for I had a long business to do in a very short space--I intimated to Sheikh Said and the Beluch guard my intention of taking them with me to the lake, and ordered them to prepare for the journey by a certain date. Said demurred, saying he would give a definite answer about accompanying me before the time of starting, but subsequently refused (I hear, as one reason), because he did not consider me his chief.[50] I urged that it was as much his duty as mine to go there; and said that unless he changed his present resolution, I should certainly recommend the Government not to pay the gratuity which the Consul had promised him on condition that he worked entirely to our satisfaction, in assisting the expedition to carry out the Government's plans.

The Jemadar of the Beluch guard, on seeing the Sheikh hold back, at first raised objections, and then began to bargain. He fixed a pay of one gora or fifteen cloths per man, as the only condition on which I should get their services; for they all declared that they had not only been to Ujiji, the place appointed by Sultan Majid and their chief before leaving Zanzibar, but that they had overstayed the time agreed upon for them to be absent on these travels--namely, six months. I acceded to this exorbitant demand, considering the value of time, as the dry season had now set in, and the Arabs at this period cease travelling to Zanzibar, from fear of being caught by droughts in the deserts between this place and the East Coast Range, where, if the ponds and puddles dry up, there is so little water in the wells that travelling becomes precarious.

Further, I had not only to go through a much wilder country than we had travelled in before, two and a half degrees off, to discover and bring back full particulars of the N'yanza, but had to purchase cattle sufficient for presents, and food for the whole journey down to the coast, within the limited period of six weeks. Ramji's slaves all came back to us here, and begged we would take them into our service again. I wanted to do so, as Snay not only strongly advised me to have as strong an escort as possible, but thought that their knowledge of treating with native chiefs would be of the greatest value to me. Captain Burton, however, would not listen to my request, as he insisted they would only prove of more expense than profit to the expedition; but instead, he employed them himself, after I had gone, in repairing our damaged property, and in laying in supplies for our future journey home. I regretted the loss of these men the more, as they all so warmly volunteered to go with me. The Arab depot now came into play to satisfy this sudden and unexpected call upon our store of cloths. There were ten Beluches fit for service, and for each of them a gora was bought at the depot, at a valuation of ten dollars each, or a hundred the lot. In addition to this they received an advance of fifteen maunds of white beads in lieu of rations--a rate of 1 lb. per man per day for six weeks. The Kirangozi now returned with many excuses to escape the undertaking of guiding me to the lake. He declared that all the roads were rendered impassable by wars, and that it was impossible for him to undertake the responsibility of escorting me in so dangerous a country. After a good deal of bothering and persuading he at length acceded, and brought fifteen pagazis or porters from his own and some neighbouring villages. To each of these I gave five cloths as hire, and all appeared ready; but not so. Bombay's Seedi nature came over him, and he would not move a yard unless I gave him a month's wages in cloth upon the spot. I thought his demand an imposition, for he had just been given a cloth. His wages were originally fixed at five dollars a-month, to accumulate at Zanzibar until our return there; but he was to receive daily rations the same as all the other men, with an occasional loin-cloth covering whenever his shukka might wear out. All these strikes with the Beluches and Bombay for cloth were in consequence of their having bought some slaves, whose whims and tastes they could not satisfy without our aid; and they knew these men would very soon desert them unless they received occasionally alluring presents to make them contented. But finessing is a kind of itch with all Orientals, as gambling is with those who are addicted to it; and they would tell any lie rather than gain their object easily by the simple truth, on the old principle that "stolen things are sweetest." Had Bombay only opened his heart, the matter would have been settled at once, for his motives were of a superior order. He had bought, to be his adopted brother, a slave of the Wahha tribe, a tall, athletic, fine-looking man, whose figure was of such excellent proportions that he would have been remarkable in any society; and it was for this youth, and not himself, he had made so much fuss and used so many devices to obtain the cloths. Indeed, he is a very singular character, not caring one bit about himself, how he dressed or what he ate; ever contented, and doing everybody's work in preference to his own, and of such exemplary honesty, he stands a solitary marvel in the land: he would do no wrong to benefit himself--to please anybody else there is nothing he would stick at. I now gave him five cloths at his request, to be eventually deducted from his pay. Half of them he gave to a slave called

Mabruki, who had been procured by him for leading Captain Burton's donkey, but who had, in consequence of bad behaviour, reverted to my service. This man he also designated "brother," and was very warmly attached to, though Mabruki had no qualifications worthy of attracting any one's affections to him. He was a sulky, dogged, pudding-headed brute, very ugly, but very vain; he always maintained a respectable appearance, to cloak his disrespectful manners. The remainder was expended in loin-cloths, some spears, and a fez (red Turkish cap), the wearing of which he shared by turns with his purchased brother, and a little slave-child whom he had also purchased and employed in looking after the general wardrobe, and in cooking his porridge dinner, or fetching water and gathering sticks. On the line of march the little urchin carried Bombay's sleeping-hide and water-gourd.

Before my departure from Kaze, Captain Burton wrote the Royal Geographical Society to the following effect:--"I have the honour to transmit a copy of a field-book with a map, by Captain Speke. Captain Speke has volunteered to visit the Ukerewe Lake, of which the Arabs give grand accounts."

9th July 1858.--The caravan, consisting of one Kirangozi, twenty pagazis, ten Beluches as guard, Bombay, Mabruki, and Gaetano, escorting a kit sufficient for six weeks, left Kaze to form camp at noon. The Beluches were all armed with their own guns, save one, who carried one of Captain Burton's double rifles, an eight-bore by W. Richards.[51] I took with me for sporting purposes, as well as for the defence of the expedition, one large five-bore elephant-gun, also lent by Captain Burton; and of my own, one two-grooved four-gauge single rifle, one polygrooved twenty-gauge double, and one double smooth twelve-bore, all by John Blissett of High Holborn. The village they selected to form up in was three miles distant on the northern extremity of this, the Unyanyembe district.

I commenced the journey myself at 6 P.M., as soon as the two donkeys I took with me to ride were caught and saddled. It was a dreary beginning. The escort of Beluches who accompanied me had throughout the former journeys been in great disgrace, and were in consequence all sullen in their manner, and walked with heavy gait and downcast countenances, looking very much as if they considered they had sold themselves when striking such a heavy bargain with us, for they evidently saw nothing before them but drudgery and a continuance of past hardships. The nature of the track increased the general gloom; it lay through fields of jowari (holcus) across the plain of Unyanyembe. In the shadow of night, the stalks, awkwardly lying across the path, tripped up the traveller at every step; and whilst his hands, extended to the front, were grasping at darkness to preserve his equilibrium, the heavy bowing ears, ripe and ready to drop, would bang against his eyes. Further, the heavy sandy soil aided not a little in ruffling the temper; but it was soon over, though all our mortification did not here cease. The pagazis sent forward had deposited their loads and retired home to indulge, it is suspected, in those potations deep of the universal pombe (African small-beer) that always precede a journey, hunt, or other adventure--without leaving a word to explain the reason of their going, or even the time which they purposed being absent.

10th July.--The absence of the pagazis caused a halt, for none of them appeared again until after dark. The Beluches, gloomy, dejected, discontented, and ever grumbling, form as disagreeable a party as it was ever the unfortunate lot of any man to command.

11th.--We started on the journey northwards at 7 A.M., and, soon clearing the cultivated plain, bade adieu to Unyanyembe. The track passed down a broad valley with a gentle declination, which was full of tall but slender forest-trees, and was lined on either side by low hills. We passed one dry nullah, the Gombe, which drains the regions westward into the Malagarazi river, some pools of water, and also two Wasukuma caravans, one of ivory destined for the coast, and the other conveying cattle to the Unyanyembe markets. Though the country through which we passed was wild and uninhabited, we saw no game but a troop of zebras, which were so wild that I could not get near them. After walking fifteen miles, we arrived at the district of Ulekampuri, and entered a village, where I took up my quarters in a negro's hut. My servants and porters did the best they could by pigging with the cattle, or lying in the shade under the eaves of the huts.

Up to this point the villages, as is the case in all central Unyamuezi, are built on the most luxurious principles. They form a large hollow square, the walls of which are the huts, ranged on all sides of it in a sort of street consisting of two walls, the breadth of an ordinary room, which is partitioned off to a convenient size by interior walls of the same earth-construction as the exterior ones, or as our sepoys' lines are made in India. The roof is flat, and serves as a store-place for keeping sticks to burn, drying grain, pumpkins, mushrooms, or any vegetables they may have. Most of these compartments contain the families of the villagers, together with their poultry, brewing utensils, cooking apparatus, stores of grain, and anything they possess. The remainder contain their flocks and herds, principally goats and cows, for sheep do not breed well in the country, and their flesh is not much approved of by the people. What few sheep there are appear to be an offshoot from the Persian stock. They have a very scraggy appearance, and show but the slightest signs of the fat-rumped proportions of their ancestors. The cows, unlike the noble Tanganyika ones, are small and short-horned, and are of a variety of colours. They carry a hump like the Brahminy bull, but give very little milk. In front of nearly every house you see large slabs of granite, the stones on which the jowari is ground by women, who, kneeling before them, rub the grain down to flour with a smaller stone, which they hold with both hands at once. Thus rubbing and grinding away, swaying monotonously to and fro, they cheer the time by singing and droning in cadence to the motion of their bodies.

The country to the east and north-east of this village is said to be thinly peopled, but, as usual, the clans are much intermixed, the two principal being Wakimbu and Wasagari. I here engaged a second guide or leader for five shukkas (small loin-cloths) merikani, as a second war, different from the one we had heard of at Kaze, had broken out exactly on the road I was pursuing, and rendered my first leader's experience of no avail. The evening was spent by the porters in dancing, and singing a song which had been evidently composed for the occasion, as it embraced everybody's name connected with the caravan, but more especially Mzungu (the wise or white man), and ended with the prevailing word amongst these curly-headed bipeds, "Grub, Grub, Grub!" It is wonderful to see how long they will, after a long fatiguing march, keep up these festivities, singing the same song over and over again, and dancing and stamping, with their legs and arms flying about like the wings of a semaphore, as they move slowly round and round in the same circle and on the same ground; their heads and bodies lolling to and fro in harmony with the rest of the dance, which is always kept at more even measure when, as on this occasion, there were some village drums beating the measure they were wont to move by.

12th.--The caravan got under way by 6 A.M., and we marched thirteen miles to a village in the southern extremity of the Unyambewa district. Fortunately tempers, like butterflies, soon change state. The great distractor Time, together with the advantage of distance, has produced such a salutary effect on the Beluches' minds, that this morning's start was accomplished to the merry peals of some native home-ly ditty, and all moved briskly forward. This was the more cheering to me because it was the first occasion of their having shown such signs of good feeling as singing in chorus on the line of march. The first five miles lay over flattish ground, wind-ing amongst low straggling hills of the same formation as the whole surface of the Unyamuezi country, which is diversified with small hills composed of granite out-crops. As we proceeded, the country opened into an extensive plain, covered, as we found it at first, with rich cultivation, and then succeeded by a slender tree-forest, amongst which we espied some antelopes, all very wary and difficult of approach.

At the ninth mile was a pond of sweet water, the greatest luxury in the desert. Here I ordered a halt for half an hour, and made a hearty breakfast on cold meat, potted Tanganyika shrimps, rozelle jelly, with other delicacies, and coffee. The lat-ter article was bought from the Kaze merchants. Towards the close of the journey a laughable scene took place between an ivory caravan of Wasukuma and my own. [52] On nearing each other, the two Kirangozis or leaders slowly advanced, march-ing in front of the single-file order in which caravans worm along these twisting narrow tracks, with heads awry, and eyes steadfastly fixed on one another, and with their bodies held motionless and strictly poised, like rams preparing for a fight, rushed in with their heads down, and butted continuously till one gave way. The rest of the caravan then broke up their order of march, and commenced a general melee. In my ignorance--for it was the first time I had seen such a scrimmage--I hastened to the front with my knobbed stick, and began reflecting where I could make best use of it in dividing the combatants, and should no doubt have laid on if I only could have distinguished friend from foe; but both parties, being black, were so alike, that I hesitated until they stopped to laugh at my excited state, and assured me that it was only the enactment of a common custom in the country when two strange caravan-leaders meet, and each doubts who should take the supremacy in choice of side. In two minutes more the antagonists broke into broad laughter, and each went his way.

The villages about here are numerous, and the country, after passing the forest, is highly cultivated, and affords plenty of provisions; but unfortunately as yet the white beads which I have brought have no value with the natives, and I cannot buy those little luxuries, eggs, butter, and milk, which have such a powerful influence in making one's victuals good and palatable; whereas there is such a rage for coloured beads, that if I had brought some I might purchase anything.

13th.--The caravan started at 6.30 A.M., and after travelling eight miles over an open, waving, well-cultivated country, stopped at the last village in Unyambewa. The early morning before starting was wasted by the pagazis "striking" for more cloth, and refusing to move unless I complied with their demand. I peremptorily refused, and they then tried to wheedle me out of beads. In demanding cloth, they pretended that they were suffering from the chilling cold of night--a pretence too absurd to merit even a civil reply. I then explained to my head men that I would rather anything happened than listen to such imposture as this; for did the men once succeed by tricks of this sort, there would never be an end to their trying it on, and it would ultimately prove highly injurious to future travellers, especially to merchants. On the route we had nothing to divert attention, save a single Wasuku-ma caravan proceeding southwards to Unyanyembe. A sultana called Ungugu governs this district. She is the first and only female that we have seen in this position, though she succeeded to it after the custom of the country. I imagine she must have had a worthless husband, since every sultan can have as many wives as he pleases, and the whole could never have been barren. I rallied the porters for pulling up after so short a march, but could not induce them to go on. They declared that forests of such vast extent lay on ahead that it would be quite impossible to cross them before the night set in. In the evening I had a second cause for being vexed at this loss of time, when every mile and hour was of so much importance; for by our halt the sultana got news of my arrival, and sent a messenger to request the pleasure of my company at her house on the morrow. In vain I pleaded for permission to go and see her that moment, or to do so on my return from the N'yanza; her envoy replied that the day was so far spent I could not arrive at her abode till after dark, and she would not have the pleasure of seeing me sufficiently well. He therefore begged I would attend to the letter of her request, and not fail to visit her in the morning.

The lazy pagazis, smelling flesh, also aided the deputy in his endeavours to detain me, by saying that they could not oppose her majesty's will, lest at any future time, when they might want again to pass that way, she should take her revenge upon them. Though this might seem a very reasonable excuse, I doubt much, if their interests had lain the opposite way, whether they would have been so cautious. However, it was not difficult to detect their motives for bringing forward such an urgent reason against me, as it is a custom in this country that every wealthy traveller or merchant shall pay a passport-fee, according to his means, to the sultan of the country he travels through, who in return gives a cow or goat as a mark of amity, and this is always shared amongst the whole caravan.

14th.--The sultana's house was reported to be near, so I thought to expedite the matter by visiting her in person, and thus perhaps gain an afternoon's march: otherwise to have sent the Jemadar with a present would have been sufficient, for these creatures are pure Mammonists. Vain hope, trying to do anything in a hurry in Negroland! I started early in the morning, unfortified within, and escorted by two Beluches, the Kirangozi, three porters, Bombay, and Mabruki. The necessary presents were also taken: these consisted of one barsati,[53] one dhoti merikani,[54] and one shukka kiniki.[55] This last article was to be kept in reserve, to throw in at last and close with, as further demands beyond what is given are invariably made. After walking six miles over a well-cultivated plain, I felt anxious to know what they meant by "near," and was told, as usual, that the house was close at hand. Distrustful, but anxious to complete the business as speedily as possible (for to succeed in Africa one must do everything one's self), I followed the envoy across one of the waves that diversify the face of the country, descended into a well-cultivated trough-like depression, and mounted a second wave six miles farther on.

Here at last, by dint of perseverance, we had the satisfaction of seeing the palisadoed royal abode. We entered it by an aperture in the tall slender stakes which surround the dwellings and constitute the palisadoing, and after following up a passage constructed of the same material as the outer fence, we turned suddenly into a yard full of cows--a substitute for an anteroom. Arrived there, the negroes at once commenced beating a couple of large drums, half as tall as themselves, made something like a beer-barrel, covered on the top with a cow-skin stretched tightly over, by way of a drum-head. This drumming was an announcement of our arrival, intended as a mark of regal respect.

For ten minutes we were kept in suspense, my eyes the while resting upon the milk-pots which were being filled at mid-day, but I could not get a drop. At the expiration of that time a body of slaves came rushing in, and hastily desired us to follow them. They led us down the passage by which we entered, and then turned up another one similarly constructed, which brought us into the centre of the sultana's establishment--a small court, in which the common negro mushroom huts, with ample eaves, afforded us grateful shelter from the blazing sun. A cow-skin was now spread, and a wooden stool set for me, that I might assume a better state than my suite, who were squatted in a circle around me. With the usual precaution of African nobles, the lady's-maid was first sent to introduce herself--an ugly halting creature, very dirtily garbed, but possessing a smiling contented face. Her kindly mien induced me, starving and thirsty as I was after my twelve miles' walk, to ask for eggs and milk--great luxuries, considering how long I had been deprived of them. They were soon procured, and devoured with a voracity that must have astonished the bystanders.

The maid, now satisfied there was nothing to fear, whether from ghost, goblin, or white face, retired and brought her mistress, a short stumpy old dame, who had seen at least some sixty summers. Her nose was short, squat, and flabby at the end, and her eyes were bald of brows or lashes; but still she retained great energy of manner, and was blessed with an ever-smiling face. The dress she wore consisted of an old barsati, presented by some Arab merchant, and was if anything dirtier than her maid's attire. The large joints of all her fingers were bound up with small copper wire, her legs staggered under an immense accumulation of anklets made of brass wire wound round elephant's tail or zebra's hair; her arms were decorated with huge solid brass rings, and from other thin brass wire bracelets depended a great assortment of wooden, brazen, horn, and ivory ornaments, cut in every shape of talismanic peculiarity.

Squatting by my side, the sultana at once shook hands. Her nimble fingers first manipulated my shoes (the first point of notice in these barefooted climes), then my overalls, then my waistcoat, more particularly the buttons, and then my coat-- this latter article being so much admired, that she wished I would present it to her, to wear upon her own fair person. Next my hands and fingers were mumbled, and declared to be as soft as a child's, and my hair was likened to a lion's mane. "Where is he going?" was the all-important query. This, without my understanding, was readily answered by a dozen voices, thus: "He is going to the Lake, to barter his cloth for large hippopotami teeth." Satisfied with this plausible story, she retired into privacy, and my slave, taking the hint, soon followed with the hongo (present or tax), duly presented it, and begged permission in my name to depart. But as she had always given a bullock to the Arabs who visited her, I also must accept one from her, though she could not realise the fact that so scurvy a present as mine could be intended for her, whose pretensions were in no way inferior to those of the Unyanyembe Sultan. An Arab could not have offered less, and this was a rich Mzungu!

Misfortunes here commenced anew: the bullock she was desirous of giving was out grazing, and could not be caught until the evening, when all the cattle are driven in together. Further, she could not afford to lose so interesting a personage as her guest, and volunteered to give me a shakedown for the night. I begged she would consider my position--the absolute necessity for my hurrying--and not insist on my acceptance of the bullock, or be offended by my refusing her kind offer to remain there, but permit our immediate departure. She replied that the word had gone forth, so the animal must be given; and if I still persisted in going, at any rate three porters could remain behind, and drive it on afterwards. To this I reluctantly consented, and only on the Kirangozi's promise to march the following morning. Then, with the usual farewell salutation, "Kuahere, Mzungu," from my pertinacious hostess, I was not sorry to retrace my steps, a good five hours' walk. We re-entered camp at 7.20 P.M., which is long after dark in regions so near to the equator. All palaces here are like all the common villages beyond Unyamuezi proper, and are usually constructed on the same principle as this one. They consist of a number of mushroom-shaped grass huts, surrounded by a tall slender palisading, and having streets or passages of the same wooden construction, some winding, some straight, and others crosswise, with outlets at certain distances leading into the different courts, each court usually containing five or six huts partitioned off with poles as the streets are. These courts serve for dividing the different families, uncles and cousins occupying some, whilst slaves and their relatives live in others. Besides this they have their cattle-yards. If the site of the village be on moist or soft ground, it is usual, in addition to the palisading, to have it further fortified by a moat or evergreen fence.

15th.--We left Unyambewa at 7 A.M., and reached a village in the Ibanda district, having marched seven miles over flat ground, growing fine crops in some places, with the remainder covered by the usual slender forest-trees. The road was very good and regular. In the afternoon the three porters arrived with the sultana's bullock, and were attended by her nephew and managing man, and by some of her slaves as drivers. The nephew asked first for more presents in her name; as this was refused, he requested something for the drivers. I gave them a cloth, and he then pleaded for himself, as he had sacrificed so much time and trouble for me. I satisfied him with one fundo of beads (a bunch of beads sufficient to form ten khetes or necklaces), and we parted: a full khete is a string of beads double the length of the fore-arm, or sufficiently long to encircle the neck twice. The Beluches, finding that nothing but the coarsest grains were obtainable with the white beads they had received, petitioned for and obtained a shukka, but under the proviso of their always assisting me to urge on the lazy porters. This they not only agreed to do, but also declared themselves willing to execute any orders I might give them: they looked upon me as their Ma, Bap (mother and father, a Hindostani expression, significant of everything, or entire dependence on one as a son on his parents), and considered my interests their interests.

16th.--We started at 6 A.M., and travelled eleven miles to Ukamba, a village in the district of Msalala, which is held by a tribe called Wamanda. The first four miles lay over the cultivated plain of Ibanda, till we arrived at the foot of a ridge of hills, which, gradually closing from the right, intersects the road, and runs into a hilly country extending round the western side of the aforesaid plain. We now crossed the range, and descended into a country more closely studded with the same description of small hills, but highly cultivated in the valleys and plains that separate them. About twelve miles to the eastward of Ukamba live a tribe called Wasongo, and to the west, at twenty miles' distance, are the Waquanda. To-day was fully verified the absolute futility of endeavouring to march against time in these wild countries.

The lazy pagazis finding themselves now, as it were, in clover, a country full of all the things they love, would not stir one step after 11 A.M. Were time of no consequence, and coloured beads in store, such travelling as this would indeed be pleasant. For the country here, so different from the Ujiji line, affords not only delightful food for the eyes, but abounds in flesh, milk, eggs, and vegetables in every variety. The son of the Msene Sultan, who lives between Unyanyembe and Ujiji, and became great friends with us when travelling there, paid me a visit to-day. He caught me at work with my diary and instruments, and being struck with veneration at the sight of my twirling compass and literary pursuits, thought me a magician, and begged that I would cast his horoscope, divine the probable extent of his father's life, ascertain if there would be any wars, and describe the weather, the prospects of harvest, and what future state the country would lapse into. The shrewd Bombay replied, to save me trouble, that so great a matter required more days of contemplation than I could afford to give. Provisions were very dear when purchased with white beads, for they were not the fashion, and the people were indifferent to them. I paid him one loin-cloth for four fowls and nine eggs, though, had I had coloured beads, I might have purchased one hen per khete (or necklace). Had this been a cloth-wearing instead of a bead-decorating nation, I should have obtained forty fowls for one shukka (or loin-cloth), that being the equivalent value with beads, equal, according to Zanzibar money, to one dollar. It is always foolish to travel without an assortment of beads, in consequence of the tastes of the different tribes varying so much; and it is more economical in the long-run to purchase high-priced than low-priced beads when making up the caravan at Zanzibar, for every little trader buys the cheaper sorts, stocks the country with them, and thus makes them common.

17th.--This day, like all the preceding ones, is delightful, and worthy of drawing forth an exclamation, like the Indian Griff's, of "What a fine day this is again!" We started at 7 A.M., and travelled thirteen miles, with fine bracing air, so cold in the morning that my fingers tingled with it. We were obliged here to diverge from the proper road *via* Sarenge, to avoid a civil war--the one before alluded to, and to escape which I had engaged the second guide--between two young chiefs, brothers of the Wamanda tribe, who were contending for the reins of government on the principle that might ought to give the right. Our new course led us out of the Msalala into the Uyombo district, which is governed by a sultan called Mihambo. He paid me a visit and presented a sheep--a small present, for he was a small chief, and could not demand a hongo. I gave in return one shukka merikani and one shukka kiniki. Here all the people were very busily engaged in their harvest, cutting their jowari, and thrashing it out with long sticks.

The whole country lies in long waves, crested with cropping little hills, thickly clad with small trees and brushwood. In the hollows of these waves the cultivation is very luxuriant. Here I unfortunately had occasion to give my miserable Goanese cook-boy a sound dressing, as the only means left of checking his lying, obstinate, destructive, wasteful, and injurious habit of intermeddling. This raised the creature's choler, and he vowed vengeance to the death, seconding his words with such a fiendish, murderous look, his eyes glistening like an infuriated tiger's, that I felt obliged to damp his temerity and freedom of tongue by further chastisement, which luckily brought him to a proper sense of his duty.

18th.--We left at 7 A.M., and travelled ten miles to Ukuni. The country still continues of the same rich and picturesque character, and retains daily the same un-varying temperature. On the road we met a party of Wayombo, who, taking advan-tage of the Wamanda disturbances, had lifted some forty or fifty head of their cattle in perfect security. I saw two albinos in this village, one an old woman with greyish eyes, and the other young, who ran away from fright, and concealed herself in a hut, and would not show again although beads were offered as an inducement for one moment's peep. The old lady's skin was of an unwholesome fleshy-pink hue, and her hair, eyebrows, and eyelashes were a light yellowish white. This march was shortened by two pagazis falling sick. I surmised this illness to be in consequence of their having gorged too much beef, to which they replied that everybody is sure to suffer pains in the stomach after eating meat, if the slayer of the animal happens to protrude his tongue and clench it with his teeth during the process of slaughtering. At last the white beads have been taken, but at the extravagant rate of two khetes for four eggs, the dearest I ever paid.

19th.--The caravan proceeded at 6 A.M., and after going eight miles re-entered the Msalala district's frontier, where we put up in a village three miles beyond the border. The country throughout this march may be classed in two divisions, one of large and extensively cultivated plains, with some fine trees about; and the other of small irregularly-disposed hills, the prevailing granitic outcrops of the region. There is no direct line northwards here, so we had to track about, and hit upon the lines between the different villages, which enhanced our trouble and caused much delay. At this place I witnessed the odd operation of brother-making. It consists in the two men desirous of a blood-tie being seated face to face on a cow's hide, with their legs stretched out as wide to the front as their length will permit, one pair overlapping the other. They then place their bows and arrows across their thighs, and each holds a leaf: at the same time a third person, holding a pot of oil or butter, makes an incision above their knees, and requires each to put his blood on the other's leaf, and mix a little oil with it, when each anoints himself with the brother-salve. This operation over, the two brothers bawl forth the names and extent of their relatives, and swear by the blood to protect the other till death. Ugogo, on the highway between the coast and Ujiji, is a place so full of inhabitants compared with the other places on that line, that the coast people quote it as a wonderful instance of high population; but this district astonished all my retinue. The road to-day was literally thronged with a legion of black humanity so exasperatingly bold that nothing short of the stick could keep them from jostling me. Poor creatures! they said they had come a long way to see, and now must have a good long stare; for when was there ever a Mzungu here before?

20th.--We broke ground at 6 A.M., and after travelling through high cultivation six miles, were suddenly stopped by a guard of Wamanda, sent by Kurua, a sultan of that tribe, and chief of the division we were marching in. Their business was to inform us that if we wished to travel to the Lake, the sultan would give directions to have us escorted by another route, as his eldest brother was disputing the rights of government with him along the line we were now pursuing; and added, that our intentions would be only known to him by the part we might choose to take. These constant interruptions were becoming very troublesome; so, as we were close to the confines of these two malcontents, I was anxious to force our way on, and agreed to do so with the Beluches. But the tiresome, lazy, flesh-seeking pagazis saw a feast in prospect by the sultan's arrangement, and would not move an inch. Further, the Kirangozi requested his discharge if I was otherwise than peacefully inclined. The guard then led us to Mgogua, the sultan's village, a little off the road.

Kurua is a young man, not very handsome himself, but he has two beautiful young wives. They secured me a comfortable house, showed many attentions, and sent me a bowl of fresh sweetmilk, the very extreme of savage hospitality. In the evening he presented me with a bullock. This I tried to refuse, observing that flesh was the prime cause of all my hindrances; but nothing would satisfy him; I must accept it, or he would be the laughing-stock of everybody for inhospitality. If I gave nothing in return, he should be happy as long as his part of host was properly fulfilled. Salt, according to the sultan, is only to be found here in the same efflorescent state in which I saw it yesterday--a thin coating overspreading the ground, as though flour had been sprinkled there.

21st.--Halt. I gave the sultan, as a return present, one dhoti merikani and six cubits kiniki, what I thought to be just the value of his bullock. His kindness was undoubtedly worthy of a higher reward, but I feared to excite these men's cupidity, as there is no end to their tricks and finesse whenever they find a new chance of gain, and I now despaired of accomplishing my task in time. However, Kurua seemed quite happy under the circumstances, and considered the exchange of hongo a bond of alliance, and proclaimed that we were henceforth to be brothers. He then said he would accompany me back to Unyanyembe, on my return from the Lake, and would exchange any of his cows that I might take a fancy to for powder, which I said I had there. The quantity of cattle in Msalala surpasses anything I have seen in Africa. Large droves, tended by a few men each, are to be seen in every direction over the extensive plains, and every village is filled with them at night. The cultivation also is as abundant as the cattle are numerous, and the climate is delightful. To walk till breakfast, 9 A.M., every morning, I find a luxury, and from that time till noon I ride with pleasure; but the next three hours, though pleasant in a hut, are too warm to be agreeable under hard exertion. The evenings and the mornings, again, are particularly serene, and the night, after 10 P.M., so cold as to render a blanket necessary. But then it must be remembered that all the country about these latitudes, on this meridian, 33o east, is at an altitude of from 3500 to 4000 feet. My dinner to-day was improved by the addition of tomatos and the bird's-eye chili--luxuries to us, but which the negroes, so different from the Indians, never care about, and seldom grow.

The cotton-plant is as fine here as at Unyanyembe or Ujiji, and anything would grow with only the trouble of throwing down the seed. It is a great pity that the country is not in better hands. From all I can gather, there is no fixed revenue paid to these sultans; all their perquisites are occasional hongos received from travellers; a percentage on all foreign seizures, whether by battle or plunder; and a certain part of all windfalls, such as a share of the sportsman's game-bag, in the shape of elephants' tusks or flesh, or the skins of any wild animals; otherwise they live by the sweat of the brow of their slaves, in tilling their ground, tending their cattle, or trafficking for them in slaves and ivory. It seems destined that I should never reach the goal of my ambition. To-day the Jemadar finds himself too unwell to march, and two other Beluches say the same. This is an effectual obstacle; for the guard declares itself too weak to divide, and the sultan blows on the fire of my mortification by saying that these are troubled times, and advises our keeping all together. He says that his differences have been going on these five years with his eldest brother, and now he wishes to bring them to a crisis, which he proposes doing after my return, when he will obtain powder from me, and will have the preponderating influence of Arab opinion brought to bear in his favour by the aid of their guns--an impressive mode which Africa has of proving right in its own way.

22d.--After much groaning and grumbling, I got the sick men on their legs by 7 A.M., and we marched eight miles to Senagongo, the boma[56] (palisade) of Sultan Kanoni, Kurua's second brother. These two younger brothers side together against the eldest. They are all by different mothers, and think the father's property should fairly be divided among them. It is a glaring instance of the bad effects of a plurality of wives; and being contrary to our constitutional laws of marriage, I declined giving an opinion as to who was right or wrong.

To avoid the seat of war my track was rather tortuous. On the east or right side the country was open, and afforded a spacious view; but on the west this was limited by an irregularly-disposed series of low hills. Cultivation and scrub-jungle alternated the whole way. The miserable Goanese, like a dog slinking off to die, slipped away behind the caravan, and hid himself in the jungle to suffer the pangs of fever in solitude. I sent men to look for him in vain: party succeeded party in the search, till at last night set in without his appearing. It is singular in this country to find how few men escape some fever or other sickness, who make a sudden march after living a quiet stationary life. It appears as if the bile got stirred, suffused the body, and, exciting the blood, produced this effect. I had to admonish a silly Beluch, who, foolishly thinking that powder alone could not hurt a man, fired his gun off into a mass of naked human legs, in order, as he said, to clear the court. The consequence was, that at least fifty pairs got covered with numerous small bleeding wounds, all dreadfully painful from the saltpetre contained in the powder. It was fortunate that the sultan was a good man, and was present at the time it occurred, else a serious row might have been the consequence of this mischievous trick.

23d.--Halt. We fired alarm-guns all night to no purpose; so at daybreak three different parties, after receiving particular orders how to scour the country, were sent off at the same time to search for Gaetano. Fortunately the Beluches obeyed my injunctions, and at 10 A.M. returned with the man, who looked for all the world exactly like a dog who, guilty of an indiscretion, is being brought in disgrace before his master to receive a flogging; for he knew I had a spare donkey for the sick, and had constantly warned the men from stopping behind alone in these lawless countries. The other two parties adopting, like true Easterns, a better plan of their own, spent the whole day ranging wildly over the country, fruitlessly exerting themselves, and frustrating any chance of my getting even an afternoon's march. Kanoni very kindly sent messengers all over his territory to assist in the search: he, like Kurua, has taken every opportunity to show me those little pleasing attentions which always render travelling agreeable. These Wamanda are certainly the most noisy set of beings that I ever met with: commencing their fetes in the middle of the village every day at 3 P.M., with screaming, yelling, rushing, jumping, sham-fighting, drumming, and singing in one collective inharmonious noise, they seldom cease till midnight. Their villages, too, are everywhere much better protected by bomas (palisading) than is usual in Africa, arguing that they are a rougher and more war-like people than the generality. If shoved aside, or pushed with a stick, they show their savage nature by turning fiercely like a fatted pig upon whoever tries to poke it up.

24th.--The march commenced at 7 A.M.; and here we again left the direct road, to avoid a third party of belligerent Wamanda, situated in the northern extremity of the Msalala district, on the highway between Unyanyembe and the Lake. On bidding the sultan adieu, he was very urgent in his wishes that I should take a bullock from him. This I told him I should willingly have accepted, only that it would delay my progress; and he, more kindly than the other chief, excused me. Finding that none of our party knew the road, he advanced a short way with us, and generously offered to furnish us with a guide to the Lake and back, saying that he would send one of his own men after us to a place he appointed with my Kirangozi. I expressed my gratitude for his consideration, and we parted with warm regard for one another. Unfortunately, Bombay, who is not the clearest man in the world in expressing himself, stupidly bungled the sultan's arrangement, and we missed the man.

To keep the pagazis going was a matter of no little difficulty; after the fifth mile they persisted in entering every village that they came across, and, throwing down their loads, were bent upon making an easy day's work of it. I, on the contrary, was equally persistent in going on, and neither would allow the Beluches to follow them, nor enter the villages myself, until they, finding their game of no avail, quietly shouldered their loads and submitted to my orders. This day's journey was twelve miles over a highly-cultivated, waving country, at the end of which we took up our abode in a deserted village called Kahama.

25th.--We got under way at 7 A.M., and marched seven and a half hours, when we entered a village in the district of Nindo, nineteen miles distant. After passing through a belt of jungle three miles broad, we came upon some villages amidst a large range of cultivation. This passed, we penetrated a large wilderness of thorn and bush jungle, having sundry broad grassy flats lying at right angles to the road. Here I saw a herd of hartebeests, giraffes, and other animals, giving to the scene a truly African character. The tracks of elephants and different large beasts prove that this place is well tenanted in the season. The closeness of the jungle and evenness of the land prevented my taking any direct observations with the compass; but the mean oscillations of its card showed a course with northing again. This being a long stage, I lent my ass to a sick Beluch, and we accomplished the journey, notwithstanding the great distance, in a pleasant and spirited manner. This despatch may in part be attributable to there being so much desert, and the beloved "grub" and the village lying ahead of us luring the men on.

26th.--We broke ground at 7 A.M., and, after passing the village cultivation, entered a waterless wilderness of thorn and tree forest, with some long and broad plains of tall grass intersecting the line of march. These flats very much resemble some we crossed when travelling close to and parallel with the Malagarazi river; for the cracked and flawy nature of the ground, now parched up by a constant drought, shows that this part gets inundated in the wet season. Indeed, this peculiar grassy flat formation suggests the proximity of a river everywhere in Africa; and I felt sure, as afterwards proved true, that a river was not far from us. The existence of animal life is another warranty of water being near: elephants and buffaloes cannot live a day without it.

Fortunately for my mapping, a small conical hill overtopped the trees in advance of our track, at twelve miles from the starting-point. We eventually passed alongside of it, and travelled on six miles farther to a village in the cultivated plain of Salawe, a total distance of eighteen miles. The whole country about here was covered with harvest-workers, who, on seeing my approach, left off work and followed me into the village. As nothing proves better the real feelings and natural propensities of a nation than the impulsive actions of the children, I will give a striking instance, as it occurred to me to-day. On seeing a child approach me, I offered him a handful of beads, upon which the greedy little urchin snatched them from my hand with all the excited eagerness of a monkey. He clenched tight hold of them in his little fists, and, without the slightest show of any emotions of gratitude, retired, carrying his well-earned prize away with a self-satisfied and perfectly contented air, not even showing the beads to his parents or playmates. I called Bombay's attention to this transaction, and contrasted it with the joyful, grateful manner in which an English child would involuntarily act if suddenly become possessed of so much wealth, by hurrying off to his mamma, and showing what fine things the kind gentleman had given him. Bombay passed on my remark, with a twelvemonth's grin upon his face, to his inquiring brother Mabruki, and then explained the matter to his sooty friends around, declaring that such tumma (avaricious) propensities were purely typical of the Seedi's nature.

At the usual hour of departure this morning, the Kirangozi discovered that the pagazis' feet were sore from the late long marches, and declared that they could not walk. To this the Jemadar replied that the best asylum for such complaints was on ahead, where the sahib proposed to kill some goats and rest a day. The Kirangozi replied, "But the direct road is blocked up by wars: if a march must be made, I will show another route three marches longer round." "That," answered the Jemadar, "is not your business: if any troubles arise from marauders, we, the Beluches, are the fighting men--leave that to us." At last the Kirangozi, getting quite disconcerted, declared that there was no water on the way. "Then," quoth the energetic Jemadar, "were your gourds made for nothing? If you don't pack up at once, you and my stick shall make acquaintance." The party was then off in a moment.

On the way we met some herdsmen driving their cattle to Unyanyembe, and inquired from them the state of the road. They said that the country beyond a certain distance was safe and quiet, but corroborated the Kirangozi's statement as to warriors being in the immediate neighbourhood, who came and visited this place from the west, where is the northern extremity of the Msalala district. Several varieties of antelopes were seen, and the Beluches fired at an ostrich. As in the last place, no milk could be obtained, for the people, fearing the Wamanda, had driven off their cattle to the northward. It is evident, from the general nakedness of the people, that cloth or beads do not find their way much here, which is accounted for by so few merchants ever coming this way. Hardly a neck here is decorated, and they seldom wear anything but the common goat-skin covering, hung over the shoulder by a strap or string like a game-bag, which covers only one hip at a time, and might as well be dispensed with as far as decency is concerned; but at night they take it off, and spread it on the ground to protect themselves from the cold and moisture of the earth. This district is occupied by a tribe called Waumba; to the east of it, thirty miles distant, are the Wanatiya, and thirty miles westward the Wazinza tribes.

27th.--At 6 A.M. we crawled through the opening in the palisading which forms the entrances of these villages, and at once perceived a tall, narrow pillar of granite, higher than Pompey's at Alexandria, or Nelson's Monument in Charing Cross, towering above us, and having sundry huge boulders of the same composition standing around its base, much in the same peculiar way as we see at Stonehenge, on Salisbury Plain. This scene strikes one with wonderment at the oddities of nature, and taxes one's faculties to imagine how on earth the stones ever became tilted up in this extraordinary position; but farther on, about five miles distant, we encountered another and even higher pillar, that quite overtopped the trees and everything about it. This and the former one served as good station-marks for the journey, the latter being visible at eight miles' distance. After the first eight miles, which terminates the cultivated district of Salawe, the track penetrated a waterless desert of thorn and small tree-forest, lying in a broad valley between low hills. As the sick Beluch still occupied my steadier donkey Ted, I was compelled to mount the half-broken Jenny--so playful with her head and heels that neither the Sheikh nor any other man dared sit upon her. The man's sickness appears to be one of those eccentric complaints, the after-effects of African fevers: it was attended with severe pain, and swelling extending over the stomach, the right side, the right arm, and the right half of the neck, depriving him of sleep and repose. In every position, whether sitting, lying, standing, rising up, or sitting down, he complained of aching muscles. I purchased a goat and sheep for the men for one dhoti merikani.

28th.--Halt. This stoppage was for the restoration of wounded feet, the pagazis' being all blistered by the last four long marches. I now slaughtered and gave the two purchased animals to the men, as no one grumbled at my refusing the last bullock, a recognised present for the whole party, though nominally given to the Sahib. These people, like the Arabs, and all those who have many wives, seem to find little enjoyment in that domestic bliss so interesting and beautiful in our English homes. Except on rare occasions, the husband never dines with his wife and family, always preferring the exclusive society of his own sex: even the boys, disdaining to dine with their mothers, mess with the men; whilst the girls and women, having no other option, eat a separate meal by themselves.

29th.--We started at 6 A.M., and marched thirteen miles to a village at the northern extremity of the district. The face of the country is still very irregular, sometimes rising into hills, at other times dropping into dells, but very well cultivated in the lower portion; whilst the brown granite rocks, with trees and brushwood covering the upper regions, diversify the colouring, and form a pleasing contrast to the scene; added to this, large and frequent herds graze about the fields and amongst the villages, and give animation to the whole. Amongst the trees, palms take a prominent part. Indeed, for tropical scenery, there are few places that could equal this; and if the traveller, as he moves along, surrounded by the screeching, howling, inquisitive savages, running rudely about and boisterously jostling him, could only divest himself of the idea that he is a bear baited by a yelping pack of hounds, the journey would be replete with enjoyment.

Crossing some hills, the caravan sprang a covey of guinea-fowls, and at some springs in a valley I shot several couple of sand-grouse, darker in plumage than any I ever saw in Africa or India, and not quite so big as the Tibet bird. The chief of the village offered me a bullock; but as the beast did not appear until the time of starting, I declined it. Neither did I give him any cloth, being convinced in my mind that these and other animals have always been brought to me by the smaller chiefs at the instigation of the Kirangozi, and probably aided by the flesh-loving party in general. The Jemadar must have been particularly mortified at my way of disposing of the business, for he talked of nothing else but flesh and the animal from the moment it was sent for, his love for butcher-meat amounting almost to a frenzy. The sandstone in this region is highly impregnated with iron, and smelters do a good business; indeed, the iron for nearly all the tools and cutlery that are used in this division of Eastern Africa is found and manufactured here. It is the Brummagem of the land, and has not only rich but very extensive ironfields stretching many miles north, east, and west. I brought some specimens away. Cloth is little prized in this especially bead country, and I had to pay the sum of one dhoti kiniki for one pot of honey and one pot of ghee (clarified butter).

30th.--The caravan started at 6 A.M., and travelled four miles northwards, amidst villages and cultivation. From this point, on facing to the left, I could discern a sheet of water, about four miles from me, which ultimately proved to be a creek, and the most southern point of the N'yanza, which, as I have said before, the Arabs described to us as the Ukerewe Sea.[57] We soon afterwards descended into a grassy and jungly depression, and arrived at a deep, dirty, viscid nullah (a watercourse that only runs in wet weather), draining the eastern country into the southern end of the creek. To cross this (which I shall name Jordan) was a matter of no small difficulty, especially for the donkeys, whose fording seemed quite hopeless, until the Jemadar, assisted by two other Beluches, with blows and threats made the lazy pagazis work, and dragged them through the mud by sheer force. This operation lasted so long that, after crossing, we made for the nearest village in the Uvira district, and completed a journey of eight miles. The country to the eastward appeared open and waving, but to the north and far west very hilly. The ground is fertile, and the flocks and herds very abundant. Hippopotami frequent the nullah at night, and reside there during the rainy season; but at this, the dry half of the year, they retreat to the larger waters of the creek. Rhinoceroses are said to pay nightly visits to fields around the villages, and commit sad havoc on the crops. The nullah, running from the south-east, drains the land in that direction; but a river, I hear, rising in the Msalala district, draws off the water from the lays we have recently been crossing, to the westward of our track, where its course lies, and empties it into the creek on the opposite side to where the nullah debouches.

31st.--On hearing that a shorter track than the Sukuma one usually frequented by the Arabs led to Muanza, the place Sheikh Snay advised my going to, I started by it at 8 A.M.; and after following it west-ward down the nullah's right bank a few miles, turned up northwards, and continued along the creek to a village, eight miles distant, at the farther end of the Urima district, where we took up our quarters. The country has a mixed and large population of smiths, agriculturists, and herdsmen, residing in the flats and depressions which lie between the scattered little hills. During the rainy season, when the lake swells and the country becomes super-saturated, the inundations are so great that all travelling becomes suspended. The early morning was wasted by the unreasonable pagazis in the following absurd manner.

It will be remembered that, on starting from Unyanyembe, these cunning rascals begged for cloth as a necessary protection against the cold. This seemed reasonable enough, if they had not just before that received their hire in cloth; for the nights were so cold that I should have been sorry to be as naked as they were; but their real motive for asking was only to increase their stock for this present occasion, as we now shall see. Two days ago they broke ground with great difficulty, and only on my assuring them that I would wait at the place a day or two on my return from the Lake, as they expressed their desire to make a few halts there, and barter their hire of cloth for jembes (iron hoes), to exchange again at Unyanyembe, where those things fetch double the price they do in these especially iron regions. Now, to-day these dissembling creatures, distrusting my word as they would their own brethren's, stoutly refused to proceed until their business was completed,--suspecting I should break my word on returning, and would not then wait for them. They had come all this way especially for their own benefit, and now meant to profit by their trouble. Fortunately, the Jemadar and some other Beluches, who of late had shown great energy and zeal in promoting my views, pointed out to them that they were really more bound to do my business than their own, as they had engaged to do so, and since they could never have come there at all excepting through my influence and by my cloths; further, if they bought their hoes then, they would have to carry them all the way to the Lake and back. The Kirangozi acknowledged the fairness of this harangue, and soon gave way; but it was not until much more arguing, and the adoption of other persuasive means, that the rest were induced to relinquish their determination.

1st August.--This day's march, commenced at 6 A.M., differs but little from the last. Following down the creek, which, gradually increasing in breadth as it extended northwards, was here of very considerable dimensions, we saw many little islands, well-wooded elevations, standing boldly out of its waters, which, together with the hill-dotted country around, afforded a most agreeable prospect. Would that my eyes had been strong enough to dwell, unshaded, upon such scenery! but my French grey spectacles so excited the crowds of sable gentry who followed the caravan, and they were so boisterously rude, stooping and peering underneath my wide-awake to gain a better sight of my double eyes, as they chose to term them, that it became impossible for me to wear them. I therefore pocketed the instrument, closed my eyes, and allowed the donkey I was riding to be quietly pulled along. The evil effects of granting an indulgence to those who cannot appreciate it, was more obvious every day. To secure speed and contentment, I had indulged the pagazis by hiring double numbers, and giving each only half a recognised burden; but what has been the return? Yesterday the pagazis stopped at the eighth mile, because they said that so large a jungle was in our front that we could not cross it during daylight.

I disbelieved their story, and gave them to understand, on submitting to their request, that I was sure their trick for stopping me would turn to their own disadvantage; for if my surmise proved true, as the morrow would show, I should give them no more indulgence, and especially no more meat. On our arrival to-day there was a great hubbub amongst them, because I ordered the Jemadar and Kirangozi, with many of their principal men, to sit in state before me; when I gave a cloth to the soldiers to buy a goat with, and, turning to the Kirangozi, told him I was sorry I was obliged to keep my word of yesterday, and, their story having proved false, I must depart from the principle I had commenced upon, of feeding both parties alike, and now they might feel assured that I would do nothing further for their comfort until I could see in them some desire to please me. The screw was on the tenderest part: a black man's belly is his god; and they no sooner found themselves deprived of their wonted feast, than they clamorously declared they would be my devoted servants; that they had come expressly to serve me, and were willing to do anything I wished. The village chief offered me a goat; but as it came at the last moment before starting, I declined it.

To-day's track lay for the first half of the way over a jungly depression, where we saw ostriches, florikans, and the small Saltiana antelopes; but as their shyness did not allow of an open approach, I amused myself by shooting partridges. During the remainder of the way, the caravan threaded between villages and cultivation lying in small valleys, or crossed over low hills, accomplishing a total distance of twelve miles. Here we put up at a village called Ukumbi, occupied by the Walaswanda tribe.

2d.--We set out at 6 A.M., and travelled thirteen miles by a tortuous route, sometimes close by the creek, at other times winding between small hills, the valleys of which were thickly inhabited by both agricultural and pastoral people. Here some small perennial streams, exuding from springs by the base of these hills, meander through the valleys, and keep all vegetable life in a constant state of verdant freshness. The creek still increases in width as it extends northward, and is studded with numerous small rocky island-hills covered with brushwood, which, standing out from the bosom of the deep-blue waters, reminded me of a voyage I once had in the Grecian Archipelago. The route also being so diversified with hills, afforded fresh objects of attraction at every turn; and to-day, by good fortune, the usually troublesome people have attended more to their harvest-making, and left me to the enjoyment of the scenery. My trusty Blissett made a florikan pay the penalty of death for his temerity in attempting a flight across the track. The day's journey lasted thirteen miles, and brought us into a village called Isamiro.

Chapter IV.

First Sight of the Victoria N'yanza--Its Physical Geography--Speculations on its Being the Source of the Nile--Sport on the Lake--Sultans Machunda and Mahaya--Missionary Accounts of the Geography--Arab Accounts--Regrets at Inability to Complete the Discovery--The March Resumed--History of the Watuta--Hippopotamus-hunting--Adventures--Kahama.

August 3d.--The caravan, after quitting Isamiro, began winding up a long but gradually inclined hill--which, as it bears no native name, I shall call Somerset--until it reached its summit, when the vast expanse of the pale-blue waters of the N'yanza burst suddenly upon my gaze. It was early morning. The distant sea-line of the north horizon was defined in the calm atmosphere between the north and west points of the compass; but even this did not afford me any idea of the breadth of the lake, as an archipelago of islands (***vide*** Map, Bengal Archipelago), each consisting of a single hill, rising to a height of 200 or 300 feet above the water, intersected the line of vision to the left; while on the right the western horn of the Ukerewe Island cut off any farther view of its distant waters to the eastward of north. A sheet of water--an elbow of the sea, however, at the base of the low range on which I stood--extended far away to the eastward, to where, in the dim distance, a hummock-like elevation of the mainland marked what I understood to be the south and east angle of the lake. The important islands of Ukerewe and Mzita, distant about twenty or thirty miles, formed the visible north shore of this firth. The name of the former of these islands was familiar to us as that by which this long-sought lake was usually known. It is reported by the natives to be of no great extent; and though of no considerable elevation, I could discover several spurs stretching down to the water's edge from its central ridge of hills. The other island, Mzita, is of greater elevation, of a hog-backed shape, but being more distant, its physical features were not so distinctly visible.

In consequence of the northern islands of the Bengal Archipelago before mentioned obstructing the view, the western shore of the lake could not be defined: a series of low hill-tops extended in this direction as far as the eye could reach; while below me, at no great distance, was the debouchure of the creek, which enters the lake from the south, and along the banks of which my last three days' journey had led me. This view was one which, even in a well-known and explored country, would have arrested the traveller by its peaceful beauty. The islands, each swelling in a gentle slope to a rounded summit, clothed with wood between the rugged angular closely-cropping rocks of granite, seemed mirrored in the calm surface of the lake; on which I here and there detected a small black speck, the tiny canoe of some Muanza fisherman. On the gently shelving plain below me, blue smoke curled above the trees, which here and there partially concealed villages and hamlets, their brown thatched roofs contrasting with the emerald green of the beautiful milkbush, the coral branches of which cluster in such profusion round the cottages, and form alleys and hedgerows about the villages as ornamental as any garden shrub in England. But the pleasure of the mere view vanished in the presence of those more intense and exciting emotions which are called up by the consideration of the commercial and geographical importance of the prospect before me.

I no longer felt any doubt that the lake at my feet gave birth to that interesting river, the source of which has been the subject of so much speculation, and the object of so many explorers. The Arabs' tale was proved to the letter. This is a far more extensive lake than the Tanganyika; "so broad you could not see across it, and so long that nobody knew its length."[58] I had now the pleasure of perceiving that a map I had constructed on Arab testimony, and sent home to the Royal Geographical Society before leaving Unyanyembe, was so substantially correct that in its general outlines I had nothing whatever to alter. Further, as I drew that map after proving their first statements about the Tanganyika, which were made before my going there, I have every reason to feel confident of their veracity relative to their travels north through Karague, and to Kibuga in Uganda.

When Sheikh Snay told us of the Ukerewe, as he called the N'yanza, on our first arrival at Kaze, proceeding westward from Zanzibar, he said, "If you have come only to see a large bit of water, you had better go northwards and see the Ukerewe;

for it is much greater in every respect than the Tanganyika;" and so, as far as I can ascertain, it is. Muanza, our journey's end, now lay at our feet. It is an open, well-cultivated plain on the southern end, and lies almost flush with the lake; a happy, secluded-looking corner, containing every natural facility to make life pleasant. After descending the hill, we followed along the borders of the lake, and at first entered Mahaya's Palace, when the absence of boats arousing my suspicions, made me inquire where the Arabs, on coming to Muanza, and wishing to visit Ukerewe, usually resided. This, I heard, was some way farther on; so with great difficulty I persuaded the porters to come away and proceed at once to where they said an Arab was actually living. It was a singular coincidence that, after Sheikh Snay's caution as to my avoiding Sultan Mahaya's Palace, by inquiring diligently about him yesterday, and finding no one who knew his name, the first person I should have encountered was himself, and that, too, in his own Palace. The reason of this was, that big men in this country, to keep up their dignity, have several names, and thus mystify the traveller.

I then proceeded along the shore of the lake in an easterly direction, and on the way shot a number of red Egyptian geese, which were very numerous; they are the same sort here as I once saw in the Somali country. Another goose, which unfortunately I could not kill, is very different from any I ever saw or heard of: it stands as high as the Canadian bird, or higher, and is black all over, saving one little white patch beneath the lower mandible. It was fortunate that I came on here, for the Arab in question, called Mansur bin Salim, treated me very kindly, and he had retainers belonging to the country, who knew as much about the lake as anybody, and were of very great assistance. I also found a good station for making observations on the lake. It was Mansur who first informed me of my mistake of the morning; but he said that the evil reports spread at Unyanyembe about Mahaya had no foundation; on the contrary, he had found him a very excellent and obliging person.

To-day we marched eight miles, and have concluded our journey northwards, a total distance of 226 miles from Kaze, which, occupying twenty-five days, is at the rate of nine miles per diem, halts inclusive.

4th.--Early in the morning I took a walk of three miles easterly along the shore of the lake, and, ascending a small hill (which, to distinguish it, I have called Observatory Hill), took compass bearings of all the principal features of the lake. Mansur and a native, the greatest traveller of the place, kindly accompanied me, and gave me every obtainable information. This man had traversed the island, as he called it, of Ukerewe from north to south. But by his rough mode of describing it, I am rather inclined to think that instead of its being an actual island, it is a connected tongue of land, stretching southwards from a promontory lying at right angles to the eastern shore of the lake, which, being a wash, affords a passage to the mainland during the fine season, but during the wet becomes submerged, and thus makes Ukerewe temporarily an island.

If this conjecture be true, Mzita must be similarly circumstanced. Cattle, he says, can cross over from the mainland at all seasons of the year, by swimming from one elevation of the promontory to another; but the Warudi, who live upon the eastern shore of the lake, and bring their ivory for sale to Ukerewe, usually employ boats for the transit. A sultan called Machunda lives at the southern extremity of the Ukerewe, and has dealings in ivory with all the Arabs who go there. One Arab at this time was stopping there, and had sent his men coasting along this said promontory to deal with the natives on the mainland, as he could not obtain enough ivory on the island itself. Considering how near the eastern shore of the lake is to Zanzibar, it appears surprising that it can pay men to carry ivory all the way round by Unyanyembe. But the Masai, and especially those tribes who live near to the lake, are so hostile to travellers, that the risk of going there is considered too great to be profitable, though all Arabs concur in stating that a surprising quantity of ivory is to be obtained there at a very cheap rate.

The little hill alluded to as marking the south-east angle of the lake, I again saw; but so indistinctly, though the atmosphere was very clear, that I imagined it to be at least forty miles distant. It is due east of my station on Observatory Hill. I further draw my conclusions from the fact, that all the hills on the country are much about the same height--two or three hundred feet above the basial surface of the land; and I could only see the top of the hill like a hazy brown spot, contrasted in relief against the clear blue sky. Indeed, had my attention not been drawn to it, I should probably have overlooked it, and have thought there was only a sea horizon before me. On facing to the W.N.W., I could only see a sea horizon; and on inquiring how far back the land lay, was assured that, beyond the island of Ukerewe, there was an equal expanse of it east and west, and that it would be more than double the distance of the little hill before alluded to, or from eighty to one hundred miles in breadth.[59]

On my inquiring about the lake's length, the man faced to the north, and began nodding his head to it; at the same time he kept throwing forward his right hand, and, making repeated snaps of his fingers, endeavoured to indicate something immeasurable; and added, that nobody knew, but he thought it probably extended to the end of the world. To the east of the Observatory, a six hours' journey, probably fourteen or fifteen miles, the village of Sukuma is situated, and there canoes are obtainable for crossing to Ukerewe, which island being six hours' paddling, and lying due north of it, must give the firth a breadth of about fifteen miles.

Whilst walking back to camp, I shot two red geese and a florikan, like those I once shot in the Somali country. This must have been a dainty dish for my half-starved Arab companion, who had lost all his property on first arriving here, and was now living on Mahaya's generosity. It appears that nine months ago he was enabled, by the assistance of Mahaya, to hire some boats and men at Sukuma, and had sent his property, consisting of fifteen loads of cloth and 250 jembis or hoes, by them to Ukerewe, to exchange for ivory. But by the advice of Mahaya, and fearing to trust himself as a stranger amongst the islanders, he did not accompany his merchandise. Sultan Machunda, a man of the highest character by Unyanyembe report, on seeing such a prize enter his port, gave orders for its seizure, and will now give no redress to the unfortunate Mansur. All Mahaya's exertions to recover it have proved abortive: and Mansur has therefore been desirous of taking his revenge by making an attack in person on Ukerewe, but the "generous" Mahaya said, "No; your life is yet safe, do not risk it; but let my men do what they can, and in the meanwhile, as I have been a party to your losses, I will feed you and your people; and if I do not succeed in the end, you shall be my guest until I can amass sufficient property to reimburse your losses."

Mansur has all this time been living, like the slaves of the country, on jowari porridge, which is made by grinding the seed into flour and boiling it in water until it forms a good thick paste, when master and man sit round the earthen pot it is boiled in, pick out lumps, and suck it off their fingers. It was a delicious sight yesterday, on coming through Muanza, to see the great deference paid to the sick Beluch, Shadad, mistaken for the great Arab merchant (Mundewa), my humble self, in consequence of his riding my donkey, and to perceive the stoical manner in which he treated their attentions; but, more fortunate than I usually have been, he escaped the rude peeping and peering of the crowd, for he did not, like his employer, wear "double eyes" (spectacles).

During the last five or six marches, the word Marabu (Arab), instead of Mzungu (European), has usually been applied to me; and no one, I am sure, would have discovered the difference, were it not that the tiresome pagazis, to increase their own dignity and importance, generally gave the clue by singing the song of "the White Man." The Arabs at Unyanyembe had advised my donning their habit for the trip, in order to attract less attention: a vain precaution, which I believe they suggested more to gratify their own vanity by seeing an Englishman lower himself to their position, than for any benefit that I might receive by doing so. At any rate, I was more comfortable and better off in my flannel shirt, long togs, and wide-awake, than I should have been, both mentally and physically, had I degraded myself, and adopted their hot, long, and particularly uncomfortable gown.

Sultan Mahaya sent a messenger to say that he was hurt at the cavalier manner in which I treated him yesterday; and, to show his wounded feelings, gave an order to his subjects that no man should supply me with provisions, or render me any assistance during my sojourn at Muanza. Luckily my larder was well supplied with game, or I should have had to go supperless to bed, for no inducement would prevail on the people to sell anything to me after the mandate had been proclaimed. This morning, however, we settled the difference, in the most amicable manner, thus: previous to my departure for Observatory Hill, I sent the Jemadar, the Kirangozi, and a large deputation of the Beluches and pagazis, to explain away the reason of my having left his house so rudely, and to tender apologies, which were accompanied, as an earnest of good-will, with a large hongo, consisting of one barsati, one dhoti merikani, and one gora kiniki, as also an intimation that I would pay him a visit the next day. This pleased him excessively; it was considered a visit of itself; and he returned the usual bullock, with a notification that I must remain where I was, to enable him to return the compliment I had paid him, for he intended walking out to see me on the morrow.

5th.--As my time was getting short, I forestalled Mahaya in his intentions, and changed ground to the Palace, a rural-looking little place, perched on a small rocky promontory, shrouded by green trees, facing the N.W. side of the lake. Mahaya received me with great courtesy, arranged a hut comfortably, and presented a number of eggs and fresh milk, as he had heard that I was partial to such fare. He is a man of more than ordinary stature, a giant in miniature, with massive and muscular but well-proportioned limbs: he must number fifty years or more. His dress was the ordinary barsati; his arms were set off by heavy brass and copper ornaments encircling the wrists, and by numberless sambo, or thin circles made from the twisted fibres of an aloetic plant, on each of which a single infi, or white porcelain bead resembling a little piece of tobacco-pipe, was strung; these ranged in massive rows down the whole of his upper arm. Just above his elbow-joints sat a pair of large ivory rings. On his forehead two small goat or deer horns were fastened by thin talismanic ornaments of thong for keeping off the evil eye; and, finally, his neck was adorned with two strings of very coarse blue beads. Mahaya has the fame of being the best and most just sultan in these quarters, and his benign square countenance, lit up with a pleasing expression when in conversation, confirms this opinion, though a casual observer passing by that dark, broad, massive face, still more darkened by a matting of short, close, and tightly-curled-up ringlets, would be apt to carry away a contrary impression.[60]

Before leaving Kaze I notified my intention of visiting Ukerewe, supposing I could do so in three or four days, and explained to my men my wishes on this point. Hearing this, they told both Mahaya and Mansur, in direct terms, that I was going, and so needlessly set them to work finessing to show how much they were in earnest in their consideration of me. However, they have both been very warm in dissuading me from visiting Ukerewe, apparently quite in a parental way, for each seems to think himself in a measure my guardian. Mahaya thinks it his duty to caution those who visit him from running into danger, which a journey to Ukerewe, he considers, would be. Mansur, on the other hand, says, as I have come from his Sultan Majid, he also is bound to render me any assistance in his power; but strongly advises my giving up the notion of going across the water. I could get boats from Sukuma, he said, but there would be great delay in the business, as I should have first to send over and ask permission from Machunda to land, and then the collecting men and boats would occupy a long time.

As regards the collection of boats taking a long time, these arguments are very fair, as I know from experience; but the only danger would consist in the circumstance of the two sultans being at enmity with each other, as in this land any one coming direct from an enemy's country is suspected and treated as an enemy. This difficulty I should have avoided by going straight to Sukuma (where the boats, I am inclined to think, usually do start from, though all concur in stating that this is their point of departure), and there obtaining boats direct. However, I told them that I should have gone if I had found boats ready at once to take me across; but now I saw the probability of so much delay, that I could not afford to waste time in trying to obtain boats, which, had I succeeded in getting, I should have employed my time not in going to Ukerewe, but to the more elevated and friendly island of Mzita, this being a more suitable observatory than the former. These negroes' manoeuvres are quite incomprehensible. If Mahaya had desired to fleece me--and one can hardly give a despotic negro credit for anything short of that--he surely would have tried to detain me under false hopes, and have thus necessitated my spending cloths in his village; while, on the contrary, he lost all chance of gaining anything by giving advice which induced me to leave him at once, never to return again to see him.

At my request, Mahaya assembled all his principal men, and we went into a discussion about the lake; but not a soul knew anything about its northern extremity, although people had sometimes travelled in canoes, coasting along its shores by the Karague district to as far, I believe, as the Line.[61] His wife, a pretty crummy little creature of the Wanyoro tribe, came farther from the north than anybody present, and gave me the names of many districts in the Uganda country, which, she says, lies along the seashore. She had never heard of there being any end to the lake, and supposed, if any way of going round it did exist, she would certainly have known it. It is well known that there is no communication between the east and west shores of the lake, excepting by a few occasional canoe-parties coasting along the southern end, because the waters are so very broad they dare not venture.[62] That there can be no high mountain-range intersecting the N'yanza from the watercourses which we hear of north of the equator, as some people have supposed, is evident from the numerous accounts given of the kingdom of Uganda being so flat and marshy from the equator to 2o or 3o north latitude; whilst I must have seen any, did they exist, on the south side of the equator, being only 150 miles from it when standing on its southern shore. Now, judging from all the information given us by the several

Egyptian expeditions and missionaries sent up the Nile, who came across small hills in 4-1/2o north latitude and 32o east longitude, which are intersected by the Nile in the same way that the East Coast Range is intersected by the interior plateau rivers (Lufiji and Kingani), as we saw on our passage inwards from Zanzibar; and further, by the Arabs telling us that all the country on the same meridian, from the Line up to the second parallel north latitude, is flat and full of watercourses; and then again, by knowing the respective heights of the N'yanza on the one side, being nearly 4000 feet, and the Nile's bed in latitude 5o N., or beyond the small hills alluded to, being under 2000 feet--it would indeed be a marvel if this lake is not the fountain of the Nile.[63] The reason why those expeditions sent up the Nile have failed in discovering the N'yanza, is clearly attributable to the important rapids which must exist in consequence of this great variation of altitude between the north end of the N'yanza (which, let us suppose, is on the equator) and the position, in 4o 44' north latitude, at which the expeditions and missions arrived, the rise of the river being 2000 feet in 300 miles.

Indeed, by all accounts of the country lying between the N'yanza, as seen by the Arabs in Uganda, and let us say Gondokoro, a mission station on the Nile, in north latitude 4o 44', which was occupied by two Austrian missionaries, Knoblecher and Dooyak, we find it is somewhat analogous to what we observed between the low Mrima or maritime plain in front of Zanzibar, and the high interior plateau, divided from one another by the East Coast Range, which is of granitic formation, the same in its nature exactly as those which they describe, and intersected by rivers so rapid and boisterous that no canoes can live upon them; as, for instance, we found the Kingani and Lufiji rivers were when passing over the East Coast Range. There the land dropped from 2000 or more feet to less than 300 in the short distance of 100 miles.

I will now proceed to give, first, the missionary account in 4o 44' N., and then the Arab one in 2o N.--a debatable bit of ground, extending over 2o 44', or 160 English miles. Talking of the missionaries, "these two men," says Dr Petermann, "kept an annual hygrometrical and meteorological register with great precision and scientific regularity.[64] They had various instruments with them; they fixed their station, Gondokoro, at 4o 44' north latitude by astronomical observations, and determined the altitude of the Nile's bed to be only 1605 feet above the sea, by numerous good barometrical observations.... Gondokoro is surrounded on three sides by small granitic hills, ranging about 2000 feet high, which are intersected by the Nile coming from the south, as the king of the Bari country says, from 200 to 300 miles;" which is equivalent to saying from the N'yanza, as it lies exactly on the place he directs us to.

As the Arabs do not keep thermometers, scientific instruments, or properly distributed months and seasons, I must say for them that from 2o to 6o south latitude we found the mean temperature in the hottest month, August, to be only 80o; that Uganda must be quite 4000 feet above the sea, to be higher than the lake which it borders; that the rainy season is during our winter months, but most so in the spring; and that the rivers, as we see by the Malagarazi, increase more after than before that date; that as the movement of the rains tends from the southward to the northward, advancing with the sun, the same influence that swells the Malagarazi would also affect the Uganda rivers, as they rise merely on opposite sides of the axis of the same mountains. The Arabs say, as we also have found it, "that thunder accompanies nearly all the storms, and the lightning there is excessive, and so destructive that the King of Uganda expresses the greatest dread of it--indeed his own palace has been often destroyed by lightning. The Kitangule and Katonga rivers are affected by the rainy season in the same proportion as the Malagarazi, and flow north-easterly towards the lake.[65] There the Kivira (island) river (Nile) of which they bring information, flows somewhere to the northward, and is not a slow sluggish stream like the other two, but is rapid and boisterous, showing that the country drops to the northward." Now here, in 3o north latitude, where this river is said to flow with such great rapidity, I think will be found the southern base-line of those small hills, 2000 feet high, lying to the south of Gondokoro, as the missionaries describe them; though these hills, to any one looking at them from the northern side, where the land is low, might appear a barrier to the waters of the lake lying beyond them. This idea would not occur to any one standing on the southern side, where the land is nearly, if not quite, as high as these hills themselves. Indeed, from the levels given, the two countries about Kibuga[66] (Palace of Uganda) and Gondokoro may be described as two landings, with the fall between them representing a staircase formed by the hills in question. The country in latitudes 2o and 5o north is therefore terraced like a hanging garden.[67]

The N'yanza, as we now see, is a large expansive sheet of water, flush with the basial surface of the country, and lies between the Mountains of the Moon (on its western side), having, according to Dr Krapf, snowy Kaenia on its eastern flank. Krapf tells us of a large river flowing down from the western side of this snowy peak, and trending away to the north-west in a direction, as will be seen by the map, leading right into my lake. Now, returning again to the western side, we find that the N'yanza is plentifully supplied by those streams coming from the Lunae Montes, of which the Arabs, one and all, give such consistent and concise accounts; and the flowings of which, being north-easterly, must, in course of time and distance, commingle with those north-westerly off-flowings, before mentioned, of Mount Kaenia. My impression is, after hearing everybody's story on the matter, that these streams enter at opposite sides of the lake, on the northern side of the equator, and are consequently very considerable feeders to it. To help at once in the argument that the N'yanza exists as a large sheet of water to the north of the equator, I will anticipate a story recorded in my diary, by adverting to it before its order of succession. On the return to Unyanyembe, a native of Msalala told me that he had once travelled up the western shore of the N'yanza to the district of Kitara, or Uddu-Uganda, where, he says, coffee grows, and which place, by fair computation of the distances given as their travelling rates, I believe to be in about 1o north lat. To the east of this land, at no great distance from the shore, he described the island of Kitiri as occupied by a tribe called Watiri, who also grow coffee; and there the sea was of such great extent, and when winds blew was so boisterous, that the canoes, although as large as the Tanganyika ones (which he had also seen), did not trust themselves upon it.

The lake has the credit of being very deep, which I cannot believe. It certainly presents the appearance of the temporary deposit of a vast flood overspreading a large flat surface, rather than the usual characteristics of a lake or inland sea lying in a deep hollow, or shut in, like the Tanganyika, by mountains.[68] The islands about it are low hill-tops, standing out like paps on the soft placid bosom of the waters, and are precisely similar to those amongst which I have been travelling; indeed, any part of the country inundated to the same extent would wear the same aspect.

Its water appears, perhaps owing to the disturbing influence of the wind, of a dirty-white colour, but it is very good and sweet, though not so pleasant to my taste as the very clear Tanganyika water. The natives, however, who have wonderfully keen palates for detecting the relative distinctions in such matters, differ from me, and affirm that all the inhabitants prefer it to any other, and consequently never dig wells on the margin of the lake; whereas the Tanganyika water is invariably shunned, nobody ever drinking it unless from necessity; not so much because they consider it to be unwholesome, as because it does not quench or satisfy the thirst so well as spring-water. Whether this peculiarity in the qualities of the waters is to be attributed to the N'yanza lying on a foundation chiefly composed of iron, or whether the one lake is drained by a river, whilst the other is not, I must leave for other and superior talents to decide.

Fish and crocodiles are said to be very abundant in the lake; but with all my endeavours to obtain some specimens, I have succeeded in seeing only two sorts-- one similar to those taken at Ujiji, of a perch-like form, and another very small, re-sembling our common minnow, but not found in the Ujiji market. The quantity of mosquitoes on the borders of the lake is perfectly marvellous; the grass, bushes, and everything growing there, are literally covered with them. As I walked along its shores, disturbing the vegetation, they rose in clouds, and kept tapping, in dozens at a time, against my hands and face, in the most disagreeable manner. Unlike the Indian mosquito, they are of a light dun-brown colour. The Muanza dogs are the largest that I have yet seen in Africa, and still are not more than twenty inches high; but Mahaya says the Ukerewe dog is a fine animal, and quite different from any on the mainland. There are very few canoes about here, and those are of miserable construction, and only fitted for the purpose they turn them to--catching fish close to the shore. The paddle the fishermen use is a sort of mongrel between a spade and a shovel. The fact of there being no boats of any size here, must be attributed to the want of material for constructing them. On the route from Kaze there are no trees of any girth, save the calabash, the wood of which is too soft for boat-building. I hear that the island of Ukerewe has two sultans besides Machunda, and that it is very fertile and populous. Mahaya says, "All the tribes, from the Wasukuma (or Northern Wanyamuezi, Sukuma meaning the north), along the south and east of the lake, are so savage and inhospitable to travellers, that it would be impossible to go amongst them unless accompanied by a large and expensive escort."

6th.--As no further information about the lake could be gained, I bade Mahaya and the Sheikh adieu, leaving as a token of recollection one shukka merikani for the former, one dhoti kiniki for his wife, and a fundo of beads for the poor Arab, and retraced my steps by a double march back to Ukumbi. Whilst passing alongside the archipelago, I shot two geese and a crested crane. What a pity it seemed I could not pluck the fruit almost within my grasp! Had I had but a little more time, and a few loads of beads, I could with ease have crossed the Line, and settled every question which we had come all this distance to ascertain. Indeed, to perform that work, nobody could have started under more advantageous circumstances than were then within my power--all hands being in first-rate condition and health, and all in the right temper for it. But now a new and expensive expedition must be formed, for the capabilities of the country on the eastern flank of the Mountains of the Moon, and along the western shores of the N'yanza, are so notoriously great that it is worthy of serious attention. My reluctance to return may be easier imagined than described. I felt as much tantalised as the unhappy Tantalus must have been when unsuccessful in his bobbings for cherries in the cherry-orchard, and as much grieved as any mother would be at losing her first-born, and resolved and planned forthwith to do everything that lay in my power to visit the lake again.

7th.--We made a march of fourteen miles, passing our second station in Urima by two miles, partly to avoid the chief of that village, a testy, rude, and disagreeable man, who, on the last occasion, inhospitably tried to turn us out of a hut in his village, because we would not submit to his impudent demand of a cloth for the accommodation--a proceeding quite at variance with anything we had met in our former receptions; and we resisted the imposition with a pertinacity equal to his own. Besides this, by coming on the little extra distance, we arrived at the best and cheapest place for purchasing cows and jembies.

8th.--Halt. I purchased two jembies for one shukka merikani, but could not come to any terms with these grasping savages about their cows, although their country teems with them, and they are sold at wonderfully cheap prices to ordinary traders. They would not sell to me unless I gave double value for them. The fauna of this country is most disappointing. Nearly all the animals that exist here are also to be found in the south of Africa, where they range in far greater numbers. But then we must remember that a caravan route usually takes the more fertile and populous tracks, and that many animals might be found in the recesses of the forests not far off, although there are so few on the line. The elephants are finer here than in any part of the world, and have been known to carry tusks exceeding 500 lb. the pair in weight. The principal wild animals besides these are the lion, leopard, hyena, fox, pig, Cape buffalo, gnu, kudu, hartebeest, pallah, steinboc, and the little madoka, or Saltiana gazelle. The giraffe, zebra, rhinoceros, and hippopotamus are all common. The game-birds are the bustard, florikan, guinea-fowl, partridge, quail, snipe, various geese and ducks, and a very dark-coloured rock-pigeon or sand-grouse. The birds in general have very tame plumage, and are much more scarce, generally speaking, than one finds in most other countries.

The traveller on entering these agricultural districts meets with a treatment quite opposite to what he does from the pastoral tribes, such, for instance, as the Somali, Gallas, Masai, &c. &c. Here they at once hail his advent as a matter of good omen, or the precursor of good fortune, and allow him to do and see whatever he likes. They desire his settling amongst them, appreciate the benefits of commerce and civilisation, and are not suspicious, like the plundering pastorals, of every one coming with evil intentions towards them. The Somali, about as bad a lot as any amongst the rovers, will not admit a stranger into their country, unless accompanied by one of their tribe, who becomes answerable for the traveller's actions, and even with this passport he is watched with the eyes of Argus. Every strange act committed by him, no matter how simple, absurd, or trifling, is at once debated about in council, and always ends to Viator's disadvantage.

They add to everything they see or hear, by conjuring up the most ridiculous phantoms; and the more ridiculous they are, the more firmly do they at last believe in them themselves. The worse their grounds are, the more jealously do they guard against anybody's seeing them; and woe betide any one who should frequent any particular spot too often: he is at once set down as designing a plot against it, to fortify the place and take it from them; this idea is their greatest bugbear. Among that tribe blood shed by any means--by the stealthy knife or in fair fight--is deemed meritorious and an act of heroism. No one is ever sure of his life unless he has force to carry him through, or can rely on the chief of the clan as his pillar of safety. This latter plan is probably the safer one, for, as the old adage goes, "There is honour amongst thieves;" so with these savages it is a matter of importance to their honour and dignity, according to their quaint notions of rectitude, to protect their trust to their utmost; whereas, on the contrary, were that trust not reposed in them, they would feel justified in taking any liberties, or act in opposition to any of those general laws which guide the conduct of civilised men.

I would not, however, desire the African agricultural people to be considered models of perfection. Individually, or in small bodies, the mass of them are very far from being so, for they would commit any excesses without the slightest feelings of compunction. The fear of retribution alone keeps their hands from blood and plunder. The chiefs and principal men, if they have no higher motives, keep their different tribes in order, and do not molest travellers without good cause, or from provocation, as they know that protecting the traveller is the only way in which they can keep up that connection with the commerce of the coast which they all so much covet. It may be worthy of remark that I have always found the lighter-coloured savages more boisterous and warlike than those of a dingier hue. The ruddy black, fleshy-looking Wazaramo and Wagogo are much lighter in colour than any of the other tribes, and certainly have a far superior, more manly and warlike independent spirit and bearing than any of the others.[69]

9th.--We started early, and crossed the Jordans by a ferry at a place lower down than on the first occasion. After leaving the low land, we rose up to the higher ground where we had first gained a sight of the N'yanza's waters, and now took our final view. To myself the parting with it was a matter of great regret; but I believe I was the sole sufferer from disappointment in being obliged to go south, when all my thoughts or cares were in the north. But this feeling was much alleviated by seeing the happy, contented, family state to which the whole caravan had at length arrived. Going home has the same attraction with these black people that it has with schoolboys. The Beluches have long since behaved to admiration, and now even the lazy pagazis, since completing their traffic, have lighter hearts, and begin to feel a freshness dawn upon them. We soon entered our old village in Nera, having completed fourteen miles. Here the chief, who had travelled up the western shore of the N'yanza, assured me that canoes like the Tanganyika ones were used by the natives, and were made from large trees which grew on the mountain-slopes overlooking the lake. The disagreeable-mannered Wasukuma (or north men) are now left behind; their mode of articulation is most painful to the civilised ear. Each word uttered seems to begin with a T'hu or T'ha, producing a sound like that of spitting sharply at an offensive object. Any stranger with his back turned would fancy himself insulted by the speaker.

The country throughout is well stocked with cattle, and bullocks are cheap, two dhotis, equal to four dollars, being the price of a moderate-sized animal; but milch cows are dear, in consequence of the great demand for sour curd. Sheep and goats sell according to their skills; a large one is preferred to a shukka, equal to one dollar; but a dhoti, the proper price of three small goats, is scarcely the value of the largest. The bane of this people is their covetousness. They do not object to sell cheaply to a poor man, yet they hang back at the sight of much cloth, and price their stock, not at its value, but at what they want, or think they may get, obstinately abiding by their decision to the last. Cattle are driven from this to Unyanyembe, and consequently must be cheaper here than in those more southern parts: still I could not purchase them so well; indeed, a traveller can never expect to buy at a reasonable rate in a land where every man is a sultan, and his hut a castle--where no laws regulate the market, and every proprietor is grasping. Bombay suggests that to buy cattle cheap from the Washenzi (savages), you should give them plenty of time to consider the advantages and disadvantages of the transaction, for their minds are not capable of arriving at a rapid conclusion; but friend Bombay forgets that, whilst waiting to beat them down a cloth or two, four or five are consumed by the caravan in waiting. The women, especially the younger ones, are miserably clad here; a fringe, like the thong kilt of the Nubian maidens, made of aloe fibres, with a single white bead at the end of each string, is the general wear; it is suspended by a strap tied round the waist. Hanging over the belly, it covers about a foot of **ground** in breadth, but not more than seven or eight inches in depth. The fibrous strings, white by nature, soon turn black, and look like India-rubber, the effect of butter first rubbed in, and then of constant friction on the grimy person. The dangling, waving motion of this strange appendage, as the wearer moves along, reminded me of the common fly-puzzler sometimes attached to horses' head-stalls. Amongst a crowd of fifty or sixty people, not more than two or three have a cloth of native make, and rarely one of foreign manufacture is to be seen. Some women have stood before me in the very primitive costume of a bunch of leafy twigs.

But far worse clad than these are the Wataturu, a tribe living to the eastward, and the Watuta, living to the westward of this place, besides the Warori and others.

Of the first mentioned, the Wataturu, a people living a little to the northward of Turu, I have only seen a few males, and they were stark naked. The Wataturu despise any one who is weak enough to cover his person, considering that he does so only to conceal his natural imperfections. Their women are currently reported to be as naked as the men, but I did not see any of them, and cannot vouch for it.

The Watuta, on the other hand, require a special notice, because they are the naked Zulu Kafirs whose peculiar costume, if such it may be called, has caused so much risibility at the Cape of Good Hope. In the very first instance, I am inclined to believe these Watuta were Cushites, who migrated from the shores of the Caspian Sea, across Arabia and the Red Sea, to Abyssinia. There, mixing with the negro aborigines, they became in process of time woolly-headed. Later still, they broke off from the parent stock, lost their original name, and took instead that of Masai. By some unaccountable means they then separated from the Masai and migrated south to the Cape of Good Hope; here they appear to have changed their name to Kafir, from which a branch of the tribe were called Zulu Kafirs. These Zulu Kafirs becoming restless, after a time migrated again to the west of the Nyassa, and there settled with their flocks and herds, devastating the Babisa's country. From thence again they have been migrating in detachments north, up the east side of the Tanganyika Lake. Whilst doing so they came at Fipa on the Wapoka, another offshoot of the Cushite-Abyssinians, who, crossing the Nile, took the name of Wahuma, and have spread as far down south as Fipa, where their name, in course of time, had changed from Wahuma to Watusi, and from Watusi to Wapoka, in the same way as the Watuta had changed their name from Masai to Kafir and Zulu Kafir, and again from that to Watuta. Now, these Watuta are still pushing northwards, fighting, plundering, and conquering wherever they go. They have knocked the Watusi out of the southern hills of Urundi, overlooking the Tanganyika Lake, and have spread to the southern limits of Usui, devastating the countries *en route*, in the same way as they have done on the west of the Nyassa. Strange as it may appear, neither these Watuta nor the Watusi know anything of their common origin. They are very different in physical form and appearance from one another; for, whilst the Watusi *alias* Wahuma retain their Abyssinian type, the Watuta *alias* Zulu Kafirs are much more like the Somali and Masai--thus, I think, showing that the Wahuma have detached themselves at a later period than the Kafirs from the parent stock. The Wahuma are certainly the finer-looking people of the two, but the Watuta are rougher in nature. Both, however, are strictly pastoral, though the Wahuma in the equatorial regions affect to maintain large kingdoms.[70]

It is to be hoped that India, when once aroused to the advantages of dealing more extensively with this country, will never lose sight of the fact that the negro as well as more enlightened man can detect the difference between good and poor stuffs; that the nation which makes the strongest stuffs will be considered to be the honestest; and the more lasting the material, the more readily it will be taken. In sending cloths great care should be taken that every piece be of the same length, and always evenly divisible by cubits, or eighteen-inch measure. If the Lion and the Unicorn, figuring on the outside of each piece--Than or Gora, as it is called respectively in India and Africa--were security of its being English manufacture, and, by being so, sure to be of uniform quality and size, much respect would be given to it; and "Shukka Anglesi" (English shukka) would soon take the place of "merikani," which are by different mills, and of different lengths and qualities. The only reason for the negro taking a large goat-skin in preference to a shukka, is because it is stronger.

On coming here I had the misfortune to make my donkey over to Bombay, to save his foot, which had been galled by too constant walking; for though unable to ride, he was too proud to say nay, and was therefore placed upon it, carrying the gun consigned to his charge, Captain Burton's smooth elephant. Now Bombay rode much after the fashion of a sailor, trusting more to balance and good-luck than skill in sticking on; and the consequence was, that with the first side-step the donkey made he came to the ground an awkward cropper, falling heavily on the small of the stock of the gun, which snapped short off, the piece being thus irredeemably damaged. At first I rated him heartily, for this was the second of Captain Burton's guns which had been damaged in my hands. I then told Bombay of the circumstances which led to the accident to the first gun. It occurred whilst hippopotamus-shooting on the coast rivers opposite to Zanzibar; and as Bombay had a little experience in that way to relate, we had long yarns about such sport, which served to improve our Hindustani (the language I always conversed with him in), as well as to divert our useless yet unavoidable feelings of regret at the accident, and also killed time.

One day, when on the Tanga river near its mouth, I was busily engaged teasing hippopotami, with one man, a polesman, in a very small canoe, just capable of carrying what it had on board, myself in the bows, with my 4-bore Blissett in hand, while Captain Burton's monster elephant-gun, a double-barrelled 6-bore, weighing, I believe, 20 lb., was lying at the stern in the poler's charge.

The river was a tidal one, of no great breadth, and the margin was covered by a thick growth of the mangrove shrub, on the boughs of which the sharp-edged shells of the tree-oyster stuck in strings and clusters in great numbers. The best time to catch the hippopotamus is when the tide is out and the banks are bared, for then you find him wallowing in the mud or basking on the sand (when there is any), like jungle-hog, and with a well-directed shot on the ear, or anywhere about the brain-pan, you have a good chance of securing him. I especially mention this, as it is quite labour in vain, in places where the water is deep, to fire at these animals, unless you can kill them outright, as they dive under like a water-rat, and are never seen more if they are only wounded. I, like most raw hands at this particular kind of sport, began in a very different way from what, I think, a more experienced hunter would have done, by chasing them in the water, and firing at their heads whenever they appeared above it; and even fired slugs about their eyes and ears, in hopes that I might irritate them sufficiently to make them charge the canoe. This teasing proved pretty successful; for when the tide had run clean out, only pools and reaches, connecting by shallow runnels the volume of the natural stream, remained for the hippopotami to sport about in; and my manoeuvring in these confined places became so irritating, that a large female came rapidly under water to the stern of the canoe, and gave it such a sudden and violent cant with her head or withers, that that end of the vessel shot up in the air, and sent me sprawling on my back, with my legs forced up by the seat--a bar of wood--at right angles to my body; whilst the poler and the big double gun were driven like a pair of shuttlecocks, flying right and left of the canoe high up into the air.

The gun on one side fell plump into the middle of the stream, and the man on the other dropped, *post* first, on to the hippopotamus's back, but rapidly scrambled back into the canoe. The hippopotamus then, as is these animals' wont, renewed the attack, but I was ready to receive her, and as she came rolling porpoise-fashion close by the side of the canoe, I fired a quarter of a pound of lead, backed by four drams of powder, into the middle of her back, the muzzle of the rifle almost touching it. She then sank, and I never saw her more; but the gun (after lying on the sandy bottom the whole of that night), I managed, by the aid of several divers, to find on the following day.

Bombay says that on one occasion, when coming down the Pangani river in a canoe with several other men, an irritated hippopotamus charged and upset it, upon which he and all his friends dived under water and then swam to the shore, leaving the hippopotamus to vent his rage on the shell of the canoe, which he most spitefully stuck to. This, he assures me, is the proper way to dodge a hippopotamus, and escape the danger of a bite from him. On another occasion, when I was hippopotamus-hunting in one of the boats of the Artemise, in an inlet of the sea close to Kaole, I chased a herd of hippopotami in deep water, till one of the lot, coming as usual from below, drove a tusk clean through the boat with such force that he partially hoisted her out of the water; but the brute did no further damage, for I kept him off by making the men splash their oars rapidly whilst making for the shore, where we just arrived in time to save ourselves from sinking.

The day previous to this adventure, I bagged a fine young male hippopotamus close to this spot, by hitting him on the ear when standing in shallow water. The ivory of these animals is more prized than that of the elephant, and, in consequence of the superior hardness of its enamel, it is in great requisition with the dentist.

Hippopotami are found all down this coast in very great numbers, but especially in the deltas of the rivers, or up the streams themselves, and afford an easy, remunerative, and pleasant sport to any man who is not addicted to much hard exercise. The Panjani, Kingani, and Lufiji rivers are full of them, as well as all the other minor feeders to the sea along that coast. If these animals happen to be killed in places so far distant from the sea that the tidal waters have not power to draw them out to the ocean depths, their bodies will be found, when inflated with gas, after decomposition, floating on the surface of the water a day or two afterwards, and can easily be secured by the sportsman, if he be vigilant enough to take them before the hungry watchful savages come and secure them, to appease their rapacious appetites. Mussulmans will even eat these amphibious creatures without cutting their throats, looking on them as cold-blooded animals, created in the same manner as fish.

The following day, 10th August, we made a halt to try our fortune again in purchasing cows, but failed as usual; so the following morning we decamped at dawn, and marched thirteen miles to our original station in Southern Nera. Here I purchased four goats for one dhoti merikani, the best bargain I ever made. Thunder had rumbled, and clouds overcast the skies for two days; and this day a delicious cooling shower fell. The people said it was the little rains--*chota barsat*, as we call it in India--expected yearly at this time, as the precursor of the later great falls.

As Seedi Bombay was very inquisitive to-day about the origin of Seedis, his caste, and as he wished to know by what law of nature I accounted for their cruel destiny in being the slaves of all men, I related the history of Noah, and the dispersion of his sons on the face of the globe; and showed him that he was of the black or Hametic stock, and by the common order of nature, they, being the weakest, had to succumb to their superiors, the Japhetic and Semitic branches of the family; and, moreover, they were likely to remain so subject until such time as the state of man, soaring far above the beast, would be imbued by a better sense of sympathy and good feeling, and would then leave all such ungenerous appliances of superior force to the brute. Bombay, on being made a Mussulman by his Arab master, had received a very different explanation of the degradation of his race, and narrated his story as follows:--"The Arabs say that Mahomet, whilst on the road from Medina to Mecca, one day happened to see a widow woman sitting before her house, and asked her how she and her three sons were; upon which the troubled woman (for she had concealed one of her sons on seeing Mahomet's approach, lest he, as is customary when there are three males of a family present, should seize one and make him do porterage), said, 'Very well; but I've only two sons.' Mahomet, hearing this, said to the woman, reprovingly, 'Woman, thou liest; thou hast three sons and for trying to conceal this matter from me, henceforth remember that this is my decree--that the two boys which thou hast not concealed shall multiply and prosper, have fair faces, become wealthy, and reign lords over all the earth; but the progeny of your third son shall, in consequence of your having concealed him, produce Seedis as black as darkness, who will be sold in the market like cattle, and remain in perpetual servitude to the descendants of the other two."

12th.--We returned to our former quarters, the village of Salawe; but I did not enjoy such repose as on the former visit, for the people were in their cups, and, *no-*

lens volens, persisted in entering my hut. Sometimes I rose and drove them out, at other times I turned round and feigned to sleep; but these manoeuvres were of no avail; still they poured in, and one old man, more impudent than the rest, understanding the trick, seized my pillow by the end, and, tugging at it as a dog pulls at a quarter of horse, roused me with loud impatient "Whu-hu" and "Hi, hi's," until at last, out of patience, I sent my boots whirling at his head. This cleared the room, but only for a moment: the boisterous, impudent crowd, true to savage nature, enjoying the annoyance they had occasioned, returned exultingly, with shouts and grins, in double numbers.

The Beluches then interfered, and, in their zeal to keep order, irritated some drunkards, who at once became pugnacious. On seeing the excited state of these drunkards, bawling and stepping about in long, sudden, and rapid strides, with brandished spears and agitated bows, endeavouring to exasperate the rest of the mob against us, I rose, and going out before them, said that I came forth for their satisfaction, and that they might now stand and gaze as long as they liked; but I hoped, as soon as their legs and arms were tired, that they would depart in peace. The words acted with magical effect upon them; they urgently requested me to retire again, but finding that I did not, they took themselves homewards. The sultan arrived late in the evening, he said from a long distance, on purpose to see me, and was very importunate in his desire for my halting a day. As I had paid all the other sultans the compliment of a visit, he should consider it a slight if I did not stay a little while with him. On the occasion of my passing northwards he had been absent, and could not entertain me; so I must now accept a bullock, which he would send for on the morrow. A long debate ensued, which ended by my giving him one shukka merikani and one dhoti kiniki.

13th.--Travelling through the Nindo Wilderness to-day, the Beluches were very much excited at the quantity of game they saw; but though they tried their best, they did not succeed in killing any. Troops of zebras, and giraffe, some varieties of antelopes roaming about in large herds, a buffalo and one ostrich, were the chief visible tenants of this wild. We saw the fresh prints of a very large elephant; and I have no doubt that by any sportsman, if he had but leisure to learn their haunts and watering-places, a good account might be made of them--but one and all are wild in the extreme. Ostrich-feathers bedeck the frizzly polls of many men and women, but no one has ever heard of any having been killed or snared by huntsmen. These ornaments, as well as the many skulls and skins seen in every house, are said to be found lying about in places where the animals have died a natural death.

14th.--We left, as we did yesterday, an hour before dawn, and crossed the second broad wilderness to Kahama. At 9 A.M. I called the usual halt to eat my rural breakfast of cold fowl, sour curd, cakes, and eggs, in a village on the south border of the desert. As the houses were devoid of all household commodities, I asked the people stopping there to tend the fields to explain the reason, and learnt that their fear of the plundering Wamanda was such that they only came there during the day to look after their crops, and at night they retired to some distant place of safe retreat in the jungles, where they stored all their goods and chattels. These people, in time of war, thus putting everything useful out of the way of the forager's prying eyes, it is very seldom that blood is spilt. This country being full of sweet springs, accounts for the denseness of the population and numberless herds of cattle. To look upon its resources, one is struck with amazement at the waste of the world: if instead of this district being in the hands of its present owners, it were ruled by a few scores of Europeans, what an entire revolution a few years would bring forth! An extensive market would be opened to the world, the present nakedness of the land would have a covering, and industry and commerce would clear the way for civilisation and enlightenment.

At present the natural inert laziness and ignorance of the people is their own and their country's bane. They are all totally unaware of the treasures at their feet. This dreadful sloth is in part engendered by the excessive bounty of the land in its natural state; by the little want of clothes or other luxuries, in consequence of the congenial temperature; and from the people having no higher object in view than the first-coming meal, and no other stimulus to exertion by example or anything else. The great cause, however, is their want of a strong protecting government to preserve peace, without which nothing can prosper. Thus they are, both morally and physically, little better than brutes, and as yet there is no better prospect in store for them. The climate is a paradox quite beyond my solving, unless the numerous and severe maladies that we all suffered from, during the first eight months of our explorations, may be attributed to too much exposure; and even that does not solve the problem. To all appearance, the whole of the country to the westward of the East Coast Range is high, dry, and healthy. No unpleasant exhalations pollute the atmosphere; there are no extremes of temperature; the air is neither too hot nor too cold; and a little care in hutting, dressing, and diet should obviate any evil effects of exposure. Springs of good water, and wholesome food, are everywhere obtainable. Flies and mosquitoes, the great Indian pests, are scarcely known, and the tsetse of the south nowhere exists. During the journey northwards, I always littered down in a hut at night; but the ticks bit me so hard, and the anxiety to catch stars between the constantly-fleeting clouds, to take their altitudes, perhaps preying on my mind, kept me many whole nights consecutively without obtaining even as much as one wink of sleep--a state of things I had once before suffered from. But there really was no assignable cause for this, unless weakness or feverishness could create wakefulness, and then it would seem surprising that even during the day, or after much fatigue, I rarely felt the slightest inclination to close my eyes. Now, on returning, without anything to excite the mind, and having always pitched the tent at night, I enjoyed cooler nights and perfect rest. Of diseases, the more common are remittent and intermittent fevers, and these are the most important ones to avoid, since they bring so many bad effects after them. In the first place, they attack the brain, and often deprive one of his senses. Then there is no rallying from the weakness they produce. A little attack, which one would only laugh at in India, prostrates you for a week or more, and this weakness brings on other disorders: cramp, for instance, of the most painful kind, very often follows. When lying in bed, my toes have sometimes curled round and looked me in the face; at other times, when I have put my hand behind my back, it has stuck there until, with the other hand, I have seized the contracted muscles, and warmed the part affected with the natural heat, till, relaxation taking place, I was able to get it back. Another nasty thing is the blindness which I have already described, and which attacked another of our party in a manner exactly similar to my complaint. He, like myself, left Africa with a misty veil floating before his eyes.

There are other disorders, but so foreign to my experience that I dare not venture to describe them. For as doctors disagree about the probable causes of their appearance, I most likely would only mislead if I tried to account for them. However, I think I may safely say they emanate from general debility, produced by the much-to-be-dreaded fevers.

15th.--The caravan broke ground at 4 P.M., and, completing the principal zig-zag made to avoid wars, arrived at Senagongo. Kanoni, followed by a host of men, women, and children, advanced to meet the caravan, all roaringly intoxicated with joy, and lavishing greetings of welcome, with showers of "Yambo, Yambo Sanas" ("How are you?" and, "Very well, I hope?") which we as warmly returned: the shakings of hands were past number, and the Beluches and Bombay could scarcely be seen under the hot embraces and sharp kisses of admiring damsels. When recovered from the shock of this great outburst of feelings, Kanoni begged me to fire a few shots, to apprise his enemies, and especially his big brother, of the honours paid him. No time was lost: I no sooner gave the order than bang, bang went every one of the escort's guns, and the excited crowd, immediately seeing a supposed antagonist in the foreground, rushed madly after him. Then spears were flourished, thrust, stabbed, and withdrawn; arrows were pointed, huge shields protected black bodies, sticks and stones flew like hail; then there was a slight retreat, then another advance--dancing to one side, then to the other--jumping and prancing on the same ground, with bodies swaying here and bodies swaying there, until at length the whole foreground was a mass of moving objects, all springs and hops, like an army of frogs, after the first burst of rain, advancing to a pond: then again the guns went off, giving a fresh impulse to the exciting exercise.

Their great principle in their warfare appears to be, that no one should be still. At each report of the guns, fresh enemies were discovered retreating, and the numbers of their slain were quite surprising. These, as they dropped, were, with highly dramatic action, severally and immediately trampled down and knelt upon, and hacked and chopped repeatedly with knives, whilst the slayer continued showing his savage wrath by worrying his supposed victim with all the angry energy that dogs display when fighting. This triumphal entry over, Kanoni led us into his boma, and treated us with sour curd. Then, at my request, he assembled his principal men and greatest travellers to debate upon the N'yanza. One old man, shrivelled by age, stated that he had travelled up the western shores of the N'yanza two moons (sixty days) consecutively, had passed beyond Karague into a country where coffee grows abundantly, and is called Muanye. He described the shrub as standing between two and three feet high, having the stem nearly naked, but much branched above; it grows in large plantations, and forms the principal article of food. The people do not boil and drink it as we do, but eat the berry raw, with its husk on. The Arabs are very fond of eating these berries raw, and have often given us some. They bring them down from Uganda, where, for a pennyworth of beads, a man can have his fill.

When near these coffee plantations, he (our informer) visited an island on the lake, called Kitiri, occupied by the Watiri, a naked lot of beings, who subsist almost entirely on fish and coffee. The Watiri go about in large canoes like the Tanganyika ones; but the sea-travelling, he says, is very dangerous. In describing the boisterous nature of the lake, he made a rumbling, gurgling noise in his throat, which he increased and diversified by pulling and tapping at the skin covering the apple, and by puffing and blowing with great vehemence indicated extraordinary roughness of the elements. The sea itself, he said, was boundless. Kanoni now told me that the Muingira Nullah lies one day's journey N.N.W. of this, and drains the western side of the Msalala district into the southern end of the N'yanza creek. It is therefore evident that those extensive lays in the Nindo and Salawe districts which we crossed extend down to this periodical river, which accounts for there being so many wild animals there: water being such an attractive object in these hot climes, all animals group round it. Kanoni is a dark, square, heavy-built man, very fond of imbibing pombe, and, like many tipplers, overflowing with human-kindness, especially in his cups. He kept me up several hours to-night, trying to induce me to accept a bullock, and to eat it in his boma, in the same manner as I formerly did with his brother. He was much distressed because I would not take the half of my requirements in cattle from him, instead of devoting everything to his brother Kurua; and not till I assured him I could not stay, but instead would leave Bombay and some Beluches with cloth to purchase some cows from his people, would he permit of my turning in to rest. It is strange to see how very soon, when questioning these negroes about anything relating to geography, their weak brains give way, and they can answer no questions, or they become so evasive in their replies, or so rambling, that you can make nothing out of them. It is easily discernible at what time you should cease to ask any further questions; for their heads then roll about like a ball upon a wire, and their eyes glass over and look vacantly about as though vitality had fled from their bodies altogether. Bombay, though, is a singular exception to this rule; but then, by long practice, he has become a great geographer, and delights in pointing out the different features on my map to his envying neighbours.

16th.--We came to Mgogua this morning, and were received by Kurua with his usual kind affability. Our entrance to his boma was quiet and unceremonious, for we came there quite unexpectedly--hardly giving him time to prepare his musket and return our salute. Though we were allowed a ready admission, a guinea-fowl I shot on the way was not. The superstitious people forbade its entrance in full plumage, so it was plucked before being brought inside the palisade. Kurua again arranged a hut for my residence, and was as assiduous as ever in his devotion to my comforts. All the elders of the district soon arrived, and the usual debates commenced. Kurua chiefly trades with Karague and the northern kingdoms, but no one could add to the information I had already obtained. One of his men stated that he had performed the journey between Pangani on the east coast of Africa and the N'yanza three times, in about two months each time. The distance was very great for the little time it took him; but then he had to go for his life the whole way, in consequence of the Masai, or Wahuma, as some call them, being so inimical to strangers of any sort that he dare not stop or talk anywhere on the way.[71] On leaving Pangani, he passed through Usumbara, and entered on the country of the warring nomadic race, the Masai; through their territories he travelled without halting until he arrived at Usukuma, bordering on the lake. His fear and speed were such that he did not recognise any other tribes or countries besides those enumerated.

Wishing to ascertain what number of men a populous country like this could produce in case of an attack, and to gain some idea of savage tactics, I proposed having a field-day. Kurua was delighted with the idea, and began roaring and laughing about it with his usual boisterous energy, to the great admiration of all the company. The programme was as follows:--At 3 P.M. on the 17th, Kurua and his warriors, all habited and drawn up in order of battle, were to occupy the open space in front of the village, whilst my party of Beluches, suddenly issuing from the village, would personate the enemy and commence the attack. This came off at the appointed time, and according to orders the forces were drawn up, and an engagement ensued. The Beluches, rushing through the passages of the palisaded village, suddenly burst upon the enemy, and fired and charged successively; to which the Wamanda replied with equal vigour, advancing with their frog-like leaps and bounds, dodging and squatting, and springing and flying in the most wild and fantastic manner; stabbing with their spears, protecting with their shields, poising with bows and arrows pointed, and, mingling with the Beluches, rushed about striking at and avoiding their guns and sabres. But all was so similar to the Senagongo display that it does not require a further description. The number of Kurua's forces disappointed me,--I fear the intelligence of the coming parade did not reach far. The dresses they wore did credit to their nation--some were decked with cock-tail plumes, others wore bunches of my guinea-fowl's feathers in their hair, whilst the chiefs and swells were attired in long red baize mantles, consisting of a strip of cloth four feet by twenty inches, at one end of which they cut a slit to admit the head, and allowed the remainder to hang like a tail behind the back. Their spears and bows are of a very ordinary kind, and the shield is constructed something like the Kafir's, from a long strip of bull's hide, which is painted over with ochreish earth. The fight over, all hands rushed to the big drums in the cow-yard, and began beating them as though they deserved a drubbing: this "sweet music" set everybody on wires in a moment, and dancing never ceased till the sun went down, and the cows usurped the revelling-place. Kurua now gave me a good milch cow and calf, and promised two more of the same stamp. Those which were brought by the common people were mere weeds, and dry withal; they would not bring any good ones, I think, from fear of the sultan's displeasure, lest I should prefer theirs to his, and deprive him of the consequent profits. My chief reason for leaving Bombay behind at Senagongo was, that business was never done when I was present. For, besides staring at me all day, the people speculated how to make the most of the chance offered by a rich man coming so suddenly amongst them, and in consequence of this avariciousness offered their cattle at such unreasonable prices as to preclude the transaction of any business.

18th.--Halt. My anticipations about the way of getting cows proved correct, for Bombay brought twelve animals, which cost twenty-three dhotis merikani and nine dhotis kiniki. Kurua now gave me another cow and calf, and promised me two more when we arrived at the Ukumbi district, as he did not like thinning one herd too much. I gave in return for his present one barsati, five dhotis merikani and two dhotis kiniki, with a promise of some gunpowder when we arrived at Unyanyembe, for he was still bent on going there with me. Perhaps I may consider my former obstruction in travel by Kurua a fortunate circumstance; for though the eldest brother's residence lay directly in my way, he might not possess so kind a nature as these two younger brothers.

Still I cannot see any good reason for the Kirangozi abandoning the proper road: there certainly could be no more danger on the one side than on the other, and all would have been equally glad to have had me. It is true that I should have had to pass through his enemies' hands to the other brother, and such a course usually excites suspicion; but, by the usual custom of the country, Kurua should have been treated by him only as a rebellious subject, for though all three brothers were by different mothers, they are considered in line of succession as ours are, when legitimately begotten by one mother. Some time ago the eldest brother made a tool of an Arab trader, and with that force on his side threatened these two brothers with immediate destruction unless they resigned to him the entire government, and his rights as senior. They admitted in his presence the justness of his words and the folly of waging war, as such a measure could only bring destruction on all alike; but on his departure they carried on their rule as before.

Bombay, talking figuratively with me, considers Kurua's stopping me something like the use the monkey turned the cat's paw to; that is, he stopped me simply to enhance his dignity, and gain the minds of the people by leading them to suppose I saw justice in his actions. Pombe-brewing, the chief occupation of the women, is as regular here as the revolution of day and night, and the drinking of it just as constant. It is prepared from bajeri and jowari (common millets): the first step in the manufacture is malting in the same way as we do barley; then they range a double street of sticks, usually in the middle of the village, fill a number of pots with these grains mixed in water, which they place in continuous line down the street of sticks, and, setting fire to the whole at once, boil away until the mess is fit to put aside for refining: this they then do, leaving the pots standing three days, when fermentation takes place and the liquor is fit to drink. It has the strength of labourers' beer, and both sexes drink it alike. This fermented beverage resembles pig-wash, but is said to be so palatable and satisfying--for the dregs and all are drunk together--that many entirely subsist upon it. It is a great help to the slave-masters, for without it they could get nobody to till their ground; and when the slaves are required to turn the earth, the master always sits in judgment with lordly dignity, generally under a tree, watching to see who becomes entitled to a drop.

In the evening my attention was attracted by small processions of men and women, possessed of the Phepo, or demon, passing up the palisaded streets, turning into the different courts, and paying each and every house by turns a visit. The party advanced in slow funereal order, with gently springing, mincing, jogging action, some holding up twigs, others balancing open baskets of grain and tools on their heads, and with their bodies, arms, and heads in unison with the whole hobbling-bobling motion, kept in harmony to a low, mixed, droning, humming chorus. As the sultan's door was approached, he likewise rose, and, mingling in the crowd, performed the same evolutions.

This kind of procession is common at Zanzibar: when any demoniacal possessions take place among the blacks, it is by this means they cast out devils. While on the subject of superstition, it may be worth mentioning what long ago struck me as a singular instance of the effect of supernatural impression on the uncultivated mind. During boyhood my old nurse used to tell me with great earnestness of a wonderful abortion shown about in the *fairs* of England--a child born with a pig's head; and as solemnly declared that this freak of nature was attributable to the child's mother having taken fright at a pig when in the interesting stage. The case I met in this country was still more far-fetched, for the abortion was supposed to be producible by indirect influence on the wife of the husband taking fright. On once shooting a pregnant doe waterboc, I directed my native huntsman, a married man, to dissect her womb and expose the embryo; but he shrank from the work with horror, fearing lest the sight of the kid, striking his mind, should have an influence on his wife's future bearing, by metamorphosing her progeny to the likeness of a fawn.

19th.--We bade Kurua adieu in the early morning, as a caravan of his had just arrived from Karague, and appointed to meet at the second station, as marching with cattle would be slow work for him. Our march lasted nine miles. The succeeding day we passed Ukumbi, and arrived at Uyombo. On the way I was obliged to abandon one of the donkeys, as he was completely used up. This made up our thirty-second loss in asses since leaving Zanzibar. My load of beads was now out, and I had to purchase rations with cloth--a necessary measure, but not economical, for the cloth does not go half as far as beads of the same value. I have remarked throughout this trip, that in all places where Arabs are not much in the habit of trading, very few cloths find their way, and in consequence the people take to wearing beads; and beads and baubles are the only foreign things much in requisition.

As remarks upon the relative value of commodities appear in various places in this diary, I shall endeavour to give a general idea how it is that I have found this plentiful country--quite beyond any other I have seen in Africa in fertility and stock--so comparatively dear to travel in. The Zanzibar route to Ujiji is now so constantly travelled over by Arabs and Wasuahili, that the people, seeing the caravans approach, erect temporary markets, or come hawking things for sale, and the prices are adapted to the abilities of the purchasers; and at such markets our Sheikh bought for us, and transacted all business. It is also to be observed that where things are brought for sale, they are invariably cheaper than in those places where one has to seek and ask for them; for in the one instance a livelihood is the consequence of trade, whereas in the other a chance purchaser is treated as a windfall to be made the most of. Now this line is just the opposite to the Ujiji one, and therefore dear; but added to those influences here, the sultans, to increase their own importance whilst having me their guest, invariably gave out that I was no peddling Arab or Msuahili, but a great Mundewa, or merchant prince of the Wazungu (white or wise men), and the people took the hint to make me pay or starve. Then again, not having the Sheikh with me, I had to pay for and settle everything myself; and from having no variety of beads in this exclusively bead country, there was great inconvenience.

Kurua now joined us, and reported the abandoned donkey dead. A cool shower of rain fell, to the satisfaction of every thirsty soul. It is delightful to observe the freshness which even one partial shower imparts to all animated nature after a long-continued drought.

Chapter V.

General Character of the Country Traversed--The Huts--The Geology--
Productions--Land of Promise--Advice to Missionaries--Leave Ulekam-
puri--Return of the Expedition--Register of Temperature--Wages and Kit.

24th August.--During the last four days we have marched fifty-eight miles, and
are now at our old village in Ulekampuri. As we have now traversed all the ground,
I must try to give a short description, with a few reflections on the general character
of all we have seen or heard, before concluding this diary.

To give a faithful idea of a country, it is better that the object selected for comparison should incline to the large and grander scale than to the reverse, otherwise
the reader is apt to form too low an idea of it. And yet, though this is leaning to the
smaller, I can think of no better comparison for the surface of this high land than
the long sweeping waves of the Atlantic Ocean; and where the hills are fewest, and
in lines, they resemble small breakers curling on the tops of the rollers, all irregularly arranged, as though disturbed by different currents of wind.

Where the hills are grouped, they remind me of a small chopping sea in the
Bristol Channel. That the hills are nowhere high, is proved by the total absence of
any rivers along this line, until the lake is reached; and the passages between or over
them are everywhere gradual in their rise; so that in travelling through the country, no matter in which direction, the hills seldom interfere with the line of march.
The flats and hollows are well peopled, and cattle and cultivation are everywhere
abundant. The stone, soil, and aspect of the tract is uniform throughout. The stone
is chiefly granite, the rugged rocks of which lie like knobs of sugar over the surface
of the little hills, intermingled with sandstone in a highly ferruginous state; whilst
the soil is an accumulation of sand the same colour as the stone, a light brownish
grey, and appears as if it were formed of disintegrated particles of the rocks worn off

by time and weathering. Small trees and brushwood cover all the outcropping hills; and palms on the plains, though few and widely spread, prove that water is very near the surface. Springs, too, are numerous, and generally distributed. The mean level of the country between Unyanyembe and the lake is 3767 feet; that of the lake itself, 3750. The tribes, as a rule, are well disposed towards all strangers, and wish to extend their commerce. Their social state rather represents a conservative than a radical disposition; their government is a sort of semipatriarchal-feudal arrangement; and, like a band of robbers, all hold by their different chiefs from feeling the necessity of mutual support. Bordering the south of the lake there are vast fields of iron; cotton is also abundant, and every tropical plant or tree could grow; those that do exist, even rice, vegetate in the utmost luxuriance. Cattle are very abundant, and hides are found in every house. On the east of the lake ivory is said to be very abundant and cheap; and on the west we hear of many advantages which are especially worthy of our notice. The Karague hills overlooking the lake are high, cold, and healthy, and have enormous droves of cattle, bearing horns of stupendous size; and ivory, fine timber, and all the necessaries of life, are to be found in great profusion there. Again, beyond the equator, of the kingdom of Uganda we hear from everybody a rapturous account. That country evidently swarms with people who cultivate coffee and all the common grains, and have large flocks and herds, even greater than what I have lately seen. Now if the N'yanza be really the Nile's fount, which I sincerely believe to be the case, what an advantage this will be to the English merchant on the Nile, and what a field is opened to the world, if England does not neglect this discovery!

But I must not expatiate too much on the merits and capabilities of this part of inner Africa, lest I mislead any commercial inquirers; and it is as well to say at present, that the people near the coast are in such a state of helplessness and insecurity, caused by the slave-hunts, that for many years, until commerce, by steady and certain advance, shall in some degree overcome the existing apathy, and excite the population to strive to better their position by setting up strong constitutions to protect themselves and their property, no one need expect to make a large fortune by dealing with them. That commerce does make wonderful improvements on the barbarous habits of the Africans, can now be seen in the Masai country, and the countries extending north-westward from Mombas up through Kikuyu into the interior, where the process has been going on during the last few years. There even the roving wild pastorals, formerly untamable, are now gradually becoming reduced to subjection; and they no doubt will ere long have as strong a desire for cloths and other luxuries as any other civilised beings, from the natural desire to equal in comfort and dignity of appurtenances those whom they now must see constantly passing through their country. Caravans are penetrating farther, and going in greater numbers, every succeeding year, in those directions, and Arab merchants say that those countries are everywhere healthy. The best proof we have that the district is largely productive is the fact that the caravans and competition increase on those lines more and more every day. I would add, that in the meanwhile the staple exports derived from the far interior of the continent will consist of ivory, hides, and horns; whilst from the coast and its vicinity the clove, the gum copal, some textile materials drawn from the banana, aloe, and pine-apples, with oleaginous plants such as the ground-nut and cocoa-nut, are the chief exportable products. The cotton plant which grows here, judging from its size and difference from the plant usually grown in India, I consider to be a tree cotton and a perennial. It is this cotton which the natives weave into coarse fabrics in their looms. Rice, although it is not indigenous to Africa, I believe is certainly capable of being produced in great quantity and of very superior quality; and this is also the case with sugar-cane and tobacco, both of which are grown generally over the continent. There is also a species of palm growing on the borders of the Tanganyika Lake, which yields a concrete oil very much like, if not the same as, the palm-oil of Western Africa; but this is limited in quantity, and would never be of much value. Salt, which is found in great quantity in pits near the Malagarazi river, and the iron I have already spoken about, could only be of use to the country itself in facilitating traffic, and in maturing its resources.

These fertile regions have been hitherto unknown from the same cause which Dr Livingstone has so ably explained in regard to the western side of Africa--the jealousy of the shortsighted people who live on the coast, who, to preserve a monopoly of one particular article exclusively to themselves (ivory), have done their best to keep everybody away from the interior. I say shortsighted; for it is obvious that, were the resources of the country once fairly opened, the people on the coast would double or triple their present incomes, and Zanzibar would soon swell into a place of real importance. All hands would then be employed, and luxury would take the place of beggary.

I must now (after expressing a fervent hope that England especially, and the civilised world generally, will not neglect this land of promise) call attention to the marked fact, that the missionaries, residing for many years at Zanzibar, are the prime and first promoters of this discovery. They have been for years past doing their utmost, with simple sincerity, to Christianise this negro land, and promote a civilised and happy state of existence among these benighted beings. During their sojourn among these blackamoors, they heard from Arabs and others of many of the facts I have now stated, but only in a confused way, such as might be expected in information derived from an uneducated people. Amongst the more important disclosures made by the Arabs was the constant reference to a large lake or inland sea, which their caravans were in the habit of visiting. It was a singular thing that, at whatever part of the coast the missionaries arrived, on inquiring from the travelling merchants where they went to, they one and all stated to an inland sea, the dimensions of which were such that nobody could give any estimate of its length or width. The directions they travelled in pointed north-west, west, and south-west, and their accounts seemed to indicate a single sheet of water, extending from the Line down to 14o south latitude--a sea of about 840 miles in length, with an assumed breadth of two to three hundred miles. In fact, from this great combination of testimony that water lay generally in a continuous line from the equator up to 14o south latitude, and from not being able to gain information of there being any land separations to the said water, they very naturally, and I may add fortunately, put upon the map that monster slug of an inland sea which so much attracted the attention of the geographical world in 1855-56, and caused our being sent out to Africa. The good that may result from this little, yet happy accident, will, I trust, prove proportionately as large and fruitful as the produce from the symbolical grain of mustard-seed; and nobody knows or believes in this more fully than one of the chief promoters of this exciting investigation, Mr Rebmann. From these late explorations, he feels convinced, as he has oftentimes told me, that the first step has been taken in the right direction for the development of the commercial resources of the country, the spread of civilisation, and the extension of our geographical knowledge.

As many clergymen, missionaries, and others, have begged me to publish what facilities are open to the better prosecution of their noble ends in this wild country, I would certainly direct their attention to the Karague district, in preference to any other. There they will find, I feel convinced, a fine healthy country; a choice of ground from the mountain-top to the level of the lake, capable of affording them every comfort of life which an isolated place can produce; and being the most remote region from the coast, they would have less interference from the Mohammedan communities that reside by the sea. But then, I think, missionaries would have but a poor chance of success unless they went there in a body, with wives and families all as assiduous in working to the same end as themselves, and all capable of other useful occupations besides that of disseminating the Gospel, which should come after, and not before, the people are awake and prepared to receive it. As that country must be cold in consequence of its great altitude, the people would much sooner than in the hotter and more enervating lowlands, learn any lessons of industry they might be taught. To live idle in regard to everything but endeavouring to cram these negroes with Scriptural doctrines, as has too often been and now is done, is, although apparently the straightest, the longest way to reach the goal of their desires.

The missionary, I think, should be a Jack-of-all-trades--a man that can turn his hand to anything; and being useful in all cases, he would, at any rate, make himself influential with those who were living around him. To instruct him is the surest way of gaining a black man's heart, which, once obtained, can easily be turned in any way the preceptor pleases, as is the case with all Asiatics: they soon learn to bow to the superior intellect of the European, and are as easily ruled as a child is by his father.[72]

25th.--We left Ulekampuri at 1 A.M., and marched the last eighteen miles into Kaze under the delightful influence of a cool night and a bright full moon. As the caravan, according to its usual march of single file, moved along the serpentine footpath in peristaltic motion, firing muskets and singing "the return," the Unyanyembe villagers, men, women, and children, came running out and flocking on it, piercing the air with loud shrill noises, accompanied with the lullabooing of these fairs--which, once heard, can never be mistaken. The crowd was composed in great part of the relatives of my porters, who evinced their feelings towards their adult masters as eagerly as stray deer do in running to join a long-missing herd. The Arabs, one and all, came out to meet us, and escorted us into their depot. Captain Burton greeted me on arrival at the old house, and said he had been very anxious for some time past about our safety, as numerous reports had been set afloat with regard to the civil wars we had had to circumvent, which had impressed the Arabs as well as himself with alarming fears. I laughed over the matter, but expressed my regret that he did not accompany me, as I felt quite certain in my mind I had discovered the source of the Nile. This he naturally objected to, even after hearing all my reasons for saying so, and therefore the subject was dropped. Nevertheless, the Captain accepted all my geography leading from Kaze to the Nile, and wrote it down in his book--contracting only my distances, which he said he thought were exaggerated, and of course taking care to sever my lake from the Nile by *his* Mountains of the Moon.

It affords me great pleasure to be able to report the safe return of the expedition in a state of high spirits and gratification. All enjoyed the salubrity of the climate, the kind entertainments of the sultans, the variety and richness of the country, and the excellent fare everywhere. Further, the Beluches, by their exemplary conduct, proved themselves a most efficient, willing, and trustworthy guard, and are deserving of the highest encomiums; they, with Bombay, were the life and success of everything, and I sincerely hope they may not be forgotten.

The Arabs told me I could reach the N'yanza in fifteen to seventeen marches, and I returned in sixteen, although I had to take a circuitous line instead of a direct one. The provisions, too, just held out. I took a supply for six weeks, and completed *that* time *this* day. The total road-distance there and back is 452 miles, which, admitting that the Arabs make sixteen marches of it, gives them a marching rate of more than fourteen miles a- day.

The temperature is greater at this than at any other time of the year, in consequence of its being the end of the dry season; still, as will be seen by the annexed register of one week, the Unyamuezi plateau is not unbearably hot.

Thermometer hung in a passage of our house showed--Morning, Noon, and Afternoon respectively--

6 A.M. 9 A.M. Noon. 3 P.M. 6 P.M.

73o   75o   84o   86o   84o   Mean temperature during
                                     first week or seven days
                                     of September 1858.

71o   ---   ---   88o   ---   Extreme: difference, 17o
                                     of variation during 12
                                     hours of day.

Thermometer suspended from ridge-pole of a one-cloth tent pitched in a close yard:--

6 A.M. 9 A.M. Noon. 3 P.M. 6 P.M.

65o   85o   108o   107o   80o   Mean temperature.

63o   ---   ---   113o   ---   Extreme: difference, 50o
                                     of variation.

List of Stores along this Line.

Rice is grown at Unyanyembe, or wherever the Arabs settle, but is not common, as the negroes, considering it poor food, seldom eat it.

Animal.

Cows, sheep, goats, fowls, donkeys, eggs, milk, butter, honey.
P.S.--Donkeys are very scarce; only found in a few places in the Unyamuezi country.

Vegetable.

Rice, jowari, bagri, maize, manioc, sweet potatoes, yams, pumpkins, melons, cucumbers, tobacco, cotton, pulse in great varieties, chilis, benghans, plantains, tomatoes, sesamum.

The Quantity of Kit taken for this Journey consisted of--

9 Gorahs merikani; 1 Gorah or piece of American sheeting, = 15
               cloths of 4 cubits each.
30 Do. Kiniki; 1 Gorah Kiniki, a common indigo-dyed stuff, = 4
               cloths of 4 cubits each.

1 Sahari, a coloured cloth. | These cloths are more expensive being of
1 Dubuani, a coloured cloth. | better stuff, and are used chiefly by the
2 Barsati, a coloured cloth . | sultans and other black swells.

20 Maunds white beads = 70 lb.
3 loads of rice grown at Unyanyembe by the Arabs.

Expenditure for the Journey from 9th July to 25th August 1858.

	Value.
10 Beluches' wages, 150 shukkas, or 4 cubits apiece merikani,	100 dols.
10 Beluches' rations, given in advance, 30 lb. white beads,	5
15 Pagazis' wages, 75 shukkas merikani,	50
26 Men, including self, rations, 60 lb. white beads,	10
2 Pagazis, extra wages, 7 shukkas of merikani and	

kiniki mixed,	5
6 Sultans' hongos or presents, 22 shukkas of merikani and kiniki, mixed,	16
6 Do. Do. Do. 2 barsatis,	2

Total expenditure,		188 dols.
		Or L39, 3s. 4d.

The Indian Government also very generously authorised me to pay, on my last expedition, those poor men who had carried our property down from Kaze to Zungomero; but unfortunately for them, as well as for our own credit, I could not find one man of the lot.

The End.

Notes

[1] Without exception, and after having now shot over three quarters of the globe, I can safely say, there does not exist any place in the whole wide world which affords such a diversity of sport, such interesting animals, or such enchanting scenery, as well as pleasant climate and temperature, as these various countries of my first experiences; but the more especially interesting was Tibet to me, from the fact that I was the first man who penetrated into many of its remotest parts, and discovered many of its numerous animals.

[2] Lieutenant Burton received L100 from the Royal Geographical Society to cross Africa from west to east, and whilst attempting that journey he got drifted off

with the flood of pilgrims to Mecca. See his book.

[3] I had then mapped Tibet, and had laid down several new districts which even to this day have not been trodden by any European but myself.

[4] *Wadi*, river or nullah.

[5] It is questionable whether or not these Christians were driven south, fought at Mombas, were repulsed, and since have crossed the Nile to where we now find them, under the name of Wahuma. People may argue against the possibility of this, as the Wahuma do not keep horses; but the only reason, I believe, why they do not, is simply because horses won't live in those rich regions.

[6] Lieutenant Cruttenden, in his geographical treatise, describes the Darud family as being divided into four tribes, and, in addition to the three of which I heard, places the fourth or Murreyhan in his map to the southward of the country of Ugahden, lying between his Wadi Nogal and the Webbe Shebeli river.

[7] The Somali, in their own country, consider the Arab's gown and trousers effeminate; so on return to Africa they throw off the Arab costume again.

[8] This proved a great mistake. By having both men of the same tribe for my entire dependence, they invariably acted in concert against me like two brothers.

[9] Akil, *plural Okal*--chief or elder.

[10] The sultan has four sons.

[11] This gazelle is slightly different from the Dorcas, and, I believe, has never been obtained before.

[12] In talking of white men or Europeans, the Somali always say English French, those two branches of the European community being all they are acquainted with.

[13] Tobe, properly *thobe*, the dress used by Somali of both sexes. It consists of a white cloth, eight cubits long, frequently adorned with gaily-coloured edges; by the men it is worn loosely round the body with the end thrown over the shoulder, very much like the Roman toga. The women gather it in folds round the waist, where it is confined by a string, and both ends are fastened in a knot across the breast.

[14] It may appear strange that these men would not accept anything from me in payment except such things as they were accustomed to; and many of the pretty baubles which I brought from Calcutta, and considered would allure them by their

beauty, proved of no use here as a medium of exchange.

[15] Tug, in the Somali language, signifies a periodical river, or water-course, the same as Wadi in Arabic, and Nullah in Hindustani.

[16] *Durbar*--Eastern Court.

[17] Lions, as well as other large animals, are said to come into the Nogal during the rainy season, when water and grass are abundant.

[18] Unfortunately, when sent on this mission, I was not furnished with a chart, and had never seen any works written on the subject.

[19] For the advancement of future investigations, I would here notice the reported existence of a large reptile like the armadillo--probably a Manis--which the Somali think a very remarkable animal. It is said by them to be common in Haud, is very slow in motion, has a hard scaly exterior coating, invulnerable to their spears, and capable of supporting the weight of a man without any apparent inconvenience to the creature who bears it.

[20] From the presence of these crosses, it would appear as though in ignorance they had adopted the emblem of their Christian predecessors.

[21] *Ras* means point or headland.

[22] This interesting little animal has since been compared by Mr Blyth, curator of the Asiatic Society, Calcutta, and determined to be a new genus, and was named by him *Pectinator Spekei*.

[23] Then changed to Colonel Coghlan.

[24] These notes were reported in an Appendix in the 'First Footsteps in East Africa,' by Lieutenant Burton, with his other reports of this expedition.

[25] To say the least of it, this was a very dangerous policy to play with a people who consider might right, and revenge to death.

[26] Since this was written I have asked Lieutenant-Colonel Playfair his opinion on this matter, and the subjoined is the reply:--"In this Lieutenant Burton erred; and this was the *termina causa* of all the mishaps which befell the expedition. The institution of Abbanage is of great antiquity, and is the representative amongst a barbarous people of our customs laws, inasmuch as every trader or traveller pays to his Abban a certain percentage on the merchandise he buys or sells, and even on the food he purchases for his own use.

"A traveller who hopes for success in exploring a new country must accept the institutions he finds in existence; he can hardly hope, by his simple *fiat*, to revolutionise the time-honoured and *most profitable* institutions of a people, amongst whom precedent is a law as unchangeable as that of the Medes and Persians."

[27] Siyareh, a fort and small village belonging to the Makahil branch of the Habr Awel, is the watering-place of Berbera, and derives a small revenue from the boats which touch there *en route* to, and returning from, the Berbera fair. During this year it attained an unenviable notoriety as the rendezvous for the slaves intended for export to the Persian Gulf. Many of these were free Somali girls, sold by their relatives or kidnapped by their friends. Colonel Playfair wrote to me that one hundred and forty boys and girls were rescued here in the early part of this year by H.M.S. Lady Canning.

[28] Colonel Playfair thinks 20,000 men nearer the right number.

[29] I must here notice, although I have endeavoured to stick as closely as possible to the narration of my own story in these pages, that I saw Herne, who had been guarding the rear, opposed to the whole brunt of the attack, fighting gallantly with his sable antagonists; and from the resolution with which he fired at them, he must have done some damage.

[30] Articles of peace and friendship concluded between the Habr Owel tribe of Somali on the one part, and Brigadier William Marcus Coghlan, Political Resident at Aden, on behalf of the Honourable East India Company, on the other.

"Whereas, on the 19th of April 1855 (corresponding with the 1st of Shaban 1271), a treacherous attack and murder were perpetrated at the port of Berbera by a party of Habr Owel tribe, upon a party of British officers, about to travel in that country with the consent and under the protection of the elders of the tribe, in consequence of which outrage certain demands were made by the Government of India, and enforced by a blockade of the Habr Owel coast; and whereas it has become apparent that the said tribe has fulfilled these conditions to the utmost of its ability, and has prayed to be relieved from the blockade; therefore it is agreed,--

"1st, That the elders of the Habr Owel will use their best endeavours to deliver up Ou Ali, the murderer of Lieutenant Stroyan.

"2d, That, until this be accomplished, the sub-tribe Esa Moosa, which now shelters, and any other tribe which may hereafter shelter, harbour, or protect the said Ou Ali, shall be debarred from coming to Aden.

"3d, That all vessels sailing under the British flag shall have free permission to trade at the port of Berbera, or at any other place in the territories of the Habr Owel; and that all British subjects shall enjoy perfect safety in every part of the said territories, and shall be permitted to trade or travel there under the protection of the elders of the tribe. In like manner shall the members of the Habr Owel tribe enjoy similar privileges at Aden, or in any other part of the British possessions.

"4th, The traffic in slaves through the Habr Owel territories, including the port of Berbera, shall cease for ever; and any slave or slaves who, contrary to this engagement, shall be introduced into the said territories, shall be delivered up to the British; and the commander of any vessel of Her Majesty's or the Honourable East India Company's navy shall have the power of demanding the surrender of such slave or slaves, and of supporting the demand by force of arms, if necessary.

"5th, The Political Resident at Aden shall have the power to send an agent to reside at Berbera during the season of the fair, should he deem such a course necessary, to see that the provisions of this agreement are observed; and such agent will be treated with the respect and consideration due to the British Government.

"6th, That on a solemn promise being given by the elders of the Habr Owel, faithfully to abide by the articles of this agreement, and to cause the rest of the tribe to do so likewise, and to deliver up to the Political Resident at Aden any party who may violate it, the blockade of the Habr Owel coast shall be raised, and perpetual peace and friendship shall exist between the British and the Habr Owel.

"Done at Berbera this seventh day of November, one thousand eight hundred and fifty-six of the Christian era (corresponding with the eighth day of Rabea-el-Owel, one thousand two hundred and seventy-two of the Hejira).

MAHOMED ARRA'LEH,   \
AHMED ALI BOOKERI, | Ayal Yoonus.
NOOR FA'RRAH,   /

AHMED GHA'LID,   \
MAHOMMED WA'IS, | Ayal Ahmed
MUGGAN MAHOMMED,   /

ROOBLIE HASSAN,   \
ATEYAH HILDER, | Makahil.
FARRAH BENI'N,   /

AWADTH SHERMARKIE,   Ayal Hamood.

"Signed in my presence at Berbera, on the 7th November 1856.

R. L. PLAYFAIR, Assistant Political Resident, Aden.
W. M. COGHLAN, Political Resident.

"Aden, 9th November 1856.

"Ratified by the Right Honourable the Governor-General of India in Council, at Fort William, this 23d day of January 1857.

    CANNING.
    And Five Members of Council of India."

[31] I was first blinded by ophthalmia when a child, which had ever since rendered reading a very painful task; and again I suffered from snow-blindness whilst crossing over the Himalayas into Tibet.

[32] The cheque, I found, after my arrival in England, was not credited in my account, so I had, after all, to pay my own passage.

[33] I must add here, to show that the generous hospitality of the Indian navy was now as strong in force as ever it was, that the wardroom officers, not being aware of the intended generosity of the Government to supply us with messing gratis, had laid in an extra store of provisions for the purpose of making us their guests.

[34] Banyans are the only class of coloured men who have the ability to be accountants. They fill this office properly, and are therefore always selected for it.

[35] On starting to the rescue, my companion complained of the shock his

nerves had received since the Somali encounter, and this appeared to affect him during the whole of this journey.

[36] Caravans have also reached the shores of the N'yanza at 1o S. lat., and entered Usoga, rounding its north-east corner.

[37] See further description of this, page 185.

[38] See Bombay's history, page 210.

[39] In future I shall call this fringe or mountain-chain the East Coast Range, in contradistinction to the same hill-formation on the western coast of Africa; for it must be remembered that there are three great leading features in the geographical formation of Africa--viz., a low exterior belt of land, or margin to the continent, varying in breadth according to circumstances, which is succeeded by a high belt of mountains or rugged ground, separating the lowlands from a high interior plateau, lying like a basin within the fringe of hills.

[40] The officers of state cannot receive a present without the sanction of the government.

[41] The murderers of Dr Boscher were sent to Zanzibar by the chief of their tribe, and were executed by orders of the Sultan.

[42] To save repetition, I may as well mention the fact that neither Captain Burton nor myself were able to converse in any African language until we were close to the coast on the return journey.

[43] Another question suggests itself. How did Ptolemy hear of the two lakes which he considered were the sources of the Nile? It is obvious he could not have done so by the channel of the Nile, for the Anthropophagi barred all communication in that direction. Here, however, the route from Zanzibar to the Tanganyika Lake and the Victoria N'yanza, in all probability, was kept open by the trading "Men of the Moon;" and thus two lakes were heard of situated east and west of one another, just in convenient situations to fit on to the two branches of Ptolemy's Nile.

[44] *Khambi*--Encampment.

[45] The Babisa purchase ivory at Luwemba for the Kilua merchants, and are met there by the Kaze merchants.

[46] I have since heard from Colonel Rigby (Colonel Hamerton's successor) that Hamed and all his slaves were murdered on their journey to Uruwa, and their property was seized by the natives.

[47] Here is the confusion again of the Nile and the lake as one water. The Nile was in reality five marches east of Kibuga, and the boundary of the lake one march to its southward. Snay obviously meant it so, for it was the river he thought was the Jub, but I did not understand him.

[48] See Dr Beke's paper on 'The Sources of the Nile,' printed 1849.

[49] *Kirangozi*--leader of a caravan.

[50] Sheikh Said has since declared, in "the most solemn manner, that Captain Burton positively forbade his going." This happened when we were at Usenye, and immediately after I first asked the Sheikh.

[51] Captain Burton started with two huge elephant-guns, one double rifle, one pea-rifle, one air-gun, two revolving pistols, and a cross-bow, all of which he used for display to amuse the Arabs.

[52] Sukuma means north, and the Wasukuma are consequently northmen, or northern Wanyamuezi.

[53] *Barsati*--a coloured cloth.

[54] One dhoti = 2 shukkas; 1 shukka = 4 cubits, or 2 yards, merikani (American sheeting).

[55] *Kiniki*--a thin indigo-dyed cloth.

[56] *Boma*--a palisade. A village or collection of huts so fortified is called so also.

[57] This, I maintain, was the discovery of the source of the Nile. Had the ancient kings and sages known that a rainy zone existed on the equator, they would not have puzzled their brains so long, and have wondered where those waters came from which meander through upwards of a thousand miles of scorching desert without a single tributary.

[58] This magnificent sheet of water I have ventured to name VICTORIA, after our gracious Sovereign. Its length was not clearly understood by me, in consequence of the word Sea having been applied both to the Lake and to the Nile by my local informants; and there was no recent map of the Nile with the expedition by which I might have been guided.

[59] I now think the breadth is over one hundred miles.

[60] Mahaya said he was of Wahinda extraction, or from the princes of the Wahuma; but this I do not believe, for his features bore the strongest possible tes-

timony against him.

[61] The King of Uganda has sent presents by boat to Machunda, Sultan of Uk-erewe, coasting along the western shore of the lake. Mtesa told me this himself, and asked me if I knew Machunda personally.

[62] The Waganda also send boats for salt to the Bahari (Lake) Ngo, at the north-east corner of the lake.

[63] On my return to England I constructed a map representing this view, and lectured on the same in presence of Captain Burton, who then raised no objections to what I said.

[64] In England geographers doubted this; and after it was printed, Dr Peter-mann had reason to change his opinion. However, Knoblecher was not far wrong, as I have since made the latitude of Gondokoro 4o 54' north.

[65] The rising of the Katonga still puzzles me.

[66] Kibuga means palace.

[67] There are three cataracts between the N'yanza and Gondokoro: 1. from Ri-pon Falls to Urondogani; 2. from Karuma Falls to Little Luta Nzige; 3. from Apuddo to near Gondokoro.

[68] Captain Burton, by way of having a special Lunae Montes of his own, calls these mountains a "mass of highlands, which, under the name of Karagwah, forms the western spinal prolongation of the Lunar Mountains." See his 'Lake Regions,' vol. ii. p. 144.

[69] There are exceptions to the rule in the instance of the Waganda, who are of an earth-red colour; for these men never fight excepting in overpowering num-bers.

[70] The history of the Wahuma has been given in 'The Discovery of the Source of the Nile.' The Watuta also have been alluded to, for they were fighting on my line of march. I heard then of the arrival of a recent detachment from the west of the Nyassa, and subsequently I heard they had invaded Usui.

[71] The Wahuma are a link between the Masai and the Kafirs, so far as I can judge of the common origin of this migratory pastoral race. The ethnologist ought to look well into this matter, and treat it without regard to change of language or names, as time will efface and create both anew.

[72] Since writing this, as I have had more insight into Africa by travelling

from Kaze to Egypt down the whole length of the Nile, I would be sorry to leave this opinion standing without making a few more remarks. Of all places in Africa, by far the most inviting to missionary enterprise are the kingdoms of Karague, Uganda, and Unyoro. They are extremely fertile and healthy, and the temperature is delightfully moderate. So abundant, indeed, are all provisions, and so prolific the soil, that a missionary establishment, however large, could support itself after the first year's crop. Being ruled by kings of the Abyssinian type, there is no doubt but that they have a latent Christianity in them. These kings are powerful enough to keep up their governments under numerous officers. They have expressed a wish to have their children educated; and I am sure the missionary need only go there to obtain all he desires on as secure a basis as he will find anywhere else in those parts of Africa which are not under the rule of Europeans. If this was effected by the aid of an Egyptian force at Gondokoro, together with an arrangement for putting the White Nile trade on a legitimate footing between that station and Unyoro, the heathen would not only be blessed, but we should soon have a great and valuable commerce. Without protection, though, I would not advise any one to go there.

Now, for the use of commercial inquirers, I may also add, that it may be seen in my 'Journal of the Discovery of the Source of the Nile,' that the kings of these three countries were all, more or less, adverse to my passing through their countries to the Nile; but they gave way, and permitted my doing so, on my promising to open a direct trade with this country and theirs by the channel of that river. I gave them the promise freely, for I saw by the nature of the land, subjected as it is to frequently recurring showers of rain all the year round, that it will be, in course of time, one of the greatest nations on the earth. It is nearer to Europe than India; it is far more fertile, and it possesses none of those disagreeable elements of discontent which have been such a sharp thorn in our sides in India--I mean a history and a religion far anterior to our own, which makes those we govern there shrink from us, caused by a natural antipathy of being ruled by an inferior race, as we are by them considered to be. These countries, on the contrary, have no literature, and therefore have neither history nor religion to excite discontent should any foreigners intrench on their lands. By this I do not wish it to be supposed that I would willingly see any foreign European power upset these Wahuma governments; but, on the contrary, I would like to see them maintained as long as possible, and I seriously trust some steps may speedily be taken for that most desirable object. Should it not be so, then in a short time these kingdoms will fall into the hands of those vile ruffian traders on the White Nile, in the same way as Kaze has been occupied by the Arabs of Zanzibar. To give an instance of the way it most likely will be effected, I will merely state that the king of Unyoro begged me repeatedly to kill some rebel brothers of his, who were then occupying an island between his palace and the Little Luta Nzige. I would not do it, as I thought it would be a bad example to set in the country; but some time afterwards I felt sorry for it, for on arrival in Madi, where I first met the Nile traders, I found that they were in league with these very rebels to dethrone the king. The atrocities committed by these traders are beyond all civilised belief. They are constantly fighting, robbing, and capturing slaves and cattle. No honest man can either trade or travel in the country, for the natives have been bullied to such an extent that they either fight or run away, according to their strength and circumstance. That a great quantity of ivory is drawn from those countries I must admit, for these traders ramify in all directions, and, vying with one another, see who can get most ivory at the least expense, no matter what means they employ to obtain their ends.

At the same time, I have no hesitation in saying that ten times as much merchandise might be got at less expense, if the trade were protected by government means, and put on a legitimate footing. Those countries teem with cattle. The indigenous cotton is of very superior quality. Indigo, sugar-cane, coffee, tobacco, sesamum, and indeed all things that will grow in a tropical climate, may be grown there within 3o of the equator, in luxurious profusion, and without any chance of failure owing to those long periodical droughts which affect all lands distant more than 3o from the equator.

When I was sailing down the Nile, I could not help remarking to all the pashas I visited how strange it appeared that men so civilised as they were should be living in such a barren, hot, and glaring land as Egypt, when the negroes on the equator were absolutely living in the richest and pleasantest garden in the world, so far as nature has made the two countries.

Now, though I have dwelt so markedly on the surprising fertility of Uganda and Unyoro in particular, I do not wish it to be supposed that I consider those countries alone to be exclusively rich, for I believe there is a continuous zone of fertility stretching right across Africa from east to west, affected only by the nature of the soil. In advancing this argument, I hold that the greatest discovery I have made in Africa consists in my positive knowledge regarding the rainy system of Africa; and to exemplify it irrespectively of my meteorological observations, I will state emphatically that as surely as I have determined the source of the Nile to lie within 3o of the equator, and that it cannot emanate from any point farther south, because all the lands beyond that limit are subject to long periodical droughts--so certain am I that the Tanganyika is supplied from the same source, or rainy zone, though draining in the opposite direction. Again, to its west also, from the same source of supply, the head-waters of the Zambezi take their origin. Still farther west, the fountains of the Congo must have their birth. Again, farther west still, the Chadda branch of the Niger can alone be thus supplied, and the same must be the case with the Gaboon river.

To carry this argument still farther, I would direct attention to the periodical conditions of the Blue Nile and Niger rivers. Both of these rivers rise in high mountains on the coast-range, at about 10o north latitude, but on opposite sides of the continent. They are considered large rivers, but only in consequence of their great floodings, when the sun, in his northern declination, brings the rains over the seats of their birthplaces; for when the sun is in the south they shrink so low that the waters of the Blue river would never have power to reach the sea were they not assisted by the perennial stream of the White Nile.

The most important exploring expedition that any one could undertake now, would be to cross Africa from east to west, keeping close to the first degree of north latitude, to ascertain the geological formation of that parallel. Within the coast-ranges, in consequence of the great elevation of the land, the temperature is always moderate, and it is proved to be much more healthy than any of those parts of Africa subjected to periodical seasons. Next to this scheme, I would recommend this fertile zone to be attacked from Gondokoro on the Nile, and from Gaboon (the French port) on the equator. The Gondokoro line, being known to a considerable extent, is ready for working, and only requires government protection to make it succeed; but the other line from the Gaboon should first be inspected by a scientific expedition.

The Codes Of Hammurabi And Moses
W. W. Davies

QTY

The discovery of the Hammurabi Code is one of the greatest achievements of archaeology, and is of paramount interest, not only to the student of the Bible, but also to all those interested in ancient history...

Religion   **ISBN:** *1-59462-338-4*   **Pages:132**
MSRP $12.95

The Theory of Moral Sentiments
Adam Smith

QTY

This work from 1749. contains original theories of conscience amd moral judgment and it is the foundation for systemof morals.

Philosophy   **ISBN:** *1-59462-777-0*   **Pages:536**
MSRP $19.95

Jessica's First Prayer
Hesba Stretton

QTY

In a screened and secluded corner of one of the many railway-bridges which span the streets of London there could be seen a few years ago, from five o'clock every morning until half past eight, a tidily set-out coffee-stall, consisting of a trestle and board, upon which stood two large tin cans, with a small fire of charcoal burning under each so as to keep the coffee boiling during the early hours of the morning when the work-people were thronging into the city on their way to their daily toil...

Pages:84

Childrens   **ISBN:** *1-59462-373-2*   **MSRP $9.95**

My Life and Work
Henry Ford

QTY

Henry Ford revolutionized the world with his implementation of mass production for the Model T automobile. Gain valuable business insight into his life and work with his own auto-biography... "We have only started on our development of our country we have not as yet, with all our talk of wonderful progress, done more than scratch the surface. The progress has been wonderful enough but..."

Pages:300

Biographies/   **ISBN:** *1-59462-198-5*   **MSRP $21.95**

The Art of Cross-Examination
Francis Wellman

QTY

I presume it is the experience of every author, after his first book is published upon an important subject, to be almost overwhelmed with a wealth of ideas and illustrations which could readily have been included in his book, and which to his own mind, at least, seem to make a second edition inevitable. Such certainly was the case with me; and when the first edition had reached its sixth impression in five months, I rejoiced to learn that it seemed to my publishers that the book had met with a sufficiently favorable reception to justify a second and considerably enlarged edition. ..

Pages:412

Reference   ISBN: *1-59462-647-2*   *MSRP $19.95*

On the Duty of Civil Disobedience
Henry David Thoreau

QTY

Thoreau wrote his famous essay, On the Duty of Civil Disobedience, as a protest against an unjust but popular war and the immoral but popular institution of slave-owning. He did more than write—he declined to pay his taxes, and was hauled off to gaol in consequence. Who can say how much this refusal of his hastened the end of the war and of slavery ?

Law   ISBN: *1-59462-747-9*

Pages:48

MSRP $7.45

Dream Psychology Psychoanalysis for Beginners
Sigmund Freud

QTY

Sigmund Freud, born Sigismund Schlomo Freud (May 6, 1856 - September 23, 1939), was a Jewish-Austrian neurologist and psychiatrist who co-founded the psychoanalytic school of psychology. Freud is best known for his theories of the unconscious mind, especially involving the mechanism of repression; his redefinition of sexual desire as mobile and directed towards a wide variety of objects; and his therapeutic techniques, especially his understanding of transference in the therapeutic relationship and the presumed value of dreams as sources of insight into unconscious desires.

Pages:196

Psychology   ISBN: *1-59462-905-6*   *MSRP $15.45*

The Miracle of Right Thought
Orison Swett Marden

QTY

Believe with all of your heart that you will do what you were made to do. When the mind has once formed the habit of holding cheerful, happy, prosperous pictures, it will not be easy to form the opposite habit. It does not matter how improbable or how far away this realization may see, or how dark the prospects may be, if we visualize them as best we can, as vividly as possible, hold tenaciously to them and vigorously struggle to attain them, they will gradually become actualized, realized in the life. But a desire, a longing without endeavor, a yearning abandoned or held indifferently will vanish without realization.

Pages:360

Self Help   ISBN: *1-59462-644-8*

The Rosicrucian Cosmo-Conception Mystic Christianity *by Max Heindel*   ISBN: *1-59462-188-8*   **$38.95**
The Rosicrucian Cosmo-conception is not dogmatic, neither does it appeal to any other authority than the reason of the student. It is: not controversial, but is: sent forth in the, hope that it may help to clear...   New Age/Religion Pages 646

Abandonment To Divine Providence *by Jean-Pierre de Caussade*   ISBN: *1-59462-228-0*   **$25.95**
"The Rev. Jean Pierre de Caussade was one of the most remarkable spiritual writers of the Society of Jesus in France in the 18th Century. His death took place at Toulouse in 1751. His works have gone through many editions and have been republished...   Inspirational/Religion Pages 400

Mental Chemistry *by Charles Haanel*   ISBN: *1-59462-192-6*   **$23.95**
Mental Chemistry allows the change of material conditions by combining and appropriately utilizing the power of the mind. Much like applied chemistry creates something new and unique out of careful combinations of chemicals the mastery of mental chemistry...   New Age Pages 354

The Letters of Robert Browning and Elizabeth Barret Barrett 1845-1846 vol II   ISBN: *1-59462-193-4*   **$35.95**
by Robert Browning and Elizabeth Barrett
Biographies Pages 596

Gleanings In Genesis (volume I) *by Arthur W. Pink*   ISBN: *1-59462-130-6*   **$27.45**
Appropriately has Genesis been termed "the seed plot of the Bible" for in it we have, in germ form, almost all of the great doctrines which are afterwards fully developed in the books of Scripture which follow...   Religion/Inspirational Pages 420

The Master Key *by L. W. de Laurence*   ISBN: *1-59462-001-6*   **$30.95**
In no branch of human knowledge has there been a more lively increase of the spirit of research during the past few years than in the study of Psychology, Concentration and Mental Discipline. The requests for authentic lessons in Thought Control, Mental Discipline and...   New Age/Business Pages 422

The Lesser Key Of Solomon Goetia *by L. W. de Laurence*   ISBN: *1-59462-092-X*   **$9.95**
This translation of the first book of the "Lernegton" which is now for the first time made accessible to students of Talismanic Magic was done, after careful collation and edition, from numerous Ancient Manuscripts in Hebrew, Latin, and French...   New Age/Occult Pages 92

Rubaiyat Of Omar Khayyam *by Edward Fitzgerald*   ISBN:*1-59462-332-5*   **$13.95**
Edward Fitzgerald, whom the world has already learned, in spite of his own efforts to remain within the shadow of anonymity, to look upon as one of the rarest poets of the century, was born at Bredfield, in Suffolk, on the 31st of March, 1809. He was the third son of John Purcell...   Music Pages 172

Ancient Law *by Henry Maine*   ISBN: *1-59462-128-4*   **$29.95**
The chief object of the following pages is to indicate some of the earliest ideas of mankind, as they are reflected in Ancient Law, and to point out the relation of those ideas to modern thought.   Religion/History Pages 452

Far-Away Stories *by William J. Locke*   ISBN: *1-59462-129-2*   **$19.45**
"Good wine needs no bush, but a collection of mixed vintages does. And this book is just such a collection. Some of the stories I do not want to remain buried for ever in the museum files of dead magazine-numbers an author's not unpardonable vanity..."   Fiction Pages 272

Life of David Crockett *by David Crockett*   ISBN: *1-59462-250-7*   **$27.45**
"Colonel David Crockett was one of the most remarkable men of the times in which he lived. Born in humble life, but gifted with a strong will, an indomitable courage, and unremitting perseverance...   Biographies/New Age Pages 424

Lip-Reading *by Edward Nitchie*   ISBN: *1-59462-206-X*   **$25.95**
Edward B. Nitchie, founder of the New York School for the Hard of Hearing, now the Nitchie School of Lip-Reading, Inc, wrote "LIP-READING Principles and Practice". The development and perfecting of this meritorious work on lip-reading was an undertaking...   How-to Pages 400

A Handbook of Suggestive Therapeutics, Applied Hypnotism, Psychic Science   ISBN: *1-59462-214-0*   **$24.95**
by Henry Munro
Health/New Age/Health/Self-help Pages 376

A Doll's House: and Two Other Plays *by Henrik Ibsen*   ISBN: *1-59462-112-8*   **$19.95**
Henrik Ibsen created this classic when in revolutionary 1848 Rome. Introducing some striking concepts in playwriting for the realist genre, this play has been studied the world over.   Fiction/Classics/Plays 308

The Light of Asia *by sir Edwin Arnold*   ISBN: *1-59462-204-3*   **$13.95**
In this poetic masterpiece, Edwin Arnold describes the life and teachings of Buddha. The man who was to become known as Buddha to the world was born as Prince Gautama of India but he rejected the worldly riches and abandoned the reigns of power when...   Religion/History/Biographies Pages 170

The Complete Works of Guy de Maupassant *by Guy de Maupassant*   ISBN: *1-59462-157-8*   **$16.95**
"For days and days, nights and nights, I had dreamed of that first kiss which was to consecrate our engagement, and I knew not on what spot I should put my lips..."   Fiction/Classics Pages 240

The Art of Cross-Examination *by Francis L. Wellman*   ISBN: *1-59462-309-0*   **$26.95**
Written by a renowned trial lawyer, Wellman imparts his experience and uses case studies to explain how to use psychology to extract desired information through questioning.   How-to/Science/Reference Pages 408

Answered or Unanswered? *by Louisa Vaughan*   ISBN: *1-59462-248-5*   **$10.95**
Miracles of Faith in China
Religion Pages 112

The Edinburgh Lectures on Mental Science (1909) *by Thomas*   ISBN: *1-59462-008-3*   **$11.95**
This book contains the substance of a course of lectures recently given by the writer in the Queen Street Hail, Edinburgh. Its purpose is to indicate the Natural Principles governing the relation between Mental Action and Material Conditions...   New Age/Psychology Pages 148

Ayesha *by H. Rider Haggard*   ISBN: *1-59462-301-5*   **$24.95**
Verily and indeed it is the unexpected that happens! Probably if there was one person upon the earth from whom the Editor of this, and of a certain previous history, did not expect to hear again...   Classics Pages 380

Ayala's Angel *by Anthony Trollope*   ISBN: *1-59462-352-X*   **$29.95**
The two girls were both pretty, but Lucy who was twenty-one who supposed to be simple and comparatively unattractive, whereas Ayala was credited, as her Bombwhat romantic name might show, with poetic charm and a taste for romance. Ayala when her father died was nineteen...   Fiction Pages 484

The American Commonwealth *by James Bryce*   ISBN: *1-59462-286-8*   **$34.45**
An interpretation of American democratic political theory. It examines political mechanics and society from the perspective of Scotsman James Bryce   Politics Pages 572

Stories of the Pilgrims *by Margaret P. Pumphrey*   ISBN: *1-59462-116-0*   **$17.95**
This book explores pilgrims religious oppression in England as well as their escape to Holland and eventual crossing to America on the Mayflower, and their early days in New England...   History Pages 268

QTY

The Fasting Cure *by Sinclair Upton*   ISBN: *1-59462-222-1*   **$13.95**
In the Cosmopolitan Magazine for May, 1910, and in the Contemporary Review (London) for April, 1910, I published an article dealing with my experiences in fasting. I have written a great many magazine articles, but never one which attracted so much attention... New Age/Self Help/Health Pages 164

Hebrew Astrology *by Sepharial*   ISBN: *1-59462-308-2*   **$13.45**
In these days of advanced thinking it is a matter of common observation that we have left many of the old landmarks behind and that we are now pressing forward to greater heights and to a wider horizon than that which represented the mind-content of our progenitors... Astrology Pages 144

Thought Vibration or The Law of Attraction in the Thought World   ISBN: *1-59462-127-6*   **$12.95**
by William Walker Atkinson   Psychology/Religion Pages 144

Optimism *by Helen Keller*   ISBN: *1-59462-108-X*   **$15.95**
Helen Keller was blind, deaf, and mute since 19 months old, yet famously learned how to overcome these handicaps, communicate with the world, and spread her lectures promoting optimism. An inspiring read for everyone... Biographies/Inspirational Pages 84

Sara Crewe *by Frances Burnett*   ISBN: *1-59462-360-0*   **$9.45**
In the first place, Miss Minchin lived in London. Her home was a large, dull, tall one, in a large, dull square, where all the houses were alike, and all the sparrows were alike, and where all the door-knockers made the same heavy sound... Childrens/Classic Pages 88

The Autobiography of Benjamin Franklin *by Benjamin Franklin*   ISBN: *1-59462-135-7*   **$24.95**
The Autobiography of Benjamin Franklin has probably been more extensively read than any other American historical work, and no other book of its kind has had such ups and downs of fortune. Franklin lived for many years in England, where he was agent... Biographies/History Pages 332

Name	
Email	
Telephone	
Address	
City, State ZIP	

☐ **Credit Card**   ☐ **Check / Money Order**

Credit Card Number	
Expiration Date	
Signature	

Please Mail to: *Book Jungle*
PO Box 2226
Champaign, IL 61825
or Fax to: *630-214-0564*

ORDERING INFORMATION

web*: www.bookjungle.com*
email*: sales@bookjungle.com*
fax*: 630-214-0564*
mail*: Book Jungle PO Box 2226 Champaign, IL 61825*
or PayPal *to sales@bookjungle.com*

Please contact us for bulk discounts

DIRECT-ORDER TERMS

**20% Discount if You Order
Two or More Books**
Free Domestic Shipping!
Accepted: Master Card, Visa,
Discover, American Express

www.ingramcontent.com/pod-product-compliance
Lightning Source LLC
Chambersburg PA
CBHW080901020726
47502CB00008B/2303